HERO

AT THE FALL

HERO
AT THE FALL

A REBEL OF THE SANDS NOVEL

ALWYN HAMILTON

VIKING

VIKING
An imprint of Penguin Random House LLC
375 Hudson Street
New York, New York 10014

First published in the United States of America by Viking,
an imprint of Penguin Random House LLC, 2018

LIBRARY OF CONGRESS CATALOGING-IN-PUBLICATION DATA IS AVAILABLE
ISBN: 9780451477866

Printed in U.S.A.

1   3   5   7   9   10   8   6   4   2

Set in Fiesole Text

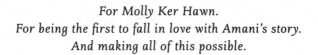

For Molly Ker Hawn.
For being the first to fall in love with Amani's story.
And making all of this possible.

HERO

AT THE FALL

To GALLANDIE / ALBIS / GAMANIX
Der's Valley
Ghasab
Saramotai
Fahali
Dassama
REBEL CAMP
AMONPOUR
SAND SEA
Deadshot
Dustwalk
Sazi
MIRAJI

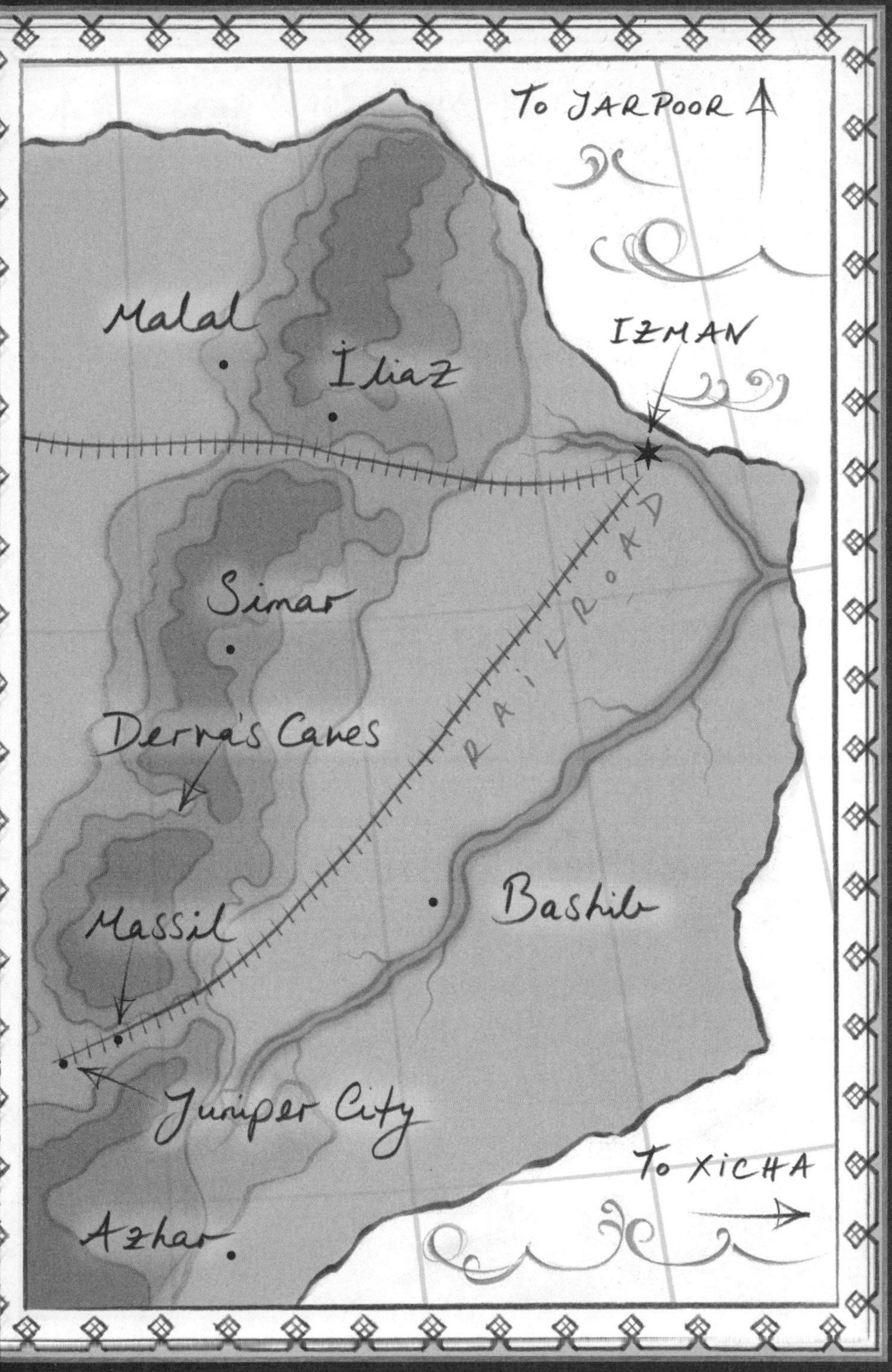
To JARPOOR
Malal
Iliaz
IZMAN
RAILROAD
Simar
Derra's Caves
Bashib
Massil
Juniper City
To XICHA
Azhar

CAST of CHARACTERS

THE REBELLION

Amani Sharpshooter, Demdji marked by blue eyes, able to control desert sand, goes by the moniker of the Blue-Eyed Bandit. Current de facto leader of the Rebellion in absence of Prince Ahmed. Seventeen years old.

Prince Ahmed Al-Oman Bin Izman The Rebel Prince, leader of the Rebellion. Currently captured. Nineteen years old.

Jin Prince of Miraji, brother of the Rebel Prince Ahmed, full name Ajinahd Al-Oman Bin Izman. Nineteen years old.

Prince Rahim Prince of Miraji. Half brother to Ahmed and Jin. Full-blooded brother of Leyla. One-time military commander of Iliaz. Currently captured. Nineteen years old.

Shazad Al-Hamad Daughter of a Miraji general, among the original members of the Rebellion, well-trained fighter, strategist. Currently captured. Eighteen years old.

Sam Albish Army deserter

turned thief. Can walk through stone. Eighteen years old.

Tamid Amani's former best friend, Holy Father in training, walks with a limp due to a deformity at birth. Seventeen years old.

Delila Demdji marked by purple hair, able to cast illusions out of light in the air, Ahmed's sister by blood, Jin's sister by adoption. Currently captured. Fifteen years old.

Hala Demdji marked by golden skin, able to twist people's minds into hallucinations. Nineteen years old.

Izz and Maz Twin Demdji, marked by blue skin and blue hair respectively, able to shapeshift into any animal form. Seventeen years old.

Navid Imin's husband. Captured. Fate unknown.

Sara Guardian of the Hidden House in Izman.

Fadi Shira's son with the Djinni

Fereshteh. Demdji born with blue hair. Named after his grandfather. Smuggled out of the palace to safety.

◆―――◎―――◆

NORTHERN MIRAJI

Sultan Oman   Ruler of Miraji, Ahmed and Jin's father.

Leyla   Daughter of the Sultan, and full-blooded sister of Prince Rahim. Skilled inventor. Betrayed the Rebellion. Fifteen years old.

Lord Bilal   Emir of Iliaz. Currently dying of a long-drawn-out illness. Nineteen years old.

General Hamad   General feigning loyalty to the Sultan. Shazad's father.

Samira   Daughter of the deceased Emir of Saramotai. Newly appointed leader of Saramotai in the name of the Rebellion. Seventeen years old.

THE DJINN

Bahadur   Immortal Djinni. Amani's Father.

Fereshteh   Immortal Djinni. Fadi's father. Killed so that his energy could be turned into electricity in the Sultan's machine. The First Djinni to die since the First War.

◆―――◎―――◆

THE LAST COUNTY

Farrah Al-Fadi   Amani's aunt, eldest sister to her mother.

Asid   Farrah's husband, a horse trader in Dustwalk.

Nasima   One of Amani's young cousins.

Olia   One of Amani's young cousins.

Fazim Al-Motem   A resident of Dustwalk. Formerly Shira's lover. Amani's enemy.

Noorsham   Demdji marked by

blue eyes, able to produce Djinni fire that can annihilate a whole city. Born in the mining town of Sazi. Missing since the battle of Fahali.

◆————◎————◆

THE FALLEN

Zahia Al-Fadi Amani's mother, hanged for the murder of her husband.

Hiza Amani's mother's husband. Not Amani's father by blood. Killed by his wife.

Nadira Ahmed and Delila's mother by blood, killed by the Sultan for bearing a child to a Djinni.

Lien Xichian woman, wife of the Sultan, Jin's mother by blood, Ahmed and Delila's mother by adoption. Died of an illness.

Bahi Childhood friend of Shazad, disgraced a Holy Man, killed by Noorsham.

Prince Naguib Al-Oman One of the Sultan's sons, army commander. Killed by the Rebellion in the battle of Fahali.

Malik Al-Kizzam Usurper of Saramotai. Killed by Shazad.

Ranaa A young Demdji who could conjure light in her hands. Killed in a skirmish.

Sayidda A spy for the Rebellion in the palace. Tortured to insanity in the Sultan's machine. Killed in the flight from the rebel camp.

Mahdi Sayidda's lover. Betrayed the Rebellion to try to save Sayidda. Killed in the flight from the rebel camp.

Ayet, Uzma, and Mouhna Wives of Prince Kadir. Tortured to insanity in the Sultan's machine.

Shira Amani's cousin. Wife of Prince Kadir. Sultima. Executed by order of her husband for giving birth to a Djinni's child.

Prince Kadir The Sultan's eldest son, Sultim, heir to the throne of Miraji. Killed by the Sultan.

Imin   Demdji marked by golden eyes, able to shapeshift into any human form, Hala's sibling. Executed in order to save Ahmed, assuming his identity.

Princess Hawa   Legendary Princess who sang the sun into the sky.

The Hero Attallah   Lover of Princess Hawa.

<hr />

Myths & Legends

First Beings   Immortal beings made by God, including Djinn, Buraqi, and Rocs.

The Destroyer of Worlds   A being from the darkness of the earth who came to the surface of the world to bring death and darkness. Defeated by humanity.

Ghouls   The Servants of the Destroyer of Worlds, includes Nightmares, Skinwalkers, etc.

The First Hero   The first mortal created by the Djinn to face the Destroyer of Worlds. Made out of sand and water and air and brought to life with Djinni fire. Also known as the First Mortal.

ONE

I woke from a sleep filled with nightmares to the sound of my name.

I was already reaching for a gun when I recognized Sara's face above me, swimming in and out of focus as my eyes blurred with exhaustion.

My grip on the trigger eased. It wasn't an enemy, just Sara, the guardian of the Hidden House. She was holding a small lamp that lit up only her face. For a moment she looked like a disembodied head floating in the dark, like the ones in the dream that was fading now as I woke:

Imin wearing Ahmed's face going willingly to the executioner's stage.

My cousin Shira screaming her defiance as she was forced to her knees in front of the block.

Ayet, with eyes full of madness, awaiting the death that would come from having her soul drained out of her.

Ranaa, the Demdji child who had carried the sun in her hands and died by a stray bullet in a battle she shouldn't have been fighting.

Bahi, who'd burned in front of me at my brother's hand.

My mother, who'd swung from a rope back in Dustwalk for shooting her husband, the man who'd never been my father anyway.

People I had watched die. People I had let die. The accusation was all over their faces.

But Sara was real. Sara was still alive. And so were others.

When the Sultan ambushed our camp in the city, many were captured. But there was only one execution.

Imin. Our Demdji shapeshifter.

Imin had died wearing Ahmed's face to deceive the Sultan and all of Izman into thinking the Rebel Prince was dead, while Delila cast an illusion to hide her real brother, still jailed with the rest of the Rebellion's leaders.

Ahmed was still alive. So was Shazad, our General, even if she didn't like being called that. We needed her back to lead us in the fight against the Sultan. And Rahim, another of the Sultan's sons who had held a grudge against our exalted ruler since he caused his mother's death. He was our key to a whole army in the mountain who had never been loyal to the Sultan, but to him instead.

And now it was up to me to rescue them and all the others captured rebels. With the help of a handful of others who'd escaped capture that night: our reluctant Prince Jin, our professionally difficult golden skinned Demdji Hala, our shapeshifting twins Izz and Maz, and our semi-reliable foreign thief Sam. Not exactly an army, but it was what we had left.

I'd fallen asleep in a chair in some corner of the Hidden House, our last refuge in Izman, where what was left of the Rebellion had retreated. A faint glow coming in through the window danced across Sara's face, enough for me to see the worry etched there. Her hair was tousled from a restless night, and a dark red robe hung loosely over her nightclothes, like she'd tied it in a hurry.

It must have been dawn. My body still felt heavy with exhaustion, like I'd slept only a few hours. But I reckoned I could sleep a year and I still wouldn't shed this tiredness from my bones. It was the exhaustion of pain and of grief. My side still throbbed from the effort of using my powers a few hours ago, and for a second my vision tilted dangerously to one side, like I might lose my footing.

"What's happening?" My voice came out a croak as I stretched my aching body, still sore from being cut open by my aunt just yesterday. A necessary evil to get out the iron the Sultan had put under my skin to keep me from accessing my Demdji power. "Is it morning?"

"No, it's late. I got up because the baby was fussing." As my eyes slowly adjusted, I noticed the sleeping infant balanced in the crook of her left arm. It was little Fadi, my cousin Shira's newborn Demdji son. If there was any justice in the world he'd be with his mother now. But Shira had lost her head on the chopping block, too. I remembered the accusation in Shira's gaze in my nightmare. That her son would grow up without a family, all because of me. "When I woke up, there was . . ." Sara hesitated. "I think you'd better see for yourself."

That didn't sound good. I pressed my palms against my tired eyes. What else could *possibly* have gone wrong in the last few hours? Behind my lids I saw Imin's head falling onto that stage all over again. I dropped my hands away from my face. Better to face reality than nightmares. "All right," I said, slowly getting to my feet. "Lead the way."

Cradling the small, blue-haired Demdji in her arms, Sara led me up the dark, winding staircase to the rooftop that gave the Hidden House its name. The garden that topped the flat building was surrounded on all sides by trellises thick with flowers that concealed the house from prying eyes and kept Sara and all the women under her charge safe.

I knew something was wrong before we fully emerged onto the roof. It was late at night. But there was a dim glow outside, like the red of an angry dawn, that didn't make any sense this near midnight, not even in summer.

Sara reached the roof ahead of me and then quickly stepped out of the way, giving me an unobstructed view. And I saw what she was talking about.

The city of Izman was domed by fire.

Rippling flames hung over my head and to every side of us, like an immense vault placed over the city. I could just see the stars on the other side, but it was like looking through warped glass; they were blurry and indistinct. To the west I could see the fire arching down toward the walls of the city, and to the north, it plunged down toward the sea. A memory came to me from nowhere, of my mother in our kitchen when I was little, slamming a glass over a beetle as it scurried across the kitchen table, capturing it inside. I'd watched curiously as the thing scrambled up the side of the glass frantic and confused. Trapped. Staring up at the dome of fire over us, I understood that little Dustwalk beetle pretty well right now.

"It's magic," Sara said, gazing grimly up at the stars through the sheen of flames.

"No." I might've believed that, too, once upon a time. But I recognized it, this flickering, too-bright, not entirely natural fire. It was the same one I'd seen bloom in the vaults under the palace when the Djinni Fereshteh had been killed in the Sultan's machine. It was the same stolen fire that I had seen light up the Abdals, the Sultan's mechanical soldiers, who, even now, patrolled the streets below us, keeping the curfew. "It's an inventor's trick." Some new creation of Leyla's, the Sultan's inventor daughter, designed to keep us imprisoned here. Except, even though this was new, there was something strangely familiar about it.

And lo, a great wall of flames did enclose the mountain, trapping her for all eternity.

Those words from the Holy Books sprang into my mind fully formed. Dustwalk had drummed scripture into me for the first sixteen years of my life. I knew the story of Ashra's Wall as well as anyone: the great barrier of fire that imprisoned the Destroyer of Worlds at the end of the First War.

Killing Immortal beings. Resurrecting ideas from the Holy Books. The Sultan really was playing at being a god now.

Except this wasn't to protect us from some great evil. And this was far from holy work.

We were trapped here *by* the great evil.

• • •

I DIDN'T WAKE the rest of the house, just Jin. Though it took me longer than I would've liked before I finally found him in one of the many rooms of the house. He'd fallen asleep fully clothed on top of an unmade bed with his arm flung over his face against the light. I didn't even have to shake him awake. The moment my hand touched his shoulder, his eyes snapped open, his hand clamping painfully over my wrist, moments away from breaking it before he recognized me.

He cursed in Xichian, his grip loosening quickly as he sat up. He fought for alertness through the exhaustion. "You startled me, Bandit."

"Don't try to tell me this is the first time you've been woken up by a girl in the dead of night." My lightness was strained as I pushed a strand of dark hair out of his face with my now freed hand so I could see him clearly. He needed to cut it. But it'd been a long time since we'd had the luxury of time for frivolous things. Not since we were pushed out of our camp in the desert.

Jin caught my hand again, but more gently this time, and for a moment there was a ghost of that old smile, one that meant simpler trouble than the kind we were in right now. But before he could give voice to whatever thought it was that went with that smile, my words reached his tired mind. "It can't be the dead of night." He glanced at the light leaking through the window. And my brief moment of dodging the real world was gone.

I told him what Sara had shown me as we waited anxiously for the real dawn. The house woke little by little around us, and the same unsettled feeling draped over everyone's shoulders, one by one, as they saw the dome. Each of them looking at me for answers I didn't have.

How is it made? Can we get through it? Is it here to keep us in?

Finally, the very first spark of dawn leaked through the veil of fire, signaling the end of curfew. Finally, Jin and I could move.

The streets were already flooding with people, men and women stumbling out of their houses, eyes upon the fire-filled sky above us. The same questions that the Rebellion had been asking me were on everyone's lips. Jin and I dodged around them as quickly as we could without attracting suspicion. Both of our gazes were fixed on the compass in Jin's hand. The one that was paired with Ahmed's. Our Rebel Prince had had his compass with him when he was taken prisoner. "He still has it," I said out loud to be sure, as we rushed through the tight streets of the city. I could feel my breath coming short the closer we got to the palace. That was where the prisoners had been held yesterday, before Imin's execution. They had to still be there. Or somewhere else in the city. But as we neared the wide, richer streets that surrounded the palace, the compass needle didn't swing toward the Sultan's wall. Instead it kept pointing south.

We passed the palace, my heart feeling tighter with every step we took away from the palace. We'd figured our rebels were still being held within the palace walls. Hell, we'd counted on it. Now all I had to cling to was a faint hope that they were at least still in the city. That Jin's compass might track down its pair before we reached the wall.

It didn't.

The sky outside the wall of fire had gone from pink to gold as we reached the south gate. Zaman's Gate, named for the first Sultan of Miraji.

Just beyond it, the wall of fire rose.

It looked a whole lot more imposing up close than it had standing under it. It seemed to snap and crackle angrily. Sparking at intervals, like it was hungry for destruction. Like it would consume anything that dared try to cross it.

And the compass in Jin's hand was pointing straight toward it.

They were outside the city. The Sultan had sent the prisoners beyond the city and put a wall up around us. We were trapped here while they were out there. Taken somewhere to be imprisoned for the rest of their lives without trial—our Sultan's version of mercy.

We could feel the heat pouring off the wall from here.

But Jin picked up a stone from the street. He bounced it up and down in his palm a few times; it made him look young, like a kid about to cause mischief. And then he chucked the stone at the wall. It didn't bounce back toward us as it would against a regular wall, or pass through as it would normal fire. It incinerated as it hit, turned from stone to ash in the space of a heartbeat.

We would burn even faster than that if we tried to walk through.

My first thought was that the Sultan was trying to keep us from getting to the prisoners. To keep me from getting away, so he could sink his hooks into me again and drag me back to the palace. But Jin said my next thought before I could.

"It doesn't make sense." He pushed a hand through his hair, dislodging his sheema. I glanced around quickly, to see if there was anyone who might spot us. "Not if he thinks Ahmed is dead. All this . . . it can't be for our benefit."

He wasn't wrong. In the Sultan's mind, we were defeated. An act of war against us this large would be wasted. "Then who do you reckon it is for?"

We got our answer before the sun set. As we were waiting anxiously for news from the palace. For something the Sultan might say to his people about what we had all woken up to. The twins circled above the palace in the shapes of larks, taking turns to dash back to the house and report on the comings and goings. But there was nothing much of interest. That was, until just before sunset.

Izz and Maz returned together, two sand-colored birds crisscrossing each other frantically in the sky before they landed on the rooftop, becoming boys again as they did.

"Invaders." Izz spoke first, trying to catch his breath. "Coming from the west."

"Blue-and-gold banners," Maz added, breathing hard, his chest rising and falling. My heart faltered. The Gallan were marching on the city. The desert's all too familiar occupiers. Come to take our country for themselves once and for all.

That was what the wall was for. Not to keep us in. To keep them out.

The city was protected. But we were trapped.

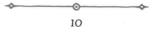

TWO

THE DEATHLESS SULTIMA

Once, there was a desert under siege and a Sultan without an heir to defend it.

The desert had many enemies. They came from the east and the west and the north to occupy the desert's cities, enslave its people, and steal its weapons to fight other wars, in faraway lands.

The Sultan saw his desert was under siege from many a side, and that his own forces were outnumbered man to man. And so he summoned his enemies' kings, queens, and princes to his palace.

He called it a truce.

His enemies saw it as surrender.

It was neither. In truth, it was a trap.

The Sultan turned soldiers made of metal and magic on his enemies, and reduced their leaders to dust.

Many of the Sultan's enemies retreated, but the great empire spreading across the north heard the Sultan's declaration of war against them and resolved to answer it. They were enraged by the slaughter of their king and their soldiers. And so their young, impulsive prince, soon to take his father's place, ordered his forces to march on the great desert city and destroy it.

The Sultan heard of the approaching threat, and he had no small number of sons whom he might have sent into battle to face the approaching armies. But he had no heir. His firstborn had died at the hands of the Rebel Prince, who was consumed by jealousy and sought the throne for himself.

Or so it was said by some.

There were others who said that the Rebel Prince was no traitor, but rather a hero. And those men and women cried out that the Rebel Prince should be the one to defend the desert—not any of the Sultan's sons raised in the palace but his true prodigal heir.

But even as the enemy's army approached, the Rebel Prince was captured. No matter that the people cried out for him to save them, they could not save him as he was delivered to the executioner's block. For the people of the desert knew that it did not matter if he was a rebel or a traitor or a hero, all men were only mortal in the end.

And yet, when the axe fell, some who saw it swore that he seemed to be more than a mere mortal, that they witnessed his soul leave his body in a great light and transform into a shield of fire around their city. They whispered that the Rebel Prince had answered their call for succor even in death. Just as Ashra the Blessed had answered the desert's call in time of need thousands of years ago.

And sure enough when the invaders arrived, they found a great barrier of fire protecting the desert city. The invaders could not attack, and the people of the desert praised the Rebel Prince for shielding them. The invaders could do nothing except surrounded the city and wait for the wall of fire to fail or for the Sultan to send a champion— a prince and heir—to lead his armies against them.

• ● •

ON THE FIRST day of the siege, the Sultan's eldest surviving son, a great swordsman, came to him and asked that he might bear the honor of leading their armies in battle against the invaders at their gates. But the Sultan refused him. He did not know if this son was worthy.

On the second day, the Sultan's second-eldest son, a great archer, came to him and asked that he might have the honor of leading men in raining arrows down on the enemies who surrounded them. But again the Sultan refused, unsure if he was worthy.

On the third day, the Sultan's third son came. And he, too, was refused.

Days passed, then weeks, with no heir chosen to fight the enemies. The people of the city grew restless.

Finally the Sultan, having rebuffed every one of his

sons old enough to fight, declared that a new heir would be chosen by trial in battle. As had been the way of the desert since the time of the first Sultan.

The people flocked to the palace to see the trial, crowding around the steps for a glimpse of the men who each might become their ruler. The Sultan appeared before his people and told them that though he still grieved his first-born son, he saw now that a new heir must be chosen, for the good of his country and his people.

But the Sultan had scarcely begun to speak when the people watching heard another voice.

He lies.

It was the voice of a woman. She did not shout; she whispered. But they heard her clearly all the same, as if she had spoken in their ears. Or from within their own minds.

The assembled people cast around in astonishment, looking for the woman bold enough to speak of their exalted ruler so. And as they did, they saw a thing that was scarcely to be believed. The woman who had spoken stood not at their side but before them, holding her severed head between her hands, pressed close to her heart.

Where her head should have been, her neck ended in a bloody stump.

Those who recognized her passed the word on to those who did not, and soon it swept through all the onlookers that standing before them was the Blessed Sultima. The traitor wife to their now dead Sultim, executed by her husband's order.

Returned from the dead.

Though her lips did not move, they all heard her speak.

He lies, she said again, hair fluttering freely over her fingers as she stared accusingly out across the crowd. *And lying is a sin.*

Scarcely had she spoken when the sky darkened. And when the people of Izman looked up, a great sandstorm had rushed in to crown the city and hide the sun, plunging the palace into shadow, even as the Blessed Sultima glowed ever more brilliantly. The people cowered under this wrathful storm, which the dead girl had brought to hang over their heads like an axe that might fall and kill them before her very eyes, just as she had been killed before theirs. They dropped to their knees, praying for mercy, though they did not know if they prayed to God or the dead girl.

But the dead Sultima was not interested in mercy. Only in truth.

It was not the Rebel Prince who killed the Sultim. Her voice was clear even over the rising wind that balanced the sand over their heads.

It was his own father. The Sultima's bloody hand shot out, pointing toward the Sultan on his balcony high above his people. Her head spilled from her hands and toppled to the ground so that its eyes stared angrily up at him. But her voice never wavered. *He killed his son in cold blood, as he did his brothers and his father. And he now stands before you pretending grief while he prepares to send more of his sons to their deaths against the invaders he has brought down on this city.*

On their knees in front of this miraculous apparition, the citizens of Izman believed her. For what reason would the dead have to lie?

Then the Sultima lifted her head from the ground where it had fallen, turning it to fix her eyes on the princes behind her. One dropped to his knees. Another drew a bow, firing an arrow toward her already blood-soaked chest. It passed straight through the deceased Sultima, as if through water, planting into the ground behind her.

The Sultima looked at the arrow dispassionately before turning back to the princes, who were helpless against her words.

No new Sultim will be chosen from this pack of unworthy princes. The true Sultim was already chosen, and I come here with a warning.

Later, those among the crowd would tell of how she cradled her head in her hands like it was the child who had been taken from her too soon, the child who had not been born of her husband but, some said, of a Djinni. Of course they should choose the mother of one of their children as their messenger from beyond this world.

The Rebel Prince is the true heir. He must rule in Miraji or else no Sultan will ever rule again. Our country will fall to war and conquest and the very armies who wait by our gates. It will be divided and bled dry by our enemies.

This Sultan can bring only darkness and death. Only the true heir to Miraji can bring peace and prosperity.

A great cry rose from the crowd then, though all heard the words she spoke next.

The Rebel Prince will rise again.

He will bring a new dawn. A new desert.

THREE

I zman looked different from above.

I was standing on the ledge of the great prayer house and I could see the crowd assembled for the Sultim trials far below us. That was why we'd picked this spot, to keep an eye on this morning's proceedings. Because it sure as hell wasn't for the comfort of it.

I shifted as much as I dared on the narrow ledge, trying to get a better view of what was going on. I teetered forward a little as gravity reached up for me, and to my right Jin instinctively grabbed my arm, steadying me before I could plunge hundreds of feet to my death.

"I don't have it in me to lose you, too, Bandit," he said as he anchored me to our perch.

Maz and Izz flanked us. They'd flown us up here, taking the form of two giant Rocs, just before daybreak, when people started to gather. The sun hitting the golden dome of the prayer house made it blaze so bright it almost blinded me, even with my back to it. Which meant it would blind anyone in the crowd who might happen to glance up our way, making us seem like kaleidoscopic illusions in the light instead of flesh and blood.

When I was down in the streets, the city was a latticed puzzle box. Sharp corners, hidden alcoves, unexpected dead ends. Long streets pierced occasionally by windows that leaked whole other worlds onto the dusty paving stones. Narrow passages made all the narrower for being lined by market stalls and a steady stream of people. The whole thing lidded by colorful canopies blotting out the sky. I still hadn't managed to solve the city, even after nearly a month of being trapped inside it by the great dome of fire.

I knew it was one of Leyla's unnatural inventions the moment I saw it. But the people had drawn the same conclusion as Sara that first night. That it was ancient magic, the likes of which hadn't been seen since the end of the First War.

Many were calling it Ahmed's Wall. Some had even begun praying to it. *Ahmed's Acolytes*, so called. Men and women who singed their clothing and smeared their faces in ash and spent their days trying to get as close to the great barrier of fire as they could in order to pray for it to hold against the invaders at our gates. No matter how many times the Sultan's soldier's turned them away, they kept coming back, dawn after dawn. A few had even died getting too close to the barrier. Disintegrating like the stone Jin had thrown at it the day it appeared. They preached that Ahmed had saved us all.

Though I hated to admit it, it was possible the barrier *had* saved us. Even if I knew it was nothing to do with Ahmed.

From up here on our perch I could see the lines of blue tents encircling our city with military precision. Waiting. Just as they had been for weeks. After the twins saw them on the horizon, it wasn't long before they got to the city. But that was where their invasion stalled. They couldn't get through the barrier on their side any more than we could. Their bullets had disintegrated against the barrier of fire, too. Soon enough the Gallan had gone silent. Even if they hadn't gone anywhere else. We all knew better than to think they would give up so easy.

The Gallan had occupied our desert for nearly two decades. They had put our Sultan on his throne, helping him usurp his father and brother. And in return he had let them impose their laws on us. Let their twisted beliefs guide them to kill Demdji and First Beings. Force our poorest people into dangerous labor to churn out enough weapons for them to fight their wars. Inflict their violence on us without fear of repercussion from the law. The Sultan had let it happen and waited until the Gallan didn't serve his purposes anymore. Only then had he tried to annihilate them using Noorsham, my brother, a Demdji who could flatten cities. He had turned the thing they hated most, magic, against them. But we'd gotten in the way before Noorsham could finish them off. I wanted the Gallan out as much as anyone, but he would've killed a whole lot of Mirajin citizens in his path, too. In the end, the only thing the Sultan achieved was making enemies of our occupiers.

And now here we were, under siege from the largest empire in the world.

They seemed to think they could wait us out on the other side of that wall of fire. Izman was bound to run out of supplies eventually. But I knew a thing or two about the Sultan. He didn't play games he didn't think he could win.

I wondered how many Mirajin villages and towns the Gallan had stormed through on the way to Izman. How many people had died in their path as the Sultan waited for them to come to him.

The Sultan had claimed to me once that his purpose was to protect his country. That he would make Miraji a force to be reckoned with, one that no foreign army would occupy ever again. And maybe he'd do it. But every step toward that looked to me like a little more power in the Sultan's hands, and bodies trampled on the way. The people of Miraji had not agreed to be pieces in this game the Sultan was playing against foreign invaders.

The rebellion was going to end the game. As soon as we figured out how the hell to get out of this city.

We were going to get Ahmed back. And Rahim back. And Shazad. And Delila. And all the others who had been captured. And we were going to end this.

A bead of sweat tracked its way from under my sheema, down my neck, and under my kurta.

"You all right, Bandit?" Jin asked me, his voice low next to my ear.

I'd have liked to have been able to lie and tell him that I was fit as a fiddle, but since I couldn't I didn't answer at all. "It's time," I said, spreading my hands out across the city below, sprawling my fingers as far as they would go. "Get ready."

I might not be able to reach the dunes beyond the Sultan's artificial barricade, but this city was full of desert dust. It was in its bones. Its very soul.

I pulled. The wound in my side twinged with pain like a muscle protesting use. It had been doing that ever since the metal was removed from my skin. The scar on my side pained me like it remembered the iron and was fighting back against my Demdji power. It was getting worse every time. And once or twice I felt like the sand might slip out of my grip altogether.

I ignored it as best I could, as the dust rose out of the streets in a golden haze, like steam rising off a bath. From between cobblestones and where it was trapped in folds of clothes and resting on leaves in roof gardens. Filling the air, swirling up, and gathering together. A thousand tiny grains of sand, nothing on their own, scattered across the city but joining together into a riotous storm.

Somewhere below us in the crowd gathered to watch the Sultim trials was Hala, bundled up to her eyebrows against prying gazes that might notice her golden skin.

She was with two other rebels who'd escaped with us, Riad and Karam. I trusted them both to keep her safe—or carry her away if the illusion became too much for her.

It was an illusion on a bigger scale than Hala had ever managed before: the Blessed Sultima come back to life. My cousin Shira, exactly as she looked in my nightmares, her head detached, her eyes full of accusations, projected into thousands of people's minds at once to deliver a message designed to spark doubt over the Sultan and stall the Sultim trials.

It was a desperate, risky thing to do, stretching Hala's powers to their limit. But we had to do something. The last thing we needed was the country falling in line behind a new prince while we were trying to rescue the old one. Besides, stalling the Sultim trials was only our second purpose.

Hala was the distraction. I was the cover.

What we really needed was to get into the palace.

Things can be a distraction and serve the cause at the same time.

Shazad had told me that once, when she'd first tried to rescue me from the harem, with pamphlets raining from the sky. But then, Shazad made everything seem easy.

Two targets. One bullet. That I could understand. *Two purposes. One plan.*

I heard a shout from below as Hala's illusion crept into the minds around her, and for a moment my own focus faltered, my power slipping out of my grip. I felt the burning pain in my side start to ease. It was such a relief that for just a second it made me want to let go, to drop the storm and stop the pain. To just let everything go and rest.

I wrestled the sand back hastily, and instantly the pain came back with it as I fought for control. I worked until the sandstorm covered the square below in a swirling mass, shielding us from sight. My side still ached. I shifted, trying to ease the pain, and the storm shifted with me unexpectedly. I couldn't stall giving the signal any longer. I was struggling to hold on already. I turned my head just far enough toward Jin and the twins to be heard over the storm, and said, "Now."

They didn't need to be told twice. Maz had been bursting for hours, shifting restlessly from one shape to another, waiting for the order. Now a huge grin spread over his face as he flung aside the cloak he was wearing, sending it tumbling down into the sandstorm below as he jumped from the edge of the roof without a second thought. For a moment he was just a boy in midair, at the pinnacle of a leap, before the inevitable fall, the moment when you stopped flying and came crashing back down to earth. And then he stopped being just a boy. His body shifted, arms turning to wings, feet becoming claws, skin exploding into feathers. Izz followed, flinging the bundle on his back around into his mouth as it turned into a beak before he launched himself from the edge.

If the crowd below us had been able to see, it might have looked like a pair of Rocs had just burst from the golden dome of the prayer house, like some mystical egg had hatched them. They soared gracefully above the storm that hid them, desperately happy to be moving again.

Unlike the twins, Jin had barely moved since we got up here. He was good at that—at stillness when everyone around us was restless. But I could read it in him all the same, there below his skin: impatience waiting to burst into action. It'd been there for weeks now. Since the day we saw Imin executed as Ahmed. Since the night we found out we were trapped here, unable to get our people back. Unable to save the family that he had protected for years. Sometimes I caught him with his hand opening and closing over the brass compass compulsively, but that was the only sign he gave that he was as worried as the rest of us. Now he spared me a sideways glance, a heartbeat, just long enough for me to give him a nod, assurance that I was fine. That I could hang on. I wasn't about to tell him pain was searing through my side from the old wound and I didn't know how long I could keep this up.

Jin gave me a small, wry smile back, a ghost of the one he used to have back when things were simpler and there were other people running this rebellion for us. The smile that said we were about to get into trouble. We were already in trouble now.

And then he stepped into thin air.

Maz soared below him, catching Jin on his back easily, then shifting directions with one effortless beat of his wings to carry him toward the palace, where Izz waited in all his blue-feathered glory.

I let out an uneasy breath, fighting the urge to drop one of my hands and press it against my aching side. We needed a way through this impossible wall and out of the city. We'd already searched the whole perimeter of Izman for some kind of gap—a gate, a fissure we could squeeze through, something, anything. But the city was locked up tight as a drum. Which meant we needed to look somewhere else for a way out. Somewhere like the mess of papers strewn across the Sultan's desk that included everything from supply routes for the army to letters addressed to foreign rulers inviting them to Auranzeb, the celebration of the Sultan's ascendancy to the throne. I'd rifled through these same papers during my own time in the palace.

Only we didn't have a spy in the palace anymore. So we needed to get back in if we were going to get information out.

This was far from our first try at getting in. Sam had made a stab at going through the palace walls first a few weeks back. His strange Albish magic allowed him to slip through solid stone like it was water. It was a gift no one in Miraji had ever seen, and so nobody knew to guard against it.

Only we'd shown our hand when the Sultan ambushed us.

After our narrow escape, the Sultan knew exactly what extraordinary powers we had up our sleeves. The walls of the palace were now lined on the inside with wooden panels, which were as solid to Sam as to anybody else.

And more than that, they were expecting us to try that night.

The bullet would have torn straight through his heart if Sam hadn't moved at the last second, unable to resist leaning back through the wall to where we waited, cloaked in Hala's illusion, to toss some offhand sarcastic comment. The gunshot caught him in the shoulder instead. There was a lot of blood. Everywhere. Smeared on the stone of the wall as he stumbled out, with no retreat except into the open. On my hands when I caught him as he lost consciousness. On Jin's shirt when he heaved him over his shoulder hastily. Soaked into the once clean linens of the bed when we finally got him back to the Hidden House, still breathing. Barely.

Not that saving him did us much good in the long run.

But that was how we learned our lesson. We had to wait for a cleaner shot. Even if every second we waited meant the prisoners were getting farther away from us. Meant they might be getting tortured. Might be killed. We had to wait. The Sultim trials was the shot we'd been waiting for. So we had to take it. No matter how desperate it was.

Below me Izz spread his huge blue wings, riding an updraft from the sandstorm I was creating, letting it carry him over the palace, his huge shadow skimming easily over the walls and the gardens of the harem, then over the glass dome that crowned the Sultan's chambers.

We couldn't get in through the walls. Fine. We'd try something less subtle.

Izz dropped the explosives he was carrying, sending them careening down toward the glass. The dome exploded, shattering into a rain of shards that caught the sun like stars falling from the heavens. Jin and Maz plunged through the new entrance to the palace, straight into the Sultan's rooms, even as Izz circled back for me.

He soared below me, and I took a deep breath, fighting to keep the sandstorm under my control even as I split my attention. The pain was distracting, but I had to trust that if I jumped Izz would catch me. So, bending my knees just a little, spreading my body flat, I leapt into nothingness. I landed on Izz's back, and the impact knocked the air out of my lungs, turning my vision black. But I didn't let go. I fought to hold on both to his back and to the desert as he soared upward.

We didn't have much time.

Hala's illusions ought to work on the people of Izman, get them to believe Shira really had come back from the dead, but the Sultan would guess it was us easily enough. And it wouldn't take him long to figure out that we were doing more than just whipping his people into a frenzy against him and his sons. He would come looking for us. I was going to have to buy Jin some more time.

Izz looped us around in the air until we were over the shattered dome. Jin and Maz had disappeared from sight, retreating to the Sultan's study. I could just make out the edge of the table where the Sultan and I had once sat, eating a duck I had killed in his gardens while he needled at my mind, making me doubt Ahmed.

It was covered in shards of glass now.

Ignoring the shooting pain in my side, I pushed away

from Izz's back, so I could see the sand. I fought to keep my balance, even as the wind whipped through my hair, lashing it around my face, tugging at my clothes. I took a deep breath and gathered the sand back toward us, tightening my grip. I lifted my arms, pulling upward, as I would if I were clearing the sandstorm. But instead of letting it scatter through the streets of Izman, I whipped it in a great swirling vacuum toward us.

The sand shot past me, narrowly missing Izz's wing, the force buffeting him upward. I didn't lose my grip as he beat his wings, frantically trying to regain his balance. I plunged every grain of sand I'd drawn from Izman's streets down through the broken glass dome in a tightly controlled cascade, ignoring the twisting agony. I focused the sand toward the hallway that led into the Sultan's chambers, flooding it, blocking the entrance like a stopper in a bottle, cutting off any access the soldiers might have to Jin.

I let go. The pain finally eased, going from a sharp stab to a dull ache as it retreated. I slumped down onto Izz's back as I looked down on my work. It wouldn't last forever. It was sand; they would dig through it eventually. But it ought to take long enough for Jin to find what we needed. If it was even there.

With a few powerful beats of his wings, Izz carried us up and out of reach of gunfire from the ground. The palace spread out below us like a little toy model. Soldiers were already running toward the Sultan's chambers. Men and women in the square dropped to their knees as the vision of Shira dissipated from their minds. The twelve princes stood in shock, one standing, sword drawn, with nothing to fight. Others fled the sandstorm and the sound of the explosion nearby and the sudden appearance of a giant Roc hovering above them.

And then I spotted a lone figure in the gardens of the harem, staring up at us. It was her stillness that caught my eye. I knew her on sight, even this far away, from the way she tied her hair and the slope of her shoulders. She was like a statue, as motionless as one of her Abdals before they moved in for the kill.

Leyla.

Our traitor princess.

FOUR

She looked tiny from up here. Like a mouse staring up at a falcon, too foolish to run from it.

I leaned down to Izz's head, pointing past him toward her. He might be in an animal shape, but he could understand me just fine. I wanted him to take me down to her.

I felt him hesitate below me for a few huge ponderous wing beats. He didn't want to enter the harem. It wasn't part of our plan. I could almost hear Shazad's voice in my mind. *No, by all means, Amani, we only spent months trying to get you out of the harem. But go ahead, go straight back in when I'm not there to bail you out.* If it were Ahmed, he would listen to her good counsel, like he always did. He would be cautious.

But Shazad and Ahmed had been captured. Because of Leyla. And that left me in charge of this rebellion, with no good counsel to listen to.

I voiced the command. "Izz, take me to the ground."

This time he obeyed. I tightened my grip on his back as he plunged, diving straight toward the gardens of the harem.

Leyla realized she was our target far too late. We were on her as she tried to look for cover, the force of the air from Izz's wings knocking her down. As she scrambled backward clumsily, I slid off Izz's feathered back, my feet landing in the harem for the first time since I'd escaped. Izz took the shape of a huge blue lion, springing for her before she could find her footing, front paws pinning her to the ground. She didn't scream as he flattened her out on her back, razor teeth inches from her face. She just squeezed her eyes shut. Like she thought she was ready to die.

She was trying to be brave. She was good at it, too. Leyla had spent several days with us, her enemies, pretending to be on our side, without so much as flinching. I might admire her if she weren't our enemy.

"Izz," I ordered, "let her up." He did what I said, pulling back his snarling face and slowly removing his weighty paw from her chest. As soon as she was released Leyla scrambled backward, her shoulders bumping into the wall behind her, halting any farther retreat. We were both silent for a long moment, Leyla breathing hard as she watched me. I pulled out my gun, deciding exactly what I wanted to do with her. I hadn't thought that far when I'd plunged us down here.

"So." I'd better start us off. "My guess is that we have your brilliant mind to thank for this"—I glanced up at the dome of fire in the sky, looking for the right word, even as I pulled out my gun—"this whole mess." I opened the chamber of the pistol and checked how many bullets I had. Six whole shots. Good.

"My father's guards—" Leyla started, a slight tremor in her voice.

"My guess would be that your father's guards are going to get sent to check on his paperwork before his daughter." The whole of the harem was strangely quiet around us. There was only the sound of Leyla's panicked gasps and the loud click as the chamber of the gun snapped back into place.

She winced at the sound. Or maybe it was at hearing that truth so plainly laid out.

"You're not going to kill me." But her eyes flicked to the gun all the same, like she wasn't sure. I only had a year or two on her, but she seemed a whole lot younger. I'd grown up fast in the desert. She was a child from the palace. I searched myself for some sympathy, but I didn't have any left for this girl who had betrayed me. Who had cost us so much because of my carelessness in believing she was as innocent as she looked.

"Want to bet your life on that?" I pointed the gun at her head, and Leyla cringed away, like she could make herself too small a target to hit. She was underestimating what a good shot I was. But I didn't fire. "Here's how this is going to go." I tried to sound sure of what I was doing, like this was a real plan and not some stupid idea I'd thought up halfway through doing it. Like I wasn't just a girl from Dustwalk with a gun, pretending I could get information out of the brilliant little head of a girl born so far above me she shouldn't even be able to see me if she deigned to look down. "I'm going to ask you a question and pull this trigger. And if you answer me truthfully, the bullet will hit that wall behind you. If you lie to me, the bullet is going to draw blood. Is that clear?"

It sure looked like it was clear from the sudden fearful understanding on her face. I was a Demdji. I could only speak the truth, and now I wasn't the one deciding whether that bullet would hit her, she was. From where he was sitting, still wearing the shape of a lion, I thought I saw Izz shift uneasily. I knew what he was thinking. I was getting myself into awfully deep waters here. But it was too late to go back now.

"Now"—I took aim—"how do we bring it down? This little wall of fire you've got around the city?"

Leyla looked me in the eyes. "You can't."

I pulled the trigger before she'd even finished speaking and before I could think twice about what I was doing. The bullet hit her in the arm. The scream that tore through her was all the confession I needed. I swept my gaze over the garden behind us quickly. That wasn't going to have gone unheard. Not even in the harem, where the women were practiced at ignoring the terrible things happening around them.

"Remember how much that hurts when you answer that again," I said as I turned my gaze back on a now bleeding Leyla, trying to hide my nerves while I pulled back the hammer, letting the next bullet slide into place. "Tell me how, or this bullet is hitting your knee, and if you ever want to walk again, you'll have to get yourself a metal leg like the one you got Tamid. You remember Tamid, don't you? A friend of mine? The one you convinced me you had a soft spot for so you could use him to lure your father to us?"

Leyla was breathing through her nose, pain written all over her, but muddling with rage now. Getting shot would do that to you. "You can't bring the wall down," she spat back. But before I could fire again she kept babbling quickly. "Because I haven't *built* the way yet. Until I do, the only way to get rid of the wall is to disable the machine." She meant the great contraption she had built under the palace that had killed and trapped the Djinni Fereshteh, turning him into energy to feed her unholy machines, like the Abdals. And now the contraption was powering this great dome of fire surrounding the city. "And for *that* you'd need the right words."

We needed the words that would free the Djinn from the trap I had summoned them to. With those we could free the living Djinn as well as Fereshteh's energy, which was powering the machine that fed life into all of Leyla's little inventions.

Tamid had found the right words to summon and

trap the Djinn. Just words unless they were spoken by a Demdji, and suddenly they became an all-powerful truth. That was how I had trapped them all in the palace when the Sultan had forced me to summon them while I was his prisoner. Tamid had been searching for the words that would free the Djinn for the past month. But so far we had nothing.

I pulled the trigger again. This time the bullet buried itself in the wall behind her. Damn, she was telling the truth.

"Do *you* know the words to release a Djinni?" I asked. She'd told us she didn't. But that was back when she'd been play-acting as a teary-eyed lost little princess and I'd been too trusting to question her about it.

"No." The third bullet buried itself in the wall, sending stone spraying violently as it did, making her flinch out of the way. Well, at least she had been honest about that.

Leyla started to cry, her sobs echoing loudly around the walls of the garden.

That was the third gunshot inside the harem. Someone ought to have reached us by now. Something was wrong. I listened carefully under the sound of Leyla crying. Far off I thought I could hear the screams of excited birds. Probably the ones trapped in the menagerie, startled by the loud noise and unable to get away. But there were no other screams to go with them—no women calling out for help or panicking at the sound of gunshots so near them. Just the bubble of fountains and, far off in the distance, the noises of the city.

"Why is it so quiet?" My question hadn't actually been for Leyla, but she answered it all the same.

"There's no one else here," Leyla said through a sob. "My father sent them all far away, to safety out of the city." She didn't say it, but I almost heard the *so there* that she was longing to tack onto the end. Like she wanted me to think I was wrong for judging her father the villain of this story. That he was a man who cared about his wives and his sons and had hurried them off to safety. But I didn't care what she wanted me to think about her father. What I did care about was the way she had said that. *He sent them all far away.*

I'd asked the wrong question, I realized. We needed to get out of the city. But we didn't need a way to bring down the magical barrier keeping us in. We needed a way *around* it. "So you're saying there's a way out of the city."

Leyla's already tormented expression shifted as she realized what she'd revealed to me. "No." I raised the gun and pointed at her. "Yes," she admitted quickly, amending the lie before I could fire again. "Yes."

The bullet struck the wall behind her, sending a spray of stone debris across her face. She was telling the truth, or else that bullet would've wound up in her shoulder. It was as if a weight that had been sitting on my chest since the moment we realized we were trapped had been lifted and I could breathe again. There was a way out. And I had someone who knew where it was at gunpoint. We were almost free.

"How do we get out of the city, Leyla?"

She had stopped crying. She considered me for a moment with those dark eyes under long lashes, rimmed in red from her tears. She ran a sleeve across her nose, sniffling like a little girl. There was almost nothing of her brother Rahim in her. Or of the Sultan, for that matter. There was more in that face of her pale Gamanix mother—an inventor's daughter from the same northern land that had made Jin's and Ahmed's compasses. Her features were more delicate than her brother's or father's, and though she was as dark as any Mirajin girl, it was obvious she hadn't seen as much sun as a girl ought to have, trapped behind these walls. The harem had made her look soft and childish, where Rahim looked hardened by his years in the mountains. But that didn't mean that was what they were: a hardened son and a gentle daughter. Rahim had looked broken by his sister's betrayal of him in favor of their father, the man who cost their mother her life. And, in turn, Leyla had seemed to be sharpened by her loyalty to their father, those fine features turning cruel. I saw it now, that nastiness in the curl of her lip as she stared down the barrel of my gun and answered me. "There's a gap in the barrier, by the northernmost gate, big enough for a person to slip through."

I fired, and the bullet hit her in the leg. She screamed again, doubling over in pain as the consequence of the lie made her bleed. Fresh anger bloomed in me, that she would start trying to trick me now that we were so close. "Now, why did you think that lie would work?" I asked her.

"Because you're almost out of bullets."

She was right, I realized. Five shots. I'd taken five shots at her. Which meant this was my last one.

And then I saw it above me: the shape of a giant Roc shooting back into the air from the ruins of the palace dome. Jin and Maz, leaving the inner sanctum of the palace, making a run for it. Meaning we were out of time. That was when I heard the sound of approaching footsteps and shouts far off in the harem. The guards were finally coming for the Sultan's favorite daughter.

It was time to get out.

I aimed the gun at her. "Leyla, how do we get out of this city? Tell me the truth and this bullet will miss you. Lie and it's going to bury itself in your skull."

Leyla was shaking a little as she stared me down. She was scared. She was a traitor to us, but I was the enemy to her. This was war, after all.

"Why should I tell you if you're just going to kill me anyway?" she shot back at me. "That bullet might miss me, but there are other ways you could kill me. You could break my neck or choke me to death." A memory passed between us: Leyla gently inspecting the bruises on my neck after the Gallan ambassador had almost squeezed the life out of me. "Why would you leave me alive?" She had a good point: she was a danger to us alive. And if she gave me this information, she was no more use to us. "I'd rather die than be a traitor to my father and my ruler. I'll *never* tell you." I kept my finger on the trigger. But I didn't squeeze. *I'll* never *tell you.* I didn't want to know if that was true. And if it was a lie, then I needed her without a bullet in her skull.

Damn her.

"You're right." I pulled the hammer back on the gun. It made her flinch. Not as ready to die as she wanted us to think she was. "I can't afford to leave you here alive." I holstered the pistol quickly, releasing the trigger, leaving the bullet in the chamber. I grabbed her, wrenching her to her feet. "Let's go."

Izz was changing shapes again, bursting into that of the enormous Roc. Leyla kicked and screamed, but she was small and I was stronger than her. I got her onto Izz's back before she could start to fight and claw in earnest. We were in the air and out of range of guns before the guards could even get close enough to shoot.

FIVE

"**W**ell, that was useless." Hala slammed the door behind herself loudly.

I'd been half dozing in the windowsill, but Hala's rage was enough to jolt me awake.

We'd shoved Leyla into the room I'd been sharing with Hala. In stories, princesses stolen from their father got hidden away in towers in the desert or palaces above the clouds. But all we had was a room with a half-decent lock in the Hidden House. And we barely had that. Most of the Rebellion had been captured with Ahmed, but there were still enough of us left that we didn't all fit into the Hidden House along with the women and children who already claimed it as home. We had everyone stacked three or four to a room, sleeping on makeshift pillow beds or straight on the floor. Even more folks slept on the roof, under the fiery sky that kept it from ever being properly dark, shielding their eyes from it as best they could. Which meant our precious prisoner had more space to herself than anyone else in this house.

Hala and I had moved our meager collection of belongings to the neighboring bedroom, which belonged to Sara and her child. Fadi, Shira's son, now slept in there as well since Sara had taken up care of him. It seemed natural, since she was the only one of us who actually knew what she was doing with a baby. Although I'd seen Jin soothe him once or twice when Sara was asleep. It was all a temporary solution though. He wasn't Sara's or Jin's or even mine. He was an orphan now, and when this war was over I'd have to find somewhere he belonged. *If* we won this war. If we didn't . . .

Now, in our new shared room, I was sitting on the windowsill and Jin was on the floor next to it, head tipped back against the wall below me. My hand had dropped to the crown of his head as I dozed, like I needed to make sure he was still there. Both of us were awake now, watching Hala tiredly. We were all exhausted from this morning's invasion of the palace and the unexpected princess kidnapping.

Sara sat in the corner, one hand rocking the cradle she'd dug out for Fadi. As it swung back and forth, I could just see his dash of blue hair in between the blankets. Another Demdji. Another child who would die if this country fell to the Gallan who waited outside our gates. In the room's only bed, Sara's small son stirred just a little, uneasy in his sleep, his fist stuck in his mouth. It was evening, still light out, and the sunlight streaming through the lattice pattern of the window next to me drew shadowy patterns across his face. Shazad had said once that the little boy's father was Bahi, her oldest friend, who had died at the hand of my brother, Noorsham. I hadn't known Bahi long, but even I could see the resemblance. The unruly dark curls and the soft open expression that had made me trust Bahi when I still wasn't even sure I could learn to trust Jin again, now worn by a little boy who would never know his father because of this war.

We kept losing people. And not just our people. People who belonged to others. People whose lives we'd had no right to lay down for them. And the people we had left were being taken farther and farther away from us every day. With no way for us to follow.

"Weren't you supposed to come back with papers?" Hala slumped against the door heavily, her anger fading, like a puppet whose strings had just been snipped, finally releasing her from some great show. The skin below her eyes was dark from lack of sleep, and she seemed thinner than she once had. "Or some sort of map that says, *Secret doorway through the barricade here*, maybe? Instead you bring me back a princess who already led her father to us once." She dropped, her back sliding slowly down the door until she was sitting on the ground. "Next time I'd appreciate a better gift after all my efforts to get you into the palace. I'm very partial to rubies for instance. Sapphires are also acceptable."

"I grabbed everything I could." Jin stretched out his shoulders, bumping against my leg as he did. "I guess there's a separate office for maps of secret doorways. They probably keep the sapphires in there, too."

The documents Jin *had* found in the Sultan's desk weren't exactly full of good news. There was the intelligence that the Gallan army was coming our way. I didn't need a piece of paper to warn me of that, now that they were camped on our doorstep. But there was also intelligence saying that they were a first wave and reinforcements would come a few weeks after, which would explain why the Sultan was waiting to deploy the Abdals against the foreigners. He was holding off until he could annihilate them all at once. There were some notes on sending extra troops to the south, where things were starting to fall into ungoverned chaos, people in those territories seeming uncertain of whether they were still under the influence of the now defunct Rebellion or whether they were subject to the throne.

Then there was the little fact that the Sultan knew that Bilal, Emir of Iliaz, had offered to betray him for us. Which could only mean trouble for Bilal. Although our exalted ruler didn't seem to know that Bilal was dying, or that the young emir's price for changing sides had been marriage to one of Ahmed's Demdji. Which wasn't a price we were going to pay, since none of us belonged to Ahmed. So we'd planned to take control of Bilal's army another way, by having Rahim usurp him, counting on the loyalty of the soldiers of Iliaz whom he used to command.

But Rahim was imprisoned along with Ahmed now. We needed them both back if we were going to take that army.

And then there was the note that sent my blood cold. A quickly dashed-off missive, dated the same day that the Rebellion was ambushed. It was an order to send soldiers after Shazad's father, General Hamad. He had been stationed on our westernmost border, staving off invasion via our neighboring country of Amonpour as this war raged on. With his daughter revealed as a traitor, he was to be executed for her crimes. Word had been sent before the city was locked down, a man's life ended in a few scribbled lines, while we were trapped in the city with no way to warn him.

Shazad would find a way to save her father if she were here. To warn him. But she wasn't. And I couldn't get to either of them. And now, her father was going to die. A man who had risked his life passing information to us. Who had helped soldiers who showed signs of turning against the Sultan find their way to us. Who had even helped some of his soldiers' wives into the Hidden House when men in his command proved to be poor husbands. He had worked quietly against the Sultan while trying to keep his family safe, and now I was going to get them all killed.

"I gather somewhere in all this chatter is the bad news that you haven't been able to get Leyla to talk?" I returned my attention to Hala as I unfolded myself from the windowsill. It was nearing sunset, and I'd been watching the people of Izman rush back and forth on the streets, completing their errands in a hurry. At sunset, the Abdals would flood the streets to enforce the citywide curfew that was still in place.

Hala scraped her pale gold nails through her dark hair. "It's a lot more difficult to trick someone when they know what you can do." The idea had been simple: Hala would slip into Leyla's mind and fool her into telling us the information that we needed. Hala was good at that. She had deceived my aunt into thinking I was my mother. And today she had conned an entire city. But Leyla was not some unsuspecting bystander. She knew what a Demdji could do. "And I will remind you that I wouldn't *have* to trick anyone if you'd brought back answers instead of more questions."

Silence dropped like a stone. I knew what Ahmed would've done in the old days. Gathered everyone to hear what we all reckoned we should do, listened to good counsel, figured out a plan. But nowadays this was everyone. Imin was dead. Ahmed, Shazad, and Delila were gone. Rahim, our newest ally, was captured with them. Sam was . . . missing. The twins were asleep somewhere. And all that left was me, Jin, and Hala. Two tired Demdji and one reluctant prince: that was all we had left. An awfully small, sad collection compared to the lot of us that used to gather in Ahmed's pavilion back in the oasis.

And then a voice boomed from outside, shattering the silence.

"Hear me now, my subjects."

Sudden terror bloomed in my chest. I would know the

Sultan's voice from a single word. I would know it if I heard it in my ear in the middle of nowhere on the other side of the world. I knew that voice better than I knew even Jin's. And right now there was absolutely no doubt in my mind that it was his voice coming from immediately below our window. He had found us.

We—I—had taken his daughter and I'd led him straight to us, and now we were done for. He would execute Jin on the stage, another rogue son to be rid of. And he would enslave us Demdji. And the rest of the Rebellion would die in some desert prison with no rescue ever coming for them.

For a second I was rooted. All the blood had rushed out of my body and I was just a shell of fear. Almost as if I was standing outside myself, I looked around the room, seeing equally frozen expressions on every other face.

Jin moved first, drawing his gun as he pressed himself into the space next to the window. I moved to follow him as the blood returned to my body, drawing my own weapon as I plastered myself to the wall, glancing outside. I prepared to see the Sultan standing below our window, shouting up at us. Like Bashir the Brave from the legends, calling up to Rahat the Beautiful when she was locked in the Djinni's tower.

Instead, on the street below us was an Abdal in all its gleaming bronze glory, staring straight ahead with its sightless eyes. The Sultan's mechanical soldiers, lit with Djinni fire.

"I speak to you now not as your ruler but as a father."

The Sultan's voice was coming from the Abdal. The machine was speaking, although its metal lips never moved. "A father to you, my people, and to my innocent daughter, your princess Leyla. Who has been kidnapped from the very heart of the palace by dangerous radicals acting in the name of the dead traitor prince." He didn't say Ahmed's name, stripping him of all identity except that of traitor.

The Sultan's voice was louder than any normal man's ought to be. As I craned my neck to peer down the street I could see another Abdal on the corner, the same voice presumably speaking out of it. People still on the streets were pressed against the walls as if they could retreat into them, taking in every word that was being spoken. . . .

This was not just happening here. My guess was that the Sultan had dispersed his mechanical soldiers across the city to stand in every neighborhood and speak this same message. Our exalted ruler was talking to thousands of people in his city at once with one voice we all had to heed.

"How is he doing that?" I hissed under my breath. I wasn't sure whether the Abdals could hear us or not.

Jin's gaze was fixed on the street. He looked grim, the lattice window casting strange patterns on his face. He shook his head.

"Some of you will understand the grief of losing a child." The Sultan's voice echoed out of the machine. Across the room I caught Hala's gaze just as she rolled her eyes so far back in her head I thought she might lose them there. "If you stood in my place now," the machine went on, "there is nothing any of you would not do that was within your power to retrieve your own daughters." The unspoken words seemed to echo just as loudly as those that spilled from the Abdals' unmoving lips: *and there is nothing that is not within my power.* "Any person who retrieves my daughter from these radicals and returns her to me will be rewarded with their weight in gold." My finger, which had been tightly wound around the trigger, eased a little. Bribes of gold were nothing new. There was no one in the Rebellion who would betray us for the Sultan's money. If this was all he had to offer his people—

"But," the voice spoke again, stopping the creeping relief in its tracks, "for every dawn that my daughter has not been returned to the palace, another man's daughter will die."

The ground tilted below me so suddenly that for a moment I had to squeeze my eyes shut and lean back against the wall to keep myself steady. But the words didn't stop coming from outside. And with my eyes shut it sounded like the Sultan was speaking within my own mind.

"I have forgiven you, my people who allied yourselves with my traitor son. Your crimes were put aside with his death. A new dawn . . . a fresh start for traitors." The voice trailed off mockingly as it turned Ahmed's words against us. "But do not mistake my forgiveness for ignorance. I know which of you turned your backs on me for the false promises of those renegades. And it is within my power to take your daughters' lives in exchange for the absence of mine."

It wasn't a lie or a bluff. The Sultan was a man of his word. I didn't know what I had imagined would happen as a consequence of kidnapping Leyla. I hadn't really thought much about it in that moment of diving down into the harem. I'd been reckless. Like I always was. And this time Shazad wasn't here to sweep up behind me. Or Ahmed to take the consequences of it.

"My message is simple. Return my daughter or yours will start dying tomorrow at sunrise," the Sultan's voice finished below us. "The choice is yours."

A long moment of silence stretched out from the streets. I opened my eyes. Below us the Abdals stood still, sightless and pitiless, as if they were waiting for their message to sink in. And then the machine below our window took a step, and I heard the crash of a dozen more metallic feet against stone, as the Abdals began to march in perfectly timed step. Returning to the palace to wait for the city's reply.

I pushed away from the wall, as the sound of thousands of mechanical feet echoed through the streets. I was still gripping the gun as I moved across the room. I didn't have to shove Hala aside; she knew exactly where I was going. She stepped away from the door that led to Leyla.

I slammed the door open. Our princess had moved as close to the window as she could with her hands chained to the frame of the bed. Her head snapped around as I entered.

"What the hell was that?" Behind me I heard Fadi start to cry. I'd woken him up. I cast a glance over my shoulder. Sara gave me a reproachful look as she picked him up, bundling the baby out of the room.

"I could've told you taking me was a mistake," Leyla gloated. She'd heard it, too, every word.

"What the *hell* was that?" I repeated, taking a threatening step toward her. But Leyla didn't flinch.

"A Zungvox." She sounded disgustingly pleased with herself. "Clever isn't it? They use it in my mother's land. I adapted it so that one could speak through my Abdals. I meant it to be so that the Holy Father's prayers could be heard all through the city, to quell those idiots worshipping the fire barrier like it was God's work and not mine." She shifted awkwardly back toward the bed, making herself comfortable. "I guess my father found another use for it."

"He's not a father who cares about getting his daughter back, you know." I tasted the spite in the words even as they spilled out. "He's a ruler who just wants his inventor back."

"Well, at least my father cares if I live or die," Leyla brought her bound hands up to her face, pushing the hair out of her eyes defiantly. "Can you say the same?"

I took another swift step toward her, and this time Leyla retreated against the headboard. I didn't realize I was still holding the gun until Jin's fingers brushed over the back of my hand. He had come up behind me, his broad hand closing gently over mine, his other arm circling my waist, pulling me back, away from her.

"Don't." He spoke quietly into my ear, so only I heard. "Let it go." I opened my fingers and released the gun into his grasp. As we turned away from Leyla, retreating from her prison, I realized I'd been clutching the gun so hard the mark of the handle was imprinted in my palm.

"I know you're afraid of him," Leyla called out from behind me as I started to close the door between us. "And you should be." She raised her voice so I could still hear her from the other side of the wall. "When they die, it's going to be your fault."

I ignored her. I didn't need her to tell me that. I already knew it was my fault.

● ● ●

I SLAMMED AS many things in the kitchen as I could before I found a half-stale loaf of bread. I started to tear off pieces. Sara had kicked us all out of the room while she dealt with the children we'd disturbed. Hala had gone to find the twins. They had been sleeping in the shapes of various animals since we got here—lizards and birds, for the most part. They were trying to take up as little room as possible when we had so little to spare, but it didn't always make them the easiest to track down. And we needed them. We needed everyone if we were going to make a plan, since we didn't have Shazad to do it for us anymore.

"We can't turn her back over." I said what we'd all been thinking. "She's the best shot we're likely to get at finding a way out of this city."

"I know," Jin replied absently, running his hand along his jaw, his eyes fixed on me. "If you give Hala a few more days with her, we might be able to trick something out of her when her guard's down. But—"

"But we don't have a few more days until the Sultan starts killing off girls," I completed. Jin was leaning against the door, arms crossed, like he could stand between me and the whole world.

"You did the right thing," he said after a moment, "with Leyla. Even if it was stupid as hell, it's still a shot to get out of here, and we've got to take all of those we can get."

"What if she really does keep her mouth shut?" I lifted my head, looking at him straight on across the kitchen. "What do we do then?"

We were tangling with a man who had armies and Djinni fire at his fingertips. And what was I? I was no-body. A girl with a gun from the end of the desert. To most people I didn't even have a name. I was just the Blue-Eyed Bandit.

I'd forgotten my place, after Imin's execution, when I stood up and volunteered to lead us. I'd forgotten that I was no one in this fight and there were dozens of men and women in this rebellion who were born better than me. Raised better than me. Educated better than me.

Shazad would have a strategy. Ahmed would wait until

he was sure of what to do. Rahim had armies that would march for him. I was just taking random shots in the dark and hoping to hit something.

"We figure it out," Jin said. "Like we always figure it out." It wasn't much of an answer, but it was all we had. I felt suddenly restless. I started moving again. Opening and closing cupboards. Like one of them might have the answer. Or at least some coffee.

"You don't look like you've been sleeping much," Jin said behind me.

I slammed another cupboard. "Have you been?"

I meant it as a challenge. But the question somehow felt more dangerous than it should have. We'd been separated by everyone else for the last month, in a house too crowded to ever find privacy. It was only then that I realized Jin and I were alone for the first time in as long as I could remember.

And now here he was asking me about sleeping. Because we'd been sleeping seperately. Which suddenly put into my head thoughts of sleeping . . . not separately. Which was ridiculous. We were both trapped in the middle of something bigger than what was between us. So all-consuming it didn't leave a whole lot of room for each other. But still, we'd been inching closer and closer to something more lately. Toward unknown waters—or unknown to me. And I knew that of the two of us, I was the one keeping us docked.

"No," Jin replied even as I stilled. He seemed to read what I was thinking and suddenly it was as if the kitchen had been emptied of air and I couldn't breathe for wanting to reach out for him. "I haven't been."

I moved first but he was quicker. It took only a few steps for him to reach me, backing me up against the table. But he stopped just before we touched. I didn't move either. I could tell he was being careful with me. Everything felt more fragile lately. He was close enough that I could feel the warmth from him even in the kitchen. I tilted my head back, finding the corner of his mouth with mine. Jin's hands had dropped to my waist, something solid to hang on to. His hands curled around the dusty shirt I hadn't had a chance to change out of, tugging it up just enough so that I felt his thumb graze over skin, sending a trail of heat behind it. He hadn't shaved today, and I found myself grazing my lips over the stubble at his jaw. The coarseness sent a shiver through my body.

Jin let out a breath that sounded like surrender a second before his arms went fully around me, lifting me to sit on the table as if I were light as anything. My shirt bunched under his arms, riding most of the way up my spine, his hands following my skin farther up, grazing the bottom of my shoulder blades, making me shiver all over again.

"You need to shave." I broke away from him, breathless, rubbing one hand along his jaw. We were face-to-face like this, with me sitting and him standing. Eye to eye. But it was hard for me to look at him straight on—it was too much, and if I did, everything I'd been holding back for weeks would rush into my blood and burn me alive from the inside. I might as well try to stare into the midday sun.

Jin grinned wryly against my hand on his jaw. "Later," he said, before claiming another kiss from me.

Without thinking I wrapped my legs around his middle, pulling him closer.

"And here I thought the rumors that Sara was running a brothel out of here were supposed to be false." The bitterness in Hala's voice split Jin and me apart.

"I'm no expert, but I figure doors in brothels have locks. So people have to knock," I retorted. Jin hadn't let me go, and with his back to Hala I was the only one who could see the smile that danced over his face before he stepped away, leaving me to get my feet back on solid ground.

She was leaning in the doorway, flanked by the twins. They were wrapped in robes, their blue and black tousled hair sticking up at strange angles, but grinning at the spectacle all the same.

"Is this you two coming up with a plan?" Hala asked, rolling her eyes and pushing into the kitchen.

"I have a plan." I could feel my face still flushed with heat as I straightened my shirt. "We don't return Leyla; we save the girls instead."

"Good plan," Izz chimed in cheerfully.

"Great plan," Maz chorused. "I love that plan."

"Yes, wonderful, what else could we possibly need other than a vague statement." Hala looked annoyed. "That's not a plan; it's barely an idea. Besides what makes you think we can save anyone else when you couldn't even save Imin?" That blow was meant to sting and it did, but

I wasn't going to stand here and argue with Hala. She couldn't be argued with lately; all she did was spit back the grief over losing Imin like poison.

"That's why you're here." I said, turning toward everyone. "To hash out the details." Night had fallen outside, and the only light in the kitchen was from the embers of the fire that cast everyone in a half-light, making them look like they were only half there. I needed to draw them back. "Now do you want to help, or do you want to just let them die?"

Nobody wanted to see anyone else die.

We put together something that was about halfway between a vague idea and a real plan with a few hours left to go until sunrise. A few precious hours in which we agreed we all ought to try to get some sleep. The Hidden House was quiet when we left the kitchen. Hala and I retreated to Sara's room through darkened hallways while the boys went the other way.

We were about midway up the many flights of stairs when I noticed light flooding from under one door: Tamid, reading late into the night.

My old friend wasn't a true rebel. He just had nowhere else to go after Leyla betrayed us. He'd claimed a whole room to himself, which most thought was petty when space was so valuable. But I'd allowed it because he had a job to do, burning oil between dusk and dawn as he searched for the words to free Fereshteh's energy and disable the Sultan's machine. And I'd allowed it because I didn't need to give him more reasons to despise me.

I paused on the landing that headed toward his room. Hala stopped climbing when she realized I wasn't beside her anymore. She gave me a withering look from three steps above me. "He doesn't want to talk to you," she told me, not for the first time. I knew that. Hala had reveled in telling me that, since he *did* want to talk to her.

Tamid and I hadn't spoken in weeks, and I'd steered clear of his room. But this was different. This wasn't about what either of us wanted. It was about what we needed to do.

"Get some sleep," I said to Hala by way of dismissal.

She looked like she might say something else for a moment, then she threw her hands up above her head as if to say she couldn't help it if I was going to do something stupid, and she left me.

When I couldn't hear her footsteps, I rapped gently at the door. "Come in," Tamid's voice said sharply from the other side, seeming unsurprised by a visitor in the middle of the night. Still, when I pushed the door open, I could see all over his face that he hadn't expected me.

He'd probably thought the knock was Hala bringing him more books to study. The collection she'd already acquired for him was strewn around the room. I could barely see the floor under stacks of open tomes piled one on top of another, or discarded in frustration in a corner. The books were lifted from libraries at the university or from the vaults of prayer houses. Hala's Demdji gift meant she could walk out of any building in Izman with a pile of books in her arms without drawing so much as a glance her way. And she'd been putting it to good use, with minimal complaining. I reckoned she just liked being kept busy. Or she half enjoyed the possibility that she was walking into peril. It distracted her from her grief.

Against all odds, Hala and Tamid seemed to get along decently enough. Maybe because they were both angry at me—Tamid for dragging him into this rebellion, Hala because I hadn't saved Imin. I knew they'd been talking about me behind my back. How else would Hala know he didn't want to see me?

Tamid looked back down at the book sprawled open on the desk in front of him. He was sitting at an uncomfortable-looking angle, his amputated leg propped on a stool. His fake leg was leaning up against a wall, not even in reach. He'd been using crutches instead. The beautifully engineered metal leg that Leyla had made for him had been lost when we'd escaped the Sultan. After our exalted ruler had taken it off him, revealing the device Leyla had hidden inside to guide her father to our hiding place. His new leg was a simple piece of wood, measured and cut to the right length to fit into the gap where his articulated bronze leg had been, designed to be attached by a crude system of leather straps. It was far from as sophisticated as Leyla's. But then, it had the advantage that it couldn't be used to sell us out to our enemy. I'd call that an even trade.

I glanced down at a book cast aside on the corner of the desk. It was open to an illuminated picture of the fall of Abbadon, in all its glory of flames and tumbling stones.

"Any luck?" I asked, trailing a finger absently along the outline of the flames consuming the city.

"It's not about luck," Tamid said sharply. "If I had any of that, I wouldn't be here."

"I'll take that as a no," I said. Tamid had been scouring the books for weeks now, looking for the words we needed to free the Djinn.

Words in the first language, which existed before lies were invented. And a Demdji tongue that couldn't tell a lie.

It was a powerful combination: with the right words in the first language, I could make anything happen. By just saying it like it was the truth, I could make money fall from thin air, or topple kings, or raise the dead.

Hell, I could use some decent magic words right now, to get us out of here.

But the first language was fragmented and lost. So I would settle for the words to disable the machine and stop our army from being burned alive. Once we had an army.

We'd had the shape of a plan before the ambush and the execution and the city being locked down around us: to get Rahim to Iliaz and take control of men that were once his. They were still loyal to him as their one-time commander. And then, once we had them, we could get me inside the palace to disable the machine and deactivate the army of Abdals. And from there we had a real chance of taking on the Sultan's army, and taking the throne. One mortal army against another.

Except, for the plan to work, we needed the right words in the first language. And judging by the ever-growing library in Tamid's room we were no closer to finding them than we'd been a month ago. I wondered whether those words might've been lost forever. It seemed very human that we'd have managed to hang on to the words to capture a Djinni and compel it to do our bidding, but not the ones we'd need to return the Djinni's freedom. It was as shortsighted as we usually were as a species. But all we could do was search.

"You're not here to ask me about that." Tamid rubbed his eyes tiredly. "What do you want, Amani?"

"We've got a prisoner." I ought to choose my words carefully here, but there wasn't a whole lot of time for subtlety. "It's Leyla." Tamid winced at the name of the princess. We'd both been fooled by her, both been betrayed. We'd thought she was an innocent, helpless girl stuck in the harem. But she'd meant something more to Tamid once. And Leyla had used that relationship to get Tamid out of the palace with her and lead her father straight to us. She might've taken a whole lot of people from me, but I was far from the only person she'd hurt.

"Because bringing Leyla to a rebel hideout worked out so well for you the last time?" Tamid asked, sharper than he needed to.

"I know," I said. I felt suddenly exhausted, like I wanted to slump down, but there was nowhere to sit among the books, so I just leaned against the door. "But she knows things. Things *we* need to know."

"Unless she knows the right words to free a Djinni from their bonds, I'm not interested," Tamid said.

"She doesn't have those," I said. "But she might have a way to get us the hell out of this city." Tamid finally looked at me, interest sparked. "But she's not talking. Leastways not to me. Any chance you think she'd talk to you?"

"Doubtful," Tamid scoffed, too quick to make me believe he had even given it any consideration.

"I wouldn't ask if we weren't desperate, Tamid. But the Sultan is going to start killing people if we don't give her back to him, and we need a way out. Can you at least *try* before telling me it won't work?" I tried to draw his gaze back to me, but he'd returned to his books, angry at me all over again. "Tamid." I heard the desperation creeping into my own voice. "I need your help."

"Of course you do." Tamid scowled at the book. "Because *everything* is always about you. Everything in my life has been about you since you came into it. I'm here because of you. Leyla used me to get to *you*. Even *this*"—he waved at his books—"is about you."

Tamid's sudden outburst left silence in its wake. I wanted to tell him that it wasn't true. That it wasn't fair. That if his life in Dustwalk had been about me, that was his fault, not mine. Then again, I'd been the one who'd always wanted to drag him out with me into the great, wide world. He'd been the one who'd tried to hold me back there. In the end, I'd pulled stronger. But Leyla—that was something he couldn't lay at my door. "Am I wrong"—I tried to keep the accusation out of my voice, lest I sound like a wife jealous of a husband's lover—"or did she make you that leg before I ever came around? If you want to be a martyr, Tamid, I can't stop you, but don't let other people die who haven't gotten to make a choice."

Tamid stared at the page for a long moment. "I'll talk to her. But I have a condition."

Name it. But I didn't say that. "What is it?"

"If she does have a way out of this city, I'm coming with you. I don't want any part of this. This rebellion, or this suicide mission of a rescue you think you're going to go on. I never did. I just want to go home." Home. Back to Dustwalk. "I never wanted to leave in the first place." I'd never understood what made him want to stay there. All he'd ever hoped for was to train as a Holy Father and take over the prayer house in Dustwalk one day. But I'd give just about anything not to have to go back to Dustwalk with him. It felt like a trap still waiting for me at the end of the desert. Like if I returned to the place I was born, the town might close its iron jaws around me and never let me leave again.

"And where that does that leave us?" I asked. "Nobody else knows how to read the first language here." Nobody else had been trained by the Holy Father down in the Last County, where old traditions and old languages had hung on better than in the northern cities. "We don't stand a chance against the Sultan if we can't find a way to disable that machine."

"So what then? You keep me locked up here on the off chance that I'll find something?" Tamid retorted. "I hate to tell you this, but if I was going to find the words we need, I think I would have by now." He waved around the room angrily. "Because believe you me, I've been trying."

He wasn't wrong.

"Fine," I conceded. "If we can get out of here, we'll get you as close to Dustwalk as we're able. Just talk to Leyla. Soon." I turned to go, but Tamid's voice stopped me.

"Amani." I turned back, door halfway open. He finally looked at me, a pained expression on his face, before glancing away again. "There's something else." His eyes roved over the books strewn across his room. Like he was looking for another answer at the last moment. "It's not—I *have* found something. Not the words you need to disable the machine, don't get excited. But . . ." Now he seemed like the one trying to pick his words carefully. "There are accounts, from the First War, of Djinn dying. In every single one, without fault, their death destroyed everything for miles around them. They're made of fire. And their death . . . it's like an explosion. They raze towns, battlefields, dry up rivers, split the earth itself, before vanishing into the sky to become stars. Leyla's machine . . . When Fereshteh died, it contained that power, trapped it, harnessed it for the wall and the Abdals. But if you disable the machine, all that power, it won't be contained anymore . . ." He trailed off uncomfortably.

I understood what he was saying. "If I disable the machine and release Fereshteh's power, you reckon there's a chance it'll destroy me." Tamid didn't need to answer me. I understood why he wouldn't meet my eye now. No matter how complicated our history was, it didn't mean either of us wanted to see the other dead.

I glanced down at the destruction of Abbadon again, in the open book. I could see it clearly, all that fire from Fereshteh's soul, unleashed from the Gamanix machine Leyla had made, burning everything in those vaults. Inlcuding me. I tried to wrap my tired mind around that. My own death. But it seemed far away right now. There were a whole lot of other things that could possibly get me killed before I risked being burned alive by Djinni fire. Right now, amid uncooperative princesses and threats of dying girls, it seemed like some remote nagging issue.

"One problem at a time, Tamid." I ran my hand over my face, trying to scrub away my exhaustion. "Right now, there's someone scheduled to die before me. And we've got to try to save her."

SIX

It wasn't easy to move through the streets of Izman in the dark during curfew, with Abdals patrolling the streets. In fact, it was impossible for most people. But we weren't most people. We were Demdji. And by the time the sky started to lighten behind the wall of fire, we had managed to make our way to the outskirts of the palace.

We stayed hidden until the streets finally began to fill around us, until finally the square in front of the palace was busy enough to hide us in plain sight. We moved out into the open, taking our places among the people of Izman. There was an unusual restlessness to the crowd. They had gathered here just yesterday for the Sultim trials, which we'd interrupted. But today they didn't know what they were going to see, an execution or a hostage exchange. I glanced at the faces around me as I pushed through the crowd. Something felt different today than it had for Ahmed's execution, or Shira's. Both of them had been accused of crimes. They'd been brought before the crowd to face what passed for justice in the Sultan's world. This time, though, whoever appeared on that stage would be unquestionably innocent, standing there for crimes that were not her own. And I saw, in some of the grimly pressed-together mouths and downcast eyes, that I wasn't the only one who recognized that.

But still, the people of Izman crowded in, even as the shadows of night retreated. We had split up: Jin and I at two different vantage points with guns at our hips, Izz and Maz in the shapes of starlings, perched on a rooftop nearby, Hala at the back so she could keep everyone in view. The way we saw it, our biggest threat was the Abdals. They were the reason I hadn't been able to save Imin. Hala's illusions didn't work on them. And besides, they could burn us alive if we got too close. Shooting them through their metal chests didn't work—we had to destroy the word inscribed on their heels that gave them life. Which Leyla had helpfully covered with metal armor. I was hoping a jaguar's claws could pry those off—Izz would take care of that. Then either Jin or I would take the shot, depending on which one of us was closer. And then, under Hala's illusion, Maz could swoop down and pick the girl up in his talons. It wasn't a foolproof plan, but it was better than nothing, which was what we'd had when Imin died right in front of us.

I shifted restlessly, watching the place where Imin and

Shira had both lost their lives. Finally dawn broke in earnest. All eyes were fixed on the stage now, waiting for the appearance of the girl who would die for our crimes. Minutes passed slowly as I touched the gun by my side over and over, making sure it was still there. But there was no movement from the palace. The doors didn't swing open, no sign of an Abdal and a struggling girl.

"Do you think the princess was sent home?" a voice asked in the crowd behind me.

"Maybe it was a bluff," another voice considered. But I knew that neither of those could be true. So what was the Sultan waiting for?

I caught movement from the corner of my eye. Not on the stage, but up above us and to the side, on the palace walls. When I glanced up, there was nothing there at first, and for a moment I thought I was seeing things, a trick of the light. But something kept my eyes fixed on that point on the wall, as if I could see through stone by sheer force of will.

And then the Sultan stepped into view, holding a girl around the waist.

He cut an impressive figure in the dawn light, dressed in a scarlet kurti with a bright gold sheema draped around his neck: the colors of blood shed over a dawn sky. He was flanked by his Abdals, the bronze of their artificial skin glinting in the sunlight. The rush of anger and hatred and humiliation was almost too much to take. Like it might send me doubling over.

The young girl was dressed in white nightclothes that

whipped and twisted around her legs in the morning air, her dark hair falling around her shoulders in a wild tumble. She would've looked leached of all color, if it wasn't for the flash of red at her neck. For a moment I feared her throat had already been slashed and she was being brought out here to die slowly. But no, it wasn't blood, just a bright red cloth. From far away it looked like a sheema thrown loosely around her neck as any desert girl might wear it. But there was another flash of red identical to it, tied around the crenellations of the palace walls. The same walls that Jin and I had jumped from in the chaos of Auranzeb, trusting a rope to get us to safety. But this rope wasn't securing her.

He wasn't going to execute her on the stage. He was going to hang her.

My heart started to beat frantically as I cast around, looking for the others. I couldn't reach her up there. I desperately searched for the twins to give them a sign to forget the plan and fly to the walls of the palace. But we'd split ourselves up, scattering through the crowd that now hid the others from me.

I was on my own. And I was too far away.

I started to move all the same, pushing my way through the mass of gawkers, praying I might be able to get close enough to the twins to call out to them, or to Hala to tell her to draw something up in the Sultan's mind that would stall him. Or even close enough to fire off a shot, a bullet straight between the Sultan's eyes. To do something other than watch a girl die. But the crowd fought against me like

I was trying to push my way upstream in a raging river. Around me faces started to turn upward, noticing that something was happening high above us.

The Sultan stepped up to the very edge of the palace walls.

I was close enough to see that the girl was shaking and crying as she stood on the precipice. Close enough to see the Sultan turn her away from him, toward the rising sun. To see him lean over the girl and whisper something in her ear. To see the girl squeeze her eyes shut.

But too far away to do anything.

He pushed her.

It was one swift, violent motion that sent her over the edge of the wall, falling fast. Her scream ripped the air open like a knife through cloth, drawing up every eye that hadn't noticed her. Some cries from the crowd mingled with hers as the whole of the square watched helplessly as she fell. Nightclothes twisted cruelly around her flailing legs, feet frantically searching for a purchase they wouldn't find. As she dropped, the long, colorful rope of the noose unfurled like a sheema caught in the desert wind, whipping behind her in a trail of red.

Until there was none of it left to unfurl.

It snapped taut. The noose around her throat pulled tight, bringing her fall to a wrenching stop.

Her scream cut off with sickening suddenness. And I knew it was over.

• ● •

HER NAME WAS Rima. She was from a poor family that lived by the docks. Her father's door had a sun emblazoned on it in scarlet paint, left over from the Blessed Sultima's Uprising. That was why she had been taken. Ahmed's sun had turned from a symbol of defiance into a target.

She was the middle daughter of five. The Sultan could have plucked any one of them from their beds that night. But Rima was closest in age to me.

• ● •

THE SECOND GIRL was named Ghada. We never even got a chance to save her. We never so much as saw her alive. Dawn found her body already hanging from the palace walls next to Rima's. She'd been killed inside, where we didn't have a hope of reaching her. The Sultan wasn't foolish enough to repeat the same trick twice.

On the afternoon after Ghada's death, her father, who had rioted in the streets against the Sultan, stood in the square before the palace and denounced the rebellion that had condemned his innocent daughter. I didn't blame him for his words. He had another daughter he needed to save.

• ● •

NAIMA WAS THE name of the third girl. The third one we failed to save. The third one who died for our crimes.

No matter what we did, what we tried, we were too late. Too slow. We would have to get into the palace to save them before they died. And we didn't have any way in with Sam gone. Hell, we hadn't managed to get in back when he was still with us.

"No living parents." Sara was telling me what she had learned about Naima, as she rocked Fadi in her arms. "But she has four brothers." Curtains were pulled against prying eyes, but early morning light leaked through the lattice of the window to dance anxiously across her face as she moved. There was something else she wasn't telling me.

"What is it?"

"You don't need to torture yourself." Jin interrupted Sara before she could get out with it. He was leaning against the far wall, watching me. "You're not responsible for every death in this rebellion any more than Ahmed was."

It was good advice, the sort that Shazad might give me if she were still here. But she wasn't. And I wasn't Ahmed, either. I had told Tamid that I had changed, that I wasn't someone who let folks die on my account. But there were three bodies hanging from the palace walls to prove me wrong. Maybe I hadn't changed from that selfish Dustwalk girl as much as I'd thought. Maybe going back with Tamid really would take me right back to where I'd started. "I am responsible for this one, though."

No one contradicted me. It was the truth, after all.

Sara's eyes flitted between Jin and me for a moment before continuing. "They're saying it was a neighbor who denounced them to the palace as allies of the Rebellion.

Someone her brothers thought was a friend, who was just as much a part of the riots as they were."

"The neighbor sold them out to save his own family," Jin filled in, looking grim.

Sara nodded gravely. "Naima's brothers figured out he was responsible. He was just found beaten to death in his home." I felt sick to my stomach. A violent act of revenge and grief. Brothers trying to make *someone* pay for a dead sister since they couldn't reach the Sultan.

"This is what the Sultan wants," Jin said. "For what's left of the Rebellion's support in the city to turn on itself."

"Well, nice of us to make it so easy for him, then," I muttered.

"You know," Hala interjected, "we can wallow and continue to watch people die. Or we could just *fix* the mistake you made and give that useless princess back to her father."

"No." I shook my head emphatically. "Even if she does turn out to be useless to us, she's not useless to her father." I glanced at the closed door. Tamid was talking to Leyla again on the other side of it now. He hadn't gotten anything useful out of her yet, but he wasn't ready to give up. He'd returned the second day carrying one of the tomes of the Holy Books. He seemed to think he could compel her to repent with religion. She'd killed an immortal being, so I had to guess that it wasn't going to work, but I was ready to try anything by now.

"I didn't say we should give her back alive," Hala said, drawing my attention sharply back to her. Her words shifted the mood in the room instantly. I searched her face for a sign that she was being sarcastic; Hala had a cruel sense of humor. But I hadn't seen her laugh a whole lot since Imin died.

"We're not going to kill her," Jin said, raising his dark eyebrows at her, like he thought she wasn't serious.

"Why not?" Hala raised her own in a mocking imitation. "Because she's your *sister*? She'd jump at the chance to kill every single one of *us*. And the Sultan's demand never said whether he wanted her returned dead or alive."

"I feel like *alive* was implied," Jin said drily. "That's usually the way with hostages."

"He ought to know better," Hala said. "We're Djinn's children; we take things by the letter." She offered him a sarcastic smirk. The twins shifted where they were sitting on the windowsill, looking uneasy at being dragged into this talk of murder. "Besides," Hala added, finally breaking her staring contest with Jin, "I don't think it's your decision." And then she looked at me.

I could feel Jin's eyes on me, too. He was expecting me to say no right away, to side with him against Hala's idea to murder his sister.

I hesitated.

The Sultan was trying to turn the city against us. He'd gotten away with killing three girls so far because in this story he was spinning, we were the villains. Kidnapping princesses wasn't the sort of thing a hero did; that was the monster's role. Heroes saved the princess. And heroes didn't stand idly by when innocent girls were killed.

The people would forget that the Sultan was the one doing the killing. All they would remember was that we were the ones who had sent them to the gallows. Killing Leyla wouldn't get us out of the city, but it might at least stop more girls from dying in our name. Might stop the whole city turning against us before we could ever get Ahmed back to lead them.

But what kind of monsters would we be to lay his daughter's body on his doorstep?

I was saved from answering when the door to Leyla's bedroom prison opened. Tamid joined us, holding his Holy Book.

"Any luck?" I asked without much hope but grateful for the distraction all the same.

"No, but . . ." He hesitated, looking at his feet, like he was already dreading what he was about to say. "I have an idea of what might make her talk."

"If it's death threats, don't bother," Hala said. "She's already made it clear she's not afraid to die. Or at least she thinks she isn't." She gave me a pointed look, like that entirely justified her whole *kill the princess* plan.

"No," Tamid agreed, "but there's something she *is* afraid of. One thing she values more than anything."

Everyone was hanging on Tamid's words now, even as he hesitated. He knew that whatever he was about to tell us, we would use it, and it would be because of him. But instead of speaking to me, he glanced at Hala. "Is it true," he asked her, "what they say you did to the man who took your fingers?"

Even I'd never dared ask Hala about that. Most of the Demdji didn't like to talk about their lives before the Rebellion. It was difficult being what we were in an occupied country that wanted to kill us. And even without the Gallan, Demdji tended to get sold, used, killed, or worse. We all knew Hala hadn't had it easy. We all knew that her mother had sold Hala. But the rumor around camp, back when we'd had a camp, was that Hala had gotten her revenge on the man who'd cut off her fingers. That she had used her Demdji gift and torn his mind asunder. That she had driven him so deep into madness that he'd never see the light of sanity again.

And I understood what Tamid meant. Death was one thing, but Leyla's life without her intellect—well, that was something else. It would make her useless to her father, for one. And she'd seen madness before. Her mother had been driven mad trying to build a version of what Leyla had successfully completed. It was what made Rahim turn on his father. And Leyla had driven her brother Kadir's wives to madness—Ayet, Mouhna, and Uzma, three jealous but harmless girls in the harem whom she had put through her machine as sacrificial test subjects before using the full force of the machine to harness a Djinni's energy.

She might not fear losing her head. But she would fear losing her mind.

"Is it true?" Tamid pressed.

Hala was running the thumb of her three-fingered hand in a slow, thoughtful circle over her golden mouth as she thought. "No," she admitted finally. "What I did to him was worse than you've ever heard."

• • •

WHEN I LET myself into her room, Leyla was curled up on her side. She reminded me of my cousin Olia sulking in our shared room back in Dustwalk, when she clearly wanted someone to pay attention to her but wanted it to look like she didn't.

"Are you here to shoot me again?" Leyla muttered into her pillow. The way she was lying made the bandages on her arm conspicuous. I guessed Tamid had sewn her up, too. Probably smart; we didn't want her to bleed out on us. Though I could've let her suffer for a bit.

"No." I leaned against the door. "I'm here to give you one last chance to keep that clever little head of yours screwed on the right way." I sat down at the end of her bed. "Have you ever seen anyone go sun-mad, Leyla? I have—once—a man named Bazet, back in the town where I grew up. It was like watching someone whose head had been set on fire from the inside and he couldn't put it out. He went absolutely raving, babbling, screaming, seeing things, and in the end my uncle shot him like a dog in the middle of the street out of mercy."

Leyla sat up, her hand pressing hard into the pillow, leaving a small indent next to where her face had been.

"Hala's power, it's a bit like sun-madness. She can make you see things for a little while, sure, but if she wants to, she can also rip your mind into such fractured pieces you'll never again be wholly sure what's just in your head and what's really there. And believe me, she really wants to do that to you."

Leyla's mouth had parted slightly, her eyes looking huge and childlike. "You wouldn't do that. You need me."

"Right now you're costing us a lot more lives than you're helping us save," I said. "And here's the thing: I don't think your father can keep this city on lockdown forever. Eventually, I reckon this siege will end and we'll get out. But, see, I want people to stop dying before that. And if I return you to him without your head screwed on straight, the killings stop, and I don't think you'll be much good to him anymore either, when you can't build him little toys for his wars. Do you reckon you'll still be his favorite daughter when you've lost your mind?"

I could see her churning it over, the cost of telling.

"Where will you go?" she asked finally. And then, more quietly, "Are you going to rescue my brother?"

The question caught me off guard. I hadn't thought Leyla gave a damn about Rahim. She'd let him be imprisoned with the rest of the Rebellion. She blamed him as a traitor. But she sounded tentative, almost shy. I supposed he was still her brother, the only one of the Sultan's many children who shared a mother with her.

"That's the plan."

In fact, the plan was to rescue two of her brothers, but she didn't need to know Ahmed was still alive, even if she didn't have any way of getting that information to her father.

Leyla chewed on her lip thoughtfully for a long moment before finally answering me. "There are tunnels. Below the city." She started talking quicker, as if she could get all the treasonous words off her tongue at once. "I needed a way of feeding the power all the way out to the walls. So my father had tunnels dug from the palace, running wires through them to feed the walls with fire from the machine. His wives and the children of the harem slipped out through one of the tunnels to a waiting ship before the Gallan invaders arrived. But the exits are all bricked up now."

Bricked up wasn't so bad—easier to get through than a wall of fire. I stood. "I'm going to get a map of the city, and I'm going to want you to tell me where these tunnels run, every single one of them. And I'll know if you try to lie to me again." I gave the bandage on her wounded arm a pointed glance.

"It won't *matter*, you know." Leyla interrupted my retreat from the room. She was awfully chatty now that she'd started talking. I ignored her. "Even if you can get through this wall, you won't get through the next."

I stopped, my hand resting on the door. She was baiting me, I could tell by the way her words rose at the end mockingly. She wanted me to ask. Which was exactly what made me not want to ask. Except I probably ought to. Pettiness wasn't the right hill to make my stand on in this war.

I turned around and gave her what she wanted. "What do you mean, the *next* wall?"

"The one around the prison where the traitors have been sent." She looked all too pleased with herself now she had regained the upper hand, knees pulled up to her chin. There was an annoying singsong quality to her words when she asked, "Where do you think my father got the idea to protect our city this way?"

Ashra's Wall. The story had leapt into my mind the moment I'd seen the great barrier of fire. And I wasn't alone in that. Everyone had been whispering Ashra's name around the city since we saw the wall of fire. It was impossible not to think of the legend from the Holy Books. But there was no way that was what Leyla was talking about. Because that would mean that Ahmed and the others were being kept prisoner in . . .

"Eremot." Dark satisfaction was scrawled all over Leyla's face. "They've been sent to Eremot."

The ancient name sent a feeling of wrongness through me, an unease that went deeper than my skin and bones and seemed to churn even my soul into unrest. Half of me was immortal. Half of me had been there, at Eremot in the ancient days. Half of me remembered.

Eremot was a name that belonged in the Holy Books. It was the place where the Destroyer of Worlds had emerged, leading her army of ghouls, and the place she had been imprisoned again at the end of the First War. Behind Ashra's Wall, a great barrier of fire to keep the dark at bay.

"Eremot is . . ." *not real.* Only that wouldn't get past my lips.

"The stuff of legends," Leyla finished for me, with a pinched, self-satisfied look on her face. "Past the end of civilization where no one can find it. But I found it."

She meant to intimidate me. But I'd grown up past the end of civilization and Jin had found me just fine. "We've got our own ways of finding it." Jin's compass would lead us to wherever the prisoners were being held. Whether that was Eremot or not.

"Well." Leyla shrugged. "Even if you do find it, do you really think you can cross *a great and impenetrable barrier against evil, risen from the trueness of sacrifice and which—*"

"*And which will stand un-breached until such time as humanity's courage fails,*" I finished for her. "I can quote the Holy Books, too, when I want to."

Ashra had been a carpet weaver's daughter born when the First War was coming to an end. The ghouls were being driven into hiding and darkness, skulking the desert alone at night instead of swarming in armies. The Destroyer of Worlds' greatest monsters were dead, slain by the First Hero and all the heroes that came after him: Attallah, the Gray Prince, Sultan Soroush, and the Champion of Bashib. The Destroyer of Worlds was being beaten back to the darkness of the earth from whence she came.

But she could not be held back permanently. Each time, she burst free from her prison again to roam and terrorize the desert. And the Djinn looked on in despair at the humans who had defended them for so long and feared that they would not be able to accomplish this final task. So they made it known among the humans that they would grant immortality to whichever man could imprison the Destroyer of Worlds forevermore. Many a hero died trying.

Ashra was not a hero. She was just a girl from a small village in the mountains, the eldest of twelve children, who spent her days helping her father dye wool and her evenings helping her mother cook meals for her eleven brothers and sisters.

Until the day the Destroyer of Worlds came to her village.

The villagers had no weapons, and they lit torches against the Destroyer of Worlds, placing them in a circle as they huddled together, trying to stay alive until dawn, when they would be able to flee.

The Destroyer of Worlds stalked through the dark in one great circle around the village, around their torches. And then she laughed, and with her breath she extinguished all the torches. All except one, which stood by Ashra and her family.

Before the Destroyer of Worlds could attack, Ashra seized the last torch and set herself on fire with it. A body does not burn much, but it was said that she swallowed a spark, just enough to light her soul as well as her body. And her soul burned much brighter than her body ever could. And when the burning girl took a step toward the

Destroyer of Worlds, the Destroyer of Worlds took a step back. So Ashra took another step, then another, and another, and slowly the Destroyer of Worlds retreated.

Ashra walked the Destroyer of Worlds all the way back toward Eremot. And as she walked, she did as her father had taught her and wove the fire burning inside her body together, as one would a carpet, until it became an impenetrable wall. By the time they reached Eremot, she had made it so high and wide that it held back even the Destroyer of Worlds. It was wide enough to encircle the entrance to Eremot and keep the Destroyer of Worlds trapped inside the mountain forever.

The Djinn saw her sacrifice, and they kept their promise. They granted Ashra immortal life so that her soul would burn forever as the great wall she had made. They said that as long as Ashra's Wall stood, the Destroyer of Worlds would be imprisoned. If it fell, so would a new age of darkness fall on the world.

So that was why Leyla had asked if we were headed to rescue Rahim. Not because she had had a change of heart about her brother, but because she wanted to know for sure that even if she betrayed her father and let us through this wall, we would still fail. There was another wall between us and our purpose.

"What does your father want to send prisoners to Eremot for?" Just saying the name made me feel uneasy. "If he was going to break his promise to his people of granting the Rebellion mercy, there have got to be easier ways to kill them."

Leyla looked at me through dark eyelashes. "He doesn't want them dead. He just doesn't care if they die. There's a difference. He's after something in Eremot. And people who go in there don't come back out—eventually the hours and hours of digging in the dark will wring all the life out of them. So he sends in expendable lives."

But I wasn't listening to her gloating. There was only one possible thing the Sultan could have his prisoners digging out in Eremot. "Your father wants them to find the Destroyer of Worlds."

I might know better than anyone the distance between legends and the truth, that stories were not always told whole. The monsters in them were less fierce in reality, the heroes less pure, the Djinn more complicated. But there were some things you didn't prod at to find out if their teeth were really as big at the stories said. Because on the off-chance that the stories were really true, you were about to lose a finger. The Destroyer of Worlds was at the top of the list of things I didn't want to find out the truth about. "I don't know how close you've read the Holy Books, but there are a whole lot of reasons why letting her out of that prison is a bad idea. Starting with the destruction of all of humanity."

"Oh, he doesn't want to let her out," Leyla said earnestly. "He wants her for the same reason he wants the Djinn. My father is a hero. He's going to end her once and for all. And use what's left of her for good. Just like Fereshteh."

He was going to kill her, turn her immortal life into power that he could use. I remembered something he had said to me once: that the time for immortal things was over. Now was the time for us, time to stop living so attached to our legends and to magic. And sure enough, he was destroying our legends one at a time, dragging Miraji into a new age, whether it wanted to come or not. Whether letting great evils out of the earth was a good idea or not.

"He can't do it without you, though, can he?"

Leyla's satisfaction drifted back to fear. "If you kill me, he will find another way. My mother's homeland is full of people like me, makers of new ideas and new inventions." Some who would even be prepared to defy the laws of religion and good sense, too, I was sure.

I didn't want to kill her. But we couldn't keep her either. We might have a way out, but we couldn't just vanish from the city without doing *something* about Leyla—not with girls dying every dawn in her name.

The beginning of a plan had started in my mind. Only we were missing someone if we were going to pull it off.

I needed to get Sam back.

SEVEN

I t took me the better part of the day to track Sam down, which didn't exactly do a whole lot for how angry I was at him. I started imagining creative ways to kill him sometime around midday, when the sweat had soaked into my shirt in earnest and my hair was sticking to my sheema from the heat. By the time I finally ran him to ground just before sunset, I had built a very vivid image of how he'd meet his end at my hands.

We'd been damn lucky that Sam hadn't bled out that day he'd tried to slip into the palace. After he'd gotten himself shot, it was only thanks to Hala and Jin that we got him back to the Hidden House still breathing. The hours that followed had been a frenzy of trying to keep our foreign friend alive, as well as get everyone ready to flee if we had to. I didn't know if we'd been followed from the palace. But I'd already led the Sultan to one of our hideouts once. I wasn't taking chances.

Finally Sam had stopped bleeding and kept breathing. Though barely on both counts. And no soldiers came knocking at the door of the Hidden House.

I'd spent the night keeping watch over him while everyone else kept watch over the streets. If we had to flee, I wasn't sure we'd be able to take Sam with us, wounded as he was. So we'd waited and kept watch. I'd prayed a whole lot.

Then, three days after Sam got shot, I woke up next to an empty bed. My face had been pressed so hard into the stitching of the blanket that it had left a mark on my cheek. Where Sam had been, there was nothing but tangled sheets faintly stained with blood. My first thought was that Sam had died sometime in the night and Jin had moved the body to spare me. But then I saw the golden cuff set with emeralds, slipped onto my wrist while I slept. It was Shazad's, one of the pieces of jewelry she'd paid Sam with, back when he was running information between the palace and the Rebellion.

I read it for what it was, a farewell note. *No amount of money is worth dying for*, it said. He wasn't wrong, either. Money was a damn stupid thing to die for. I'd just been figuring Sam was still with us for something more.

Still, leaving me the bracelet seemed like it was more symbolic than anything, since he took everything else Shazad had paid him, down to the very last of her rings.

Shazad's jewelry was how I found him in the end. There was a goldsmith on the corner of Moon Street who was known to trade coin for material without questions. It took a bit of bribery, but he told me Sam had been by. He was on his way to the White Fish, a bar on the docks that normally served sailors of all sorts passing through Izman. It'd become glutted with the same sailors lately, seeing as no one was getting in or out of the city. The barricade of fire even plunged deep into the sea.

Only there was a rumor going around that there was a man who knew how to get through the barricade, and for the right price, he'd give you passage. He was rounding up anyone with the right money at the White Fish.

I'd heard that rumor, too. I'd ignored it since it was so obviously a scam. Only it seemed Sam was stupid enough to fall for it.

The heat of a long day of trawling the city streets clung to me as I pushed through the doors of the White Fish. A dozen pairs of men's eyes joined it. I knew what they were seeing. It didn't matter that I was dressed in sturdy desert clothes or that I was armed: I was a woman in a place where only men belonged. I half missed the days when I was a scrawny girl from Dustwalk and could still pass for a boy when I needed to. But it had been a year of decent meals, and there was too much of me to hide what I was now.

Most of the men turned back to their drinks and their gambling, shrugging me off as I pressed farther into the bar, searching for a familiar face. But one man stepped square in my path, quickly enough that I had to pull up short to keep from running straight into him.

"How much?" he asked without preamble.

"For you to get out of my way?" My hand was already on the gun at my belt. "I'll do you a favor, and until the count of three, I'll let you move for free. After that, I might start charging you in toes." When he looked down, the pistol was pointed at his boot. It was an easy shot to pull off in close quarters.

I recognized Sam's laugh a second before his arm draped itself over my shoulder. "Don't mind my lady friend." His voice was too bright, like he was trying to cut through the tension, like sun through clouds. "She's too much for you to handle anyway." He winked at the man across from me. In a low voice, in Albish, slow enough so I could understand, he said, "Put your gun away before he does something stupid and you and I have to do something heroic."

I bit my tongue angrily, but he was right. I wasn't here to draw attention to myself by starting a bar brawl. The man gave us a once-over before taking a step back. Sam pulled me around, turning me toward a table lined with men holding cards, watching us with interest. "Sorry about that interruption, boys," Sam declared too loudly. "Just had to go get my good luck charm." He sat back down abruptly, pulling me into his lap so fast I didn't think about swatting him away until I was already sitting.

I moved the most painful means of death to the top of the list I'd spent this afternoon constructing.

Still, I had to admit, the too-interested eyes that had strayed toward us were moving away, a smug, knowing look crossing the faces of the other gamblers at his table. Now they thought they understood what I was and who owned me. Sam knew what he was doing.

"You're going to need a lot more than luck tonight, my foreign friend," a man with a dark green sheema draped loosely around his neck said with a laugh. "With cards like those."

"You looked at my cards?" Sam slapped a hand dramatically to his chest in feigned shock, like he'd just been shot through the heart. "You curs, you cheaters, you—" I didn't have time for this.

"Sam," I interrupted his mock tirade. "Buy me a drink." When he looked about to protest, I toyed pointedly with the sleeve of the arm slung around my shoulder. I could feel the cards tucked inside his shirt pressing against me. "Now, before I say something that might get *you* shot." He took my meaning as I got to my feet, freeing myself of the indignity of his lap.

"Gentlemen," he said dramatically as he rose, kicking his chair back out of the way, "your infidelity leaves me no choice but to fold this hand. But I will return when I've had some luck rub off on me." He winked widely, pulling me tight against him by the waist. Thumbscrews. The way I murdered him was going to include thumbscrews.

"So here's what I'm thinking," Sam said. He drew me toward a table in a dark corner and gestured to the barkeep with two fingers. "Your timing is perfect to help me cheat my way to victory." The barkeep set down two glasses of amber liquid in front of us, sliding mine to me with a careful once-over. I met his gaze steadily in return. "All we need to do is work out some sort of code between us," Sam went on blithely, clearly not caring who overheard.

"Selling Shazad's jewelry wasn't enough? Are you just getting greedy now?" I ran a finger along the rim of the glass of liquor that had just been put down in front of me.

"Oh, don't be like that." He jostled me, like it was all some big joke. "My friend over there is charging an arm and a leg to get smuggled out of here." He nodded toward a man at the bar who was still looking at us. "And the only people who can get away with missing their limbs and still being as dashing as I am are pirates. I have no interest in spending the rest of my life eating fish with my hook hand."

"Why would anyone replace their hand with a hook?" Sam didn't used to give me this much of a headache.

He opened his mouth like he was going to explain to me some foreign concept that had gone far over my head, like he used to in our meetings at the palace, but then seemed to change his mind and took a sip of his drink instead. "The point is," Sam ploughed on a nervous energy seeming to animate him, "that if I want to get out of this city *and* keep all my appendages, I've got to find something else to offer him."

I glanced over at the man leaning on the bar. If he actually had a way out of this city, then *I* was the Queen of Albis.

"So, tell me, what exactly is your plan here?" I shifted my chair so that I had him in my sights. "Even if you can get out of Miraji, you're a deserter, Sam." I didn't bother softening the blow. "I don't know what they do in Albis, but here if you turn your coat on the army, they take your head off your shoulders."

"In Albis, they let you keep your neck and use it to hang you from a tall tree." He didn't sound all that bothered by it. "An oak, if there's one immediately available, but ash or yew will do in a pinch. And since it'd be criminal to rob the world of me, I'm not going back to Albis. I hear the Ionian Peninsula has beautiful women and good food and the sun lets up every once in a blue moon, unlike here."

"So you got shot once and now you're running scared?" We'd all gotten ourselves shot once or twice in this war. I'd dug a bullet out of Jin's shoulder before I even knew his name. I had a scar across my stomach from a wound that had nearly killed me. Sam lost a little bit of blood and suddenly he was deserting all over again.

But Sam didn't look as cowed as I'd hoped he would. "Yes," he said, like I was the one being unreasonable. "Anyone who isn't afraid of dying is stupid or lying." He tipped his drink at me like a bow. "And I'm a better liar than that."

I tapped my glass, thinking of what Tamid had told me about the likelihood of me burning alive when I released Fereshteh's energy from the machine. "We're all going to die some day or another, Sam. What else are you going to do? Keep running from one country to another until you die from a knife between the ribs because you walked through the wrong wall in the next city? Or from poison in your glass because you charmed the wrong woman in the one after that? Or do you think it might be worth standing still for once?" I asked. "Here with us."

A wry smile crossed his face. "They talked a lot about making a stand when I joined the army, too. Turns out what that means for boys who were born farmers' sons is that they wanted us to stand in front of enemies' cannons so the rich men's sons behind us could go home with the glory."

"I don't care about glory," I challenged. "I care about getting our people home. People I know you care about, too."

Sam leaned his head back against the wall, like he was truly considering it. Out of the corner of my eye, I realized the man at the bar was looking at us again. His eyes darted away, like he'd been caught. There was something unsettling about him.

"Sam," I said carefully, keeping my tone neutral, "did that friend of yours happen to say how it was he's able to sail out of Izman now when no one else has managed it in weeks?"

"Mmm?" Sam scratched his eyebrow with a thumb evasively. "I don't recall."

That sounded as good as a no to me. The man's foot was tapping out a frantic timpani against the edge of the bar. Almost like he was nervous. Or waiting for something.

"How about a price?" I asked. "Was there a number mentioned before you turned up here with your money, or did you get here to find out that whatever amount you brought wasn't enough?"

"Well . . ." Sam looked thoughtful. The drinks were dulling him. "That's how business works. When a service is so in demand . . . it would be stupid to set his going rate too low . . ." Now even he sounded skeptical.

"You don't think it's strange"—my hand strayed to my pistol even as I kept my voice steady—"that this is all happening now, right when the Sultan is especially desperate to get his daughter back? And that you just *happened* not to have the right amount of money so that you'd have to stick around, gambling for a shot at getting out?"

It finally dawned on Sam what I was saying. He cursed in Albish, looking more annoyed than anything else. "It's a trap."

EIGHT

I was on my feet, pistol in hand. That was my next mistake, showing alarm. A shrill whistle went up from the same man who'd tried to stop me when I walked in. Suddenly three more men were on their feet, pulling out guns I hadn't seen before.

I was already moving, headed for the bar, firing as I went, Sam close behind me. One shot struck a wall, the next struck a man in the chest, the last sent a bottle exploding, forcing two men to cover their faces as we dove over the bar. Sam slid across after me, his foot catching a drink, sending it flying into the wall, spraying liquor and shattered glass. The barman flinched from where he was crouched, trying to stay covered. We were going to get him killed if we stayed back here.

My mind raced. They'd set this as a trap to lure in someone from the Rebellion. That was why they'd staged it here, in this floating box of wood, far from the reach of the desert. They'd been warding against both me and Sam. And the twins, too, since it left nowhere to fly out of if they'd been here. They knew too much about us.

Gunfire started again, shattering the shelves above our heads, raining clear booze and glass over us. I reached up and grabbed a half-empty bottle, shooting a few times over the bar.

"Sam!" I could feel the sand deep below the sea's waters. It was heavy and sluggish, nothing like the wind-quick grace of pure desert sand. But it was still sand. "You can swim, can't you?"

"What?" Sam's eyes were wide with panic. "Why?" That was as good as a yes, as far as I was concerned.

"Give me your sheema." I held out my hand to Sam.

"No! Why? Use yours," Sam protested.

"I'm not going to use mine," I said, uncorking the bottle. I took a swig for good measure. "Sentimental value."

"Well, maybe I'm sentimental about mine, too," Sam protested. "It was given to me by the wife of—"

"No it wasn't." I pulled the sheema from his neck, the badly done knot coming apart easily. "That," I said, shoving the cloth into the mouth of the bottle, "is your own fault for never learning how to tie a sheema properly."

"Okay, I was lying about the sentimental value." Sam flinched as a new volley of gunfire started. They were being careful; they wanted us alive. But not *that* careful.

"Mostly I'm sentimental about not having my skin peeled off by the sun without my sheema. And also I'm *very* concerned you're going to get us both killed and—"

"Hey," I said to the bartender. I shoved the bottle bomb into Sam's hands as I turned away. "Matches. I know you have them."

With shaking hands, he retrieved a box of matches from under the bar, holding them out to me.

I struck a match, setting it to the sheema wick of the makeshift bomb. Sam raised an eyebrow at me. "Nice to know my fear of you doing something that would get us killed was baseless."

"You should probably toss that, unless you really want to be proved right," I offered. "Now!"

We moved as one. Whatever else he was, Sam had always been good in a crisis. It was that same survival instinct that made him run out on us. We made a good team. He surged to his feet as I pulled my Demdji energy into my fingertips. Pain flooded in with it, making me stagger for a moment, almost tripping, almost losing my grip.

Sam flung the bottle, sending it smashing to the floor in a burst of glass, fire, and, best of all, smoke.

I whipped my arms upward. The sand surged up with all the strength I had in me. The thin, cheap floorboards never stood a chance. They splintered under the force, creating a gash in the building straight down into the water below.

I grabbed Sam by the collar and hauled him through.

He was going to need to come up with a better answer than "What?" to my question about swimming pretty quick. At least one of us needed to be able to stay afloat.

I just had time to suck in a lungful of air before we plunged into the sea. It was like stepping off a cliff into nothingness as the rest of the water rushed up around me. I started to panic as the unnatural feeling assaulted me. Then arms around me, fastening us together, buoyed me up in the waves, keeping me from plunging to the depths and getting lost there. I latched my own arms in a death grip around Sam's shoulders as he propelled us back up, toward air. We broke through the surface, our heads bobbing in the narrow space between the bottom of the dock and the surface of the water.

"Here's a tip," Sam sputtered in my ear as we broke free. I coughed up salt water across his shoulder. "Don't try to inhale the sea."

I hung on to him for dear life as he kicked, swimming us away from the bar and our pursuers. I tried to focus through the sensation of salt water clawing at my nose until we came to a stop bobbing in the narrow space between the hulls of two huge ships. It was dark now, and I could still hear shouting, but it was far away. It was possible we'd lost them.

We floated for a second, listening, breathing hard, both of us shaking. I could feel the dull pain in my side from using my power so much, and my head was spinning. I'd almost lost my grip on it that time. Almost killed us both.

"Well." Sam finally spoke up, low so his voice wouldn't

carry back to our pursuers. "Seems I'm a bit lower on options than I thought. What was it you said about me using my exceptional skills to heroically get you out of here?"

Thumbscrews and a knee splitter. That was how I was going to kill him.

"Who said anything about needing you to get out?" I said. "How do you feel about getting me *in* somewhere?"

NINE

"For what it's worth, I still think we should have killed her." Hala kept her head and her voice low, letting her hood obscure her face as the crowd pressed in around us.

"I know you do," I said under my breath, glancing over my shoulder to the palace walls behind us for the thousandth time, as we shuffled toward the huge doors of the prayer house with painstaking slowness. The bodies of the three girls were still hanging there. No fourth body yet. We had some time to save this morning's victim. A little time, at least.

Above us, the predawn light glinted off the great Golden dome. The sound of bells rocked through the city. They were calling the people to prayers, and today, we were answering.

Prayers had been better attended since the city had come under siege. Hundreds were flocking in every day, driven by the sight of the unholy barricade all around us. Or by the enemies at our gates. Or the fear that their daughters would be stolen from them.

The latest girl had been taken in the night, probably right around the time Sam and I were getting back to the Hidden House, drenched from our accidental dip in the ocean. Jin had raised his brows at us curiously. "Do I even want to ask?"

"Probably not," I offered as I went in search of dry clothes while Sam stood dripping and grinning like an idiot.

Her name was Fariha. She was only fourteen. I was praying we weren't too late to save her this morning. Even if I wasn't sure anyone was listening to my prayers anyway.

"And," Hala added, "I think *this* is a terrible idea."

"I know," I said again, not sure if I meant that I knew what she thought or that I knew it was a terrible idea.

"Even if we're not going to kill her, you really ought to let me take her mind away," Hala muttered as we followed the flow of people into the great domed building. "She's a menace."

"I heard you the first three times you said that."

We were both tense and irritable. I didn't even blame Hala for it. I'd only had a few hours of sleep. And we might both be walking to our demise. All because I didn't want to deliver Leyla back to her father dead or insane.

Hala had pointed out that he wouldn't hesitate to do it to us if the roles were reversed. And that was exactly why I couldn't. We weren't the Sultan. We were supposed to be better than him.

So we'd both agreed we weren't leaving this city without doing something. Even if doing something meant we might not get out of the city at all.

The throng of people pushed us forward. We were close enough now that I could make out some of the details of the gold panels in the door, the First Hero swinging his sword through a monster's neck in one. Below it, the Sin Maker standing behind him with a knife, ready to betray him. In another panel, the other Djinn surrounded the Sin Maker, casting him out in shame for his treason. We passed close enough that I found myself glancing at the faces of the Djinn, trying to recognize my father among them. But their faces had been worn down over the centuries. If they had ever looked like anyone, they were anonymous now. Faded even as the Djinn drew away from the everyday life of mortals.

And then the doors and their golden panels were behind me, and Hala and I were passing under the towering blue-and-gold arch and into the warm embrace of the prayer house. Outside, some of the cool of night was still clinging on, but inside, fires were burning all around in grates set into the terracotta-tiled walls, and the air was thick with the smell of burning oil and incense.

I hadn't been able to tell in the dark last night, while we were making our preparations, but I could see clearly now that the tiles of each wall were a different bright color, with the same swirling circular patterns repeated over and over again. The north wall was two shades of blue, representing water. The west was gold and brown for earth. Those were the two elements that were blended together to make up a human body when the Djinn created us. The south wall was a startling white and silver for the air that molded the clay into the shape of our bodies. And the east wall was a violent red and gold for the fire that sparked us to life. They all converged together on the tiled floor, like some great flood of colors spilling from the walls. And above it all, the golden dome crowned us.

I could see now, with the fires burning, the bronze wire that was wound all the way around the inside of the dome in a spiral. A clear marker of Leyla's inventive hand in things. And, descending from the apex of the dome on the same wire, a bronze face, mouth open as if in a scream. Leyla's speaking machine, the one she had called the Zungvox. Meant so that prayers could be dispersed throughout the city in a vain attempt to control the people as more and more turned to worshipping at the wall. Used instead by the Sultan to speak through the Abdals and threaten us across the whole city.

Hala and I moved through the crowd as everyone around us found a place on the cool marble floor.

Everyone except us. We kept heading forward. Toward where I could see the young man at the front, standing next to the Holy Father, as he fussed with incenses and a huge gold-paged copy of the Holy Book. He stood out with his finely embroidered kurti and the fact that he had his father's chin.

It was well known that at least one of the Sultan's sons attended morning prayers every single day among the people. It was an attempt to calm the restlessness that was building in the city. The Sultan had sent a prince among his people to remind them we were all here together.

Hala and I were about to make a scene. Hopefully enough of one to save Fariha and every girl after her, too. Even if it meant us dying. Hala had made me swear to that. We made it out of here alive or we stayed behind dead— nothing in between.

We were almost at the front when the Holy Father standing on the dais above us raised his tattooed palms over the crowd, a gesture that everyone should kneel. With some shuffling and jostling, everyone did.

Everyone except us.

"Ready?" I whispered to Hala, my hand closing over a knife at my side. I was shaking. I was never nervous before a fight. But this wasn't a fight; it was a performance.

"Oh, don't tell me now is when you decide to turn coward on me." I couldn't see Hala's face, but I could practically hear the roll of her eyes in her voice. "Your guts are one of the things that I actually like about you."

I decided to take that as a yes.

It was like a curtain dropping at a show, a sea of people descending to their knees as we stayed standing. And then we moved together, Hala tipping her head back and dropping her hood even as I pulled out the knife and placed it at her collarbone. Then I let out a long whistle. Around us, all the heads that had dropped, ready for prayers, shot back up. Attendants dotted around glanced our way, ready to move to stop the disturbance. Even the Holy Father looked up, brow furrowed in annoyance. But his expression quickly changed as he caught sight of us.

No one looking at us would see two Demdji. Instead, they would see Princess Leyla with the Blue-Eyed Bandit holding a knife to her throat, though none of them would know exactly how they recognized the pair. Princess Leyla had never been seen by most of the people of Izman. And there were so many stories of the Blue-Eyed Bandit swirling around that no one was sure whether I was a girl, a man, or a legend. But Hala would slip into every single one of their minds, and they would all be perfectly sure of who we were.

"Your Highness," I called over the cacophony of whispers. The prince at the front in his elaborately stitched robes looked our way.

I didn't know the name of this particular prince, who was now staring at us with guileless eyes. It didn't much matter. There were hundreds of princes. According to Leyla, the youngest princes had been sent to safety, stored away somewhere, until the storm passed and they could be brought home. And then the Sultan could mold one of them into the heir he really wanted. One who wouldn't disappoint him like Kadir had. Who wouldn't rebel like Ahmed had. Who wouldn't resent him like Rahim still did. But in the meantime, the other sons were being used. I wondered if they knew that no matter what they did they wouldn't be chosen as heirs.

"I believe your father wants this back." I pressed the knife firmer against Hala's throat. The young prince winced, thinking it was his sister whimpering under my blade. "Now, here's what I want. Give us back Fariha Al-Ilham, the girl he currently has imprisoned in the palace. And I want her alive. Do you reckon you can get that message to your father before the sun rises?" The young prince looked bewildered. He definitely didn't take after his father with brains like that. "That means you'd better run."

The boy took off like a hare who'd just spotted a hawk, dashing the short distance back to the palace to fetch his father and hopefully a still-living Fariha. As he disappeared, I addressed the crowd kneeling around us, turning to face them, still holding Hala. "The rest of you ought to get out of here if you don't want to get caught up in this." My voice echoed around the high dome of the prayer house like the words of the Holy Father did when he stood here, making them sound like they were sent from a greater power.

No one moved right away, staying kneeling all around me. Staring up, at me. Drinking in my words.

"Now," I barked. And they obeyed, scrambling to their feet, almost creating a stampede in their rush to get out of the line of fire. It didn't matter what happened from here on out. Or what the truth of matters was. The men and women now rushing out would tell the story of what they had seen: the Blue-Eyed Bandit returning the Sultan's daughter. There would be no convincing the city that it hadn't been real. Belief was a foreign language to logic. Jin had told me that long ago. And I was counting on him being right—that if the city really believed that the Sultan had his daughter back, it would be enough to stop the executions. The Sultan would have no more justification for them in the eyes of his people.

I turned my attention now toward the attendants and the Holy Father, still lingering, uncertain of what they should do. "'The rest of you' means everyone," I ordered. They almost tripped over themselves gathering the Holy Father's heavy robes around him, bundling him hastily out as they gratefully fled. The great golden door that led onto the square closed behind them, leaving us alone in the huge prayer house.

I let the knife fall away from Hala's throat now we didn't have an audience. I turned my attention to the ground. The riot of colors in the tiles was chaos as they spilled down from the walls. But slowly they converged and coalesced into order as they swept into the dead center of the floor, where a huge golden sun painted into the tiles aligned perfectly with the dome above. I started counting from the center of the sun. Five tiles toward the dais and six to the right. Hala and I moved without speaking, in careful steps, checking our path like our lives depended on it. Which they did, really.

"It's this one, genius." Hala pointed, finding the right tile a fraction of a second before I did. "Don't they teach you to count at the dead end of the desert?"

"Sometimes you have to do it on your hands," I dead-panned, "Four fingers plus one thumb makes this fist I'm real tempted to knock you out with. How's that?" We took up our position carefully, making sure we were standing exactly where we were meant to on the tile.

The small side door swung open just as I settled my knife against Hala's throat again. It led directly from the palace to the great prayer house, a passage so the Sultan and princes could attend prayers without having to pass among their people. And sure enough, the Sultan appeared through it, trailing four Abdals behind him. One of them was holding a young crying girl: Fariha.

I had to remind myself that she was not Rima or Ghada or Naima. They were hanging from the palace walls. I had failed them. But Fariha could still be saved. And a hundred other girls in this city could, too. Girls whose names I would never know, so long as we saved one last girl whose name I did.

"Amani." The Sultan greeted me with a slow, luxuriant smile. I hated that voice. I hated that even now it made me want to straighten my spine and lean in to hear what he would say to me.

He'd shown me a whole lot of faces before. The benevolent arbitrator at his petitioners' court, the concerned father, the man with the heavy weight of a whole country on his shoulders across from me at dinner. But all those masks had been discarded now. Here in front of me, the Sultan looked like what he honestly was: a ruler descended from hundreds of legendary rulers before him who had fought and clawed for that throne. And grabbed it. And then held it. He was the blood of Imtiyaz the Blessed; Mubin, the victor against the Red-Eyed Conqueror; Fihr, who built the city of Izman from the dust.

And I was just a discarded Djinni's daughter from a dead-end desert town who was scraping tricks from the bottom of the barrel. I heard it again, that voice at the back of my head, getting louder every day that the eyes of the Rebellion turned to me for orders I didn't want to give. And answers I didn't have. Who did I think I was to face this man, the descendant of conquerors and legends?

"And who's this?" The Sultan's eyes skated to Hala, who was still holding the illusion of looking like Leyla in everyone's minds. Though not doing a good enough job of it to fool the princess's father. I hadn't counted on it fooling him. It didn't need to. It was enough that it had tricked the people.

"Does it matter?" I dropped the knife and the pretense, although Hala didn't discard the illusion right away, still wearing Leyla's face. "Everyone thinks I walked in here with your daughter. And now I reckon it would be a good idea for you if they saw Fariha walk out. Or else some folks are bound to wonder why their Sultan doesn't seem to be a man of his word now he's got his daughter back."

I hated the slow, wry smile that spread over his face, the one Jin had inherited from him. I hated that as I saw it, I realized I had wanted it. That some part of me had wanted to impress him by pulling off this trick. I had cared that he understood that I knew he was toying with us by killing those girls. Some part of me even wanted praise for playing my own game right back.

"There were easier ways than this, of course." The Sultan took a step toward us, his four Abdals following in one perfectly timed military step, forcing the crying girl forward. I resisted the urge to take a step back. We couldn't move from here, not if we wanted at least a chance at getting out alive. "*Someone* must have suggested returning Leyla to me dead." He was using that infuriatingly patient voice, like he was my father teaching me something that was very important for me to understand.

Hala helpfully raised her hand. "Oh, believe me, I did. So, so many times." The illusion changed in the blink of an eye, the way a scene changed without explanation in a nightmare. She wasn't a living, breathing Leyla anymore but Leyla's body, hanging from the ceiling with a long red rope, just like the three girls who hung from the walls of the palace, her feet scraping along the tiles below her as she swung. But the Sultan just stared dispassionately at the illusion. It didn't matter how real it appeared, it wasn't enough to move him. Instead, his attention turned back to me.

"You had good counsel. And you didn't listen." He sounded like he'd expected as much. As if he'd had absolutely no fear of his daughter dying at my hands. "That's why you lost, you know—trying to play at heroes."

"We haven't lost yet." I meant to fire it back at him, but

I knew I sounded like a child stomping my foot. And he was baiting me into delays. Almost baiting me into telling him our secret: that Ahmed was still alive. We were running out of time. The day was nearly finished breaking. The dawn bells would start soon—our signal for Sam to get us out of here. And we needed to get the girl out first. "Now, I'm going to ask you again: let Fariha go, for your own good."

There was a long moment of silence as the Sultan considered me. I could almost hear the moments dropping away, sand running too quickly through the hourglass. Counting down the precious seconds until we would be pulled out of here, leaving Fariha behind. Then, finally, he nodded, conceding a small loss to my move. "Release her," he commanded the Abdal. Immediately its metal hands loosened. The girl stumbled out of the machine's grasp, eyes wide and terrified. And then she ran, bolting toward the door and safety.

I'd meant to keep my eyes on the Sultan. But I couldn't help it. I had to watch her go. I turned my head just a little, to see her step over the threshold to safety. It was a mistake. I knew it as soon I heard the click, like a bullet slipping into place before it shoots you.

My head snapped around to see a small sphere, no bigger than a child's ball but made of metal and gears, roll toward us, coming alive with a sickening whirring noise. It was one of Leyla's inventions.

I was reaching for my gun when the explosion came. Not of fire and gunpowder, of dust. Suddenly a gray cloud enveloped us. I inhaled before I could think better of it and tasted the metallic tang. I realized what it was, even as I glanced over at Hala and saw her as she was, all illusions gone, just a golden-skinned girl doubled over, coughing violently.

Iron dust. It was a bomb of iron dust that the Sultan had thrown at us, draining our powers for as long as any of it clung to our skin, our tongues, our throats.

"Hold them," he ordered, and I heard the whirr of the Abdals as they started to move. I yanked my sheema up quickly, shielding myself from inhaling any more and covering my eyes as best I could. I might be powerless for now, but I hadn't come unarmed either.

I saw a glint of bronze through the cloud of dust, and I dove, knife in hand, swinging for the heel. The blade plunged through soft bronze, mangling the word below that powered the Abdal, sending it slumping over. I felt a metal hand on my shoulder. I moved like Shazad had taught me. I wasn't nearly as good with a knife as she was, but I had the upper hand just long enough to slice the Abdal's arm open savagely before I yanked my gun out of its holster and shot the mechanical soldier in the foot. It collapsed as I rounded away from it, pushing my way out of the cloud of iron dust.

I turned, ready to face the next opponent. Instead I saw the Sultan standing a few feet away from me, his arm braced around Hala, holding her firm against him, a knife at her throat. Just like I'd held her while she wore the illusion of Leyla's face.

She was helpless, her golden skin covered in clinging iron dust, turning its sheen a mottled gray. I'd never seen anyone look so furious and so frightened at the same time.

I held the gun pointed toward him. It didn't shake, even though my heart was hammering out a violent beat.

"Go ahead. Kill me," the Sultan taunted. "Then what, Amani? With our enemy at the gates and a city without a ruler or an heir, how do you think that will end? Conquest or civil war?" He was right and I knew it. But my gun wasn't pointed at him anyway. I was aiming at Hala.

Because we had a deal. She'd made me promise. An unbreakable Demdji promise.

Last night, in the dark, in our shared room, we'd agreed that if it all went wrong, neither of us would leave the other to be used against the rest of us. The Sultan could do a whole lot more harm with a Demdji under his control than just hanging girls from the palace walls.

It had reminded me of a thousand and one conversations Shazad and I had at night in our tent back in the rebel camp. In the dark it felt safer to do so somehow. Like we could confess anything there. Trust each other with our lives.

I caught Hala's eyes, dark in her beautiful golden face. Her lips moved ever so slightly. *Do it.*

Now in the cold light of dawn I wondered if it had been a trick, her Djinn side showing itself as she fooled me into agreeing to this. As if either one of us might surrender her life for this. When really she knew only one of us truly risked dying here. When she knew she had no gun, no fight in her if this went wrong, when she knew she was going to throw herself at the Sultan to spare me. When what she really wanted was assurance that I wouldn't leave her behind to be used again like she had once been.

My hand started to shake, and I saw the sunlight dance over the end of my pistol.

The Sultan was saying something else, something I didn't hear. All I could see were Hala's lips moving, mouthing what she wanted me to do. She couldn't speak into my mind, not with the iron still clinging to her skin. But I could almost hear her all the same.

I was running low on time, but still I hesitated until the last possible moment, my mind scrambling for any other way out of this. I wasn't going to pull the trigger until I absolutely had to.

In the grip of our enemy, on the brink of death, Hala rolled her eyes at me. And I heard her words from earlier clear as a bell in my head.

Oh, don't tell me now is when you decide to turn coward on me. Your guts are one of the things that I actually like about you.

And then the bells in the great prayer house chimed. That was our signal and that meant I was out of time. There was no other way out of this for Hala. I had to keep my promise.

Everything happened at once.

I sucked in a deep breath and held it.

Hala smiled.

My finger squeezed the trigger.

I closed my eyes, too. It didn't matter. I wouldn't miss.

A gunshot echoed around the huge gold dome just as hands closed over my feet. I felt the floor give way below me, like it was turning to water. I couldn't help it. I opened my eyes for a fraction of a second even as I sank quickly through the floor. Even as the moment that it would be too late rushed toward us. I had to see. I had to make sure I hadn't broken my promise.

She was slumped in the Sultan's arms, red blood smearing her still-smiling face. Her fingers dragged on the floor. Only eight of them. That was how I knew she was dead. If she was living she would be trying to hide that wound, one way or another. Like she always did.

For a moment as I sank, my eye caught on the broken Abdal. And I realized Hala looked the same, her glowing gold skin like their polished bronze. If she'd been left alive she would have been just like them, a thing to be used. A mechanical Demdji.

The floor rushed up and I shut my eyes again, like Sam had always taught me. When I hit solid ground again, I opened them. I was standing in the dark, broken only by the faint flicker of an oil lamp by Sam's feet.

We'd found the tunnels Leyla had told us about last night and worked out an escape route, a way to get out when Fariha was safe, one the Sultan wouldn't be able to anticipate. The floor was stone, which meant Sam could pass his arms through it and pull us down through the floor and out of the prayer house into the tunnels below. We'd marked the spot on the roof of the tunnel, figuring out which tile above corresponded to it. We'd been stand-ing exactly where we needed to stand to get to safety. To get out of there alive.

If it wasn't for the iron-dust bomb.

Sam opened his mouth, a question in his pale eyes. *Hala?* But before he could ask it, I shook my head quickly.

He understood.

She had died so that others could live. So that we could save them. So that other girls wouldn't die while we were gone. Maybe she had even walked in there knowing one of us had to die. Deciding it would be her. So that we could live. Escape.

So we did what she had died for. We ran.

TEN

THE GIRL MADE OF GOLD

Once there was a woman so greedy she gave birth to a daughter made of gold.

The Girl Made of Gold knew what it meant to be used. By a greedy mother. Then by a greedy husband. But the Girl Made of Gold had a secret: she could remake the world in the mind of others.

And one day she used her gift to escape all those who would have used her against her will.

She saw that there were others in the world who were being used against their will. But unlike the Girl Made of Gold, they were powerless to escape.

She resolved that she would not only remake the world in people's minds, she would dedicate her life to remaking it in reality, too. And she vowed that she would die before anyone ever used her against her will again.

And she kept that vow.

ELEVEN

It was the middle of the day by the time we reached the mountains of Iliaz.

I felt weighed down with grief over Hala, like I ought to be too heavy to fly through the desert skies like this. Too heavy for Maz to carry me, even with those immense wings that cast such a long shadow across the sand below. But somehow we were soaring through the air, leaving Izman far behind, racing toward the mountain fortress of Iliaz ahead of us. Jin's compass would lead us to Ahmed, but we had a pit stop to make first. Our destination was only a few short hours due west of Izman, as the magical shape-shifting Roc flew.

I was keenly aware that we were missing a soul every time I glanced over at Izz, flying parallel with his brother, carrying Sam, Tamid, and Leyla, while Maz carried just me and Jin.

It shouldn't have been this way. We'd had a plan.

I'd waited at the Hidden House while Sam and Hala accompanied the others into the tunnels Leyla had located for us. Sam got them through the bricked-up exits of the tunnels and out beyond the barrier. And then Hala used her Demdji gift to walk them through the Gallan siege around the city unseen. Then, once the others were out of sight beyond the city, Hala and Sam came back to the Hidden House, to wait until it was time to pull off our grand trick in the prayer house.

And then . . . iron dust, blood, bullets . . . and we were left without our golden-skinned Demdji.

I'd felt Hala's absence as soon as Sam and I emerged through the bricks and the sand, out of the tunnel, into broad daylight, facing our enemies with no cover from a Demdji illusion.

"So what do we do now?" Sam had asked in a low voice that carried far too much for my liking, as we'd crouched just outside the walls of Izman, facing the Gallan military tents ahead of us. And suddenly I felt like a child again.

I'd grown up in a desert full of monsters, but I'd never feared Nightmares or Skinwalkers as much as I did the Gallan.

For a moment I wasn't a rebel anymore. I was a little girl hiding under the house when the Gallan came to Dustwalk. I was watching through the windows when they dragged a man out of his house for spitting at their boots and shot him. I was seeing a woman swing because a Gallan soldier had caught her alone in the dark and everyone had closed their ears to her screams. I was helpless in Fahali, watching a bullet go through a Demdji's head before I even knew what a Demdji was.

I was helpless back then. I wasn't helpless now.

I was a Demdji now. I had all the more reason to fear them for that. But I also had more weapons than I used to.

I was a Demdji. I wasn't a little girl. I repeated that over and over even as I dredged up enough power from inside myself to raise a small sandstorm around us, leaning on Sam for support as I did. It was enough to give us cover to get to the other side, where the others were waiting for us.

Now Maz spread his wings, just barely brushing my knees as I clung to him against the wind. Jin's arm went around me as Maz prepared to drop down, steadying me against his solidness.

Last time I was in these mountains I was shot through the stomach, and Jin carried me to safety—barely. This place didn't exactly hold wonderful memories for me. But even I had to admit that Iliaz was a sight to behold. Half our country might be desert, but the rainclouds that gathered over the sea always broke across the mountains, making the soil here rich. The slopes were laced with vines and fields and orchards. And at the highest point, governing over the only pass through the mountains, was the great fortress.

Jin's compass pointed south, toward Eremot if Leyla was to be believed. But even I wasn't reckless enough to think we could pull off a rescue with only eight of us—

seven now, I reminded myself. A Blue-Eyed Bandit and an imposter Blue-Eyed Bandit, a Foreign Prince, a reluctant one-time friend, shape-shifting twins, and an enemy princess. Not exactly an army.

We needed help.

The twins landed us just out of view of the fortress. Approaching by flying shape-shifter seemed like a good way to get ourselves shot. I figured we ought to at least wait until we'd been out of Izman a whole day before anybody else died. On principle.

I staggered off Maz's back as we set down. My cramped legs almost gave out below me as I hit the ground. Jin slid down behind me, stretching out sore shoulders in a way that made his shirt pull up just enough to show the edge of the tattoo on his hip bone, drawing my eyes there.

And then Izz landed nearby, bringing Tamid, Leyla, Sam, and all our problems crashing back down to earth. Maz was returning to his human shape, letting the bags we'd slung over him slide away as his body drew into itself, feathers shifting to skin, wings into arms, until instead of a Roc, he was a skinny boy with blue hair.

Jin tossed him a pair of trousers from the bag. "Right." Maz caught them in the air, tugging them on. "There are ladies present."

"Since when are you a lady?" Sam asked me, unceremoniously scooping Leyla up under her bound arms, like she was an unruly child, and easing her to the ground. We didn't exactly *want* the traitor princess with us, but we didn't have a whole lot of choices.

Sam dropped down behind her easily, leaving Tamid

sitting awkwardly astride the huge bird. His bad leg was keeping him where he was, between Izz's enormous wings.

He looked shaken and angry, staring intently at Izz's feathered shoulderblades. I offered my hand to help him off, but he refused to meet my gaze as he slung his fake leg over one side and carefully slid down. He landed badly, crumpling to the ground in a heap. I rushed to help him up, but he waved me away. I stood back, watching him pull himself to his feet with agonizing difficulty.

He was angry at me about Hala. Now he'd lost another person, someone he'd formed an unlikely bond with in all the late nights when she couldn't sleep for grief and he was poring over the books she'd brought him, looking for an answer that wasn't there.

"Can you walk?" I asked. Izz had slipped back into his human shape and found some clothes of his own. We were ready to start moving.

"I can walk," he replied bitterly, pushing past me. And we started to make our way up to the fortress to have some words with Lord Bilal, Emir of Iliaz.

• **•** •

WE HADN'T BEEN walking long when we came across the first body.

It was partly covered by dirt, like someone had heaped soil on it. And then someone—or something—else had started trying to dig it out. Whatever had been digging had managed to drag an arm and part of the torso out of the ground. There were teeth marks on the skin, like maybe a ghoul had made a start on its meal before sunrise drove it away.

The arm was wearing a deep green uniform trimmed with gold. Those were Albish colors. And the hair that poked out of the grave was the same bright gold as Sam's. What was an Albish soldier doing covered in dirt outside Iliaz?

Iliaz was the most significant passage from east to west in Miraji. The bastion against invasion of Izman. The fighting here was frequent, and so the soldiers were the best trained in the country, and the most likely to die, as well. It was where Rahim had been sent as a boy, with the expectation that he wouldn't last long. An easy way for his father to get rid of him. But he'd thrived instead, becoming the soldiers' commanding officer, first under Bilal's father and then under Bilal. Iliaz defended the country against invaders. So how come now there was an invader so close to the fortress, and on the wrong side of the pass, no less?

A little way farther, there was another pile of dirt similarly disturbed. And another one after that. A whole line of them.

"What is this?" I asked.

"They tried to bury them." Jin sounded grim. We were close to the fortress now, and the stone walls loomed above us, casting this side of the mountain in shadow as the afternoon moved on.

"Why would anyone do that?" We passed another mound of earth, this one undisturbed. It was marked with a stick, standing straight in the ground, snapped off one of the vines that climbed up the mountain.

"In the north, we don't burn our dead like you do here," Sam spoke up from where he had dropped to the back of the group. He looked uneasy. "We bury them. Return them to the earth they came from. In Albis, you're supposed to put them in soft earth and plant a tree to mark the spot."

That didn't make any kind of sense. Bodies *had* to be burned. Leaving a corpse lying around was like inviting ghouls to come feast on it.

"They don't have the same problems with ghouls in the north as here in the desert," Jin said absently. "There are only five graves. That's not enough for this to have been a battle."

Before I could ask what he meant, we rounded a turn in the path leading up to the fortress. A half dozen Albish soldiers' heads shot up from where they were gathered around a freshly dug hole. Their uniform jackets were slung over nearby stones, shirts rolled up to their elbows, brows sweating under the Mirajin sun. We'd interrupted them in the middle of burying another body.

My gun was in my hand in a blink—Jin's, too. But the soldiers were scrambling for their own weapons, diving for discarded gun belts. We were outnumbered if they got there.

We'd have to shoot first.

My finger was on the trigger when the ground moved below my feet. It wasn't like the mountain itself shifting— more like the skin of it was trying to shake us off, like we were an itchy nuisance. Dirt slid away under our feet, pitching Sam off balance and sending him crashing to the ground. I fought to steady myself, but it was no good. The wind picked up from nowhere, slamming me backward, sending me sprawling, opening the skin at my elbow and knocking the gun from my hand.

And then, as fast as it had started, everything stopped. The mountain stilled. The wind died.

"What just happened?" I asked, cradling my bleeding elbow.

Sam groaned, clutching his side as he rolled over. He'd scratched up his face. That would dent his vanity for sure. "The ones in the dark green uniforms," he said. "They're like me. Well, I guess more like you." He amended quickly, looking sour. I glanced over at the men. Two among them were in different uniforms than the others, the green of the fabric pattered with bright gold leaves, like vines twisting up and around their bodies. And they were un-armed, unlike all the others who were now pointing guns at us. One of the men in the gold vine uniform had the most brilliant pair of unnaturally green eyes I'd ever seen. The other had a faint tint of gray to his pale skin, like it might be made of stone.

Sam might have immortal blood in him from some an-cestor or other, but he had two mortal parents. These men were true Demdji. Or whatever it was the Albish called their Demdji. Jin had told me once that their immortal creatures weren't made of fire and wind and sand but of water and clouds and soft earth. Their gifts were differ-ent, but there was no mistaking them. And they weren't hidden away—they were standing proudly, wearing their country's symbol emblazoned on their chests, using their powers to fight.

The twins, Leyla, and Tamid had been knocked down, too. They stayed there looking dazed as Jin, Sam, and I traded looks from our new positions on the ground. Sam didn't need to translate what they were shouting across the short distance. I knew what to do when a gun was pointed at my head. I'd been on the other side of it often enough.

We raised our hands in surrender.

TWELVE

Lord Bilal, Emir of Iliaz, looked like what he was: a dying man.

We'd been marched the rest of the way to the fortress at gunpoint by the Albish soldiers. Leyla cried and protested the whole way that she was a prisoner, that they had to help her. But her words were falling on ears that either didn't care or didn't understand Mirajin. Finally Jin leaned into her and quickly whispered, "Do you really want our country's enemies to know you're a princess?" After that, she fell into sullen silence. She might want an escape, but an escape into enemy hands was worse than no escape at all.

If Iliaz was occupied by foreign soldiers with enough authority to arrest us, it must mean the fortress had fallen. I'd figured we'd find Iliaz invaded, Lord Bilal and his men dead or imprisoned.

But when we reached the gates to the fortress, they were opened by Mirajin soldiers wearing the uniform of Iliaz. No words passed between the Albish soldiers holding us at gunpoint and the Mirajin soldiers, only brusque nods. The Iliazin soldier standing at the gate took us all in, one by one. If he was surprised by the rabble that we were, he was too well trained to show it. Beyond him, I could see into a large courtyard that encircled the fortress.

Dozens of Albish soldiers milled about in their dark green uniform, methodically cleaning guns, sharpening blades, or running through drills. And beside them, though not among them, were the men of the Iliaz garrison. Mirajin men coexisting with these foreigners on their territory.

Not invaders, then. Allies. Well, that was an unexpected development.

"Identify yourselves," the Mirajin soldier at the gate had demanded, talking to us all at once.

I didn't bother lying to him about who we were. We'd come here looking for Bilal, after all. Evidently we were expected. Before I knew what was happening, I was being ushered into Bilal's chambers. The others came only as far as the long stone hall just outside his rooms. I could feel Jin's eyes on my back just before the door slammed between us.

On the other side, Bilal was waiting for me as if I were an invited guest instead of a prisoner. He sat flanked by a servant and one of his soldiers, propped up by dozens of pillows at the end of a low table that had been set with dozens of dishes so decadent I wasn't sure I recognized most of them.

Bilal was the same age as Rahim. They had grown up together, both raised by Bilal's father, as brothers. Both of them were still shy of two decades. But now, with the illness destroying him, Bilal looked as if he might be ninety rather than nineteen.

To his right sat a man in an Albish uniform more elaborate than those of the younger men who'd brought us here. He didn't have vines all over his uniform, but there were gold tassles on his shoulders and gold buttons that marked him apart. I guessed he was their general or captain. He seemed to be suffering in the heat, his pale face slightly flushed. His hair was a reddish color, one I'd only ever seen before on foxes, and a carefully trimmed moustache adorned his upper lip. He was shifting uncomfortably on the pillow next to the low table, as if he'd prefer a chair. He wouldn't find one here.

I guessed this was the outer receiving chamber of Bilal's set of rooms, but it didn't look like it was really meant to receive anyone. It reminded me of Tamid's room back in the Hidden House, crowded with tables, stacked up with books and jars of powders labeled in a language I didn't know.

"Amani," Bilal greeted me. At least he was calling me by my name instead of *Demdji*. "Please." He waved one thin hand at the meal laid out around the table. "Do join me and Captain Westcroft." I didn't move, glancing from Bilal to the Albish officer at his right. "I should get to know my bride, after all."

There was no mistaking that Bilal was closer to the end than he'd been a mere month ago in Izman, when he'd issued his ultimatum to us. He'd wanted a Demdji wife to tie his life to, in order to keep that life going. So it figured Bilal thought he knew why I was here.

I didn't sit. "I'm not here to marry you."

The servant to Bilal's left flinched. I didn't blame him. I waited for Bilal's anger. I remembered Prince Kadir's barely restrained violence when he'd been told he couldn't have me. Men raised in privilege were not accustomed to being refused. But Bilal simply dropped his shaking hand to his plate, then smoothed out a crease in the cloth draped over the table, buying himself time to compose his features

"Well, then, to what do I owe the dubious honor of this visit?" He was thinner than he'd been when he left Izman, and his eyes looked sunken with pain and lack of sleep. But that imperious look hadn't left him. Even now, on the edge of death, he wasn't going to admit defeat.

I glanced at the Albish soldier to his right again, who was still watching me. "Don't trouble yourself." Bilal waved a hand. "The captain here doesn't understand a word of what you're saying, and I will instruct Anwar not to enlighten him." He waved to the soldier standing between the two of them. "Anwar's Albish is as flawed as any man's who learned it from a woman." The soldier, Anwar, looked embarrassed as his emir said this, but he held his tongue. "But it's passable for our present purposes. And it's the best we have at the moment."

The Albish captain was watching me with an air of studied blankness I didn't entirely trust, but I turned my attention back to Bilal all the same.

"I came here with a warning." I tried to hold myself with the same easy authority Shazad had when she was talking, like I held the upper hand here, not him. Me with my four rebels and two reluctant tagalongs on the run. Him with a fortress and an army and an arsenal. "And an offer."

Bilal inclined his head. "I'll take the warning first, I suppose. It couldn't get much worse."

"The Sultan knows that you met with Ahmed before leaving the city." I reached into my pocket, pulling out a piece of paper, one of the letters that Jin had stolen from the palace. I passed it to the servant, who handed it down to Bilal, holding it open for him to read. "Our exalted ruler knows you're a traitor. After he deals with the foreign threat at his gates"—my eyes flicked hesitantly toward the fox haired captain—"you're his next target."

Bilal didn't look unduly distressed by this as he scanned the paper in the servant's hands. After all, Iliaz was supposed to be the impregnable city, the fortress that guarded one of the only passages between western and eastern Miraji. The ultimate strategic land, according to Shazad.

"And your offer?" He sounded bored as he flicked two

fingers at the servant, dismissing him and the letter that spelled out his destruction as if it was nothing. The servant carefully set the paper aside on one of the tables that was already overflowing with scraps and scribbles. "Well?" he prompted when I didn't speak right away.

My eyes darted again to the others in this room before I spoke. "My offer is that if you help us rescue Rahim"—Anwar, the soldier at Bilal's side, snapped to attention at the mention of Rahim; the mere sound of his captain's name seemed to straighten his spine—"and Ahmed, we will do our best to take the throne from the Sultan and make sure the ruler of this country isn't someone who wants to kill you."

Mention of Rahim didn't seem to do as much to get Bilal's attention as it had Anwar's. I'd figured Bilal must be something close to a brother to him. That Bilal would care that Rahim was going to die if we didn't rescue him.

But Bilal just spread his hands wide, indicating the man at his side in the Albish uniform. "Does it look to you as if I'm trying to hide my treason, Amani? What kind of ruler would I be if I wasn't prepared to face the consequences of it?"

"Maybe one who doesn't care about consequences because he's a dead man anyway." The words were out before I could decide whether or not I ought to say them. I could swear that I saw the Albish soldier's eyebrows rise just a little at the unchecked words. But Bilal let out a sharp laugh that turned quickly into a cough. It racked painfully through his worn body, seeming to rattle his very bones. The servant stepped forward, but Bilal waved him off quickly, composing himself.

"You think I'd throw our country to the dogs out of spite?"

My eyes flicked to the Albish captain to see whether he had any reaction to his army being called dogs. But his face was studied blankness again. "I think what you're treating like an alliance looks a lot like an invasion."

"Invasions don't usually come with an invitation." Bilal smoothed his hand over the table again, a tic he couldn't seem to help, trying to hide his shaking hands. "Though I appreciate that with those two words sounding so similar, it might be confusing to simpler folk."

I tried to ignore the flash of shame as his voice took on a mocking twinge of my thick accent on the last handful of words. Like I was stupid just because I didn't talk like he did.

"A breach was inevitable, Amani." Bilal's words took on a patronizing tone now. "The Sultan's army at our western border is in shambles. The rumor is that General Hamad has gone missing and they are without leadership." General Hamad. That was Shazad's father. Missing, he said. Not dead. Shazad's father must have escaped the Sultan's attempt to apprehend him after his daughter's treason. "Without a decent line of defense, it was easy for my new friends to walk into the desert from Amonpour. Our ruler is struggling to hold onto this country, Amani. You really think he has the resources to come after me for my choice of allies?" He sounded so smug, sitting up here in his fortress. But I had just come from Izman and I knew better than to underestimate the Sultan.

"So, what about all those bodies buried in the dirt outside? That sure doesn't look like an easy alliance to me."

"A run-in with a pack of Nightmares farther down the mountain, not with my men. My new allies were not prepared, foreign as they are." Bilal looked at me like I was a child whose wild ideas he was entertaining for his own amusement. "Do you really want to debate me on the difference between cooperation and invasion? Because I can promise you that my education in history, strategy, and vocabulary was far more expensive than yours."

It was like I was back in the palace, sitting across from the Sultan, unable to defend my Rebel Prince against his twisted logic. Shazad, who was better read, would have had some smart retort for him, or Ahmed, who was sure of his intentions, would have been able to stand his ground better than I could. I just stood, taking the blows of his words as he batted away my arguments effortlessly. "Captain Westcroft and his army are here at my invitation, because I do not intend to die."

"Lots of people wind up dead without meaning to, you know." Out of the corner of my eye, I saw the Albish captain brush a hand across his moustache quickly, as if he was hiding a smile.

"Yes, well"—Bilal's shaking hand twitched—"as amusing as your sense of self-importance is, you don't really think *you* were my last resort, do you?" He waved an arm weakly around himself, at the chaos that dominated the rest of the room. "I have tried a thousand ways to stay alive already. This is just one more. See for yourself."

A few steps took me to the table where the servant had tossed the letter that acknowledged Bilal's treason. I could barely see the table itself under the chaos. "I have tested and used and searched for every single piece of Mirajin sorcery to save me. Without any result. It is time to move away from desert magic." My fingers danced across the papers and scribbled, half-mad notes. There were pages violently ripped out of books, the torn edges painted with bright pigmented flowers and gold-leaf animals. "The Albish know how to heal with water and earth instead of fire and words. You've already seen what they are capable of in battle." So he was trading our country to foreigners for a chance at a cure.

A page on the corner of the table caught my attention. The whole thing was taken up by a drawing of a mountain, a single gray peak that stretched up from the bottom of the page, and invaded the sky. Except this mountain was hollow, and inside it was a man with crimson skin, like shifting fire, and chains around his arms. In bright gilded letters the words inscribed below him glinted at me: *The man below the mountain.*

I ran my finger along the jagged edge of the paper, where it had been torn out of a book. I had seen this image before, though never this finely done. There was a pale illustration in cheap water paints from one of Tamid's books back in Dustwalk. In his, the man was an angry, violent shade of purple, and he had huge, sharp teeth that protruded from his mouth in a snarl. Not a man but a monster. But otherwise, the image was the same, down to the particular peaks on the mountain.

"This is a story they used to tell to scare us back home," I said, pulling out the page from the pile. I was six years old and being scolded by Tamid's mother. *Be good, or the monster in the mountain will get you. He eats naughty children alive, you know.* "They told us there was a monster who had done such a great wrong to the Djinn that he'd been locked under a mountain for all eternity. That he survived by eating children who disobeyed their parents."

Bilal shook his head. "Trust them to get it wrong all the way south." He said *south* like it was an insult. "Not a monster, just a man. And he didn't wrong the Djinn; they wronged him. They stole his true love. Like many Djinn steal good men's wives." His eyes danced across me pointedly. "But this man, unlike the others, dared to take vengeance on them. Or he tried. The Djinn put him in chains and locked him below the mountain until he repented. But if any man freed him early, that man would be granted his heart's greatest desire."

So that was why Bilal had this. Another way out of death—a wish granted by some impossibly immortal man below the mountain. "You shouldn't trust stories," I said. But I was still holding the page. I'd never seen the picture like this. He didn't look like a monster, but not quite like a man either. He looked like a creature made of fire. "They're never true all the way through." It reminded me of the game we used to play as children, where one child whispered a sentence into the ear of another, who whispered it on and on, until the last child spoke aloud some distorted version of the original. Only I didn't know which one was the copy. The man or the monster.

"Is it just a story, though?" Bilal was watching me intently. "Because I sent a dozen soldiers down south to find this man below the mountain, and they didn't come back. And I don't think it was make-believe that killed them."

No, it was probably Skinwalkers, or a foreign army, or the Sultan's army, or hungry Mirajin people, or any other number of things they could've encountered on their fool's errand.

I put the page down reluctantly. "There's no such thing as *just* a story."

Another coughing fit seized Bilal, doubling him over, and this time he didn't have the strength to wave away the servant who stepped forward. The coughing didn't abate. The servant and the soldier helped Bilal to his feet, supporting him through a door that led to the more private areas of his chambers.

His coughs echoed noisily back down the hallway long after the door had closed behind him, leaving me alone in the room with the fox-haired Albish captain.

I dropped down heavily into the seat that Bilal had indicated I ought to take, at his other side, across from the captain. I picked up a stuffed vine leaf and shoved it in my mouth. "So," I addressed the captain in Mirajin around the mouthful of food. I hadn't been raised finely—that much Bilal had been good enough to remind me of—so there was no point acting like I had been. "Are you really going to cure him? Or is this some story you're peddling to get a foothold in my country?" The captain watched me for a moment, the studied blankness slipping before reappearing. But I wasn't in the mood to play games. "I know you can understand me," I said. "And if you want to pretend you can't, I've got my own translator I can bring in here. But be warned, he's more annoying than me."

"Yes, well." The captain cleared his throat. Even with those few words I could tell his Mirajin was near perfect, tinged with even less of an accent than Sam's. "I hope you'll forgive the attempt at deception. It was not for your benefit. I learned your language in the first Mirajin war, two decades past, when we regrettably lost this country to your current Sultan and his Gallan allies." The captain picked up a pitcher and started to pour wine into a clear glass. "And my wife makes sure we use Mirajin at home, of course, for the children's sake. They should speak both their parents' languages." He extended the glass of wine out for me. "Do have some; it really is very good."

I took a sip of the wine. He wasn't wrong. It really was very good. And I was thirsty. "And this is your second stab at taking the desert, is it?" I asked. "After you lost the first time? That's why you're using Bilal, and pretending you can save him?"

"We'll certainly do our best to cure him." He stepped neatly around my question. "Our druid is trying to draw the sickness out of his blood. Though it may be in his bones now, in which case . . . But it is not my intention to let an ally die for no good reason. Though, as you say, sometimes intentions mean very little when death comes to the door."

"So, what is your intention?" I asked.

The captain didn't answer right away, pouring himself a glass of wine to match mine, buying himself time to think. "Miss Amani," he said finally, in a very proper tone of voice that didn't sound like he was going to answer my question straight. "I heard with great interest what you said to good Lord Bilal. But—and I hope you won't mind me putting this so indelicately—according to our intelligence, the Rebel Prince is dead." Ah, damn. I hadn't exactly meant him to know that part. But it was too late now.

"Well, your intelligence isn't all that intelligent, then."

The captain turned his laugh into a polite cough. "If our intelligence is indeed flawed . . . do you truly believe your Rebel Prince can win the throne?"

That was the question, wasn't it? Did I believe that Ahmed was capable of something his father reasoned he wasn't? Did I believe that he could be the ruler this country needed, both for his people and against our enemies? When all logic said that a regime change now would doom the desert? But belief was a funny thing, foreign to logic. "If I didn't believe that, it would be an awfully strange thing for me to risk my life trying to save him."

"I see." Captain Westcroft contemplated. "And am I right in understanding you need assistance to rescue him?" I watched him warily, not sure exactly what he was getting at, but I nodded.

"You asked me our intentions." Captain Westcroft

sighed. "I don't know how much you know about the history of Albis, Miss Amani, but we have a mutual enemy."

"The Gallan Empire." The same enemy that was sitting at the gates of Izman now.

"Yes. We have held off a Gallan invasion for a thousand years because ours is a country founded on magic. I expect you better than anyone understand what Gallan occupation means for . . . those whose ancestry is not entirely mortal." I understood exactly. It meant death for Demdji, for anyone and anything they considered touched by a First Being. It meant our country being bled dry of labor to fuel their crusade against other countries who used magic, and towns like Dustwalk being wrung out for all their worth. It meant soldiers running amok and lawless, killing and raping in my country and turning it into part of their hideous empire.

"Many fled your country in fear of the Gallan twenty years ago, my wife among them. She and others, they came to us because they knew we were a country that has held fast against the enemy for centuries. When the Gallan army first marched on Albis a thousand years ago, carrying their swords and bows, our first queen raised the very land against them." He puffed out air through his moustache. "When Gallandie sent an armada against us, our queen swept the ships from the sea with one hand. But blood thins, magic fades, and technology advances. That was why our Queen Hilda came to your Sultan so readily to make an alliance during Auranzeb. And he killed her."

I remembered the night of Auranzeb, the foreign leaders burning at the hands of Abdals, a declaration of independence from all these enemies clamoring at our borders, offering friendship and hiding manacles behind their backs.

They came for an alliance. The Sultan gave them death. I had considered everyone that night enemies of Miraji. But I supposed some were more enemies than others.

"There are terrible rumors, since Queen Hilda's death, that the new young queen, her daughter, cannot even light a fire without falling into a dead faint."

"And your enemy has matches," I said.

"Precisely. Put magic against swords and magic wins every time. Magic against guns, we stand a fighting chance. But a mortal queen against the might of the Gallan, well . . ." He smiled faintly. "She has been left with very little choice but to ally or to fall. Young Queen Elinore is crafting a treaty with Gallandie, a marriage alliance with one of their own young princes. If it is ratified, we will fight alongside our oldest enemies against your Sultan. We are waiting here, poised for instructions before we join them."

I understood suddenly. The notes scribbled in the papers Jin had found in the Sultan's office—he was waiting until the whole might of our enemies was gathered outside our walls. "You're the reinforcements that the Gallan are waiting for in Izman."

"Yes." The captain looked faintly embarrassed. "There is more of their army coming, too, from Gallandie itself, headed for your northern shores." He sounded apologetic. "Your city will be surrounded."

And they might all be annihilated for it. They had no

idea what kind of force the Sultan could turn against them. Then again, even the Sultan might not be expecting two ancient enemies to join against him. The Albish magic, with the Gallan's numbers, might stand a chance at fighting the Abdals.

One way or another, this would be a massacre. And it might be the end of Miraji before we even had a chance to take the throne for Ahmed. We would be a conquered country in the Gallan Empire.

"However," the captain said, stepping into my churning thoughts carefully, "before your Rebel Prince was executed, it was made known to some that Queen Hilda might be prepared to offer her support to the Rebel Prince's in his bid for the throne." Captain Westcroft toyed with one of the gold buttons on his sleeve. "If you were amenable, I could send word back to Albis today to find out if the offer of alliance still stands with young Queen Elinore. If perhaps she might prefer it to getting into bed with our enemies. So to speak. We would have word back by tomorrow, I expect." That didn't make any kind of sense to me. Albis was oceans away, far beyond the horizon. They really must have magic that I didn't wholly understand.

"So, for an alliance you'd be willing to help us rescue Ahmed?" He was offering me what we had come to Bilal for: an army. But I hesitated.

I remembered sitting across from the Sultan at the palace, over a duck I'd killed. He was chastising me, saying that the world was not so simple as the Rebellion would like to make it out to be. That Miraji was a country that couldn't stand on its own. That it would be conquered if it did not ally. He had been toying with me then. But that didn't mean he was wrong. To help us win our country, they wanted our country. And it wasn't my country to give away.

But if we didn't manage to rescue Ahmed, if I left the Albish to ally with the Gallan, it would never be his country either.

Before I could answer, a shout came from outside. There was a commotion in the hall where I'd left the boys and our traitor princess. I was on my feet in a second, the foreign captain close behind me. I wrenched the door open just in time to see an Albish soldier with pale brown curls take a swing at Sam, two of his compatriots looking on.

Amazingly, Sam managed to look sheepish while being punched in the face.

Sam hit the ground bleeding from his nose even as Captain Westcroft barked something that sounded like an order in Albish. The two other soldiers snapped to attention, but the one who'd hit Sam either didn't hear or didn't care. He moved as if to hit him again. I stepped to stop him, but Jin was closer. Faster than I could see, he had the soldier by the front of his uniform and slammed him back into the opposite wall. He said something to him in rapid-fire Albish. It sounded like a threat but the other boy didn't take a swing at Jin. Possibly because Jin stood a head taller than him.

Only then did the soldier seem to notice his captain. He

straightened quickly, even though he was wedged against a wall, and did his best to smooth down a uniform that was still twisted in Jin's fists.

The captain said something in Albish that I could only guess was *What the hell is going on here?* I wanted to know the same thing. Jin finally let the soldier go and reached down a hand to help up Sam, who was still lying on the floor, looking stunned.

"I'm fine," Sam said, staggering to his feet. "I've just never been hit in the face before."

"I find that very hard to believe," Jin said.

"I'm just amazed one of us didn't get there first," I said, stepping away from the captain. "What did he hit you for?"

"Jealousy," Sam said, dabbing at his bloody face with his sleeve. "Over my good looks. Do you think my nose is broken?"

"Seems our friend with the decent right hook knows Sam from his days serving Her Majesty." Jin filled in the truth, quickly translating what the younger soldier was saying to his captain.

I groaned, looking at the ceiling. "So they know you're a deserter."

"I would like to remind you"—Sam did a very poor job of looking indignant with a bloody nose—"that I wouldn't even be here to be recognized as a deserter if it wasn't for you."

"No, you'd probably be flotsam outside the White Fish," Jin said before I could fire back.

"Besides," Sam went on, "that punch wasn't for patriotism. When I left the army, I needed some additional resources to finance myself. You know, until I got settled in Izman."

"So you stole from him." This was getting better by the second.

"No." Sam looked outraged. "Not just from him. I stole from a lot of people."

I pinched the bridge of my nose in exasperation. "Can you remind me when we get out of here to kill you?"

Before Sam had a chance to dig himself any deeper, the other two soldiers stepped forward, pushing past us almost apologetically to seize Sam by the arms.

"What's happening now?" I asked. Captain Westcroft was looking unhappily on, hands interlocked behind his back as he gave his soldiers orders.

"They're arresting him," Jin said, translating, as Sam was led away, his mocking incredulity shifting to something more serious. "For desertion."

"And then what?" I asked. Sam had said that in Albis they hung their deserters from trees. But we were a little low on trees up here in the mountains.

Jin hesitated; he didn't want to give me the answer.

"He'll be executed," Captain Westcroft answered me, though he didn't look happy about it, tugging on his moustache. "At dawn, by firing squad."

Seemed like I wasn't going to have to be the one to kill him after all.

THIRTEEN

I wasn't sure if we were prisoners or not.

We were divided up quickly, before I could talk to Jin about the captain's offer, each of us sent to separate rooms. They didn't lock our doors, but there were soldiers posted outside.

The room I was escorted to didn't look like a cell either. It was about the size of my aunt's whole house back in Dustwalk, dominated by a huge bed littered with colorful pillows and a carpet that stretched from one wall to the other and depicted a hunting scene, a man with arrows chasing a flock of birds around and around the border. My window overlooked the courtyard, the fortress walls, and, just beyond that, the side of the mountain that plunged down in rolling waves of green vines to a smaller village a little way below.

As I peered out, there was a knock at the door. Two servants entered, heads down. One was carrying a pitcher of water, the other a huge silver platter heavy with food. They set them down on the table before quickly leaving, closing the door behind themselves.

Whatever privileges were being given to us didn't extend to Sam.

Hala had died at dawn. It was nearing dusk now, and we were close to losing Sam, too. A third of our rebels dead in one day. Losing people this quickly was an impressive feat for any leader.

But in return, we could add hundreds to our numbers and keep two of our country's enemies from allying against us.

A whole army in exchange for the life of one boy who was a whole lot more trouble than he was worth. But he was my friend and our ally all the same. He had saved me as many times as I had saved him, and he'd brought me help when I needed it in the harem. I'd lay down my life for him in a fight. I didn't know if he'd do the same for me, but he sure hadn't given me permission to give up his life for him.

And if I did, even if I gained us an alliance, I'd be handing over my country to foreign hands, just like the Sultan had done when he'd usurped his own father. The Albish were better than the Gallan, but they were still foreigners. They were still here to occupy our desert.

Who the hell was I to make this call? This shouldn't be my decision—not Sam's life, not the throne, not the lives of our friends or the fate of a whole country. Someone else should be deciding these things, Ahmed or Shazad or even Rahim. Someone who knew a damn about *something*.

I glanced at my door. Jin had been led into a room just across the hallway from mine. With walls and doors between us, I was somehow more keenly aware of him than I had ever been.

If I tried to cross the hallway, would the soldier stop me? And if he didn't, and I took a few short steps to his room and knocked at the door, then what? I wasn't sure what I would say. What I would do. What did I even want from him—to talk? For him to tell me that I should let Sam die for the sake of the Rebellion? For his help making a plan to get our imposter bandit out of here alive? Or did I want something else? I could feel his absence like an itch below my skin.

Before I could think better of it, I was at the door, wrenching it open. The soldier standing outside was Mirajin, one of Bilal's men and too well trained by Rahim to jump at sudden noises. He glanced at me calmly from where he was standing at attention between the two doorways.

"Do you have orders to stop me?" I asked.

The soldier considered me for a long moment. "There's a rumor going around that you're headed to rescue the commander." He was talking about Rahim. Their commander, the man they were still loyal to. Anwar, the young soldier who had been translating for Bilal, must have told the rest of the men what I'd said.

"I'm going to try."

He nodded thoughtfully. "In that case, as far as I'm concerned, you can go wherever you want." He moved to let me pass. I stepped out of the room and glanced at Jin's closed door. The idea of taking another step toward it, of closing that last distance between us, sent a small thrill down my spine that felt equal parts fear and anticipation.

Fear got the better of me.

I turned, moving down the hallway and away from him quickly.

● ● ●

I FOUND THE captain on the fortress walls, surveying six of his soldiers who were lined up taking shots at a bale of hay with unnecessarily decorative rifles. They were handmade, just like all the guns that came from anywhere in the world that wasn't Miraji. That was why they needed us so badly. We could arm as many people in a day as they could in a month of making weapons.

The last of the setting sun hit the barrels of the rifles, making the gold insets gleam in the twilight. They were in the shapes of elaborate twisting vines that worked their way down into the wooden handles. They looked more ceremonial than useful. For an execution rather than for battle. I guessed the bale of hay was a stand-in for Sam.

The top of the bale came loose as the bullets struck it, and it teetered for a moment before toppling backward, off the wall. I leaned over, watching it plummet down and over the cliff face before crashing on the mountain far below.

It was a long drop.

"Miss Amani." Captain Westcroft acknowledged me, dismissing his soldiers with a quick nod. "How can I help you tonight?" If he was surprised that I'd gotten out of my room, he didn't show it.

"I want to talk to you about Sam."

"I see." Clasping his hands behind his back, he slowly began to walk along the walls, letting me fall into step behind him.

"I want to make his release a condition in our alliance." Shazad would be able to negotiate this. I wasn't her, but I could pretend I was for one conversation.

"I'm afraid that won't be possible." The captain sounded genuinely regretful. The sky was darkening around us quickly as we walked, and torches and lamps started to spring to life throughout the fortress, pushing back against the night.

"Then it better become possible." I tried to say it like Shazad would, like I wasn't asking—I was ordering. "Sam's not yours to execute; he's with us now."

"He is still a deserter. And he will always be a deserter. An army runs on discipline. In places like these, far from home, desertion and insubordination become greater threats than ever. And if I am going to ask these soldiers to march across a desert for you, they need to be disciplined." He stopped walking, turning to face me, looking grave. "Your friend needs to be made an example of for three hundred other men."

Three hundred soldiers.

It was the best chance we'd have at getting Ahmed back. The Albish might even have enough magic among them to get us through Ashra's Wall, if it was real.

I'd have to be stupid to turn that down. But then, I'd been accused of that plenty in my life. Stupid, ignorant, reckless girl from Dustwalk who wouldn't know a good deal if it was staring her in the face.

"Captain," someone called in Albish, drawing Westcroft's attention down to the courtyard below. The soldier standing guard at the gate said something too quick for me to catch.

The captain's reaction was instant, his face shifting to real worry. "Excuse me," he said swiftly before moving down the stone stairs that led from the wall toward the gate. I followed him.

I wasn't even at the bottom step when I saw what had caused the commotion. Through the fortress's gate, I could see a pale figure stumbling out of the gloom. He was clutching his side, wearing an Albish uniform covered with blood. I could just see in the faint torchlight that his face was twisted in pain.

The Albish soldiers were already rushing forward, past the gate and into the dark, to help him. The Mirajin soldiers, on the other hand, hung back, rightfully wary. There was something wrong here, something unsettling about this wounded soldier limping home through the night. All of us who'd been born in this desert could feel it. Years in Dustwalk checking over my shoulder, wary of dark corners and of things that lurked in the gloom, had trained my instincts. But I had learned some more tricks since my desert days.

"It's not human." The words fell too easily off my tongue to be anything but the truth, and I knew. I knew as the soldiers stumbled toward the edge of the light cast by the lamps burning near the gate, grasping him by either arm, holding him up.

Neither of them saw the glint of its teeth as it shifted its head toward the nearest soldier's throat to rip it out.

It was too late to cry out a warning. Too late to do anything except move.

I was quick. My hand was around the pistol holstered at the captain's side before he could so much as see me moving. The weapon came alive in my grip. I took aim quickly, as the ghoul's maw opened, ready to clamp down.

I fired.

The bullet caught the Skinwalker between the eyes.

Its stolen face didn't even have time to look surprised as it dropped dead.

Instantly, the foreign soldiers' guns were swinging back toward me, thinking I had killed one of their own. My hands were already up, finger off the trigger, trying to prove I wasn't a threat. The gun was wrestled off me, and my arms were grabbed.

"That wasn't one of your soldiers," I said in Mirajin,

loud enough for Bilal's men at the gate to hear me, even as my arms were being wrenched painfully behind my back. "It was a Skinwalker." I thought maybe understanding dawned across the captain's face, but the rest of the soldiers looked blank. They didn't understand that they had brought this upon themselves. Bilal, lingering in his sickbed, wouldn't have known what they were doing. I wondered if he even would've cared.

And suddenly I saw another flicker of movement.

And I remembered, on our climb up the mountain: there had been more than one body buried out there, half-dragged out of the dirt with teeth marks on its skin.

"And it's not alone."

The Mirajin soldiers were quick to react, guns swiveling into the darkness. But the Skinwalkers knew we were wise to them now. They kept to the shadows, darting in and out too quickly to be a useful target even as barrels tried to follow them through the night.

We didn't have any warning before the next thing sprung. Its mouth clamped over a soldier's shoulder, ripping through flesh and muscle, all the way to the bone. The man's scream echoed down the mountain.

But Rahim's men were well trained. Another soldier was on the Skinwalker in a second, his knife across its throat, sending the monster down to the ground twitching.

Then another Skinwalker surged out of the darkness toward the soldier.

"Close the gates!" the captain was calling, even as his

men took aim at the newest Skinwalker, catching it in the chest, sending it reeling back. "Close them now!" He called the same order in Albish, unsure in this muddled army who was manning what.

The soldiers started to retreat quickly, keeping their guard up, as the huge iron gate was lowered over the entrance. Albish and Mirajin guns clattered, pointing at the Skinwalkers. There were dozens of them slinking through the dark now, darting in and out of focus. Drawn out from their mountain hiding places, looking for more bodies to devour.

A shot went off by my ear. I didn't have to check if it had hit its target. I knew it hadn't by the way the soldier was holding the weapon. The Albish held their guns like they were afraid of them, too used to magic defending them. I didn't ask permission before I knocked the gun from his loose grasp and aimed. Three Skinwalkers went down in the dark before the gun clicked empty. Damn it.

"Where do you keep your ammunition?" I asked in Mirajin, not bothering to summon up the few words I knew in their language, what with the gunfire filling the air and all. The soldier shook his head blankly at me, even as I gestured with my empty weapon. I rolled my eyes, exasperated, turning to the captain.

He looked troubled. "We don't need to turn this into a battle," he said. "We can wait them out until morning behind the walls—"

"All that'll happen then is that they'll lose interest in

us and head for the houses farther down the mountain," I snapped. We could defend the fortress. The men and women of Iliaz's villages wouldn't have as many guns and soldiers "Now, where do you keep your ammunition?"

The captain looked grim. "There is a tent by the east gate."

I ran, dashing around the central building of the fortress and heading for more bullets. I saw the tent there, propped against the outer wall, sticking out like a sore thumb in the northern Albish colors, clashing against the fortress's warm stone.

Inside, the tent was lined with weapon upon weapon: guns and swords and rifles and even a few things that might've been bombs, all neatly stacked up, a little arsenal ready to march on Izman, if needed. I was reaching for a cache of bullets when I saw the gilded rifles lined up neatly to one side.

And I stopped.

Outside were raised voices, more gunshots, and, farther away now, the sounds of an invasion of ghouls being held back. I'd been in a whole lot of fights in the name of the Rebellion now. I'd been afraid in them before. Or I'd felt nothing, everything in me focused on staying alive. But the anger that I had felt tonight, that was new. It surged from some dark part of my soul, older than I was. Old as my bloodline, old as the desert. *Our* desert—not theirs to march their armies through and claim through bargains and alliances, all while putting their dead in the ground so our monsters could thrive. It was our desert, not theirs and not the Gallan's and not any other northerners' from the edges of the horizon.

And I wasn't going to let them have it.

The Skinwalkers they could handle without me. That was just one fight. I had a war to win. Quickly, I grabbed a knife from the wall and got to work on my sabotage.

FOURTEEN

I was nearly done when I realized the guns had stopped. I heard voices, the clatter of soldiers' feet. Cursing under my breath, I quickly moved things back where they ought to be.

After the near invasion of the Skinwalkers, the yard of the fortress would be crawling with soldiers. I needed some cover to get back to my room without any questions. I took a deep breath as I raised my hands a little, just enough to draw the sand up in a small cloud, low to the ground. It wasn't a sandstorm, just a bit of dust. Nothing us desert dwellers weren't used to—that's why we wore sheemas. But if the Albish didn't know enough to burn their dead, I doubted they'd be smart enough to cover their faces from the desert sand.

I could feel my powers resisting, curling away from me as I tried to draw on them for the third time in one day.

I tugged up my own sheema and ducked out into the cloud of dust. I struggled to keep up the storm as I moved back toward the entrance. But I didn't need to keep it up long, just long enough to get back inside. The pain in my side nagged at me as I moved slowly, dodging figures in the dust as I went.

It got worse with every step I took. I couldn't take the strain much longer.

And then I felt a resistance against my power, prodding at first, and then more insistent. Without warning, I felt something try to rip it away from me, like a hurricane, wanting to gather up the sand and fling it to one side. I clung to it all the tighter.

It was the Albish Demdji, or whatever they called themselves, moving the air against my sand.

I cast around for an escape as I leaned against the wall for support.

There, an open window, straight above me.

Did I have enough strength in me to reach it? I wasn't sure. Secretly, I was afraid I'd used up all my powers drawing the cover I'd needed to get this far. I sent up a silent prayer that there was no one on the other side of that window.

I moved unsteadily, shakily, my power slipping in and out of my grasp for a moment before I managed to grab a firm hold of it. The sand rushed up below me, a sudden surge lifting me, pulling at my hair and skin and clothes, driving me up the sheer wall.

My fingertips grazed the edge of the window even as the pain in my side stabbed through me like an arrow. My tenuous grip on my power faltered, and I felt it slipping away from me like a handful of sand. The more I tried to hold on to it, the faster it fell. And then, all at once, it was gone, sand dropping out from under me, and I was the one falling. My heart lurched, but my fingers found purchase on the windowsill. I scrambled, trying to pull the sand back, but it was no good. I fought to slow my panicked breathing. I'd been struggling to use my Demdji powers ever since I'd gotten them back, but they'd never completely abandoned me like this before. What if I only had so much of the power left and I had drained it? What if it was gone forever now?

I felt my fingers start to slip . . .

And then there were familiar hands on my arms, dragging me up.

"That's a hell of an entrance, even for you," Jin said, his grip on me never faltering as he pulled me through the window.

I collapsed in a messy heap below the windowsill, my hip throbbing where I'd bashed it on the ledge as I'd scrambled through. I caught my breath as my vision cleared slowly. I felt Jin's hand on my face. It came away red. "Are you aware that you're bleeding, Bandit?"

I focused on him. He was sitting back on his heels across from me, brow creased with concern. He was clad only in loose desert trousers tied at his hips by a draw-string. My earlier thoughts of crossing the hallway to find him rushed through me, making my whole body flush with heat, even through the pain. "Are you aware that you're not wearing a shirt?" I retorted.

"I was sleeping." He ran his hand over his face tiredly. Sure enough, I could see behind him the mussed bed-sheets and pillows. And sleep was still clinging to him, in the weight of his eyelids and his disheveled dark hair. I reached out, finding the shorter hair at the nape of his neck. He exhaled as I ran my fingers through it, and I shivered. My blood was still racing from the escape, and now that the pain was ebbing, I felt awake and alive and like every little sensation was magnified a thousand times.

I needed to talk to him, to tell him what I'd decided. What I'd done. What we had left to do. Instead, I moved recklessly, pressing my lips to the corner of his mouth where it had a habit of drawing up into a wry smile just for me. He made a noise, low at the back of his throat, as his hand found its way up my neck, into my hair. I shifted closer until his body met mine, wondering how far I was ready to push us into unsteady waters this time.

He caught my hand with his, our fingers lacing to-gether, our palms pressed tightly. And then he drew away just as quickly as he'd moved forward, holding my hand up to the light leaking through the window.

"Your hands are covered in gunpowder." He sounded different now, drawing away as I glanced down. Black powder was buried in the creases of my palms. A part of me wanted to draw him back, to dust off my palms and promise to explain later. To put the Rebellion aside for one night. But Jin was already on his feet, lighting the lamp by the side of his bed so he could see me clearly.

"Does this have anything to do with why I heard gunfire earlier?" he asked as he sat down on the edge of the bed, putting a safe distance between us, putting us back on solid ground, where there was a war happening. I was going to have to explain.

I sketched it out for him as quickly as I could, explaining the offer the captain had made. The price of it. What I'd decided. And my plan.

By the time I was done, Jin was watching me grimly. "Amani . . ." He hesitated, lingering on my name like he didn't know where to start. He scrubbed his hand across his jaw, an anxious gesture. "You're seriously considering turning down an army?"

"I'm not considering it," I said, my knees drawn up to my chest. I was leaning against the wall under the open window, and the cool night air spread gooseflesh along my neck. "I've decided."

"An army is what we came here for. And now suddenly you don't think that's important?"

"I don't think it's worth trading an entire country for," I argued. "Or Sam's life."

"We don't even *have* a country to trade." Jin leaned forward. "Don't you think we maybe ought to win the throne before we decide it's under threat, Bandit?"

"It *is* under threat." I hadn't meant to raise my voice, but I didn't like his reasoning, cajoling tone. I dropped to a whisper, remembering the soldiers outside. "And making alliances with foreigners is how your father wound up in this mess in the first place."

Jin's mouth pressed into an angry line. He hated being reminded that the Sultan was his father. I knew that. Because I knew him. I'd done it deliberately, to needle him. "You didn't have a problem letting Hala die for the Rebellion," he retorted. Now *that* was more than a needle. "How is Sam different?"

"Sam doesn't *have* to die." I clenched my jaw angrily. I didn't like what he was implying: that I was being governed by feelings instead of reason. That I hadn't cared about Hala.

"Hala didn't either."

"No," I snapped as quietly as I could. "You're right. I could've just left her to be tortured and manipulated by the Sultan. Then would you be questioning my reasons for wanting to save one of our own?"

"You know that's not what I—" he started to interject, but I was done letting him talk.

"Maybe this would be a whole lot easier for you if I were still the same selfish girl you met in Dustwalk, the one who left people behind to die because it benefited her in some way. But you're alive right now because I'm not that girl. And you're—" *And you're in love with me because I'm not that girl anymore.* I'd been about to say that, but the words stumbled on my tongue. "We're here . . . together because I'm not that girl anymore." I tried to glide over the hesitation, though the slight rise of his brow told me he'd caught it. "And if Sam doesn't have to die, then I'm not going to let him just because it's easier. I can't have another body in this war before we've even gotten to the real fight. Not unless I have to."

We sat at opposing ends of the room, neither of us moving, gazes locked, muscles tensing as though we might be ready for battle.

Normally, this would be the part when one of us stormed out into the desert until we cooled off. But there was a guard outside the door, and even if he had let me out, I'd have a hard time explaining how I got back here— and into someone else's room, no less.

We were trapped together. And I might not be as selfish as I used to be, but I was still just as stubborn. I wasn't going to be the one to break.

After an excruciating stretch of silence, Jin finally spoke.

"It's my family, Amani," he said more quietly. "My brother. My sister. That's whose lives you're playing with."

I could hear the pain in that voice. There was nothing in this world Jin cared about more than his family. He would die to save them, in a heartbeat.

"My country," I argued. Jin had grown up over the sea, in his mother's country. He might be half-Mirajin, but he was more foreign. "My decision." I stood firm. "I'm not asking for your help," I said. "I'm telling you what we're going to do." That thought crept up on me again. Who did I think I was to be giving orders to a prince? To someone who had been in this rebellion longer than I had? To Jin, whom I would never take an order from myself if he tried? Who was I to be leading us all down an uncertain road and acting like I was sure of it?

"Then you ought to get some sleep," Jin said finally, breaking the silence. "There's a lot to do tomorrow."

He wasn't wrong, but there was no getting back to my room, what with the soldier in the hall. I reckoned I could sleep well enough on the floor. But Jin shifted over on the bed, making room for me, even if he was staring at the ceiling.

I thought about arguing. But I was tired. God, I was tired—tired of fighting, of running, of arguing. And that soft bed looked tempting as sin. I settled on the bed as carefully as if it were made of glass, positioning myself so my back was turned to Jin, so that I was staring at the window, waiting for sunrise, the argument firmly lodged between us.

I was drifting between sleep and wakefulness when I felt Jin's hand on my face. I heard him speak, low enough that I wasn't sure I was meant to hear it.

"You're wrong, you know. I'm not with you because of who you became. I fell in love with you when I was bleeding under a counter at the dead end of the desert and you saved my life. Back when we were both who we used to be."

I woke up with my head fitted in the place between his chin and his tattoo, one of his arms draped over me, his hand curled into the fabric of my shirt.

FIFTEEN

The blue light of dawn in the mountains made Sam look even paler than he usually did as he stumbled the last few steps to the top of the ramparts that overlooked the sheer drop of the cliff, hands shackled in iron. His golden hair was tousled from lack of sleep, and the skin below his eyes was bruise dark. Soldiers held him up on either side.

The wall was lined with army men come to watch the spectacle: the deserter too cowardly to fight for his own country, being marched to his execution.

I wrapped my hands around my arms. It was cooler in the mountains than I was used to. Sam's eyes darted my way, and then they drifted beyond me, looking for the others. He wouldn't find them. It was just me on those walls, among the lines of soldiers in green uniforms that clashed with the sky and stones around them.

Sam's mouth pulled up wanly at the corners when he realized I'd come alone. "I guess it is a pretty uncivilized hour for an execution," he said, as he was jostled past me. "Can't expect everyone to be out of bed." He was out of earshot before I could say anything back.

The soldiers took him to the edge of the wall, standing him a dozen paces away from the firing squad. An Albish man in long pale robes leaned a hand on Sam's shoulder, speaking in a low voice to him.

"He's asking if he has any last words he would like passed on to his family." Captain Westcroft was standing next to me, hands clasped behind his back. He looked as tired as Sam after last night's invasion. "To give them comfort when they are told the news."

Sam considered for a moment, and then, leaning his head forward, he answered him. The man's brow furrowed before his face slid back to complacency, nodding sagely as he touched our imposter bandit over his heart. He stepped back as another soldier came forward to place the blindfold over Sam's eyes. He knotted it at the back of his head just as the sun started to rise, turning the blue dawn light into a blazing ember.

"Captain." I spoke to the man at my elbow, "I know you're not going to have a whole lot of reasons to trust me after today, but I'm going to give you some advice that I wish I'd had sooner. Don't underestimate the Sultan. If you ever think you're outsmarting him, chances are you're about to be proved wrong in a very deadly way." Captain Westcroft raised his reddish brows at me curiously, but I kept my eyes straight ahead. They were foreigners; it wasn't my job to protect them. But then, Sam was a foreigner, too. And here I was.

The robed man who had spoken to Sam crossed the short space back to us. He looked at me and then said something quick in Albish to the captain. "Your young friend's final words," the captain translated, "were that he would like it noted that he was right: being heroic leads to death."

The smile that danced across my face didn't linger there. As the soldier moved away and the dozen men with rifles stepped forward, Sam suddenly looked terribly alone. And scared.

I felt my breathing turn shallow as the sun crested the mountain. The captain shouted an order in Albish. As one, the six soldiers in uniform clattered their gilded rifles to attention.

Sam flinched at the noise.

Silence came, and it seemed like all the soldiers watching held their breath at once. From overhead I heard the whistle of a bird, three short bursts. There was a whole lot that could still go wrong, but at least we were ready.

Another shouted order came. The guns pointed at him.

I readied myself to move, legs tensing in anticipation.

"Ready," the shout came.

I rocked onto the balls of my feet, leaning forward just a little.

"Aim."

Sam tilted his head back to catch the first rays of the sun, like he wanted to see it all one last time, even though he was blindfolded. Like he wished he'd known that yesterday was the last dawn he'd get. Maybe if he had, he would've watched it instead of spending the time in the dark under the tunnels of Izman, waiting to save my life. Maybe he wouldn't be here at all.

In that second, his pale hair turned to pure gold in the sunlight.

"Fire!"

Six fingers squeezed triggers at the same moment that I moved, running forward even as the racket of shots sounded, filling the air with the familiar scent of gunpowder.

Gunpowder without any bullets.

I barreled through the smoke easily, past the men averting their eyes against the sound and noise and sight of death. I plunged toward where Sam was standing, waiting for a bullet that would never come.

I slammed into him at full speed, pushing him toward the cliff edge. He staggered back to the edge of the ramparts, and then we pitched over into nothingness.

And for just a second, we were in wide-open air, falling. Plunging toward the rocks below.

Then we hit—not jagged rocks, but cloth pulled taut, giving way beneath our bodies, bowing just enough to catch us. It was the sheets and blankets we'd smuggled out of Jin's room, strung out between Izz and Maz as they surged upward in the shape of two huge Rocs, bursting through the smoke from the gunfire. I heard surprised cries from below; their huge wings buffeting the assembled crowd violently as they flew higher over the mountains until we were out of range of both guns and any kind of air magic the Albish army could turn on us.

I was still trying to catch my breath as Sam struggled next to me, panicked and still blind. "Stop squirming!" I shouted close to his ear over the sound of rushing air as we flew.

"Am I dead?" Sam asked too loudly in his own language, still twisting.

I yanked the blindfold off, and he blinked his startled blue eyes at me, taking in my face, the wings above my head that were carrying us to safety, and the endless open sky above that. His head jerked from side to side, seeing Jin on Maz's back to our right, Tamid on Izz's to our left.

"You're not dead," I shouted over the wind, as the enormous sling swung precariously in the wind. "Now stop moving before you kill us both." He did as he was told, lying perfectly immobile as we rushed over the mountains, up, across, and down, until we were back over the desert. I could feel the sand nearby even before I felt solid ground as the twins landed, setting the sling down gently.

Jin slid off Maz's back, pulling me to my feet, while Tamid stayed stubbornly seated on Izz. Jin checked me over quickly, looking for any new wounds. He wouldn't find any. I didn't grow up in the shadow of a weapons factory without learning a thing or two, like how to turn a bullet into a blank.

Sam let us haul him to his feet, but as soon as we let him go he collapsed back to sitting on the ground. "On second thought, I'm not going to do that." His words were calm, but his voice was shaking. "Standing seems a little ambitious right now."

Jin dropped into a crouch across from Sam. "You all right there?" he asked him as he set to work on Sam's shackled hands. There was a note of tension in his voice, but Sam wasn't going to notice it. He didn't need to know what had passed between me and Jin last night about saving his life.

"Well." Sam seemed to take stock of himself. "My legs don't exactly seem to be working. And I have pledged my allegiance to so many different gods that I am not going to be able to be faithful to them all." He was babbling at a frantic pace. "I'm guessing being caught being unfaithful to a god is probably twice as unfortunate as being caught being unfaithful to a woman. And I'm still not sure I'm not hallucinating all this." He squinted up at me. "But other than that, I've had worse days."

"It's only dawn," Jin said as the shackles came free with a satisfying click, falling into the sand. "It could still get worse." He clapped Sam on the back amicably as he got to his feet.

"So, just to be clear"—Sam rubbed at his newly freed hands—"why exactly am I not dead?"

"Because you're one of us." I reached down a hand to help Sam to his feet. He looked steadier now. "Which means you're ours to execute for treason, not theirs."

Sam squinted up at me for a moment. And then a grin split his face, a real one. "Shut up," I warned him. I could already see the beginnings of something smart on his tongue.

"I always knew you had a soft spot for me." He clasped my fingers, letting me pull him up.

"Only for your knack for getting *us* out of a tight spot." I let go of his hand. "Come on, we need to keep moving."

Sam was still getting his bearings after nearly dying, but his gaze flicked quickly around from me to Jin to Tamid, who was still refusing to look at anyone from where he sat.

"Where's the princess?" he asked.

Ah . . . Leyla.

Jin's traitor sister was the one thing he and I were able to agree on. She was a burden to our rescue mission, at best, a liability at worst.

So we'd left her. And I'd scrawled out a note for Bilal that I'd handed to one of his soldiers to give to him.

Take care of her. She might be your last line of defense if the Sultan comes knocking.

Leyla might be trouble for us, but she would make a decent shield for Iliaz as a hostage. She might keep the mountain from being burned off the map before we got back.

"She was extra weight," was all I said in answer to Sam.

"And if there's one advantage to traveling without a whole army," Jin said, tossing his compass from one hand to another, the needle still pointing due south, "it's being able to move quickly."

SIXTEEN

Flying got boring after a while.

After the initial rush of leaping into the air, the desert shrinking below, the wind whistling an excited tune in our ears as we soared higher above the ground than wingless creatures were ever meant to . . . after all that wore off, it was just a whole lot of waiting. Hot sun tracking our every mile, arms cramping from clinging to Maz's back, the wind drowning out any chance to talk as we headed south, following Jin's compass. We flew farther west than the compass told us to so that we could fly close to the mountains that ran along Miraji's border. It was better than heading due south across the desert, risking running out of water before we found Eremot.

We were headed south without an army, or a plan,

or any idea what we were facing. But the way I saw it, there wasn't a whole lot else to do now except follow Jin's compass and see what we found at the end. Every day we wasted was another day our friends were imprisoned. Maybe in danger. Maybe dying.

It was the end of our first day of traveling when I noticed the landscape was starting to look familiar. A break in the thankless stretch of desert, a break in the endless view of golden sand and blue skies, a jagged break in the ground: the Dev's Valley.

My heart skipped as I craned over Maz's back, peering down below us. We were skimming over the northernmost edge of it; it was the same path that we would take home if we were coming back from the north. Returning from a mission for Ahmed. With Shazad next to me. Because somewhere far below us, hidden in the twists and turns of those canyons, was what used to be our home, the wreckage of the rebel camp.

The desperate reckless urge hit me to ask Maz to take us down. Maybe if he could just land in the valley we could go home again. I could shoo away all the sand that I'd buried the camp in when we had to escape and unearth it like some ancient relic. We could all be safe again, for a little while. But that was foolish. We were too far from that home now.

Instead we stopped near the city of Fahali just as the sun was beginning to set. As close as we dared land near civilization. A side effect of escaping by the skin of our teeth was that more than just Leyla had been left behind in Iliaz. Food, weapons, water skins . . . a whole lot of things that we were bound to need on the way south.

"Sam and I will go," Jin said, counting out the small stash of money we had. "It's not safe for Demdji these days."

"Because you both think that being from halfway around the world is less conspicuous?" I stretched my legs, sore from a day of gripping on to Maz's feathered back.

"I mean . . . " Sam scratched the top of his head. "I'd say I'm definitely less conspicuous than blue skin and blue hair."

"Hey!" Izz said, even as Maz, in the shape of a large lizard, managed to look offended.

"I ought to go," I argued, glancing at the city on the horizon. "So long as I don't look anyone in the eye it ought to be fine."

"Right," Jin said, flipping a two-louzi coin along his knuckles. "When's the last time you got in any trouble when left to your own devices?" But he flipped the coin in my direction all the same. I caught it out of the air as he handed the rest of our money over. He knew I was right. Foreigners in this part of the desert during a war would arouse suspicion.

I paused as I rewrapped my sheema.

Tamid was unstrapping his false leg, sitting on the ground. "None of us knows where the compass is leading." I could tell he knew I was talking to him, even though he wasn't looking at me. "This might be the closest thing to civilization we see for a while. You could stay here if you wanted. When this is all over there'll be trains running again, back down to Dustwalk . . ."

"No." He didn't look up "The compass points south, and south is the way to Dustwalk. I'll keep going with you as far as I need to get home."

Home. If home was Dustwalk instead of the Dev's Valley, that was the last home I wanted to go back to.

• • •

FAHALI WASN'T JUST any city. It was the first city that had knelt to Ahmed, after we'd saved it from being annihilated by Noorsham. It was one of *our* cities—or it used to be. It had been occupied by the Gallan for nearly two decades before that. Now, with the news that Ahmed was dead, it was an uncertain city. As I walked through the streets, I could feel the unease. News of impending war and invasion must've reached them. Everyone kept their eyes down, moving quickly, as if they were afraid to be outside too long.

I kept my own eyes to the ground as I navigated the city, my sheema pulled over my face. There were people here who would know me even if I didn't stand out like Jin or the twins would.

This city knew me. And once I'd known it pretty damn well, too. But it had changed since we were last here. The streets were filled with women in rags, begging, and children running around barefoot. Where the sprawling market ought to have been, the streets were empty, shops boarded up.

I felt a tug on my clothes. I snapped around quickly,

grabbing the small hand that had been trying to find its way into my pockets. It was a little girl, her eyes big in her gaunt face.

"I wasn't doing anything!" The boldness of the lie was somewhat undercut by the panic in her expression.

"It's all right." I dropped to my knees, though I didn't let her go, in case she fled. "You think you could tell me what's happening here?"

The waif looked at me warily, as if she didn't believe that I didn't know. "Food doesn't come anymore," she said finally. "My papa says it's our punishment for turning against the Sultan."

So, the Sultan was starving them out for allying with us. He could do that. Most of the desert's trade came on the caravans or on trains from eastern Miraji. If he'd cut off what was coming from across the mountains, then there wouldn't be enough for everyone.

"Well, you can tell your papa there's a difference between punishment and revenge." I let her go, pushing my sheema away as I leaned back against the wall, silently cursing the Sultan's name. Ahmed would never have let this happen if he were still here. Hell, he would never have let this happen if he were Sultan. I'd seen Ahmed give up his own food to people hungrier than him more than once.

I was going to have to leave this starving city without supplies. Izz or Maz could probably catch us a rabbit to cook up in the hills for tonight. And then after that . . . we'd have to survive. We were good at that. It was why we were still here.

I let her go, but the little girl didn't dash away like I'd expected. She was staring at me curiously now we were directly eye level. "Are you the Blue-Eyed Bandit?" she asked boldly. And then before I could answer she kept going. "Are you here to save us? The man in the uniform said you would save us."

"What man in the uniform?"

"The one who came through the city a few days ago. He said the Rebellion would save us. He said he was a general and he knew. He said his daughter was with them and that all of you would save us."

General Hamad, Shazad's father. He had come through this way. My head dashed around without thinking, like I might be able to spy him among these streets. Like he wasn't long gone.

"Was he right?" she asked insistently. "Are you here to save us?"

I wanted to lie, to tell her that I would. That I could save them. But I was just a girl from Dustwalk. "No." I straightened. "I'm not here to save you." *But I'm going to try to save someone else for you.*

They needed more than a girl from Dustwalk. They needed their prince. They needed his general. The best I could do was try to bring the real saviors back.

• ● •

IT WAS OUR sixth day of flying when the direction of Jin's compass changed abruptly in his hands. It had been pointing due south since we left Iliaz, heading over the desert as straight as a bullet. But now, suddenly, it swung back north. We'd passed over our target. Jin quickly leaned over Maz's neck, giving him instructions. Maz did as he was told, plunging us toward the sand. Izz followed behind.

I squinted through the haze of the afternoon heat as we descended. There, not far off, was a town, the first we'd seen in days. I hadn't even noticed it when we'd passed over it a moment ago, but I knew it instantly all the same: Juniper City. It was where I'd gotten on a train to Izman a year ago, and where Jin caught up with me as I tried to head north with his compass. They called it a city, and back then it was the biggest place I'd ever seen. But since then I'd seen Izman. Juniper City didn't look like much in comparison.

Jin's compass was pointing straight toward it.

Something wasn't right here. I knew I ought to be happy. I ought to feel some hope. That we were close. That we'd found our people. But this wasn't exactly Eremot, the prison of legends. It was just a big town in the desert. And I might not trust Leyla, but I knew she hadn't lied to me. Instead of hope a new fear was being born in my chest. That this was a wild-goose chase. That we were going the wrong way. That Ahmed and the others weren't going to be here.

But there was only one way to know for sure.

We walked in silence, following Jin's compass to the city. Izz became a small bird, flying excitedly ahead of us, then back again, while Maz sat on my shoulder, a little blue-headed lizard basking in the afternoon sun.

It was slow going with Tamid's bad leg, and I caught him glancing back over his shoulder more than once as we walked. Back in the direction of Dustwalk. I'd promised to get him as close to home as possible. This was pretty damn close.

By tomorrow morning he would be home. And I could tell myself all I liked that it wasn't my home anymore, but the only thing that had made it bearable that last year I'd lived there, after my mother was hanged, was Tamid. And even if he hated me, I didn't know that I had it in me to hate him. I only hated that he was going back.

That I was losing one more person. Not to death maybe, but to somewhere I'd never see him again just the same.

It was nearer to dusk than noon when we passed through the city gates. Jin and Sam wore their sheemas tight to hide their foreignness as best they could as we joined the crowds in the streets.

The war had not reached this far south yet in earnest, but there were still signs of it. Supplies from anywhere other than the desert or the nearby mountains seemed fewer in the market stalls. And there were more men carrying weapons on the street than I remembered.

We followed Jin's compass past colorful stalls in the souk, through streets that were clean and wide compared to Izman's old maze. This was a new city. Its name was in Mirajin instead of the old language. We ducked under canopies and around brightly painted buildings, past women dragging whining children away from stalls of sweets.

And then finally we rounded the corner of a bright blue house, and I saw a small boy crouched in a doorway, something glittering in his hands.

We all hung back uncertainly, watching the little boy. He couldn't have been more than six, and he was talking to himself under his breath as he turned the compass over and over, in that way children do when they are playing make-believe, spinning a story in their minds. Weaving a world where they're more than just a grubby boy on the street playing with a toy compass, or a skinny girl out the back of a house with a gun and tin cans, pretending they're a great explorer on an adventure, or a Blue-Eyed Bandit.

One of us needed to talk to him.

Jin moved first, and the rest of us watched from the mouth of an alley as he crouched down, resting his arms on his knees.

The little boy looked up, staring at Jin with big, dark eyes, wary but not afraid. "Hello," Jin greeted him, pulling down his sheema to show his full face. "What's your name?"

"I'm Oman." Of course he was. Half the little boys in this country were named Oman, after the Sultan.

"Oh, really," Jin said, leaning forward on his knees. "Oman is my father's name." I'd never heard Jin call the Sultan his father in all the months I'd known him. "Do you think you could tell me where you got that compass, Oman?"

"I found it," Oman said, gripping the compass a little tighter to his chest. "I didn't steal it."

"I believe you," Jin said patiently. I could see that he was worried, the way his thumb ran circles along the opposite hand as he clasped them together in front of him. Because if Ahmed didn't have the compass, we didn't have a way to find Ahmed. "Where did you find it?"

"Train station," the boy said finally.

"I didn't think there were any trains running these days," Jin said, looking my way. I shrugged unhelpfully. The trains from Izman had stopped months ago, best I knew, after we claimed the western desert.

"They're not leaving," the boy said, with an eye roll like we might be stupid. "But sometimes they come in. They bring people with them."

"People like soldiers and prisoners?" Jin asked. The little boy shrugged. "And where do the people go?"

The boy shrugged again. "Out of the city. Toward the mountains."

The Sultan was shipping prisoners. Juniper City was the farthest south you could get with a train. And then they were being taken on to Eremot . . . wherever that was. If it was even as real as Leyla said.

We were close, and we could find them, but every moment we wasted looking was another moment they were stuck there.

"Oman," Jin said seriously, looking at the little boy, "see, that compass belongs to my brother." He reached into his pocket, pulling out the identical, albeit more battered, one.

"It belongs to me now," Oman said stubbornly.

"I'll tell you what," Jin said. "I'll buy it off you." The ten louzi that Jin produced from his pocket was a small fortune to a little boy. Oman grabbed it eagerly, dropping the compass in the dust.

Jin returned to us, holding both compasses. His knuckles were white from clutching them so tightly. I reached out a hand, resting it over his. I couldn't tell him everything was going to be all right, because I couldn't lie.

He shifted his hand in mine, and I thought he might be pulling away, but instead he slipped Ahmed's compass into my grip.

"We need a new plan," he said.

SEVENTEEN

THE BEAUTIFUL GENERAL

Once, in a desert always at war, there was a great general who wished for an heir. Finally, after many years of prayer, his beloved wife grew great with child. But when she gave birth, it was not to a son but to a daughter.

The general put aside his disappointment, for he loved his daughter dearly, and she was a strong, healthy girl. And some years later the general's wife bore another child, this time a boy. The general and his wife rejoiced. But quickly they saw that the child was not as strong as his sister. He was often sick, and he cried frequently, sometimes too quietly to be heard.

Years passed, and the daughter grew strong and beautiful, while the son struggled. Some days, when the general's son was strong enough to go outside, his sister would sit and read to him. On one such day, another boy saw the general's frail son and began to mock him and throw stones at him, trying to goad him into fighting back.

The general's daughter stood up to fight back instead.

When the general broke up the fight, he found to his great surprise that his daughter had blood only on her fists, while the boy who had been throwing stones had blood on his face.

In that moment, the general saw his daughter for who she was. She was the heir he had prayed for after all, the heir who would defend his family and his country when he was too old and frail. And so in secret he taught his daughter to wield any weapon she chose, and he taught her how to win a battle. How to win a war, if she had to. But still he did not know what future awaited her.

Then, one hot day, as she walked through the market in Izman, the general's daughter met the Rebel Prince. And she finally found the war that she was meant to fight. And in turn, she, too, became a general to a great ruler.

The Beautiful General stood up over and over again for those who couldn't stand for themselves, and others stood with her. And she won every fight, one after the other, the way her father had taught her to.

Until the day she lost.

The general's daughter was punished for daring to ask for a better world. She was sent deep into the darkness, hidden away, where a good death would never find her.

Where she could not fight, for her jailers were not men of flesh and blood but creatures of metal and magic.

And for once she could find no escape, not even with her quick and clever mind. For the first time, the general's daughter was forced to watch instead of standing to fight.

She watched, over and over again, as men and women burned in front of her eyes.

And then the unholy creatures of metal turned their eyes on the young princess, the Demdji sister of the Rebel Prince with the strange purple hair. The Beautiful General's back ached from bowing it when she didn't want to. Her eyes hurt from turning away when men and women burned. Her throat pained from being silent.

So the general loosened her tongue, opened her eyes, and straightened her back. And she stood up to walk into death in the young princess's stead.

EIGHTEEN

I could feel time slipping away with every moment we weren't up in the mountains, hunting for Eremot.

Juniper City was struggling to govern itself without the Rebellion or the Sultan. Neighborhoods were carving themselves up. Men with guns were charging innocent folks for protection from men with knives. The Sultan's army that came through didn't care; they were just there to transport prisoners. Neither did the other soldiers who came through, foreign and Mirajin, heading into the mountains never to come back, according to the whispers on the streets.

Jin broke a man's hand when he tried to rob us at the inn we stayed at overnight. That put an end to any sign of trouble for us, though we still took turns keeping watch through the night. As if we were back in the desert and not safely behind walls.

In the morning, we were woken by a group of men preaching loudly in the streets that it was the end of times. That death was coming for us from the mountains. That any who ventured out beyond the city, and did not go with pure hearts, would find death.

I didn't know if our hearts were pure, but we were going to have to head out of the city one way or another. We had to find what was left of the Rebellion and we had to find it quickly. Every passing day was another day Ahmed or Delila or Shazad or Rahim might be dead.

Except we had a stop to make first. I'd made a promise, after all.

• ● •

IT WAS LESS than a day to Dustwalk from Juniper City as the shape-shifter traveled. Less than a day between the place Tamid and I were born and the city that had seemed impossibly far away my whole life. I wasn't sorry to get out of Juniper City, to finally be on the move, but I reckoned I could live another hundred years and never see Dustwalk again and be happier for it. Only we'd promised to take Tamid back home if we could. And Demdji kept their promises. Besides, I could feel Ahmed's compass heavy in my pocket, reminding me we didn't have any clear direction anyway.

I knew when we were getting close to Dustwalk. The

landscape didn't change. It was all barren desert flatland outside of Juniper City. But it was something I couldn't quite explain. A shift in the air, like it was wrapping itself around me, pulling me back. The accusatory glare of the sun on my neck, like I'd done something wrong by leaving. And then, suddenly, there it was in the distance, etched against the perfectly blue desert sky like a shadow against the day: the godforsaken place that had raised me.

I leaned down on Maz's feathered neck and shouted over the wind for him to take us down. I didn't need to get any nearer.

"You ought to be able to walk from here," I said to Tamid as he slid from Izz's back. "Less chance of getting shot if you don't arrive from the sky on the back of a giant bird."

Tamid stared up at me from the ground, where he was trying to steady himself on his bad leg. "You're not coming with me?"

"You're the one who wants to go back, not me."

Tamid dropped his head, nodded. "So I guess this is good-bye, then."

"I guess so." I didn't move to get off Maz's back. We still had plenty of ground to cover and we needed to use all the daylight we had.

Tamid looked like he was about to say something else, but Jin spoke first. "Something's wrong." I twisted around on Maz's back to where Jin was sitting behind me. His eyes were fixed straight ahead on Dustwalk.

I squinted against the bright desert light at the town.

It looked exactly like I'd left it. Even from this far away I could spy the wooden roof of the prayer house sticking up a little bit higher than the others around it. A few doors down would be my uncle's house. A few doors the other way was Tamid's: the only home in the whole town with two stories. I used to think Tamid's family was the richest I would ever know. Then I'd lived in a palace for a while.

I realized what Jin meant. There were no signs of life. Even on a hot day there ought to be a dash of movement, a face watching us through a window on the edge of town—something.

It looked deserted.

I cursed under my breath as I slid off Maz's back. I could feel time running away from us. But while I might not want to set foot back in Dustwalk as long as I lived, I couldn't exactly leave Tamid alone here. He'd starve to death or get killed by a ghoul or a wild animal before he could get back to civilization.

"Looks like we're coming with you after all."

It was slow going as we moved across the shifting sands, back toward the place that had made me—part of me, at least: the dangerous, angry, restless, selfish part. The one I'd been trying to discard piece by piece. Tamid pulled ahead in spite of his bad leg, anxious to get home. I found myself falling farther and farther behind. Jin noticed. He slowed down, waiting for me until I fell into step beside him.

"You know the story of Ihaf the Wanderer?" I asked. We were getting closer, no matter how slow I walked, and my breath was feeling shorter. "Ihaf was a farmer who left his home and defeated the ghoul that had been terrorizing his people. He was feasted in Izman for a hundred days for what he had done. And then, at the end of it all—"

"He returned home and went back to tilling his fields and a peaceful life," Jin filled in, tugging his sheema a little so that it covered him from the glare of the sun. "My mother used to tell us that story."

"So did mine." My eyes found the place where my mother's house used to be. Before it burned. I wondered if on some night, across desert and sea, Jin and I were hearing the same story under the same stars from our mothers. "I always hated that ending. How could you go home again after all that? After slaying monsters and saving princesses and dining in the homes of immortal beings . . ."

Jin kept his gaze straight ahead as he answered. "Back when this all started, I used to think there was nothing I wouldn't do to go home again."

It was rare for Jin to talk about Xicha. He hadn't told me much. That their small home overlooked the sea and always smelled of salt. That Jin and Ahmed shared a room, and Delila shared another with Jin's mother. That the floor was always stained with dark dye from trying to hide Delila's purple hair. They had a rotted roof that leaked so badly that when Jin was just six years old, he and Ahmed stole some wood from the docks and clambered on to the rafters to patch it up. There was a scar on his palm where he'd sliced it open with a rusty nail. I knew that place had been home for as long as he and

Ahmed had been sailing, heading from dock to dock. It had been home until Ahmed had abandoned it for the desert, and Jin's mother had died, and Jin had collected Delila to bring her to the country of their birth. To a place where they would have to make a home.

I thought of the Dev's Valley, the colorful tent I had shared with Shazad for half a year. Of nights full of stars and warmth. I would give just about anything to go back to that home, too. Except it had been taken from us. And then it had been taken again when the Sultan ambushed us that night in Izman.

This wasn't home. Neither of us had one of those anymore.

The closer we got, the more obvious it was that Dustwalk was as quiet as a dead man. I waited for the twitch of curtains that would mean we were being watched on approach, or the sound of a voice. I felt an itch start on the back of my neck, a restlessness. There was danger here.

Jin and I caught up to the others, drawing our guns at the same time on the outskirts of town. When I glanced back to my right Sam had done the same, and the twins had shifted into large dogs with sharp teeth. I lifted my finger away from the iron for a moment, moving it far enough from my skin that I was sure I could feel the sand at my fingertips, too. That my power hadn't abandoned me.

And then we moved into the town as one.

The streets were empty as a drunk's glass. The door to the house that had belonged to Amjad Al-Hiyamat was swinging in the wind, breaking the silence. Sand had built up in it, keeping it from shutting properly. I pushed it open with my foot, peering around the darkness inside. It was empty—but not wholly. A low table still sat in the middle, and in the room off to the side, I could see a large bed. But everything else was gone: clothes, food, cookware. Anything someone could carry, like they'd fled. But not in a hurry.

I emerged from the dark back into the desert sun just as Jin stepped out of the prayer house across the way. "No signs of struggle," he said. "Or looting."

"No bodies either," I said. "Folks just picked up and left, by the look of things."

Tamid pushed by us, walking as quickly as his bad leg would allow. He didn't answer when I called out after him. I followed close behind as he rushed to his house, dread already sinking into my stomach.

Walking into Tamid's house was like walking into a half-formed dream. It was exactly like I remembered it but completely different. The blue of the dining room wall, the creak in the floorboard that always caused Tamid's mother to give me a nasty look when I came over, like I was the one making her house complain—these were familiar. But the house had been stripped, just like Amjad's. Only the things that were too big to carry were left.

"Mother!" Tamid bellowed at the top of his lungs, standing at the foot of the stairs. His one good foot was on the bottom step. Stairs were hard for him with his bad leg. It was a lot of effort to make just to be disappointed at the top.

"They're not up there." I said what we already both knew.

Tamid didn't look over his shoulder as he spoke to me. He kept his eyes fixed at the top of the stairs, like he could summon them. "Where are they then?"

"I don't know," I said.

"Are they dead?"

Yes. I tried it first, because it seemed likely. Blessedly, the word wouldn't come. "No," I said with a relieved sigh. "No, they're not dead."

I headed back out into the street, leaving Tamid to have some time in the house where he was raised. It was unsettling, being outside in this quiet. I pulled my sheema away from my face as I wandered down the long row that made up Dustwalk's main street. The sun hit my head unforgivingly, like an angry parent's eye, wanting to know why I was getting home so late.

I passed by the store. I wondered if Jin's blood was still on the floorboards where I'd sewn him up.

I fell in love with you when I was bleeding under a counter at the dead end of the desert and you saved my life, Jin had said when he thought I was asleep back in Iliaz. *Back when we were both who we used to be.*

We'd started here, he and I.

My aunt's house was the last one on the row. It was exactly two hundred and fifty paces from the shop. I knew because I'd counted it on hundreds of trips between the two. Something about it seemed different from the others. The door was closed, for one. I told myself I was imagining things. It only seemed different because I knew it so well. But still I pushed inside carefully, heart pounding a frantic rhythm as the hinges creaked open for me, pouring sunlight into the dark of the house beyond.

It was as empty as Tamid's.

Where this place had always been a riot of people, of wives and children, there was nothing here now. I wasn't sure whether I felt relieved or disappointed. I walked through the house, floorboards creaking below my feet as I went to the room I'd slept in once upon a time. Light flooded in here, through the single window. One that was big enough for me to crawl in and out of in the dead of night.

It was bare as a bone. But there, in the clear light of day, I realized why it seemed different. It was empty, but it didn't look abandoned. The floor was swept clean, unlike the other houses, which were clogged up with dust and sand. The window was washed, too. Someone had been keeping this place neat. They'd been here recently, by the look of things. Very recently.

That was when I heard a shotgun being cocked behind me.

NINETEEN

"I'm raising my hands," I said automatically. As I did, my brain started scrambling for solutions to having a gun pointed at my back. I couldn't count on Jin or Sam to come looking for me quicker than a bullet could reach my spine.

"Do it," a woman's voice said. "And turn around so I can see you."

The figure behind me shifted, and I caught the glint of metal in the glass of the window. A reflection. It wasn't much, but enough that I could tell where she was. I shifted a little bit, taking stock of the sand clinging to my boots.

"Turn around, I said," the voice harped behind me, thick with Last County accent. "If you can't move faster, I can put a jump in your step."

I could move fast.

I grabbed for the desert at the same moment that I dropped to one knee in a violent twist of my body. I whipped my hand up, slamming the sand into the barrel of the gun, knocking it clean from her grasp. The shotgun clattered to the ground, skittering out of reach and into a corner.

I was already back on my feet, releasing the sand, the sudden wrenching pain fading as I did, pistol out of its holster . . .

Pointed straight at my aunt Farrah's chest.

Farrah froze where she was, staring at me, the shock as evident on her face as it must have been on mine, both of us looking for words.

She found her tongue before I did. "I'd have thought you'd at least have the decency to be dead by now." Well, that was a bold opener considering I had a gun aimed at her. But then again, this was Dustwalk. We'd all had a gun aimed at us at one point or another. You got used to it. "So, I guess you've come crawling back after it didn't work out with whoever that man was that you rode off with? Wish I could say I'm surprised. How long did it take him to realize he couldn't beat the disrespect out of you? I tried for a year, and it didn't make a lick of difference."

It seemed like a lifetime ago that I'd last had to bear my aunt's insults and beatings. I'd spent the last year forgetting about Dustwalk and the girl I used to be here. But suddenly, standing across from her, it felt like it was just yesterday. I waited for her words to open fresh wounds, to make me feel small and angry and powerless against her, no matter that I was holding a gun.

But none of that came. Her words felt hollow, like she was shouting at me from the bottom of a deep pit and I was the only one of us who could see she was trapped in it.

"Aunt Farrah." I lowered the gun, reholstering it. I could take her without a weapon if I needed to. "What happened here?" The house felt huge and empty around me. "Where is everyone?"

"Gone." Aunt Farrah spat the word, like it might be my fault. "Everybody had to pick up and leave. What was there to stay for after the factory was destroyed?" I remembered something Shira had told me, back in the harem, about how hard things had gotten in Dustwalk without the factory. So maybe it *was* my fault—or Jin's, if we were being really specific.

"So, what are you still doing here?" I asked.

"Well"—a sly smile spread over her face as she smoothed a hand over her khalat—"not that it's any of your business, but I'm waiting for a letter from my daughter." Her tone was smug and self-satisfied, but her words just filled me with dread. She was talking about Shira, my cousin. Distantly, I remembered Shira telling me that I could trust Sam because she trusted Sam with her family. That he'd arranged to get letters and money down to Dustwalk for her. But there wouldn't be any more letters coming. "She's the Sultima now, you know," Aunt Farrah said.

She hadn't heard.

"Aunt Farrah, I'm . . ." My voice caught, snagging on the words unhappily. I breathed out slowly. "Shira is . . ." I didn't want to be the one to bring this news. But it ought to be me, because I'd stood and watched as Shira was led to the execution block, as she went with every single bit of fight I'd expect from a desert girl. She'd died for the Rebellion. "Aunt Farrah, Shira was executed about six weeks back."

I waited for her face to crumble, but she just stared at me, expression frozen. "You're a liar."

I was a lot of things, but I wasn't that. "I was there. She died as bravely as anyone could. Her child—that is, your grandson—" I started, but Aunt Farrah's face dissolved into a rage before I could finish.

"Be quiet!" she snapped, her voice carrying loud enough that I reckoned the boys would hear it outside. "You're a lying little bitch, just like your mother was, and you'd better get back to whatever whorehouse you ran off to when that boy threw you out of his bed. You worthless—" I closed the space between us with one rapid step, and Aunt Farrah staggered backward, her words cutting off. It was like she, too, was still expecting me to grow small under her blows.

I suddenly realized that even though it might've been a year since I'd stood face-to-face with her, it hadn't been that long since I'd heard her voice. It was the same voice that had been whispering in my ear since Imin was executed. Demanding to know who the hell I thought I was to be taking over this rebellion, chastising me for how high and mighty I seemed to believe myself, able to give orders in the place of a prince, even though I was just a nothing girl from nowhere. From poverty and misery and Dustwalk.

Only I knew who I was. I had an answer to the stupid question that voice kept asking me: Who did I think I was? I was a Djinni's daughter. I was a rebel. I was an advisor to a prince. I had faced down soldiers and Nightmares and Skinwalkers. I had fought and survived. I had stood against a Sultan time and time again. I had summoned an immortal being to his death. I had saved lives, and I had sacrificed lives, and I had seen more and done more good than she ever would. And I had done it in the name of saving people exactly like my aunt—the people of Dustwalk, who'd been turned bitter and angry and desperate by a country that didn't care about them. I had done it for a prince who did care what happened to them.

I knew who I was. It was Dustwalk that had no idea who I'd become since I left.

"I'm going to tell you once," I said calmly. "My name is Amani—or the Blue-Eyed Bandit, if you're feeling formal." I saw understanding register on her face. My legend had made it this far. "And not anything else." I paused to make sure she understood that my name was not *bitch* or *worthless* or anything else before I stepped away from her. "Now, I have some questions, and I want straight answers. You came here to wait for a letter from Shira. Where did you come here *from*? Where did everyone go?"

Her eyes flashed with anger before she answered me. "We almost starved, you know," she hissed. "There was nothing. We were forgotten, abandoned by everyone, and then *he* came and offered us salvation."

"He?" I asked, but Aunt Farrah seemed distracted now.

"We had nothing to lose. So we followed him away from here, to a new life." Her eyes had taken on a faraway sheen as she spoke with zealous pride.

"Who did you follow?" I was treading lightly. She sounded like she might've gone sun-mad.

"The man in the mountain, of course."

Suddenly I was standing in Bilal's rooms again, holding the page from his book, staring down at the figure chained inside the rocks.

There's no such thing as just a story, I'd told him then.

"He was sent to help us in our time of need." Aunt Farrah smiled nastily at my shocked reaction, pleased to be the one to catch me off guard this time. "But he protects only the good. Any who come to him who are deemed unworthy . . ." She trailed off tauntingly. Bilal had sent soldiers to find him, this man below the mountain—soldiers who never came back. "He's not made of flesh and blood like you and me. He's made of fire. And he burns the unworthy."

A man made of fire wasn't a man. He was a Djinni.

The beginnings of an idea started to form. I had seen what Djinn could do. If there really was one in the mountains . . . It was such a tempting notion. Facing Ashra's Wall alone, we didn't stand a chance. But fighting the legendary with the legendary, fire with Djinni fire—well, that was an idea.

"Can you take me to him?" I asked her. "Your savior in the mountain?"

My aunt's expression was far too knowing and cruel. "I can," she said. "But let me warn you, *Blue-Eyed Bandit*"— she fired the name back at me—"you have no idea who you're facing. He knows your heart. And you will burn for each of your sins."

"Well," I heard Sam say behind her, making my aunt whirl, unsettling her vitriolic composure. He was standing in the doorway, Jin next to him. I wondered how long they'd been witness to our conversation. "This sounds like a terrible idea, given how many sins I have."

"We should get going then," Jin said, clapping Sam on the back jovially. "You can count them on the way."

• • •

TAMID WAS THE only one of us who wasn't apprehensive following my aunt out of the ruins of Dustwalk into the mountains. He had a family we were going to find. He had reason to be excited. I had a family, too. I just didn't want to see them again. Aunt Farrah was already enough. But still, the thought of the man in the mountain kept me putting one foot in front of the other when all I really wanted was to turn back around.

I realized where Aunt Farrah was leading us a few paces before anyone else did. It was close to dusk, and we were deep in the mountains. I'd been on this road once before, with Jin, fleeing on the back of a Buraqi from the chaos in Dustwalk. I could almost taste the iron from the mines in the air as we wound our way up the slope, getting closer, until finally, in the last of the light, we crested over a steep rise, and Sazi came into view. The ancient mountain mining town. Or at least it had been mines before my brother, Noorsham, burned them down using his power.

But this Sazi was nothing like the town I remembered.

Last time we were here, Sazi had been a desperate collection of ramshackle houses clinging to the skin of the mountain. But those were gone now, as if they'd been decimated by thousands of years, though it had only been one year. On the outskirts, we passed a lone building that hadn't completely been destroyed. One wall still stood, a colorful sign swinging above the door: the Drunk Djinni, the same bar where I'd left Jin unconscious on a table before making a run for it. Now, instead of booze-stained bar tables, in the shadow of the single remaining wall was a bright canopy, using the wall as support.

Aunt Farrah stopped walking abruptly. "There are no weapons allowed beyond this point."

Immediately the twins held up their hands. "Don't look at us."

"Or me." Tamid was breathing hard from the walk up the mountain. But he had refused my help over and over until I'd stopped offering it.

That left the three of us.

Reluctantly I unbuckled my holster. The boys followed suit. Sam gave his guns a quick, showy and totally impractical twirl around his fingers before offering them to Aunt Farrah. Jin and I handed over our knives and guns, too.

"Is that everything?" Aunt Farrah demanded as she leaned them gingerly against the wall. I could see stacks of weapons under the canopy now, guns and bombs and swords and knives. A whole arsenal stored in the crumbled building. "He will know if you've kept anything hidden."

It wasn't everything. I'd seen Jin hold back one of his pistols, tucking it into his belt before pulling his shirt over it. I fiddled with the spare bullet I'd kept in my pocket. Between the two of us we had a working weapon. "I'm all out of knives and guns." It was the closest to an honest answer I could give. But it seemed to satisfy her. "Aunt Farrah," I asked as she started walking again, "what is this place?"

"We saw the error of our ways." Aunt Farrah's hands were folded in her khalat. Her hard demeanor had suddenly changed as we passed some invisible barrier into the camp, her head bowing like she was going to prayers. "We were arrogant to try to claim this world for our own by building houses in the sands when we are meant to roam it."

Sure enough, as we pressed deeper into what was left of Sazi, there were hundreds of tents, a riot of colors dotting the otherwise bleak mountain landscape. And among them were hundreds of people, more than all of Dustwalk, Deadshot, and Sazi put together. Men and women crowded between tents and small fires, laughing and talking. Clusters of women sat together sewing a patch in a torn tent canvas. A group of men seemed to be carving things out of wood. It reminded me of the camp we'd lost, a sanctuary hidden from the world.

Two children dashed past us, screaming with laughter. And to my surprised I recognized one of them.

"Nasima!" I called out my little cousin's name without thinking. She skidded to a stop, dark braid swinging in an arc, whipping her back. She stared at me blankly, warily, like I was a stranger.

"It's me." I pressed my hand to my chest, like I might when talking to a foreigner. Only she was my blood. "Amani, your cousin. Don't you remember me?"

"No you're not." Nasima took a bold step toward me, in challenge. "Amani is dead, my mama said so." Then she retreated. "Are you a Skinwalker?" she asked. "That's what my mama says about people who pretend they're other people."

I started to tell her that if I were a Skinwalker, it would take more than a sheema to protect me from the sun. But she wasn't listening. "Skinwalker!" Nasima called out, turning and running away from me. People looked up at us as she bolted. On instinct, Jin moved between me and the staring eyes. Only there were no guns pointing our way, no knives being drawn.

They were as unarmed as we were. Defenseless.

Then we heard it through the crowd.

"Tamid?"

The voice made me stand up straight. It was a voice I was used to being scolded by, for always being around, for corrupting her son. Tamid's mother pushed her way toward us and my heart faltered a little. The last time I'd seen her had been from the back of a Buraqi, behind Jin, as we'd fled blood and chaos and she'd tried to crawl her way toward her son, who was lying bleeding in the sand with a bullet through his knee, thanks to me. Just before he'd been taken prisoner and brought to the city along with Shira.

Now as she moved toward her son, her face was full of tentative, uncertain hope.

"Mother." Tamid limped toward her. And the hope broke into joy. She rushed to him, moving faster than he could on his false leg. She was crying before she even reached him, clasping him in her arms like he was still a little boy. I caught a few words between her sobs as she clung to him. *What happened to you? What did they do to you?* And then: *You're alive. You're alive.* Over and over again.

I realized I'd been holding myself like there was an iron rod in my back, waiting for the reproach that was coming my way for what I'd done to her son. But it never came. She didn't even see me. She didn't care that he'd been taken away. Just that he'd been brought back.

"Father?" Tamid asked, pulling away, looking around, though less hopeful. His mother shook her head.

"He didn't . . ." She hesitated. "He was deemed unworthy. *He* saw what your father did to you." Tamid winced. When Tamid was born with a crooked leg, his father had wanted to kill him. Tamid's mother had saved her son. "He burned for it." Neither Tamid nor his mother looked particularly sorry about it. I couldn't say I blamed them. I wondered who else had been judged too sinful by this man in the mountain.

I looked over at my aunt. There was pain scrawled on her face. Two people had been taken from Dustwalk the day I disappeared with Jin. Only one of them would ever come back. Aunt Farrah would never be reunited with Shira this way.

"Aunt Farrah," I tried again, "your grandson . . . In the city. Shira named him—"

"What is *she* doing here?" The belligerent voice cut me off. I knew it instantly. *You have got to be kidding me.* So, my reckoning with my past wouldn't come from Tamid's mother after all.

I turned around and faced Fazim Al-Motem. If we really were being judged for our sins, then I didn't have to worry, not if Fazim was still alive. Fazim had claimed he was in love with Shira, until he tried to threaten me into marrying him so he wouldn't tell everyone I was the Blue-Eyed Bandit. All because he wanted the money I'd get for capturing a Buraqi.

If that wasn't a sin I didn't know what was. And yet, here he was, strutting toward me.

"Pretty bold for a criminal to show her face here," Fazim crowed. He looked shorter than I remembered. I vaguely wondered if I'd gotten taller. "Stealing from your own family."

"Leave it, boy." Another voice spoke. It was my uncle, I realized. I scarcely would have recognized him if my cousin Nasima hadn't been clutching his hand, still eyeing me warily. He was wearing rags instead of the fine clothes of a horse merchant, and his hair and beard had grown long.

But Fazim took another swaggering step, full of false confidence as he crossed the rocky terrain to confront me.

"Do you think he really can't see that this is a mistake?" Jin said below his breath, so only I could hear him.

"Maybe he just hasn't noticed we outnumber him," Sam suggested from my other side. He was regarding Fazim curiously, like he was a harmless oddity in our way. Fazim wasn't exactly harmless, but they were right. We could do him a lot more harm than he could do me now. "What did you do to him anyway, Amani, break his heart?"

"Not exactly." I'd been afraid of him once, too. Just like I'd been afraid of Aunt Farrah. But in the shadow of the Sultan, the monsters of my childhood seemed ridiculous now.

"Well, Amani." Fazim was very close to me. Out of the corner of my eye I saw Jin's hand make a fist. I wasn't going to let it get far enough for that. "What do you have to say for—"

I flicked my hand at the sand below his feet, between the stones of the mountain, upsetting his footing—a trick I'd picked up off the Albish in Iliaz. The stab of pain through my stomach was gone as quickly as it came. And as Fazim toppled over, landing flat on his back, it was entirely worth it.

Fazim cursed violently as he sat back up, looking embarrassed as some laughed. A few people edged forward, not entirely sure of themselves. After all, I hadn't laid a hand on Fazim. But we might be in for a fight all the same.

But then a cry came from the back. "He's coming! Make way, he's coming." The crowd split like a knife slicing cloth, clearing a straight path through the camp. Fazim scrambled out of the way and got to his feet, suddenly looking cowed.

I turned, heart pounding, waiting to see this *he*. The man in the mountain. The real monster of my childhood stories. The Djinni who had been chained up by his own brethren. The creature who burned people he deemed unworthy of being saved.

And there, standing at the other side of the camp, his hands raised either in blessing or in warning, was my Demdji brother, Noorsham.

TWENTY

F or a second our eyes locked across the rocky terrain, surprise as clear on his face as it must have been on mine. I felt Jin reach on instinct for the gun he hadn't given away. My hand dashed to his, lacing our fingers together, drawing him away from his weapon carefully. *Don't*, I willed him silently.

Noorsham started to move toward us.

He had flattened whole cities. He had burned people from the inside out. It didn't cost him anything to do it. One wrong move from us and there was no telling what would happen.

But I'd stood across from him before when he'd refused to hurt me.

I'd been there when Jin hadn't.

And he was my brother, after all. He wouldn't harm me. I had to believe that.

As Noorsham passed through the crowd slowly, everyone around him bent like blades of grass under a strong wind.

"You kneel," my aunt hissed, loud enough that it was meant to shame me. She was enjoying this, I realized.

But I ignored her. Instead, I took a step to meet him.

My aunt sucked in a breath. I knew she was thinking it would be the end of me. She was thinking I didn't know what Noorsham could do. But I knew better than anyone. I unlaced my hand from Jin's as I pulled away from him, crossing the path that had formed between the people of the camp and my brother, until we were only a few steps apart.

He looked different from when I had last seen him. His hair had grown out from the shorn cut that had been under the bronze helmet the Sultan had forced on him. And there was a small scar on his chin. He reached out a hand toward me. For just a second, even in rags instead of metal armor, he looked exactly as he had the moment before he burned Bahi alive, blazing with power and righteousness. He'd burned whole cities with that hand.

And then he clasped my face, and his palms were only as warm as flesh and blood, not immortal fire.

"Amani." Noorsham's smile could have lit up the world. "You've found your way home to me, sister."

And he embraced me.

I'd be lying if I said I didn't enjoy the stunned look on Aunt Farrah's face just a little bit.

"The Eye!" someone called from the crowd behind Noorsham. "How can we trust them without looking at the Eye?"

"We all had to go through the Eye," another person called, sounding angry.

"The Eye," someone else called from far off. "The Eye." It was picked up like a chant among the assembled people. "The Eye. The Eye. The Eye." Soon everyone was chanting it.

"The Eye!

The Eye!

The Eye!"

Noorsham turned in a slow circle. The words of the chant seemed to shake the mountain around us as he surveyed his people. Finally Noorsham moved, raising one hand ever so slightly in the air. It was as if he had flicked a switch. The whole of the mountain fell silent at his command.

Everyone waited with bated breath for him to speak.

"To the Eye, then," he declared. An uproarious cheer swelled from the mountain. Suddenly everyone was moving at once, encircling us, pushing us forward like we were dust caught in a powerful current. I felt fingernails sink hard into my arm. It was Aunt Farrah, gripping me like she was my jailer, driving me forward. Making sure I wouldn't get away from whatever this Eye was.

We didn't have to go far.

Noorsham led us to a small indent in the mountain,

where the ground sloped off. It was surrounded by prayer scarfs, making it brighter than desert ground ought to be, and the slope was strewn with bright cloths and dried flowers, the kind I'd seen in the Sultan's gardens but that never grew here on the mountain.

And in the middle of it all was a small, jagged-looking piece of mirror, a shard roughly the shape of an eye. Everyone stopped at the edge of the slope, circling around to watch, but no one passed the line of prayer flags that marked the edge, except for Noorsham, who descended confidently.

He picked up the shard of glass reverently in his palms, lifting it high so that it caught the late afternoon sun.

The shard flashed blue, and I heard Jin suck in a breath next to me. I glanced at him curiously. "That looks like a nachseen," he said in a low voice.

"A what?" That didn't sound like any language I had heard him speak.

"A Gamanix invention." Like the paired compasses or Leyla's horde of abominations. A synergy of machine and magic. "You can use them to read things in the eyes of others. Armies use them to interrogate spies."

Noorsham's blue eyes, so much like mine, turned to catch me. "Which one among you will come and face the Eye so I may see the truth of your intentions?"

We traded quick glances. One of us had to spill all our secrets for the lives of everyone else. I ought to send down one of the twins. They were more innocent than Jin or I was. But I could see the naked fear on their faces. And I could feel Noorsham's gaze boring into the back of my neck. I had volunteered to lead the rebellion. I should take responsibility.

"I will." I turned back to Noorsham. I stepped between two of the prayer flags, crossing over the invisible border and descending to stand across from my brother.

Up close I could see the Eye better. It was obviously magic, as Jin had said. At the edge of the shard of mirror's jagged outline, there was something like a crackle of energy, like the spark that fed Leyla's machines.

"Where did you get this?" I asked my brother, keeping a safe distance from the object in his hands.

"You're not the only one to come here looking for something," Noorsham said vaguely. "At first I had to guess what was in their souls. But then foreign soldiers came, and they brought this with them, a gift from God delivered to me by their hands. I use it to see who is truly looking for sanctuary and who seeks something else. And I decide if they stay or if they burn."

A chill went through me at those words. I thought of the men Bilal had sent south looking for the powerful creature below the mountain who could grant his wish to cheat death. Sure enough, half a dozen of the prayer cloths encircling us now looked like strips taken from the uniforms from the Iliaz command.

Be good, or the monster in the mountain will get you.

Noorsham extended the shard of the nachseen toward me. "Look into the Eye, Amani. Let it see you."

From the crowd above us a rhythmic noise started to

pick up: hands pounding against the mountain rock. Just a few at first and then, gradually, more, picking up the cadence. "Eye," someone chanted, more quietly this time, as their hands slapped the ground like a drumbeat. "Eye, Eye, Eye." And soon the chant had spread again, everyone speaking softly, but their voices mingling together into a loud rhythm along with the beating of their hands.

We were surrounded. I had walked us all into a trap with a ticking bomb, one I had to defuse now, or we all died.

If Noorsham saw everything that I had done . . . I didn't know that I would be seen as being sinless. But also I didn't see that I had any choice in baring my soul to him either. I did as I was told. I looked down into the glass.

It was as if a tumble of images fell out of my mind, onto the surface of the mirror, and I was watching them all play in quick succession: Shifting desert sands and walls of fire. Execution after execution. Death after death. Djinn trapped under the palace. The Sultan at gunpoint. And then one final glaring image. The thing we were really here for: the man in the mountain.

I tore my head up, breathing hard. It felt like coming up for air underneath the White Fish, except it was as if my mind was what needed to breathe. Jin was next to me, even though I didn't see where he came from, steadying me with strong arms around my middle. I leaned against him gratefully as Noorsham carefully held the shard of mirror in his hands, inspecting the contents of my mind in it for a very long moment.

"If we need to run—" Jin said, low in my ear.

"You dodge left, I go right, split them up," I agreed. It was the only chance we might have of getting out of here in one piece.

Taking his sweet time, Noorsham placed the Eye back on the makeshift altar before turning to the crowd.

I caught Izz's gaze. He gave me a slight nod, saying he understood; if we bolted he and Maz were ready to shift into something that could outfly the people of Sazi.

"I have seen her sins." My brother finally spoke. "I have passed judgment." He spread his arms as he faced his disciples, all of them hanging on his every word, leaning forward with wide zealous eyes. "They do not need to burn!" he declared loudly. And suddenly the crowd was screaming again. This time with joy.

Though the funny thing was, I didn't find it any less unsettling than when they were baying for my blood.

TWENTY-ONE

I was keenly aware of the stars watching me as I turned over in my bedroll. I hadn't bothered to pitch one of our tents. It was warm enough this far south, even at night.

Most of Noorsham's people slept out in the open air. After all, what did they have to hide from the eyes of God? Only, for me, it wasn't the eyes of God I was worried about but the eyes of the other women, asleep around me.

Unmarried men and women were separated, according to Noorsham's rules.

"It's a sin for that boy to even look at you the way he does if you're not wedded to him," one of the disciples hissed below her breath, casting a glance over her shoulder at Jin, who was watching me as they led me away to an area of Sazi that sat below a shallow dip of the rocks, just below where the mines used to be. That was where the women slept. I caught sight of my cousin Olia settling herself in under the last of the light. She caught my gaze and just shrugged. As if to ask me if I'd really expected anything to change in the Last County. I supposed I was the only thing that had, really.

I wanted to talk to Jin. I needed to talk to someone now we'd reached this godforsaken dead end to a hunt for some impossible story. We'd lost another day of searching thanks to me. Used to be I'd go looking for Shazad in the long dark nights full of doubt. But she was gone. And I was stuck separated from the boys.

And I wouldn't put it past one of these women to sell me out if I snuck off in the dead of night. I'd seen it happen already once today. After evening prayers, where the entire camp had gathered around Noorsham to be blessed by the same hands he'd used to burn people alive. Then his disciples had lined up in front of him eagerly. We looked on curiously from the side as two of his disciples appeared, hauling two huge sacks that they set down next to him. I watched as he reached inside the first and pulled out a loaf of fresh-looking bread and handed it to the first person. They moved aside quickly. I didn't realize how hungry I was until we saw the food. The next person shuffled along; the man after him got another identical loaf. A little girl stepped up next, hands extended eagerly. But before Noorsham could feed her, the woman behind her spoke up loudly.

"She wasn't at prayers today."

Noorsham drew away from the little girl as sharply as if she were a snake. "Mira, is this true?" It sounded more like an accusation than a question. The little girl went silent. "Tell me the truth, Mira," he was saying. "I'll know if you lie."

"I lost track of the sun," she admitted finally.

As he raised his hand toward her I was suddenly worried I was about to see the little girl burn alive. I started to draw forward, and I could feel Jin shifting next to me, too, neither of us sure what we were going to do. But he only rested a hand on her cheek. "If you want to eat in the morning, you will join us at worship instead of playing in the mountains." The girl was pushed out of the line without food.

Noorsham saw me watching him. I'd taken a step forward without realizing it. He reached into the bag and held out his closed hands toward me. I didn't move straightaway, but Noorsham didn't move on. Didn't turn back to the woman who had sold out young Mira and was shifting restlessly. Waiting to reclaim her leader's attention. Finally I extended my hands toward my brother. And he dropped an orange in my palms.

I stared at it, disbelieving, even as Noorsham's attention shifted back to the disciples in his line. I hadn't seen a fresh orange for the first sixteen years of my life. Not until I got to the rebel camp, far from this dusty dead-earthed part of the desert where nothing could grow. Fruit around these parts came stewed in cans so that it could survive the long desert journey to us.

It was impossible that I was holding a fresh orange. Except it was real. When I peeled it, the rind caked under my fingernails, and the intoxicating smell of fresh citrus filled the dusty desert air. And there was no mistaking the burst of sweet flavor when I ate it.

It was unsettling. Out of place. The whole thing, this whole camp. It worried me in a way I couldn't wholly put my finger on.

I turned over restlessly in my bedroll. I hated being alone with my thoughts. They churned through my head like a desert storm, dust scattering every which way, too quick to catch. I needed to talk to Jin. I didn't care that it was against whatever rules they seemed to have here. I slipped out of my bedroll as quietly as I could, casting around to make sure there were no wakeful eyes watching me sneak out as I wove my way through the rest of the bodies of sleeping women.

I was almost out when a flicker of light above us caught my eye. I stopped, ducking quickly so I was low to the ground. Too low for the light to find me among the rocks and sleeping bodies. And I waited, for whatever nighttime patrol this was to pass.

A few moments later, Noorsham appeared above me on the slope. He was moving through the dark by a dim light emanating from his hands, a dulled version of his destructive power. He was walking a few paces above me.

I hesitated. Of all the people to get caught by, Noorsham would be the worst, that was for damn sure. I ought to go back, lie down, close my eyes and pretend to be asleep until dawn, and then we could all leave in the morning with no one getting turned to ashes. But I already knew I wasn't fooling myself, pretending I might do the smart thing for once in my life. I waited a few heartbeats, until he was a safe distance ahead of me, and then I moved to follow Noorsham.

He led me past the edge of his makeshift civilization, to where the ground started to slope upward above the camp. I moved as gingerly as I could, careful to stay far out of the circle of light cast by his hands, trying to remember where to step on the uneven ground by watching the light ahead of me as we climbed further and further up the mountain slope. Until, finally, we reached the entrance to the mines. Noorsham pressed forward without hesitating, entering the dark mouth of the mountains, his hands spilling a sea of light across the rough stone walls.

I hesitated where I was crouched just below him on the slope, moving on all fours to avoid sliding rocks that would give me away. If I entered that tunnel, there was nowhere to hide.

But I'd come this far.

I moved up the last few feet to the entrance, following him into the mountain.

Ahead of me, Noorsham moved with the confidence of someone who had taken this route a thousand times before. When the path forked, he took the left tunnel without hesitation. He passed the debris abandoned by miners without so much as glancing down. He did not slow when we wove through places where the mountain had collapsed into hideous charred and melted rock. A result of the moment he had unleashed his power inside this mountain, killing most of the peope in it.

We were deep into the old mines when he turned right and walked through what looked like a solid wall. I stopped sharply behind him as he vanished, then quickly rushed forward, already afraid of losing him. As I got closer I realized it wasn't solid rock. It was a tiny side passage in the mountain, so much narrower than the tunnels made by man, I likely would've mistaken it for a fissure in the rocks if I was walking by. The light of Noorsham's hands was still just leaking out around my feet. If I waited any longer I would lose it. I would be left alone in the dark.

I plunged after him.

It wasn't a long tunnel. I'd maybe walked a dozen paces when it ended suddenly. I staggered to an abrupt stop as the narrow tunnel opened into a huge cave. Noorsham was ahead of me, moving deeper into the cavern. In the light cast by his hands I could see a perfectly formed domed ceiling above us and smooth even walls.

We were deep into the mountain now. I could feel the weight of it pressing in all around us, as if the stone was trying to reclaim this chamber. Like it knew the cave was out of place, hadn't been formed by nature. But I could tell it wasn't made by human hands, either. Not something this size, this perfectly made.

In the center of the cave sat a huge stone chest, large enough to fit a person. I ran my hand along the narrow fissure of the entrance. There was no way something that size came through this gap. As Noorsham approached it, I saw that there was no break between the chest's sides and the floor of the cave. The chest was carved out of the mountain itself. Like the whole cavern had been hollowed out around it. The light danced across its uneven surface, casting into relief the images that adorned the side. Elegantly twisting vines were chiseled into the stone, hanging heavy with etched figs and dates and grapes and oranges and pomegranates and dozens of other fruits I'd never seen in the desert. Some I didn't even recognize now. There were scrapes of color, too, as if the carved fruits had been brightly painted once upon a time.

And then Noorsham's hands dashed light across the far wall of the cave. And I forgot all about the stone chest.

The sight was gone as quickly as it had come, plunged back into darkness as my brother dropped to his knees, prostrating himself in prayer, pressing his hands into the ground so that the only lights left in the cave were two glowing embers trapped between his palms and the stone ground. I could see his lips moving in silent supplication, his features seeming to melt into the gloom as he raised his head, slowly. Then, as he raised his hands, the wall came into view again, one inch at a time, like the dawn revealing the landscape hidden by the night.

And I knew I hadn't been hallucinating.

The wall was every color we never saw in the Last County painted in intricate patterns. It was as bright as the Sultan's gardens, decorated with scenes of a great battle, of the Destroyer of Worlds emerging from Eremot, of the First Hero being made by the hands of the Djinn, of beasts never seen in the desert or the mountains. The wall looked like a twin to the one that led into our lost sanctuary in the Dev's Valley.

And just like at the rebel camp, in the middle of it all, under a long string of words in the first language, crowning it like an arch, was a painted door. Our door had led into the Rebel Camp, a valley abandoned by a Djinni and claimed as our home. Where did this one lead?

"I've come here to pray about what to do about you, you know." Noorsham's voice in the silence made me jump. He wasn't looking at me, but he must've seen me. There was no point hiding. I stepped fully into the cave, moving toward the light.

"What is this place?" I asked.

Noorsham shifted so that he was facing me, sitting cross-legged on the floor, palms turned upward. "I thought I was dead when the mountain fell on me," Noorsham said. He meant when he had first discovered his power, and the mines had collapsed around him in the fire he made. "Even though it hadn't crushed me, I was sure I would starve or suffocate, down here in the dark. And then, wandering, fleeing the fire and the death that I didn't yet understand, I found this." He rested one hand against the huge chest in the middle of the room, though he never took his gaze off me, his eyes more unsettling now that we were alone than they had been out in Sazi. "What do you most crave to eat at this very moment, sister?"

I didn't answer, but all the same an image of a peach came into my mind. I wasn't sure why. They had been in abundance at the palace—we could pick them straight off the trees in the harem.

Noorsham pushed against the lid of the chest. It slid free with a teeth-grinding screech of stone against stone.

It was filled with peaches. Hundreds of them. They were as fresh as if displayed at a market stall in Izman, as if they'd just been picked. And yet they were under a mountain far from any peach tree.

I moved forward, next to my brother, and picked one up hesitantly. I was half expecting an illusion. But the flesh was soft and downy, and when I took a bite, juice dribbled down my hands. It tasted like another world, not of this dusty desert mountain but of far-off gardens and brighter days. If it was an illusion, it was a damn good one. It seemed more like magic. Not the kind that the Gamanix invented, but the kind that came from creatures more powerful than us, left over from stories and legends and great and terrible times.

Real magic, that was how he was feeding his hungry disciples.

Noorsham watched me as I devoured the peach, right down to the stone in the middle. "I know why you're really here, you know," he said calmly. "You came looking for war and destruction. I saw it in the Eye. And yet I deceived my people for your sake."

"You know that Eye of yours isn't some God-sent tool, don't you?" I picked my words carefully; I was on unsteady ground here. "It's an invention, and you killed the people who brought it here." Noorsham just smiled placidly back at that, like he felt sorry for me being so naive. "How many more people have you killed because of that thing, Noorsham?"

"Only those I needed to, in order to protect my people." If he felt any remorse for what he'd done, it didn't show. "I am meant to do something great in this life, Amani." From another man, that might sound like pretention. But the way Noorsham said it, it was just certainty. And he was a Demdji—he couldn't lie. "My mother always said so," Noorsham said simply. "She had been promised it."

By our father, I realized. Shira had told me, in the palace prison, that Fereshteh had granted her a gift for their son: an untainted wish, freely given, so that it wouldn't turn against her as most did in the stories. Shira, trapped in an endless cycle of political machinations, had wished that her son would be Sultan one day. Hala's mother, poor and greedy, had wished for gold. And Noorsham's mother, caught in a small life in a small mountain town, had wished for greatness for her son.

I wondered, not for the first time, what my mother had wished. For me to get the hell out of Dustwalk, since she never could? For me to know a bigger world? I glanced down at the peach stone in my hand. I doubted even she could have anticipated that the world was this big.

"When the mountain fell on me," Noorsham went on, "after I was given my gift, I thought I might die before I could fulfill my destiny. And then I was rescued. I was told that I was indeed destined to do great things." He had a faraway look in his eyes. "I thought first it was to drive the foreigners out of our desert. But then I failed. And I came back here, back home. I found this desert dying. Deadshot was tearing itself apart. Dustwalk was starving. Sazi was despairing. And I understood. It was my duty to save them. I must save as many of our people as I had killed."

That would be a whole lot of people. He had flattened Dassama, an oasis city in the northern desert. He had burned men from Sazi alive in the same mines we were in now. Bahi. Bilal's men.

"You're still killing people," I said.

"Only the ones who come to me with harm in their hearts." Noorsham didn't blink. "Ones like you. Ashra's Wall is a sacred barrier, you know." So he had seen that in the Eye, too. Damn.

"I know," I said. And I did. More than anyone I understood what stories could mean when they were true. "But there are people on the other side . . . I need to get them out, Noorsham. I can't leave them there."

"Ashra's Wall is—"

"I know, I know." I raised my voice without meaning to. "But, Noorsham, this country is being ripped apart. You have only seen some of it. That's why the Last County was in trouble. That's why you had to save them. And there are people on the other side of that wall who can save a whole lot more people than this—who could change the whole country. For good."

Noorsham looked unmoved. "I believe that if God had wanted them to save people, he would have given them a gift like mine—"

"We are *not* gifted by God," I snapped, the truth boiling over onto my lips. "You and I, we're not chosen for anything. We're just *born* like everyone else. All of us. We're just a side effect of immortals not being able to resist mortal women. And these so-called gifts they give us are just powers that are bound to tear us up or get us killed before we get old enough to do *anything* at all. Great or terrible." I felt the tears start, even though I didn't know if they were anger or bitterness or grief. "Ashra was probably a Demdji, just like us, who died in a war she shouldn't have been fighting. Princess Hawa was, too." I was breathing hard. "She was also our sister—did you know that? And she died doing something great. And Hala died, and Imin died. And if Tamid is right, I might be dead soon, too. And I'm not going to let all of that be for nothing. I have to save them."

Noorsham embraced me unexpectedly, cutting off my tirade of tears as he pressed me to his chest. "I'm sorry, sister," he said close to my ear. "I see your pain." He drew away and clasped my tearstained face with his hands. "But I cannot let you release the Destroyer of Worlds."

His hands were pleasantly warm at first. Then hot—too hot. And I knew. He had made the decision to protect his people over saving mine.

It was the choice I would have made, too. I couldn't begrudge him that.

His hands were scalding now.

I shifted, just barely, dropping the peach pit I had been clutching. My hand slipped into my pocket. I found the single bullet I had saved when we'd handed over our weapons. It was seemingly useless without a gun— unless you knew what we really were. We weren't chosen by God, we were children of immortal beings, vulnerable to iron just like they were.

I knew that. Even if my brother didn't.

I clasped my hand over Noorsham's, pressing the bullet to his skin. Immediately the heat in his hands vanished. He blinked in confusion as he felt his gift leave him. His blue eyes met mine, looking for answers.

"I'm so sorry, Noorsham," I said. And then I punched him in the face.

TWENTY-TWO

"This was your plan all along, wasn't it?" Sam had his arms wrapped around me, pressing me to his chest so I couldn't escape him talking. "Lure me down to the dead end of nowhere with promises of heroic deeds, all just to get close to me."

"That's an awfully convoluted plan." I was trying to find a comfortable place to settle my arms that wasn't his shoulders, but there really weren't very many options. "If I was going to take advantage of you, I could've done it back in the harem,"

We were standing together, chest to chest, trying our hardest to choke out any air between us. It might've looked romantic if it weren't for Jin looping a rope around us, securing us like we were some ship's anchor about to be pushed overboard.

My brother was in the corner, unconscious and bound up in the shackles we'd taken off Sam after his brush with the firing squad. We needed to get this done before dawn came and Noorsham's disciples woke up and wondered where he was. They would find him and free him eventually, but I was planning on us being long gone by then.

Tamid was fretting anxiously at the mouth of the tunnel. My one-time friend might've thought he was done with our rebellion when we got here, but he was the only person I trusted to drug my brother safely. And more than that, I'd needed him to read the words in the first language scrawled over the door.

"But isn't this so much more romantic?" Sam went on wistfully. "Braving near-certain death with me." The rope tightened so that I was pressed with my ear against his shoulder. I couldn't see his face, but I was sure he was laughing at me. "Just like Cynbel and Sorcha or Leofric and Elfleda."

"I have no idea who those people are," I said into his shirt.

"Albish love stories," he said. "You'd like Leofric and Elfleda. He's a thief, she's a powerful sorceress. They both die tragically at the end. That's what happens in all great love stories."

"Well, it's a good thing we're not in love, then." Sam's flirting had gotten a whole lot less outrageous the farther south we'd gotten. Half of me thought it was because he and Jin were actually getting along. Better than I'd seen Jin get along with Ahmed in months, now I thought about it. Sam was only back to flirting with me now because he was trying to lighten the mood.

We were about to walk through solid mountain into unknown territory.

I'd made Tamid read the words carved above the doorway to me. "They're in the first language," he had said, furrowing his brow as he read them by torchlight. "Something about . . . a prisoner?" We all felt that simple word settle over us as he said it.

The man in the mountain. Monster or mortal maybe. But definitely not just myth.

Well, we'd come here looking for powerful help, and we might've found it.

"We'll need a name to open the door," Jin had said. "Like back—back in the Dev's Valley." He cut himself off before he said *back home*. But I heard it.

"There's no name." Tamid squinted at the words above the doorway. "But there is something else, I think it's—" I saw the realization settle over him a moment before he said the next words, low and reverant. "I think they're the words to free a Djinni."

There it was. The thing Tamid had been looking for in books. Our salvation. Not recorded on any paper in a northern library but buried in the mountains here far in the south. It was an answer, too. What to expect beyond that door. Not a man. A Djinni.

It didn't matter that we didn't have the right words to get the painted door to open for us. We had alternative ways in.

Nobody asked who would be going through with Sam. Nobody needed to.

Now, standing tied to Sam, I made Tamid read the words above the door out to me again. I repeated them back carefully.

"Good," he said, like a patient teacher. He really would've made a good Holy Father. "And then at the end, you would say the Djinni's true name—"

"I know," I cut him off. "I've called Djinn before." Tamid looked away, shamefaced, that brief moment between us breaking as I reminded him that he was at least partly responsible for the Djinn currently imprisoned under the palace.

Jin pulled on the knot, dragging Sam and me together a little tighter. "That's the best I can do without running out of rope," he said. The last thing I needed was to get separated from Sam halfway through the mountain. And the rope gave us something to guide us back out. Jin ran his hand along his jaw, a nervous gesture.

"I was going to say, *Just imagine it's like diving through deep water.*" He smiled at me ruefully. "And then I remembered that you're from—"

"Here?"

"I'm going to teach you how to swim someday," he promised. "Just try to stay alive long enough."

It was time to go.

"Take a deep breath," Sam said, sounding serious for the first time since we got here. "And whatever you do, don't stop walking." I did as I was told, taking in all the air my lungs would hold, and he did the same. And then he took one big step, and we were submerged in stone.

There was dark and then there was the dark of being inside a mountain wall.

It pressed in on all sides of me as we moved, fighting against the ancient stone trying to settle back into the place it had occupied for thousands of years as we squeezed through. It felt like hands pressing against me, trying to pulverize me. We took another step, and then another. The farther we went, the worse it got. I could feel my eyelashes being pressed against my cheek. My lungs were going to burst from not breathing. I was going to die entombed in a mountain.

And then air hit my body, my left arm first, then the rest of me, as we half stumbled through, plunging to the ground, ripping our bodies free of the stone. Sam collapsed on top of me, gasping for breath. We were still in the dark, but at least there was air here, even if it tasted stale, like it had been trapped in this stone chamber forever.

For a second, all I could hear was our heavy breathing echoing around cave walls. The chamber we were in was big, judging by the sound of it. I heard Sam take a breath, like he was about to say something. To ask if I was all right or make some joke.

But the voice that slid out of the darkness wasn't his. "You are very late indeed."

I fought to keep my heart slow as I fumbled for the knot that attached me to Sam. My shaking fingers finally found it and I struggled to untie it. I needed at least to face whatever this was standing up.

"I must say," the voice came again, echoing around the chamber unsettlingly as my fingers worked frantically, "your predecessors usually took the door."

Finally the rope came apart. Sam rolled off me, pushing aside the rope. His warmth and solidity disappeared, and suddenly I was alone in the dark. I fumbled for the matches in my pocket as I sat up.

I struck one, sending up a small flare of light against the total blackness. It was enough to see by. To see Sam, only a few feet away, slumped on the ground, exhausted from dragging me through stone. And, just beyond him, a man.

I stepped back instinctively, heart leaping in fear as the stranger smiled at us from the other side of the cave. I knew instantly even as he did that he wasn't mortal. He was a Djinni. I'd summoned a whole host of immortals under the palace. I knew now how to recognize them. Their human shapes were too polished, too perfect, like they were made of burnished bronze instead of flesh. They somehow looked both ancient and young at the same time, like they'd seen a great deal but still forgotten to give their bodies the nicks and wear that made mortals look human. And this Djinni, his clothes were something out of another age, one so long gone it had been forgotten.

And then there were the burning red eyes, which had a slightly wild look in them. Like a quickly catching fire that might consume everything at any moment.

I held the match higher. Tight iron shackles were strapped around his arms and legs, darkened with age but strong all the same. And around him, there was a circle of iron to contain him. It looked identical to the ones where I'd trapped the Djinn under the palace. Like it had been made by the same hands.

"Who are you?" I asked. My voice sounded raspy and unsteady even to myself as it echoed around the chamber.

"Who am I?" he rasped back in an unkind imitation, making those burning red eyes go wide. And then they narrowed, fixing on me suspiciously. "Who are *you* that you come here without knowing me?" I didn't answer. There was something about him that made me not want to give him my name. I didn't know what he might do with it. "And what is *that*?" He nodded toward Sam, who was watching from one step back, like he was ready to bolt back through the wall at a moment's notice. "He's not one of ours." He sniffed as if he could suss Sam out. "He smells like damp earth. He's a child made by our cowardly brethren in the green lands." He talked like the Holy Books, in ancient, labyrinthine language designed to ensare the listener. "He doesn't belong here. I don't trust him."

"Always nice to be wanted," Sam muttered.

Silence descended. And lasted.

This Djinni, he wasn't going to be any use to us if he was wary of Sam. He might talk to *me* though. I turned back toward my foreign friend, but I didn't need to say anything. Sam started shaking his head as soon as he saw my expression in the flickering of the match. "No, I'm not leaving. You've lost your mind."

"Don't you still owe me one for saving your life?" I tried for lightness. Like the prospect of being imprisoned in this cavern with an immortal creature alone wasn't terrifying.

"Oh, sure, I see, because if I leave now, it would make us even. Since Jin will kill me if I come back through that wall without you, thus making you saving my life entirely moot." He ticked off the life or death count on his fingers like he was doing arithmetic.

I leaned in close to him, the match flickering close between us. "And other folks might die if we don't get some help." The flame reached my fingers now, almost scalding them before I dropped the match quickly, extinguishing it on the cavern floor. "Sam," I said in the dark, fumbling for a new match. "Please."

By the time I'd lit a new one, Sam looked resigned. "I'll give you two measures of 'Whistling Jenny,' and then I'm coming back for you."

"What's a Jenny?" I asked.

"It's not a— She's— Never mind." He sounded frustrated, even though I wasn't the one who was talking gibberish. "It's a working song we use to measure time in the fields. There are ten measures of 'Whistling Jenny' in an hour."

"Give me seven measures."

"Three," Sam haggled.

"Five, and I agree not to tell Jin or Shazad about that time you tried to kiss me."

"Deal." Sam grabbed my hand, shaking it firmly. He picked up the lingering end of the rope that stretched back through solid stone all the way to the other side, where it was anchored by Jin. He quickly looped it around my waist, tying a hasty knot. "So I can find my way back to you." He grinned at me. But just before he let go, seriousness sank over him. "You'd better still be in one piece."

And then he turned away, stepping out of the narrow pool of light cast by my match, keeping hold of the rope, and with one quick look back he was gone. And I was alone. Alone in the dark with a Djinni.

He was looking at me with wide, unblinking eyes. "Who is your father, little Demdji?" he asked.

"Why does that matter?" I asked.

"You asked me who I was." He hadn't blinked at all; it was unsettling. "Mortal memories are short, but surely not so short that you've already forgotten that. Tell me who you are and I'll tell you who I am." So it was a trade he wanted. Except I knew better than to take it at face value. Djinn traded in tricks and deceit. If I gave him anything, he might gain the upper hand on me. But if I didn't give him anything, I might not gain anything. I didn't have a whole lot of time to waste debating. On the other side of that wall, Sam was counting the minutes.

"Bahadur. My father is Bahadur." A sly smile came over his face, like he'd finally solved a puzzle he'd been working at for a long time. "Your turn," I said quickly.

"Well, daughter of Bahadur"—he drew out my father's name—"I used to have a name, it's true. A long time ago. Before you were born. Before even your oldest ancestor was made," he said. "But it was taken from me some time ago. I am known without a name now. I am called only the Sin Maker."

TWENTY-THREE

I sucked in a breath so quickly the match went out. The Sin Maker's laugh filled the darkness that rushed back in around us, bouncing off the walls as I fumbled to find another.

There were stories of all the Djinn going by a hundred different names. Bahadur was also known as the Once King of Massil, the Maker of the Sand Sea, and the Breaker of Abbadon. But the Sin Maker wasn't just another campfire story. His tale wasn't that of a greedy mortal outwitted by a First Being, or a wish granted to a worthy beggar, or even a Djinni falling in love with a princess.

The Sin Maker was from the Holy Books.

After the Destroyer of Worlds brought death into an immortal world, and the Djinn created mortality, one

Djinni created sin. He betrayed all of humanity. Though he stood with the other Djinn when they created the First Hero, he did not celebrate with his brethren when they succeeded in making mortals to challenge their enemy. Instead, while the others reveled in their victory, the Sin Maker slipped away and sought to kill the First Hero before he could challenge the Destroyer of Worlds. If he had succeeded, he would have stopped the world's only hope. But the other Djinn caught him before he could slay their creation. And when they did, the Djinn knew one of their own must've made a deal with the Destroyer of Worlds behind their backs to challenge them thus.

He was a traitor to his own kind. The first traitor the world ever knew.

I finally found another match. I struck it, trying to keep my hands steady. It was useless; the flame trembled.

"They say . . ." I hesitated, not sure what to ask first. *They say you've been banished to be imprisoned among the stars.* But I could see that wasn't true. "They say you betrayed the First Hero." It came out an accusation.

"They do say that," he agreed. He tilted his head, those fiery eyes raking across me. "You look a little bit like the First Hero, you know," he said. "You would think that after thousands of years I could forget her face. But I see her every moment I sit here in the dark. That is a worse punishment than these chains."

Had he just said *her*? I thought of every image I'd ever seen of the First Hero, illuminated on manuscripts, painted on tiles in prayer houses. All of them a dark-haired, armored man, wielding a sword. But the Sin Maker had been there. "The First Mortal was a woman?"

"Of course. My immortal brethren lost their lives in the thousands when we faced the Destroyer of Worlds. We knew we were no match for her. So we didn't create a soldier in our own image; we made one in hers." His ember eyes took on a far-off look. "Her hair was like the night, her skin was like the sand, and for her eyes, we stole the color from the sky itself." He drifted back to the present. "And I didn't betray her. I loved her.

"I loved her before any of my brethren knew love. So I tried to keep her away from death. She was too brave for her own good. I feared she would die trying to face the Destroyer of Worlds. But my brethren didn't know what it was to love yet, especially not to love something that would die." His eyes swept me. "And now the whole world is marked by their hypocrisy." He despised me, I realized. Because of what I was. Proof that one of the Djinn who had punished him for loving a mortal woman had found a mortal woman to love, too. "I suppose they know now what it is to be afraid for another. But back then they only knew selfish fear. Fear of their own death, not of the death of another. And she was a shield from that. Made to be used, not saved."

The flame had burned down to my fingers without me noticing. The snap of heat made me drop the match in surprise, and it snuffed out as it hit the ground.

The Sin Maker didn't stop speaking as I fumbled for a fresh match.

"My brethren locked me in here to keep me from protecting the First Hero at the cost of their own lives." His voice echoed through the dark. "They set a mortal guard outside, and they left him with an endless supply of food and drink so that he never left his post." The chest that Noorsham had found. "The guard was to visit me once a year and ask me if I was sorry for betraying my own kind." I knew the story. The Sin Maker was doomed to be apart from the earth until the day he atoned for his sin. "Only when I said I was sorry would I be released."

I struck a fresh match.

"I was not sorry in the short life of my first guard. Especially when he told me that she had died. He told me my son was fighting in her place now, using the name of the First Hero as she had. I was not sorry in the lifetime of my next guard either, or the one who came after that. After a time, they stopped coming as often as they had. Then they stopped coming altogether. They forgot about me. Now it is only my so-called brothers who come to see me, when they remember. They bring me news. Bahadur was the last." His eyes scraped over me. "Bahadur never changes. He tries to hide his children, ever since the first one died. The princess with the sun in her hands who fell from the walls. He gives you all those eyes like hers. . . ." He trailed off. I didn't know if he meant Princess Hawa or the First Hero now. "But he never can hide you, because he gives you all far too much power. He thinks it will help keep you safe. But all it does is make you burn too brightly and too quickly, and then you snuff out." The flame in my fingers wavered; it was burning low, but it had some life left to it. "He's so desperate to protect you that he gets you all killed."

"The Bahadur you're talking about sounds real different from the one I know," I said, trying not to sound bitter. I remembered my father watching me mercilessly as the knife plunged toward my stomach, ready to let me die. I remembered railing at him for letting my mother die and finding no remorse there. I remembered the stories of Princess Hawa, his first daughter, who had died long ago fighting in the war the Djinn were too cowardly to fight on their own. She'd received no help from him.

I had wanted to know why he couldn't save them. I had my answer. Djinn who tried to save humans ended up here. Like this.

The Sin Maker smiled, like he could read some of what I was thinking in my traitor eyes. "Your father came to ask me if I was sorry. That was nearly two tens of years past," he said, like he was trying to decide how old I was. "Nearly."

Nearly. But not quite. I could guess the true number. I was seventeen. So was Noorsham. Our father had come here for the Sin Maker's penance and found our mothers instead.

"You owe me gratitude, daughter of Bahadur."

A small, almost hysterical laugh bubbled up in my chest. "Because your imprisonment made me?"

He rattled his chains conspicuously just as the light

snuffed out again, leaving only his voice in the dark. "I might know a way to thank me."

The silence in the cave was palpable as the matches in the box rattled together. I slid one of them over the sandpaper so I could see him again.

Truth was I wanted to release him. We were going up against an impossible barrier. We needed an ally like him. But I had to ask all the same. "Are you sorry?"

The Sin Maker got to his feet slowly, bringing himself to his full height as he faced me. "Have you ever been in love, daughter of Bahadur?" I was suddenly keenly aware of the rope around my waist, stretching through solid stone back to Jin's hand. I didn't answer. "Is there anything you wouldn't do to save them if you could?"

I was still silent. This time I really didn't know the answer. I would take a bullet to hold on to Jin; I had once, and I had a scar to prove it. But the Sin Maker would have doomed the whole world for the First Hero. I didn't know if I was selfish enough to doom the whole world for Jin. I didn't know that I was selfless enough not to.

"No," he said finally, watching me struggle. "I'm not sorry."

"How would you like to be freed anyway?"

I had the satisfaction of catching him off guard. The Sin Maker tilted his head to the side just a little. "And why would a daughter of Bahadur the noble do that?" he asked warily.

I ran my tongue across my dry lips before finally settling on the part of the truth I wanted to tell. "There are some people I care about, and there's a good chance they'll die if I don't get to them soon. I want to save them." *Like you wanted to save her.* It hung unsaid between us.

"So it's a trade you want? My help for my freedom?"

"Something like that." I could already see him burning a little brighter. But for once, I had the advantage on him. I might not have been alive as long as he had, but I had lived in the world with mortality a whole lot longer. And I knew centuries of stories about making deals with Djinn. Only the gifts given willingly by Djinn ever brought good. The rest—cheated or bargained out of them—brought ruin. One misplaced word brought disaster instead of fortune. One slippery, undefined turn of phrase left all the room the Djinn needed for us slower, stupider mortals to slip off the edge.

The Sin Maker hated me. I could see it written all over him. He hated me because I was mortal, because I existed through the sacrifice of a hero he had loved long, long ago. And I was the child of one who had chained him up. He wouldn't give me anything willingly. Not even in exchange for his freedom after centuries. And if he tried, I couldn't win. I couldn't outsmart him. "You're thinking that you'll trick me," I said, stilling the thoughts roiling in his mind. "That I'll try to bind you to me, to give you orders. But I don't want to do that."

"What *do* you want, then, daughter of Bahadur?"

"I don't want to fight you." I wanted to rest. I was tired. I was wrung dry by this war. By leading. By everything. "I don't want to play games where I weigh every word I say to check for loose footing and you prod at them to find the cracks to slip through. So here's my offer: I want you to agree to do what I *want*."

What I wanted was different from what I asked for. I might ask for our friends to be freed, but what I wanted was them alive, in one piece, not freed through death. I might want a way through Ashra's Wall, but I didn't want to release the Destroyer of Worlds, if she really was trapped behind it. I was asking him to agree not to the letter of my orders but the heart of them. "I want help," I said finally.

"Help?" The Sin Maker sounded interested.

"Yes, agree to my terms and I will free you from this cave now, and from servitude to me when it is done."

"You drive a hard bargain." He was watching the match in my fingers burn down. "That's your last match."

"It is," I said. "And it'll be my last offer, too. I can leave here without you. But you can't leave here without me."

"Then I agree," the Sin Maker said simply.

"Say it."

"Amani Al-Bahadur." His tone wasn't without sarcasm, but it was his words that mattered. "Your wish will be my command. I will honor what you want in exchange for my freedom from here. And eventually from you."

I turned it over carefully. But he was right, we were running out of time. It was my last match. "Tell me your name," I said.

"My name." It was my first want, my first order. I saw his jaw work, like it was unused to the word that was coming forward. "It was given to me a very long time ago. My name is Zaahir."

"Zaahir, the Sin Maker," I repeated. And then I saw the rest of the words, the ones that had been carved into the arch above the door, which Tamid had read off for me. I spoke them out loud, carefully painstakingly, ending with his name.

I finished almost breathless. Waiting for something to happen. For the circle around him to break, maybe. Or for his chains to shatter. A flash of light or fire. Or a clap of thunder to shake the mountain.

But all that happened was that Zaahir smiled at me as the flame of the match reached my fingers, close to extinguishing. The last thing I saw was him stepping over the line of the circle before the match died, plunging us both into darkness.

TWENTY-FOUR

"Well, daughter of Bahadur." A new light bloomed just enough so that I could see him, free of his prison, standing suddenly too close to me. The fire wasn't flickering across his face, I realized. It was coming from within it, a faint glow betraying that he was not quite human. "What is it that you want now?"

The sensation of power rushed in, as if to consume me. I wanted so much. I wanted the Sultan to die for what he had done to Shira, to Imin, and to Hala. I wanted to win this war for their sakes and the sakes of everyone else who had died for it. I wanted Ahmed to sit on the throne and rule it in the name of its own people instead of some foreign power. But I knew better than to ask for something that big and imprecise. I wasn't stupid. I'd heard stories of Djinn deception.

"I want you to take me to Eremot."

The Sin Maker didn't answer me. He just smiled.

And then the mountain began to move. He didn't raise his hands like I needed to when I moved the desert. He didn't strain, didn't so much as blink as earth and rocks that had remained unmoved for centuries shifted, like a behemoth awaking from a long sleep and stretching its colossal body.

A split in the mountain appeared, a tunnel. Not leading back toward the ruins of Sazi and the cave where the others awaited, but deeper into the maw of the mountain. He'd just cleaved a mountain, effortlessly.

Only then did real understanding descend on me.

This was an immortal being, a maker of humans. His power was cosmic and beyond my understanding. He could move mountains and shake the earth. He didn't care anything for the wars of men. He hadn't ever lived in our world. He was from legends, not reality.

And I'd just gone and set him free.

The Sin Maker extended one hand straight down the tunnel. "After you."

I glanced back at the wall that led back to the others.

"You want to save the people you care about." He parroted my own words back at me. "There is no one you care about more than the boy who is waiting for you on the other side of that cave, is there?" I didn't know how he knew about Jin, but I didn't like it. "You would rather die for them than have them risk their lives for you. You want to do this alone, don't you? To keep them safe."

There was no point in telling him he was wrong. So

I untied the rope around my waist, letting it slither to the ground. Useless. Untethered. And I stepped into the tunnel, Zaahir close behind me, and the entrance closed, sealing us in. When Sam came back for me, he'd have no idea where I'd gone. No way to follow me. I hoped the others would forgive me for this.

We walked in silence for a long time, the glow from the Sin Maker's body the only thing keeping the dark at bay.

Finally another light appeared ahead. Far at the end of the tunnel, like a star in the darkest night.

I'd always imagined Ashra's Wall like the walls of Saramotai: huge and impenetrable and impossible, fire guarding against ghouls and the night. But this wall was not made just to keep out ghouls. It was made to keep something in. And it didn't look anything like the messy, violent fire the Sultan had domed the city with. It reminded me of the light that had come from the machine when it killed Fereshteh, only clearer, brighter. It wasn't a Djinni's light, it was gentler. A girl's soul outside of her body, burning. As we got closer to the light of Ashra's Wall, I swore I could see patterns in it, like the weave of a carpet.

Once upon a time, this fire had been a girl. Born in a desert at war, just like I was. Now her body was long gone and all that was left was the ever-burning fire of her soul.

"Was she human?" I asked Zaahir as we stopped an arm's reach from the wall. "Ashra."

"I think you already know the answer to that, daughter of Bahadur," the Sin Maker said, his own coal-red eyes dancing over the wall of light.

I did.

I knew as soon as I saw the wall as a pinprick of light at the end of the tunnel. Ashra was another Demdji who had sacrificed herself for the wars of our fathers. Only for the stories to forget what she really was, just crowning her a hero instead. Just like they had with Princess Hawa, and probably hundreds of other Demdji.

When I was dead and gone, burned up by releasing Fereshteh's fire, and they told the story of the Rebellion, I wondered if they'd forget me as a Demdji, too, and just remember that I was the Blue-Eyed Bandit.

We were almost at Eremot. Somewhere beyond this wall was whatever remained of our rebellion.

"How do we get through?" I asked.

"Oh, it's no trouble getting in." Zaahir knelt down, his movements strange and unnatural, like he was just pretending to use human muscles when he was really bending like a flame in the wind. He peeled a small stone from the floor of the tunnel like it was a blade of grass and tossed it. The pebble passed easily through Ashra's Wall, landing on the other side with a few bounces. It didn't even look singed. "This wall wasn't made to keep anything out."

A gust of unnatural wind rose around us, picking up the stone on the other side of the barrier, shooting it back toward us at full speed, aimed straight for my head. It hit the barrier at high speed. But this time, instead of passing through, it turned to dust, incinerating as it met the barrier. Just like the stone Jin had thrown at the wall back in Izman. "It's made to keep things in."

So that was what the Sultan had done. He had sent his

prisoners in, never to come out again. Because it didn't matter to him if they died down there. He would have killed them himself if he didn't need disposable bodies.

He feigned mercy to his city, letting the rebels be imprisoned instead of executed. And then he sent them off to the dark to die quietly in a place where nothing could ever leave. Ending any trouble rebellious captives might be.

"If we go in there," I said warily, "can you get us back out alive?"

"Yes," Zaahir said cryptically. "I can." I didn't trust Zaahir as far as I could throw a horse. But he wasn't lying to me about this.

"After you, then." I mimicked his words from earlier.

Our gazes locked for a long moment, a battle of wills passing between us. Zaahir finally nodded. "As you wish." And then he moved forward. He passed through the wall as if it were nothing but air, and then he was standing on the other side, watching me expectantly.

This was a bad idea. I knew this was a bad idea. But I'd done a lot of things that were bad ideas. Usually they turned out all right. This might be different though. This was a bad idea of mythic proportions. But what else was I supposed to do? I took a deep breath and tried not to think too hard about what I was doing as I stepped through a wall made of light.

It felt like passing through a patch of sunlight in between shady trees, pleasant and warm on my skin. And then I was stumbling through to the other side, next to my dubious Djinni ally.

Beyond Ashra's wall, the mountain didn't *look* any different from the tunnel that Zaahir had created for us, but I could feel the change instantly. The air was filled with the taste of iron. Even worse than in Sazi. Probably not enough to take away my power, but I could feel my skin itching against it. I caught myself holding my breath for fear it was going to get into my lungs. I could see even Zaahir chafing against it as we moved through the dark tunnel and into the mountain.

It wasn't long before we lost the last of the light from Ashra's Wall behind us. The darkness made me nervous. It felt like we were ghouls in the night, stalking somewhere we shouldn't be. Or like there might be things in here stalking us.

The ground sloped steeply into the belly of the mountain. We quickened our steps as it descended. I kept my eyes on my feet at first, careful of any stone that might trip me up, but the ground was remarkably smooth. At first I thought it had been swept clean; then, as the path narrowed, my hand brushed against the wall. It was smooth, too. Like it had been worn down by something. And suddenly my mind summoned up every image I had ever seen in Holy Books, of the Destroyer of Worlds' enormous monstrous snake, released in the early days of the war. And I imagined it down here, roaming through these mountains impatient for its escape, wearing the walls smooth and round. . . . I stopped that thought in its tracks. That monster was dead. The First Hero had killed it.

But that didn't mean that there was nothing else down here.

For the first time in my whole life, I was alone.

I wasn't crammed into a house with my aunt's children. I wasn't with Jin and a caravan crossing the desert. I wasn't with Shazad in a tent in the rebel camp, there to watch my back if I needed her. I wasn't surrounded by women in the harem. I wasn't stacked on top of the remnants of the Rebellion in the Hidden House.

I'd wanted to keep them safe, but now I didn't have Jin to watch my back. I didn't have the twins to fly me out of this if it all went wrong. I didn't have Sam to crack a joke to break the silence that was carrying my mind away to fearful places.

I was in hell, and I'd walked into it willingly.

I began to feel exhaustion catching up to me. I hadn't slept since Juniper City, and here in the dark, I couldn't tell how long it had been since we left Sazi, though I got the feeling dawn must've come and gone. Which would mean I'd been awake a full day. I stopped, sinking to the ground, leaning back against the wall. I just needed a moment to rest. Zaahir stopped as well, watching me with a curious look on his face. Had he forgotten, after all this time, how fragile we mortal things were?

As I was leaning there, I noticed something on the ground, in the light from his skin. I reached out to pick it up. It was a button. My button. I checked the collar of my shirt, and sure enough, there was a loose strand of thread there.

"We've been this way already," I mumbled, trying to get my tired mind to focus.

"Yes," Zaahir agreed cheerfully. "You've been walking in circles for some time now."

My eyes snapped up to him, shaking off the haze of sleep. "Are we lost?"

"You are." Zaahir smirked. "I know exactly where I am."

My anger carried me to my feet, so that I was looking him in the eye instead of groveling on the ground before him. "I want you to take me to the prisoners inside this mountain," I snapped. "And you agreed to do what I wanted."

Zaahir nodded pensively, seeming unmoved. "You do want that, don't you," he said. "But you're also frightened of what you'll find there. You don't really *want* to know which of them is alive and which is dead. You're afraid of knowing that. Or else you could have found out by now, little truth-teller." He was right, all those nights in the desert. I had held my tongue against checking on the others. Finding out if I could say out loud *Ahmed is still alive. Shazad is still alive.* "You don't really want to find out whether maybe they wouldn't be dead if it hadn't taken you quite so long to get to them. You want them all to still be alive. And they won't be. See, daughter of Bahadur, you want so many conflicting things that I could lead you in circles around this mountain forever. Toward them, then away from them, then back toward them. Round and round and round we go." He spun his finger in a circle in the air above us. "Where she'll drop dead, no one knows." Zaahir looked suddenly more dangerous than he had before. The way the light shifted around him seemed to show a glint of madness across that immortal face. "I could leave you under this mountain to die, hopelessly lost until you starved. Wouldn't that be a nice revenge on my jailer Bahadur when he next came back to check on his prisoner—if your body were waiting for him instead?"

It occurred to me, not for the first time, that letting Zaahir out and putting my faith in him was an unbelievably stupid thing to do. But I'd done it now. I would have to play this game with him. And I wasn't going to die down here. Not without saving the others. If nothing else, I knew I didn't want to die.

"Yeah, well, good luck with that." I tried to sound flippant, like I wasn't gambling for my own life. "See, Bahadur is locked up right now, so chances are it'd be a while before he'd find me. Decades. By then I'd probably be nothing but bones. He might not even know it was me." *He probably wouldn't care either way.* I didn't say that though.

Zaahir's unblinking stare didn't even pretend to be human as he took in what I had said. I expected frustration at this foiled revenge. "Well then." He spoke finally, and as he did his face suddenly split into a genial grin that was somehow more disturbing than his unblinking stare. "I'd better do what it is you want, then." He raised his hand, casting light on another branch of the tunnel that I hadn't seen before. "This way, daughter of Bahadur."

• ● •

WE'D BEEN WALKING for hours more when I finally heard something up ahead. I drew my mind away from my aching, exhausted body, to listen. It sounded like the ringing of hundreds of tinny bells. The kind aunt Farrah used to call everyone in for dinner.

I quickened my pace. We were near something. I wasn't sure what, but it was something other than darkness and stone. As we kept moving, I became aware of a light up ahead. Not the sort of glowing starlight that came off Ashra's Wall—a more natural one. Like the fire of torches or oil lamps. I was practically running now. Toward the clang of metal and the faint flicker of lamplight, until finally the tunnel opened up into an immense cavern and I stumbled to a stop.

If we were being swallowed by the mountain, then we'd finally reached the stomach. The tunnel had spat us out onto a ledge that dropped off so suddenly I'd almost stepped right off it. The cavern we'd emerged into was vast, disappearing into blackness far above us. And below, in the faint glow cast by the torches affixed to the wall, I saw the prisoners.

They were chained together like cattle. Bound up in iron, hands and feet linked to each other. Each of them had a pickaxe, and they were hewing at the rock at their feet. Swinging their axes down over and over again, metal clanging against stone noisily.

I remembered what Leyla had told me. Her father had sent them here because he was searching for the Destroyer of Worlds.

There was a different quality to the darkness inside this

mountain. It wasn't dark here like a solitary desert night or like the inside of a prison cell. The air was a thicker more viscous sort of dark. A more purposeful dark that seemed to curl around me, encroaching not just on my body but on my mind and my soul.

Somewhere down here, I had no doubt, slept the Destroyer of Worlds.

I scanned the crowd, searching frantically for a familiar face. There were far more people than had been taken from us that night. Other prisoners I guessed, who had been spared execution only to be sent here. I looked for Ahmed, Shazad—someone I knew. But the faces were so marked with dirt and dust that I wasn't sure I'd know them even if they were right in front of me, let alone when I was searching from up here.

And then, just below me, I saw a soft, childlike face, dirty dyed hair sticking to her cheek, smudged in dust. She was shaking as she tried to raise her pickaxe again.

Delila.

My heart leapt. This was them. I had found our prisoners. And at least some of them were still alive. I glanced down. It wasn't an easy jump, but I could make it. I could leap down and unchain them and then make a run for it if I—

My thoughts were interrupted by the sound of footsteps. I drew away from the edge as another prisoner entered the cavern, carrying an immense empty wooden bucket in one hand and a torch in the other. As he passed near the line of prisoners, the firelight he was carrying glinted against bronze.

"You want to see clearly." Zaahir said, stepping up beside me. And before I could stop him the glow of his skin grew brighter, casting light on the scene below. There, just beyond the line of the torches that illuminated the prisoners at work were hundreds upon hundreds of bronze and clay figures standing in silent vigil.

Abdals.

The sight of them stopped all thoughts of leaping down. I knew what they could do to me if they caught me. And so did every other prisoner here, guessing by the way they worked, eyes down, arms shaking with every stroke into the earth. None of them even looking for an escape.

As I watched, one of the figures wielding a pickaxe collapsed to his knees, breathing hard. He looked skinny and emaciated, like his body had reached the end of what it could do.

Sure enough, he didn't get back up. One of the Abdals stepped forward.

No. I couldn't let this happen. I cast around for Zaahir, who was leaning over, watching the scene below. When he caught my eye he raised his eyebrows mockingly. "Do you want me to stop it?"

"Yes," I hissed back desperately.

Below, the Abdal rested a metallic palm on the top of the prisoner's head. The man didn't try to fight it off or get back up. There on his knees, he leaned forward until his brow was pressed against the wall. And he prayed.

Zaahir pulled a face. "But you also know that stopping him might compromise saving everyone else. And you want that more don't you. Dilemma, dilemma." I could've killed him.

The Abdal's hand started to glow a fierce red. The man's praying turned to screaming.

"Ah well," Zaahir said. "Too late to decide."

And then, just like that, the prisoner was ash.

"Now." The Sin Maker's voice had lost its mockery. He looked on, interested, even as I recoiled from the sight below. "That is a novelty."

I despised him in that moment. But I already knew there wasn't any easy way out of here. If there were, Shazad would've found it and they'd be free. There were so many Abdals and just me.

"So," Zaahir spoke up again. "These are the mortals you want to free. Very well." I felt the air change around us, like it was solidifying. Whatever Zaahir was doing, I couldn't stop him now. Watching the prisoners below, I saw a few of them realize that something was happening, though they didn't know what. They kept working, but some of them winced, as if they were waiting for something terrible to strike them, bowing their heads in anticipation of a blow.

It was as if the air became invisible hands. I could feel them plucking at my clothes. I could see the chains shifting down below. And then the invisible hands pulled apart the chains like they were nothing but thread.

The shackles fell away instantly, hitting the ground with an impossible clatter that filled the inside of the mountain. It was so loud I feared it would wake the Destroyer of Worlds.

Hundreds of prisoners stopped what they were doing as their shackles fell off, looking around, bewilderment overcoming fear. They stared down at their bare wrists, some of them dropping their tools.

"There," Zaahir said. "They're free. Just like you wanted. I would, however, suggest that they start running if you want them alive."

The Abdals had been staring on mutely. They were pale imitations of us, only as intelligent as they needed to be to accomplish simple mechanical tasks. They didn't understand that the humans had been released. But they did understand that they had stopped working. And they knew what to do when they stopped working.

As one, hundreds of pale metallic hands raised toward the prisoners, ready to obliterate them.

I felt my heart quicken in fear.

"Stop them!" I cried out to Zaahir, not caring about being heard now.

But he just looked on impassively. "You said you wanted to free them. They are free. Besides, death is its own sort of freedom. That's what my brethren dared say to me when they sent your First Hero to her death and locked me up."

"You know that's not what I want," I said frantically, staring over the ledge. Some of the prisoners were scrambling to get back to work. Others looked like they might make a run for it, an edge of panic visible on their faces. A few were raising their pickaxes like weapons, ready to fight, and certainly die. "I want to save them."

"I know what those creations of metal are," he said. "I recognize Fereshteh's soul scattered out among them. What is it that makes you think I would be powerful enough to conquer him when he was among those who imprisoned me?" He was seeing which one of us would blink first. He wasn't mortal. He didn't need to blink. I did.

He wasn't mortal . . . but I was. I wondered if I could get a dying wish.

The Abdals were getting closer now, raising their hands, the heat building. And I couldn't wait anymore. I could feel that I was about to do something stupid.

"If I die down here, then here's what I want: for you to stay imprisoned in Eremot until the end of time or until you're sorry for your treason. And I think we both know which will come first."

I jumped off the ledge, hitting the ground painfully hard. Faces turned toward me as I landed behind the Abdals, wondering at what they were seeing. I grabbed a pickaxe that had been discarded on the ground. I swung for an Abdal, striking it hard in the heel again and again until it stopped moving. I dropped back exhausted. Another Abdal was facing me, my annihilation ready on its hands. I couldn't take them all on. I knew that. But I raised the weapon all the same. And then suddenly, like a match coming to life in the dark, Zaahir appeared behind the Abdal.

He placed one hand on the top of its metallic head.

The Abdal dropped in the blink of an eye. It was like watching the spark of life leave him and be absorbed into

Zaahir, a small flame joining with a greater fire. He gave me a sly smile. And then he was gone again in a blink.

It happened too quickly to see. One by one in quick succession the Abdals dropped to the ground until, where there had been a wall of soldiers before, there was nothing but metal and clay corpses strewing the ground. And prisoners staring on in mute shock, trying to understand what was happening.

"Amani?"

The voice was so blessedly familiar that I almost dropped to my knees in relief just from hearing it. Like the burden of the Rebellion was being lifted from my shoulders and returned to his. I turned, to see Ahmed standing behind me. He looked nothing like a prince. He was wearing grubby, ill-fitting clothes, and iron cuffs with broken chains hung from his wrists. His face was stained with soot, and he looked like he hadn't seen a razor in weeks. No one would know him from a pauper on the street.

I dropped the pickaxe, and without thinking, I flung my arms around him, forgetting that he was my ruler. A prince when I was just a bandit. He was alive. And then he was embracing me back. His arms felt thin and weak. But they were there. He was alive. When he let me go, Delila was there, crying, tears streaking clean lines down her face blackened with dust, babbling incoherently. Rahim was behind her, looking at me like I'd just materialized from thin air, which I supposed I had, in a way. And there were others, too. So many other faces of rebels I knew well and prisoners I'd never seen before. And some missing faces, too.

I looked around for Navid, Imin's husband, who had lost his love to the execution block. For Lubna, a rebel who had lost both her children to the Gallan and used to make the best fresh bread back at camp. For Shazad.

"Where is she?" I was afraid of the answer before I was even done asking.

Ahmed's face darkened, and I felt my stomach twist. He didn't need to ask who I meant. "They sent her . . ." He stopped, gathering his thoughts, even as my heart sped up. "There was a small earthquake, three days ago. A gap opened in the ground, a small fissure, barely big enough to slip through but just wide enough for a small girl. There are soldiers camped outside here on the mountain. They're the ones who are giving orders to the Abdals, and who provide our rations. They threatened to withhold food until we told them what had happened inside the mountain. It was . . ." he glanced anxiously at his sister. Delila was looking at her feet. "It was Delila who was meant to be gathering provisions that day. She had to tell them truth. They ordered the Abdals to send Delila down into the opening to investigate. But Shazad took her place. The Abdals lowered her down into the mountain. And then"—my heart quickened—"the rope gave way. When they pulled it back up, it looked like it had been cut through by something. And Shazad . . ." He hesitated. "She didn't come back up."

TWENTY-FIVE

The fissure in the mountain swallowed the light hungrily as we peered down into it. The place where Shazad had fallen. It seemed like it might go down forever. Except I knew it didn't because . . .

"She's alive." I could breathe easier once I knew that. Once I said it out loud. She might be hurt down there. She was probably starving, since it had been three days, by Ahmed's skewed reckoning, without any dawns or dusks to gauge the time.

But at least she was alive.

I glanced at Zaahir. "I want to get her out of there."

But Zaahir was just staring incredulously down into the darkness. Finally he spoke. "Then I'd suggest you start climbing, daughter of Bahadur." He tossed me something, and I caught it midair without thinking. It was a tiny spark of fire. I almost dropped it before realizing it wasn't giving off any heat. It didn't burn my palms, just gave off light.

My first thought was that he was playing cruel games with me again, that this was some trick or negotiation. Then Zaahir took one staggering step backward, away from the gap in the ground. It was a startlingly mortal gesture. An awkward stumble, as if his body might be made of flesh and blood instead of fire. Like it might know real fear.

Fear of whatever was down there.

And I had the feeling that this time there wouldn't be any more negotiation. No way to get Zaahir any deeper into this mountain to save Shazad.

So I would start climbing.

I looped a rope around my waist the way I remembered Jin doing once. But my hands were clumsy and unused to it. Ahmed stepped forward. "Here," he said gently, as if he could read what I was thinking. That I wished Jin were here. Wished I hadn't left him behind.

"Thank you," I said, letting him tie the knots I didn't know. When he was done, he cast it over a hook hanging from the ceiling, grabbing the other end and holding on to it. Rahim took hold, too.

And then I lowered myself into the unknown.

The darkness was somehow different on the other side. In the mines there had been noise and heat, but here there was a stillness to the air. Like it was trying to swallow the light in my hand.

I descended slowly. The deeper I got, the more I felt like there was something watching me. Something breathing down my neck. I turned on the rope, dashing the light around the walls of the fissure. But there was nothing but stone.

Then suddenly I felt a tremor on the rope.

I reached out one hand to brace myself against the wall. But it was no good. The rope was still being fed in behind me. I was about to call up, to shout to Ahmed and Rahim to stop.

But suddenly it was as if a hand were covering my mouth. At the same moment I felt a brush of air on my neck. And then, without warning, I was falling.

The drop wasn't far, but I hit the ground with violent suddenness. The light in my hand didn't extinguish as I hit. I grabbed the end of the rope, tugging it to me. It looked like a clean cut, as if by a knife. Just like Ahmed had said happened to Shazad. This was not a snapped rope. This was something else.

There was a noise, as if from very far away, climbing up from the ground.

I was hearing things. I had to be. Or it was a drip of water. Or an echo of my own breathing. Except it didn't sound like that.

It sounded like someone laughing.

And it made me more afraid than anything I'd ever heard in my life.

Then the light in my hand dashed across a figure curled up on one side, dark hair falling across her face, and I forgot everything else. Even she looked like she wasn't wholly there in this darkness. I could only make out the dirty white of her shirt and the darkness of her hair.

"Shazad." I dropped next to her, relief rushing through me. I heard the sob in my own voice. She looked thinner, worn. And her eyes were shut. But she was breathing. I had to wake her up. "I'm sorry," I said to Shazad, leaning over her. I slapped her hard across the face. She came awake ready to fight—just not in any kind of state to. She flinched against the light. I'd never seen Shazad flinch at anything.

"You're not real." She shut her eyes. "You're not real. You're not real." She said it over and over again.

"Come on." I forced lightness into my voice. "You know I wouldn't lie to you."

"Prove it." Her voice rasped, and she tucked her head further into the crook of her arm.

"Will you believe I'm real if I can get us both out of here?"

Finally she opened her eyes, though they seemed unable to settle wholly on me, dancing unfocused across my face. "It would be a start."

I glanced up at the opening far above us. I couldn't see it through the inky blackness, but I knew we couldn't be that far away. I wasn't sure they would hear me if I shouted, though. And if they did and tossed us down more rope, what good would it be?

I only had one other idea. And it was an impossible

one. Even if it was our only hope. I silently prayed that I had enough of my Djinni gift left.

"Hang on to me," I urged Shazad. I closed my eyes, pouring all my concentration around me. There wasn't much in this mountain—I could already tell. In here, stone had been melted hard and the dust was made mostly of iron. The desert was far away.

But sand got everywhere. It came with me all the way from the desert, through the mountain, stuck to my skin and in the folds of my clothes. It came trapped in the hair of the other prisoners and on the metal soles of the Abdals' feet. There was no escaping it.

I took a slow, deep breath, fighting through the pain in my side. And I called it to me. All of it. Every single tiny grain of sand I could reach. I felt it start to shift above us, stirring and then scuttling toward me like hundreds of thousands of tiny insects moving across the cave floor.

It started to rain sand. Slowly at first, then more quickly, and suddenly sand was pouring in around us. I didn't stop. I was too afraid to take a moment to breathe through the pain, too afraid that if I let it go I would lose it.

I gathered the sand up below us. I tried to think of water, the way Sam and Jin swam, the way they were able to make water lift them up when it seemed to want to drown them instead. I gathered the sand, surging it up around us with everything I had in me.

I felt the sand shift, and I doubled over in pain, gasping. But I knew I couldn't let go, that if I did now, we would drown. I had to keep going. I had to. The sand poured in around us, lifting us higher and higher. I could see a sliver of light. I reached up, trying to grip the ledge, trying to find an escape from this place even as I felt the sand begin to drop away below me.

Hands were on my wrists and on Shazad's arms, pulling us out, and we collapsed on the ground. Solid ground.

I saw Shazad lying there, breathing hard, Rahim lifting her up even as Ahmed did the same for me. But she never looked away, her eyes locked on me, blinking blearily in the light.

"All right," she conceded, "you're real."

I started to laugh. But instead I burst into tears. And I was embracing her and we were both talking at once. Spilling out weeks of words we'd been saving for each other.

• ● ●

I WAS SO close to getting them to freedom. There were only two things standing between us and escape now: Ashra's Wall and, according to Ahmed and the others, the soldiers on the other side.

Shazad filled me in as she led the way out of the tunnels.

"There's a small army camp just beyond Ashra's Wall," she told me as we worked our way over unsteady ground. "That's where they control the Abdals from and keep an eye on things." She was walking slowly, breathing hard, like she was already tired from the short walk. "We're supposed to clear the debris of rocks that comes from hacking our way into a mountain, and empty them at the border of Ashra's wall where the soldiers can keep track of us. They'll be suspicious that no one has come out in a while."

"I reckon they'll be more than suspicious when everyone appears unchained," I said, casting around for Delila. She was walking with Ahmed and Rahim, both of them keeping a close eye on her. "Can Delila cover our escape?"

"I don't know." Shazad was nothing if not honest. She pulled herself up the slight incline, hanging on to the wall. "Everyone is a little worse for wear." She glanced over her shoulder. Zaahir was trailing far behind everyone else. "Your . . . new friend. He can help us, can't he?"

He could, if he was so inclined. But getting Zaahir to cooperate was easier said than done, no matter what he'd promised. I slowed my pace, letting the rest of the prisoners draw ahead of me, until I'd fallen into step with Zaahir.

"There are soldiers waiting on the other side of that wall. When we get through, I need—" I stopped myself, choosing my words more carefully. "I want you to get us past them."

Zaahir was watching me with those uncanny, inhuman eyes as I spoke. "I believe we had a deal, daughter of Bahadur: your people freed from Eremot for my freedom from you. Once all of them are through Ashra's Wall, our deal is done."

"I'm planning on keeping my side of the bargain. But our deal isn't done until they're safe." I could see a light up ahead. Daylight. We must be almost out of the mountains. Or maybe it was just the light of Ashra's Wall. But either way, we were close. "We're not done yet."

"Ah," Zaahir said, cocking his head in that curious way, looking at me. "I see. And even after you are past those soldiers, we will not be *done* yet, will we?" I didn't say anything. He wasn't wrong. After these soldiers on the mountain, there would be other fights to win. Other chances to lose everyone we had just saved. Fighting with a Djinni on our side . . . I wasn't sure I could pass that chance up. "You *want* more." Zaahir nodded knowingly. "I believe you call that *greed*, don't you? It's the downfall of many, from what I hear. We never wanted anything before your kind came to this world, you know. We just *had*. But you take and you still want. You want your prince to take the throne, don't you?" I did. And I had made him swear that he would do what I wanted. And I wanted his help in this. I *needed* Ahmed to sit on that throne. I had given up too much for us to lose. We all had.

"There is still a great battle ahead of you, isn't there?" Zaahir said. "One stray bullet, one blow, and your prince could be gone. And all this could be for nothing. Every single death. For nothing." Everything he was saying was everything I was afraid of. His words made me feel suddenly frantic. That we might have fought this hard but still lose Ahmed. That the whole of this rebellion rested on one very mortal man. "You want to save him. That is why you want to keep me imprisoned," Zaahir said. "Well, I can give you what you want."

Zaahir pulled a knife from the sleeve of his shirt, making me draw back quickly. But he didn't make a move to kill me. Instead he turned the knife over, extending the hilt to me. "Take it," he instructed.

"I already have a knife," I said carefully. We were getting closer to the light, headed for the soldiers waiting on the other side. I needed to play out this game with Zaahir before we reached them, even though I didn't understand it yet.

"Ah, but this is a knife that can save your prince's life." Suddenly the air itself seemed to close around my hand, leading my fingers to the hilt. "Use this knife to take the life of another prince, and I promise you that *your* prince will live through the battle to take the throne."

I would have dropped the knife instantly, except the air was still tightly wrapped around my hand, forcing it to clutch the blade. "A prince's life for a prince's life." Zaahir didn't laugh, but I could tell he was mocking me. A prince's life. He meant Rahim's or Jin's life. They were the only other princes here. "Or"—the air finally stopped gripping my fingers—"you can cast the knife down. And maybe he will live, or maybe he won't. It will be in the hands of fate," Zaahir said simply. "But I have never known fate to be all that kind, have you?" I hadn't, but I didn't reply.

In the space of a breath, he was standing in front of me instead of beside me, like a flame jumping from one roof to another in a burning city. I staggered to a stop. He was so close that I could see the violent color of his eyes as he hissed the next words at me. "It is a mistake to try to outwit me, daughter of Bahadur. I have been helping you thus far, but I can make things very hard if you don't release me right now, no matter what you made me promise. You have a confused heart, just like every human. You want too many things. I can turn those things against each other like animals in your chest. I can destroy you from the very inside of your soul." He drew away just as quickly as he'd descended on me.

I realized that everyone else ahead of us had stopped, too. We'd reached the mouth of the tunnel. Shazad had paused by the entrance, holding everyone back. But Zaahir didn't stop walking. The former prisoners moved out of his way as he strode forward. I trailed behind him. Shazad looked at me expectantly as I drew level with her. I didn't have an easy answer to give her. I didn't know what Zaahir was up to. He moved past her, out into the open. And I followed.

Ashra's Wall stood a hundred feet or so from the mouth of the tunnel. And just beyond that, through the shifting light of the wall, I could see the soldiers. There were lines of military tents along the slope of the mountain, supplies stacked between them, and soldiers milling around. But more importantly, I saw the glint of sunlight against metal heads.

Abdals. They had more of them outside the wall. Soldiers, we could fool. Hell, our numbers were good enough that we might even be able to take them in a fight. But not Abdals.

"Zaahir, wait." I could feel my breathing coming ragged now.

He came to a stop, right by Ashra's Wall. "Freedom for freedom, daughter of Bahadur. You made a promise." And then his arm lashed out violently toward Ashra's Wall. But when his hand met it, he didn't burn.

Instead, the barrier of light shattered.

It reminded me of the glass dome over the Sultan's chambers, breaking apart into stars. Except these didn't fall to the ground. Again, Zaahir seemed to draw the light into himself, like a hungry fire swallowing kindling. It was like watching what he had done with the Abdals, only a thousand times greater.

And then, just like that, Ashra's Wall was gone. No, more than gone. Ashra was dead. That was what he had done. That was how he had granted us our freedom from Eremot. He'd destroyed the soul that had been protecting the entire world from what was inside that mountain.

And now we were left exposed, as from the other side of where the wall had been, a dozen startled soldiers' faces turned in our direction. And a dozen more blank Abdal faces stared at us.

And then they raised their hands.

TWENTY-SIX

I dove back toward the shelter of the tunnel even as a wave of heat and fire poured out of the Abdals, flooding in behind me as people screamed and retreated back into the mountain.

Shazad grabbed me, yanking me in as I searched for my Demdji power, dragging on any dust I could find, trying to shore up the mouth of the tunnel. But whatever strength I'd had I'd used saving Shazad, and my power seemed to slip away, tumbling useless out of my grasp, abandoning me.

Out of the corner of my eye, I saw one person burn, turning to dust before the fire abated as quickly as it had come, leaving my skin feeling raw from the heat and my lungs scorched.

"We should retreat," Shazad said, breathless. Behind us, Rahim and Ahmed were trying to return some order to the panicking people in the tunnel. The rebels who had seen Abdals before were more levelheaded, but the other newly freed prisoners had never faced anything like this. They were running for anywhere that might be shelter, back into Eremot.

My mind tripped over itself looking for a way through this. We had a few hundred recently freed prisoners in no shape for fighting, a Djinni who had turned our little game on its head, and two worn-out Demdji.

Outside, I could hear the metallic steps of the Abdals moving toward the mouth of the tunnel. Coming to finish us off, forcing us back into the dark of Eremot where they would pick us off easily.

I traded a look with Shazad and saw the same naked fear on her face. That was when I knew we were in trouble. I'd never seen Shazad run out of ideas before. We were done for. I had gotten everyone this far only to lose them on the edge of freedom.

And then the metallic footsteps stopped.

I stilled, feeling my heart's panicked timpani in my chest. I could almost hear it now in the sudden silence. And then, a voice from outside, too distant to make out any words. A voice I knew, though it took me a second to place it.

Noorsham.

I was moving before Shazad could stop me, rushing back toward the mouth of the tunnel. I burst out into open air. Zaahir was nowhere to be seen. But there, standing behind the Abdals and the Sultan's soldiers, was Noorsham. Farther behind him I could make out Jin, Sam, Tamid, and the twins.

How the hell had they found me?

Ahmed's compass. My hand drifted to my side, feeling the weight still there. I'd forgotten. It was still in my pocket. I should've known better than to think Jin would just wait patiently for me to return. He'd tracked me down once from Sazi, a long time ago. And now he'd done it again. Relief and fear warred inside me. Even if this was the end, at least we were back together. Either we all survived or we all died here.

Noorsham looked terribly vulnerable next to the army of Abdals. He wasn't clad in bronze armor like they were. He was wearing nothing but simple desert clothes, standing with his hands extended as he had yesterday over the people of Sazi. And he wasn't wearing the iron shackles I'd put on him either. His power was running free.

I understood what he was about to do a second before the Abdals turned to face him, summoning their own fire against his.

"No!" The scream tore out of my throat. But I was too late. Noorsham's power swelled to meet that of the Abdals even as they flooded the mountain. Man-made stolen Djinni fire rushing to meet Noorsham's Demdji-given gift of destruction. I ran toward him, knowing there was nothing I could do. No way to stop what was going to happen.

It was as if a new sun were being born.

The explosion bloomed bright and violent, invading everything, even the air around it. It slammed into me like a javelin of heat and light, knocking me down, blinding me. But I could still smell the burning. I could taste blood. Then, I tasted ash.

● ● ●

I WOKE VIOLENTLY out of unconsciousness. I couldn't have been out long. My ears were still ringing with the aftershock of the explosion, my lungs burning. I pushed myself up agonizingly. The pain was nothing, though, compared to the heat still rising from my skin. Even my Demdji side was struggling to fight off this heat. But I found my way to my feet all the same.

The battlefield of fire had turned dark and cold.

The soldiers, who had been flesh and blood, were nothing but dust now. There was no sign of their tents or any of the camp they had built here. All of it had been razed. But there were pieces of Abdals left in the wreckage. The bronze had fused to the stones, like shiny scars on the mountain. I saw a bronze face, some of its features still intact, its nose protruding away from the stone, its mouth twisted by the heat into some grotesque scream.

I half staggered, half ran across the remnants of the brief and bloodless fight to the one body that was not metal or ash, where Noorsham was sprawled amid the destruction he had made.

I dropped to my knees next to him. His chest was rising and falling with shallow breathing. He was badly burned, half his face blackened and unrecognizable. We were Demdji; we weren't supposed to burn so easily. But this was Djinni fire, and we were only half-Djinn. Our other halves were terribly mortal.

He didn't look anything like the weapon I'd first come face-to-face with on that train. Or like the man leading all the people in his cult toward righteousness. He just looked like a desert boy, young and helpless and dying. Eyes like the sky stared up at me, wide and scared, like he couldn't understand what was happening. Like he wanted me to explain, to comfort him. Like he needed a sister.

"What are you doing here?" My lips were blistered, and my fingertips burned against the heat of his skin as I cradled him. I ought to be screaming. I remembered after Imin had died, Hala's grief had all come out in one strangled cry that filled the Hidden House. That had been the last noise she'd made before she hadn't spoken for days.

"We came to save you," his voice rasped out, his one good eye struggling to find me.

Even after I had betrayed him. After we had chained him up. After Jin had undoubtedly dragged him up this mountain as a prisoner. After all that, still, Noorsham had chosen to save us.

"Well, that was stupid." I wanted to put my hand against his heart to make it keep beating by sheer will alone, but it was pumping too slow already.

I couldn't take this. Not another Demdji burning out so young, like Hala and Imin and Hawa and Ashra. Not my brother falling now in a fight that wasn't his when he had survived so much.

A shadow fell across his face. I looked up, expecting to find Jin or Shazad or someone who could help me. Instead, Zaahir stood over me, watching me with cruel impassiveness. I wanted to scream at him that this was not fair. But Djinn didn't deal in fair. They dealt in trades and wants and desires. And the Sin Maker wanted one thing.

"Save him," I said. "You made a promise to me to do what I want, and I want to save him. Do that and we'll end this. I'll set you free. Please."

Zaahir watched Noorsham struggle for a moment longer, his breathing coming out ragged from his scorched lungs, each breath counting down to his last. "His body is too broken," he said. "I cannot repair this."

"I don't care." The sob that tore out of me came from the oldest part of me, the part of my soul that was immortal, that used not to know death. The part that understood what the First Beings had felt when they watched the first of their number die and become stars and meet their own end, when grief and despair and rage and hopelessness were all born in a single moment. "I want to save him. Save him and I'll free you. Save him and we'll end this here. Please. I'm begging you. Save him and I'll release you."

Finally Zaahir inclined his head ever so slightly. He didn't look as pitiless as he had a moment ago. He knew what it was like to lose someone when you weren't ready to. "We have a deal, daughter of Bahadur."

The sun glared down on us from high above. Zaahir pushed me back from my brother without touching me. It was as if the air clasped me gently by the shoulders, drawing me away. Like a kindly relative pulling me from a sickbed so a Holy Man could work. So I didn't have to see the worst of it.

He lifted Noorsham the same way, without touching him. I stuffed the protest down my throat that he was hurting him. That he was too weak to survive being moved.

And then . . . it was as if his body simply fell away, disappearing into the air like sand scattering on the wind, leaving Noorsham there, but instead of flesh and blood and bone, he was made of light. Like Ashra's Wall.

The rabble of prisoners parted as Zaahir moved forward, Noorsham's body floating ahead of him.

I wanted to save him. I wanted him to live. I had asked Zaahir for it. But he hadn't promised me what kind of life Noorsham would have.

And there was another power at work here. Noorsham's mother had wished that her Demdji son would do something great. Our father had granted it. And Noorsham believed he would, in the name of God.

I didn't know if there was a God. But I knew that there were monsters. And he could protect us from those.

All eyes turned as Noorsham's glowing form reached the same place where Ashra's soul had stood as a wall for thousands of years, his body shifting, seeming to grow. As I watched, Noorsham seemed to turn toward the mountain and wrap his arms around it before all sense of his body disappeared, transforming into a burning wall of light instead.

He stood where Ashra had, relieving her watch finally after thousands of years. Shielding us from the evil that lived inside. Here he would get what he had wanted. He would save far more people than he had ever killed.

And his mother would get what she had wished for. Greatness.

TWENTY-SEVEN

I woke to a setting sun and the feeling of movement below me. I blinked blearily, feeling like I was coming back to life.

"She lives," a familiar, rueful voice said quietly in my ear. I tilted my head back. Jin was behind me. I was settled against his chest, his arm around my middle steadying me. We were on a horse, I realized. A blue one. Izz. And around us, walking at a slow but steady pace, were our people. We were making our way down the mountain, by the look of things. "You passed out," Jin said from behind me. I felt his hand slip away from me momentarily, and then he was pressing a flask of water into my hands. I gulped from it gratefully.

Everything was a blur after I released Zaahir.

In the stories, Djinn appeared and vanished in great claps of thunder and smoke. But the truth was, when I released Zaahir, he was just there one moment and gone the next. It was like waking up from a dream. And all that was left was destruction.

The last thing I remembered was Jin finding me, sitting among the ashes, and gathering me to him. And then nothing.

"Tamid says you must've hit your head when you got knocked down," Jin was saying. When he spoke, I could feel the vibrations through his chest and into my spine. "Hence you passed out. But we had to keep moving. So we moved you."

We, he said. As if it was the most casual thing in the world. But it wasn't. We meant all of us now. Because we'd done it. We'd gotten everyone out.

The realization settled over me as I looked around, seeing faces in the light of day. Shazad was walking a few paces ahead, Sam next to her, talking at the rattling speed of a runaway train. I couldn't hear what he was saying, but every once in a while, a small smile danced over her face. To one side of us, Tamid was limping painstakingly down the mountain, eyes on the path to keep from tripping, sometimes leaning on Delila for help. Or maybe she was leaning on him, it was hard to tell. Ahmed led the way up ahead, Rahim next to him, the rabble of former prisoners dragging themselves to safety in his wake. We were a sorry collection: wounded, burned, half-starved, bedraggled, exhausted.

But free. We had done it. The impossible. We'd left Eremot alive.

"Where are we?" I asked. My voice came out raspy.

"Nearly at Sazi," Jin said. He nodded upward, and I noticed a small bird swooping in circles over our heads. Maz, I realized, our scout.

A sudden panic gripped my chest. We needed to slow down. We needed to be careful.

"I can walk," I said hastily. "Izz, stop." Our blue Demdji did as I said, and I swung one leg over him, sliding off his back. Jin followed close behind, steadying me as I hit the ground, head swimming.

I pushed through the tired mass of rebels and released prisoners. I needed to talk to Ahmed. We couldn't just barge into Sazi like this. But it was too late. As I broke through to the front of the pack, I saw the outskirts of Sazi. People were already gathering at the bottom of the slope, staring up at us expectantly. But I knew they weren't waiting for us. They were waiting for Noorsham.

"Where is he?" someone called out from the assembled crowd as we got closer. "What have you done with him?"

Ahmed's brow furrowed as he turned to me. "What are they talking about?" But I didn't answer Ahmed. I called out to the crowd instead.

"He's . . ." *Dead* stuck on my tongue as we drew to a stop a few paces away. That wasn't true. He wasn't dead. He wasn't alive, either.

"Noorsham is not coming back."

A rustle went through the crowd around us as this news settled. I shifted nervously; it wouldn't take long for it to turn to anger. "You killed him," an accusation came from a skinny woman at the front of the crowd.

"No," I protested, shaking my head, scrambling for the right words. Shazad pressed through to the front now to stand beside me. I could feel the tension building in her like it did before a fight.

"Liar!" another cry came up angrily from the back. The rest of the crowd was shifting uncertainly, but I didn't think it would be long before they turned against us.

"She's not lying," Tamid said, but his voice was drowned out by the shouting.

"Well." Sam came up behind me. "This doesn't look good."

Emboldened by the mob forming at his back, a man stepped toward me. Shazad might be weak, but she still moved faster than most, and she was between us in a second. "Try it," she challenged.

The man took another step, seeming like he did indeed fully intend to try to take us on. I felt drained. Too drained to fight. But we didn't have a choice. Ahmed had led us back here when we should've steered clear. And now we had a mob facing us. I had seen what they were capable of when they had forced us to confront the Eye. We might match them in numbers, but we were a sorry collection of bedraggled prisoners, and they were an angry mass of devotees.

Behind the belligerent man, a woman picked up a stone from the ground, preparing to throw it.

Then, just as the last of the sunlight started to fade, a light bloomed from the mountain face. Right between Shazad and the first man who had challenged us, the air turned itself inside out, changing the darkness into dozens of colors. And then it spread, in the open space between the belligerent inhabitants of Sazi and our people, forming into a collection of bronze soldiers facing a fiery wall. An illusion in miniature of what had awaited us outside Eremot.

The woman staggered back, dropping the stone from her hand as tiny Abdals blossomed around her feet like flowers. And Delila stepped forward, out of the crowd.

"She's not lying." Delila spoke softly, but that didn't keep her from being heard. Not when she was conjuring images from thin air. "He wasn't killed. He walked into the arms of death like a hero." Even as she spoke, a small figure of Noorsham materialized out of thin air and started to advance.

Delila's voice was gentle and melodic. It always had been. It was what made everyone think she was so fragile, that she needed to be protected. But it was a good voice for stories, too. She held the attention of the the crowd easily as her words and her illusions worked together to tell the tale. She chose her words carefully, stopping and pausing at the right moments. Delila, who had been the subject of so many stories, about the Sultan's unfaithful wife and the Rebel Prince's return, now telling one for herself. Her voice cracked as it got to the end, as Noorsham's soul evanesced from his body, taking the place of Ashra's Wall.

"So you see"—Delila's illusions melted away as she finished—"he can't come back."

Darkness and silence followed those words for a long moment. As the spell of her words slowly began to drop away.

Then a man fell to his knees. Another one dropped down behind him, and then another and another, until in the space of a few moments every single one of Noorsham's people was kneeling before Delila.

She had done it. Delila had saved us. And she'd done it without a single weapon. I'd forgotten how powerful a story could be.

Suddenly, from the middle of the crowd, a boy stood back up abruptly. I knew him, I realized. He was from Dustwalk. His name was Samir, and he was a year or so younger than I was. My hand strayed for a gun that wasn't there. But he made no move to fight.

"Are you really the Rebel Prince?" he asked.

All eyes turned to Ahmed. "I am."

"I could fight for you," the boy declared loudly. "Against the Sultan. He killed our leader. He drove us from our homes." A murmur of ascent went through the crowd. "I would fight for you."

"I would fight for you, too." Another man stood up, this one older, more hardened. "If our leader was willing to die for you, so am I."

"So would I." It was a girl who stood up now, sweeping short dark hair behind her ears, speaking a little more quietly than the men.

"And so would I." I knew that voice. It was Olia, my

cousin who was nearest to me in age now that Shira was gone. If there was ever someone I didn't think cared about a damn thing enough to fight for it, it was her. But then, Hala had been that way, too. So had I, once. I noticed Olia's mother, my uncle's second wife, grab for her arm, as if to pull her back. But Olia jerked her arm out of her mother's reach, standing tall as others rose around her, declaring their allegiance.

Delila had done a whole lot more than save us. She had rallied for us.

All eyes were on Ahmed when I noticed Shazad moving slowly away from the front of the group, melting away from all this.

Sam saw her, too. He gave me a raised brow as we caught each other's eye. I shook my head quickly. *Stay,* that gesture told him, as I slipped away behind her.

For once he did as he was told.

● ● ●

"SHAZAD." I DIDN'T call out to her until we were out of earshot of the others. Ahead of me, on the slope of the mountain, Shazad started, almost losing her footing. I'd never encountered anything quick enough or quiet enough to startle her.

"Sorry," she said when she realized it was me. "I had to go. I couldn't breathe." She dropped down to sit on the slope of the mountain. "I needed to . . ." She trailed off. Not sure what she needed. I wasn't either.

"Do you want me to go?" I hovered uncertainly.

"No," she said. "I don't want to be—" She cut herself off, laughing ruefully. "I wasn't afraid of the dark when I was young."

"We're still young," I said, dropping down next to her. She'd been alone in the dark for three days. That'd be enough to make a lot of people worse than afraid.

"So are they," she said. Her face shifted in and out of the gloom of early night, like she was slipping away, and I was struggling to hold on to her here and now. "We're going to get some of them killed, you know." I did know. But saying it out loud would make it true and I didn't want that.

"I sent Imin to die," she said, after a long moment of silence. I stayed quiet. Though I'd figured it had been Shazad who had come up with the plan to send Imin to die in Ahmed's place. She was the strategist. She was the one who made the hardest choices for us. "Which means I killed Navid, too." That one caught me off guard. I suddenly realized that I hadn't seen Navid as we fled Eremot. But there were plenty I hadn't seen. "He dropped dead in the prison below the palace. Just stopped breathing. As the sun set."

"When Imin's head was taken off," I realized. They'd made a vow when they'd married: *My life is yours to share. Until the day we die.* An oath made by a Demdji was a dangerous thing. Lord Bilal had counted on it to save his life. But it had robbed Navid's of his.

"I thought I was going to die down there. And I saw them both, over and over again. Waiting for me."

I didn't think Shazad had been alone in the dark. I didn't think those images were just guilt. But just now I didn't think telling her that would help. "I killed Hala," I offered instead, my voice cracking. Shazad's head darted up as she took in my words. Not that I had let Hala die, or sent her to her death. I had taken her life.

"How did it happen?" she asked after a moment. She sounded more measured, more like herself. Like a general absorbing every detail of this latest casualty.

"The Sultan. I had to either kill her or let him have her . . ." I trailed off. "I did what I had to do. Because it was what you would've done."

We fell silent, sitting side by side on the mountain, the rustle of the camp far below drifting up to us on the air, mourning those we had lost: Hala, Navid, Imin, Shira, Bahi, and more I couldn't count. Mourning that not everyone down below with us in Sazi tonight would live to see Ahmed sit on the throne—if he ever did.

Me among them.

"Tamid said . . ." I started, then hesitated. I had to tell someone. Nobody knew about what Tamid had told me back in the Hidden House. It hadn't mattered until today. Until Tamid had read the words painted above the doorway that led to Zaahir. The same words he had been searching for high and low, the ones that could release what was left of Fereshteh into death from the confines of the machine and give us a fighting chance against the Sultan. "Tamid reckons there's a good chance that I'll die if I release Fereshteh." Shazad's head snapped up. "But if someone doesn't deactivate the machine, then we have to face the Abdals. And no matter how many people stand up to fight with us I don't think we stand much of a fighting chance against them."

Shazad pressed her hand against her mouth as she considered this. "Have you told him yet?"

She meant Jin. Not Ahmed. We both knew without saying it that I couldn't tell Ahmed. He would try to find a way out of this for me. But I wasn't sure I had it in me to tell Jin either. I was telling Shazad because I knew she understood. She would fight for me as long as she could, and she would mourn me if she could not win. But she wouldn't try to stop me. Because she would do the same.

I remembered, way back at the beginning, on a runaway train, holding her hand, keeping her from slipping onto the tracks and dying. Her telling me to let her go, just like Hala had in the Sultan's grip. For the greater good. She'd never been afraid. I thought of what Sam had said back at the White Fish—that anyone who wasn't frightened of dying was stupid or lying. I knew I couldn't be the second. I didn't like to think I was the first. But what would I be if I asked others to die for this cause but wasn't willing to give myself up to it?

"But I'll tell you what," I said. "If I die, we sure as hell better win this war."

Shazad let out a short, honest laugh as she pushed herself to her feet. "Well then, I guess we'd better do something about our new recruits," she said, offering a hand down for me. I clasped it.

As she pulled me to my feet, I felt something knocking against my hip. When I glanced down I knew what it was, even in the barest flash of moonlight on metal. It was the knife Zaahir had given me. Somehow it had made it out of Eremot, tucked into my belt.

And I realized, with a sinking sense of dread, that I had a way to win this war hanging at my hip. One simple way to make sure that my death was worthwhile.

All I had to do was kill a prince.

TWENTY-EIGHT

The next day was a new dawn.

We didn't talk about the things that had been said in the dark the night before. We had a war to win now.

Shazad and Rahim took stock of the weapons surrendered on entry to the camp. There were enough to arm everyone, if we stretched things. Jin and Sam and I reclaimed our own guns. Nobody seemed to notice that I had a knife at my side that hadn't come from the stash of weapons.

"Who already knows how to shoot?" Shazad asked the new recruits lined up haphazardly in front of her. Most hands went up. That wasn't surprising—this was the Last County. When you made guns, you tended to know how to use them. "What about hand to hand?"

Hands dropped, and I saw Samir lean in toward his neighbor, saying something under his breath, a smirk on his face. "Something to say?" Shazad asked, never missing a thing.

I had a feeling he was wondering why he was listening to a woman when he'd pledged his allegiance to a prince. I could see that question on a few faces around us. Samir spoke up. "I was saying that it's not much good having a knife when you've got a gun pointed at you."

"Have you ever seen the streets of Izman?" Shazad didn't wait for an answer. "They're narrow enough that half the time you can't walk two abreast, let alone turn around quickly enough to get a shot off before your opponent is on top of you. *That* is when you need to be able to fight man to man."

"So how does a woman know how to fight man to man?" another boy sniggered, loud enough so that he was heard.

Shazad's eyebrows went up. I stepped back.

"I'll tell you what," Shazad turned toward him. "Why don't you come and face me? Anyone who can land a blow can take over this training." A small audience was gathering by now. Everyone who'd ever seen Shazad fight knew exactly where this was going. The rebels were elbowing one another slyly as the boy stepped forward, looking all too confident.

"Doesn't seem like a fair fight to me," the boy said, too lightly. The boy was at least twice Shazad's weight, broad where she was slim—slimmer still, after her time in Eremot.

"It's not even close to a fair fight," Jin commented from the sidelines. We'd all formed a circle now, watching.

"Oh, my friend." Sam clapped the boy on his back. "I'm so sorry for your loss."

"My loss?" The young idiot said.

"Of your dignity." He gave him a rueful smile before stepping back to stand next to me.

The challenger lunged at our general, all ungainly fists and brute force. Shazad moved like a blade through water, going for his clumsy legs. She danced under his fists easily, her foot catching him in the ankle. And just like that he was on the ground and she was on top of him with a knife at his throat. The fight had lasted less than three seconds.

"And now you're dead," Shazad said.

"That's not fair," he wheezed, fighting for breath against the knee pressed into his chest. I got the feeling she was pressing a little harder than she strictly needed to. Pressing a point home.

"You're the one who said it wouldn't be a fair fight." Shazad got to her feet, sheathing the knife. The boy stumbled to his feet as well. I realized he was going to lunge for her again a second too late to shout a warning. But Shazad didn't need one. She grabbed his hand as it closed on her shoulder, dropping to her knees, tipping him off balance as she went down. His own anger worked against him as he tumbled over her body and onto his back, slamming down hard again.

"Besides, war isn't fair." Shazad turned away, leaving

him coughing in the dust. "But if you want to see a bit more of an even fight . . ." She glanced around the circle, eyes finally landing on Jin. She summoned him forward with a nod. He stepped into the makeshift arena with her, pulling off his shirt as he went. Across from me, among the line of new recruits, I saw one of the few girls who'd stood up to fight for Ahmed dash her eyes down to her feet, embarrassed, before looking back up quickly, eyebrows traveling up her forehead. Jin looked impressive enough with his shirt on, but without it, he was a wall of bare, lean muscles and tattoos against Shazad's smaller frame. He rolled his shoulder, making his compass tattoo shift across his skin.

I stuck my fingers in my mouth, letting out a high whistle. Jin laughed, casting me a wink over his shoulder. I couldn't remember the last time things had been so easy between all of us, the last time we'd been together like this. Not fighting for our lives, just living.

"If they kill each other"—Sam slid into the space Jin had left next to me—"does it mean you and I can finally stop these games and be together?"

Neither Shazad nor Jin moved straightaway, both eyeing each other at a safe distance. I'd seen them fight separately, but never one another. They'd trained Ahmed together, I remembered. Back before the Sultim trials, when he'd faced Kadir. They knew each other's fighting styles. Neither one of them was going to strike in haste.

Shazad moved first, a straight lunge through Jin's defenses. He slammed an arm hard into hers, forearm deflecting as he aimed a blow for her side even as she twisted away from him. Breaking apart before they clashed together again. Before even catching her breath, Shazad aimed for Jin's jaw, while he ducked out of the way, gaining a brief advantage as he dodged to her left before she dropped and rolled away from the blow that came her way.

They fought like a blur. She was quicker. He was stronger.

In the end, it happened so fast I almost missed it. Shazad snaked behind Jin, ducking under an arm as he swung, his knife suddenly out at his throat. Plucked from his belt without him ever noticing it was going.

Without thinking, my hand danced to Zaahir's knife at my own side, the levity suddenly leaving me.

But Jin laughed as Shazad released him, tossing his blade back to him. "Anyone else?" Shazad asked, spreading her arms wide. Nobody stepped forward. Whatever else it might take to train our new recruits, I didn't think Shazad would have to worry about them following her lead.

"Blue-Eyed Bandit," Samir called, eyes sparkling in the way of someone who didn't really understand that fighting meant blood. Meant death, not adventure. "Are you going to fight her?"

"Now *that* wouldn't be a fair fight," Shazad said.

"No," I agreed, and when Shazad turned around, she was staring down the barrel of my gun. I winked at my friend. "It wouldn't."

Shazad pulled something out of her pocket: an orange,

harvested that morning from the chest buried in the mountain. She tossed it up in the air, a high arc. I tracked the thing with the barrel of my gun all the way to its highest point. And right before it began its descent, I fired.

The orange fell to the ground, a mess of pulp and shredded rind.

"Now," Shazad said, turning back around to the recruits, "let's start again. Who thinks that they can shoot like Amani?"

• • •

"WILL THEY BE ready by the time we reach Izman?" Ahmed asked that evening. Shazad had run everyone ragged before she finally released them to go to the prayers that Tamid was leading at sunset.

Tamid stood where, just a few days past, I'd seen my brother bless the gathered men and women. He led them in prayer for Noorsham's soul, long may it defend us. And for the safety of those who had stood up to fight with Ahmed.

It was strange watching him; he seemed at home. Like standing in front of our people, our families, was where he had always been destined to be. I'd thought we were both too crooked to fit in this place. But he belonged here in a way I never had. Or never wanted to.

I belonged with the Rebellion.

Instead of going to prayers, the Rebellion gathered in a small tent propped up against one of the few remaining walls of what used to be Sazi. The last of the daylight filtered red through the tent casting a flame-like glow across our faces.

With all of us here, it was like a faraway echo of something familiar. Of our old camp and all the times we'd gathered like this to make a plan. Except now, everyone looked like shadows of themselves. Ahmed, Shazad, and Delila were worn ragged. Smudged with pain and exhaustion, and something else, too: the firsthand knowledge of the suffering the Sultan was putting this country through. Of what one man could do to all of us from on high. Of what it would mean for those who lived if we lost this war, those we left behind under the rule of a man who had sent hordes of people to Eremot.

We were like a faded picture in a book that had lost a lot of its gilt.

"Do you think we should take the new recruits with us?" Ahmed asked.

"I don't think we can afford to turn away any extra able bodies," Shazad said.

"Even if they're extra bodies to feed and supply?" I could hear the question Ahmed was really asking: *Even if we might just be leading them to their deaths?*

Our general cast a fleeting glance my way before she carried on quickly. "Assuming we can shut that machine down then this is a fight that's going to be won on numbers."

"Hell, we might need them before we get into Iliaz. What with the new foreign friends Bilal has been making."

It slipped out irritably, though I hadn't meant it to. Rahim and Ahmed both looked at me blankly. They hadn't been gone all that long, but a whole lot of Miraji had changed in that time. I'd been leading this rebellion, and now I had to give that power back to Ahmed. I'd thought it would be a relief. I guess I'd gotten a little used to the weight while he'd been gone.

"Things have changed while you've been in Eremot. And you know, it might not kill you from time to time to talk to someone who knows about this desert." The words were coming out in a torrent now, my accent getting thicker as I went.

"For one, I reckon I could've told you how the people here would react to us returning without Noorsham. We might've spared Delila needing to save all our necks. And another thing I can tell you is that Iliaz is crawling with Albish. They're looking to make an alliance with the Gallan and move on Izman together. And the way I see it, if two of our enemies turn on us at once, we're done for. Whether we can take that throne or not. We won't hold it."

Ahmed listened to me, pressing a knuckle against a spot at his hairline as I told them what they had missed. That to get to Izman we would have to get through Leyla's inventions and our foreign enemies. That Iliaz was occupied. I pointed at Rahim. "Your Lord Bilal is helping, too, giving them passage through the mountains, and if we don't get this right, we're going to find ourselves facing more enemies than we can handle before we even see the city."

"My men are following orders," Rahim said defensively. "They're not traitors to their country."

"We're all traitors to our country," Jin pointed out. He was sitting with one knee propped up, his arm slung lazily over it, but his focus wasn't to be mistaken. He didn't trust Rahim. Not even if Ahmed and Delila were treating him as their brother. Not even if he was Jin's brother, too. "We need them to be traitors for *us*. What happens if they're not as loyal to you as you think they are?"

"Why don't we worry about that when we get there?" I interjected, breaking up this fight before it could start. "How the hell *are* we going to get there."

"We use one of our new friends from Eremot," Shazad said, without missing a beat. "Haytham Al-Fawzi. He is— was—the Emir of Tiamat before he started sheltering rebel sympathizers and wound up jailed for it. His brother is ruling in Tiamat now, but the city belongs to him, rightfully. I reckon we can take it back."

"And it's a seaport," Jin completed, understanding. "You want to sail to Iliaz from Tiamat."

"It will be easier than traveling north on foot," Ahmed said, trying to make peace. "We can dock in Ghasab and get to Iliaz from there."

"I'm not so sure I want to go back to Iliaz," Sam interjected, making sure Shazad heard what he was saying. And how could she not—we were all cramped so close together in here that our knees were touching. "What with how I almost died there." He puffed out his chest a little.

"Half the people here have almost died in Iliaz," Rahim informed him tersely.

"Amani only almost died because *you* shot her," Jin interjected, making Sam snort under his breath. I glanced around the circle, catching Shazad's eye roll as I did. But she wasn't who I'd been looking for. I realized that without meaning to, I'd been seeking out Hala. Expecting her to interject with something that would cut the bickering boys down to size.

"The only people who aren't coming to Iliaz are people who are behaving like children," Shazad snapped. "Because I don't train children in my armies." A quick silence fell over the tent as Shazad took control. "Now, here's what we're going to do."

TWENTY-NINE

The city of Tiamat never stood a chance.

It took us almost two weeks of walking to get to the sea. It would've taken half that time if we hadn't stopped quite so often.

When the Rebellion was somewhere near recovered from Eremot, we finally made ready to move. We packed as much as we could carry, as much as Sazi could spare, splitting it between the twins and the people who were on foot.

Finally we were as ready to leave as we were ever going to be.

But not all of us were leaving.

Tamid decided to stay behind. I'd known he wouldn't be coming with us, but it was unsettling to walk away without him all the same.

"You could still come back with us, you know," I said on the morning we prepared to leave. "We could use someone to patch us up on the road." He was good at what he did. I'd watched him bandage Rahim's bloody nose a few days past, when Jin had hit him in the face as they were demonstrating something to our new recruits. Ten days in Sazi and those two weren't getting along any better.

"I belong here, Amani." Tamid leaned heavily on his false leg on the unsteady ground of the mountain face. "I always have." I could tell his mind was elsewhere. "You don't have to do this, you know," he said finally. "Go back there and—" *Die*. He couldn't bring himself to say the word. "If you stayed—"

"I have to go, Tamid," I cut him off. "I belong with them." I offered him a wan smile to take the sting out off the words. "I always have."

He nodded. And I knew he understood without really understanding. The same way I understood he had to stay here even if I'd never really understand why he wanted to. So we just stood in silence on the mountain. Waiting until the moment our paths would take us far apart. Probably forever. It was early morning, and it was colder up here. A small shiver went through me. To my surprise, Tamid reached out and put his arms around me awkwardly. My onetime friend. If I was going to die in Izman, it was nice to know that we'd forgiven each other at least.

We all said our good-byes. Some eyes filled with tears as families bid farewell to the men and women who had joined us. There were about three dozen of them in the end, adding to the hundred or so we'd rescued from the mines. A few of the people who had come out of Eremot had decided not to go any farther with the Rebellion. They were too broken by the prison to fight any more fights.

"Amani." Aunt Farrah stopped me as we turned to head down the mountain. I tensed. Whatever she had to say to me, she'd waited until the absolute last minute. Which couldn't mean anything good. Shazad noticed and stopped next to me, like she was standing guard at my back. I was grateful for her. But Aunt Farrah's face wasn't full of venom this time. "Shira"—I heard the pain it took her to say her dead daughter's name—"she had a son?"

"She did." I nervously adjusted the strap on the pack of supplies I was carrying. Aunt Farrah was more family to Fadi than the Rebellion was; she was his grandmother. She had more right to raise him than we did. But he was a Demdji, too. I couldn't just hand him over to be raised here like I had been, ignorant of what I was. Like Noorsham had been, a bomb of sheer power waiting to explode. If she asked me for her only daughter's child and I had to refuse her . . . well, then I might just be leaving her on even worse terms than I did last time. But still, I couldn't stop myself from adding, "She named him Fadi. After her—our grandfather. Your father."

"If you—" Aunt Farrah started, and then she bit off her own words, like she was struggling to get them out. "I'd like to meet my grandson someday, Amani . . . if that's possible."

I waited, but there was no threat, no demand, no belittling of me to get what she wanted. I hesitated before replying.

"I don't know—" *if I trust you with him.* "I don't know how things are going to turn out here. We're at war." *Chances are I'm not going to be alive to bring him to meet you.*

Aunt Farrah nodded stiffly. "I know. But will you try?"

That I could give her. That was a promise I could keep. "I'll try." I turned away quickly before I could see the hope spark on my aunt's face, when I knew trying might not be good enough.

◦ ● ◦

WE HEADED DOWN from the mountain and toward the railway tunnel that cut from western Miraji into the east, through the middle mountains. Haytham Al-Fawzi was anxious to reclaim his city. All of us were anxious to finish this war.

On the way, we passed through both Juniper City and Massil, the place where Jin and I had joined a caravan back when I was barely the Blue-Eyed Bandit and he was just a foreigner. Not a Demdji and a prince. I hadn't known then that the Djinni they told the story of here, who'd flooded the sea with sand, was my father.

There, standing in the same pit in the middle of town where Jin had once fought to prove his prowess to the Camel's Knees, Delila told the story of Prince Ahmed again, like she had in Sazi, images that matched her words spilling from her fingers. By the time she finished, we had another half dozen recruits. Most of them were young men and women who belonged to the crumbling city, but a few split off from their caravans to fall into step with us. Leaving their traveling clan wouldn't be looked on well, but they were taking a chance and handing their lives over.

A day after Massil, we crossed through the railway tunnel that led from the desert into eastern Miraji. We started at dawn, moving as quickly as we could. We all knew that it wasn't a good idea to wind up under the mountain in the dark. And we made it to the other side before night.

Barely. The sun was setting as we stepped out.

It had been months since we'd lost the rebel camp in the attack, but for a moment as we emerged on the other side of the mountain, I thought I wasn't stepping out of a tunnel but through the secret door.

Instead of desert sands, the valley that stretched out below us was emerald with rolling fields of grass. This was another Miraji, a thousand miles away from the one I'd grown up in, it seemed. Trees hanging with the last of the summer fruits dotted the landscape between field after field, and the air smelled of rain. Abruptly, the twins were off, bursting into the shapes of two hawks and plunging down the valley, racing, their loud screeches filling the air.

Southeastern Miraji was dotted with farming villages, and we stopped in every single one we passed. In each village Delila told Ahmed's story, and in each one new people joined us, packing up their supplies to fall in line behind the hero of Miraji, the Rebel Prince brought back to life. Before we'd made it far, the story had spread ahead of us, shape-shifting as it went.

They said Ahmed was chosen by the Djinn to save Miraji. He had been brought back from the dead and re-made by the very hands of the creatures who had made us. He wasn't wholly human in some eyes. As we passed through towns, people came out of their houses to pray to him, to call out to him, just to see him. And always, some joined up with us.

Those who could fight or who were able-bodied enough to be trained, Shazad allowed to come with us. The too old or too young, Ahmed asked to stay behind, not to give their lives for him, promising to fight for them.

And then there were the stories that Ahmed was in-vincible. That he had been resurrected by the hands of the Djinn and could not be defeated. I felt my hand drift to Zaahir's knife without meaning to as I started to hear this repeated.

By the time we reached Tiamat, we were three times as many as we'd been when we'd left the mountains. We weren't just a rabble. We were an army.

At midday, we stood on the slope that overlooked the bay of Tiamat City. Shazad's arms were crossed over her chest, surveying the city like she could take it apart brick by brick. Tiamat had walls, but we could walk through those easily. And we had Delila, if we needed to hide. And we had the twins if we needed a way over the walls.

"There's not a chance the emir hasn't heard we're com-ing." Shazad thought out loud, her hair dancing backward in the warm air off the sea as she considered our target. She almost looked like her old self after weeks of walking and fresh air and sun. "There's not a chance they think they can hold against us either. He hasn't even tried to bar the gates against us."

"No," I agreed, squinting down at the city below. We were almost there, and I felt a sudden burst of impatience as I saw our target. The ships we needed docked just beyond those walls. Ready to carry us north. "So how about we just walk in?"

I suppose I expected Shazad to disagree with me. She didn't.

• ● •

WE WALKED TO the city as if we were invited, not invading. Haytham and Ahmed leading the way, with me and Shazad close behind and Jin protecting our backs. The twins kept watch overhead as hummingbirds, zipping back and forth, ready to shift to a more threatening shape if we needed help. Rahim was left with the army just outside the city. Reinforcements if we needed it.

No one stopped us at the gates of Tiamat, although plenty of people came out to gawk at us: the Rebel Prince, returned from the dead, walking side by side with their rightful emir, who had been taken away months ago. I'd never been in a city like this before. We marched through tidy, wide, well-paved streets, boxes of flowers and plants overflowing onto colorfully painted walls.

The emir's grand house stood at the eastmost point of the city, a great square structure painted pale blue and overlooking the water. So close, in fact, that the sea breeze picked up the white flag that had been raised over its roof, whipping it out for us as we approached.

So Haytham's brother had seen us coming. He was surrendering.

"If someone surrenders, does that mean you can't kill them?" Haytham asked, squinting up at the flag over his home. He was older than us by a decade or so, though he looked even older from his time at Eremot. Curly hair grew shaggy across his brow. He had been trapped there longer than our people, and he bore marks I was sure would never go away. But there was a new lightness to him now he was back in his city again.

"It is traditional not to," Shazad advised.

"But then again, we're big on breaking tradition," Jin tossed in, as we approached the doors of the house. I could sense him close behind me as we climbed up the clean white steps. When I turned back to look at him, his eyes weren't on me though. They were fixed on the ships in the harbor just below. Jin and Ahmed has spent most of their lives on ships. There was an easiness in Jin's stance I hadn't seen in a long time, now we were so close to the sea.

We were wary in spite of the white flag as we entered the house. But there was no ambush inside the door. We ventured in carefully. Marble hallways spread out around us, vacant, and room after room was empty, except for the sea air stirring the curtains. There was no one here for revenge even if Haytham had wanted it.

"He fled," Haytham declared, pushing open the door to a fine set of rooms. Those that belonged to the emir, I guess. The inside was turned over, as if someone had grabbed their belongings in a rush. His brother. "The coward."

He must've heard that we were on our way. But I had the feeling it wasn't news of our numbers or our weapons that made him flee. It was the news that the Rebel Prince had returned from the dead. We didn't even have to fight with the tale of Ahmed preceding us.

That was the power of a legend.

· ● ·

WE SPLIT UP, starting a quick search of the house. Haytham's brother couldn't have got far. Shazad and I took the ground floor, while Haytham went in search of the servants who used to work in his household. If anyone had answers, it would be them.

Shazad made a face as she pushed open a door.

"What?" I asked, reaching for my gun already.

"No, no." She stopped me quickly, opening the door fully. It gave way to a small courtyard, with a bubbling fountain set into the wall. And above that was a half-finished, multicolored mosaic. It looked like a man's face. "If I ever think it's a good idea to put a six-foot-high portrait of myself in my home, will you promise to slap me?"

I snorted, relaxing my grip on my gun. "You know it's dangerous for Demdji to make promises," I joked.

She was about to say something else when we both

heard it. It sounded like a child's cry. It was coming from just beyond the wooden doorway in the small courtyard. The lightness leached out of Shazad's face as quick as anything as she set her hand on her sword.

She didn't speak. She didn't need to. We'd fought many a fight together. I knew what she needed. I offered her a slight nod as she moved toward the door, drawing my gun. I took a deep breath as she exhaled.

Shazad shoved the door open abruptly, drawing her sword as she did, even as I moved forward, covering her with my gun.

And then we both stopped abruptly.

Beyond the door was another small garden, crowded with cowering people. I counted about two dozen women and at least twice as many children, from about thirteen years old all the way down to babes in arms.

Shazad dropped her blade even as children in the garden started to cry and women clutched their children closer to their chests.

"It's all right!" She held up her now empty hands. "We're not here to hurt you."

I knew them, I realized. The boy who was pressed behind his mother nearby—his name was Bassam. I had seen him once before, standing on the edge of a lake, bow in hand, as he came of age. His father's hand had been on his shoulder.

They were the Sultan's wives and children.

Leyla had said that the rest of the harem had been sent away as the siege approached. Sent to safety.

Tiamat had been safety. At least before we'd arrived.

"We're not going to hurt you," Shazad repeated even as I touched the knife that Zaahir had given me, hanging at my side.

Use this knife to take the life of another prince, and I promise you that your prince will live through the battle to take the throne.

A prince's life for a prince's life.

I thought he meant it as some brutal taunt, that I should kill Jin or Rahim, when he knew I never would. Some tainted offer of help that I would never get.

Except I had hung on to the knife in spite of that. And now, I was being presented with dozens of princes.

We're not here to hurt you, Shazad had told them.

Suddenly I couldn't breathe. I pressed out of the garden, ignoring Shazad calling out behind me. Quickly I laced my way back to the street. I found the road to the sea easily enough, and soon I was standing at the docks, overlooking the ships and the terrifyingly endless water. I ripped the knife out of the sheath at my side and flung it through the air. I had good aim—it arced and landed in the waves, sinking far out of my reach. Taking away the chance I might do something stupid and desperate.

"It's no wonder you wanted to rescue him." I looked up, startled by the voice. There was a man behind me, back against the wall, a small collection of coins by his grubby bare feet. "You're so afraid of making the wrong choices, aren't you?"

I glanced around, confused. But everyone else at the

docks was going about their business without so much as glancing our way. The beggar couldn't be talking to anyone other than me.

"Do you want to know what I think?" He paused and reached out a hand toward me, like he was begging for a coin. I found a loose half-louzi piece in my pocket and dropped it into his hands. "I think you're selfish." He pocketed the coin quickly. "All those princes to choose from, who don't mean anything to you, and you can't even kill one of them to save thousands of your own kind when I handed you a way to do it." That was when he looked at me straight on, and I saw that his eyes were the color of embers.

"Zaahir." I recognized him, disguised in this new human shape. "What do you want?"

"I wanted to know what you would do." He stood, gliding his back up the stone wall behind him. "But I'm also here to keep my promises," he said. As he spoke, his body shifted, morphing from the old beggar into a young man who bore an uncanny resemblance to Ahmed. "You wanted a way to put your prince on the throne, and I promised to give you one. Except that you just walked away from it."

Jin had told me once that coincidence didn't have the same cruel sense of humor as fate. The Djinn, they had a cruel sense of humor, too—and enough power to open a mountain. To turn a boy into a wall of fire. To lead me here, across a desert, and give me exactly what I'd asked for: a way to keep Ahmed alive.

"They're children."

"So are you," he said. "Does it really matter whether a life lasts one handful of years, or two, or three?" He was really asking me, I realized. He had been out of the mortal world as long as it had existed. He didn't understand us at all. Didn't understand the difference between being ten and being twenty and being a hundred. They were all young to him. "Would it be easier to kill him if he were a man?" he asked. "No, that can't be it, because then you could have killed the other two princes you travel with. But they are men you need. Each in his own way." When he smiled his face shifted again, this time turning to one that resembled Jin's. "You've killed others before, daughter of Bahadur. Don't deny it."

"Killing people to save—" I cut myself off as a sly smile spread across the face that looked unsettlingly like Jin's. "Killing people in battle is different."

"And this is a war. But if you insist, there is another gift I can give you."

He moved quicker than I could see. He didn't step toward me, just disappeared from the air where he stood, reappearing directly before me. I didn't even have time to stagger back before he caught me, holding me tighter than any mortal thing could. It was more like being trapped in the stones of a mountain than being held by arms made of flesh and blood. "This is my new gift to you, daughter of Bahadur."

He kissed me then, before I could pull away. He didn't kiss me like a mortal man, either. But his mouth wasn't stone; it was fire. My mouth was scalding under his. And then, just as quickly, it was over.

For a moment, as he pulled away, something changed in his face. The certainty shifted to the same bewildered madness I'd seen on his face in the mountain. I remembered something he had said. That I looked like her. The First Hero. He had lived with mortality as long as the other Djinn, but he had lived out of the world. He had not been blunted by time, nor by the deaths of thousands, the way they had.

"What was that?" I brought my hand to my mouth, but when I touched my lips, they were the same temperature they always were.

"A gift, of life." His grip didn't feel like warm skin—it felt like air and stone and fire. "You can't keep it for yourself. But you can pass it on to one person, and I promise you that they will live to see old age."

First he'd given me the chance to kill someone, and now he was giving me the chance to save someone with a kiss. To save Ahmed, if I wanted to.

Or I could save Jin. The selfish thought crept in faster than I could expel it.

And then I had another thought. Bilal. If I used it on him, we might be able to take Iliaz as bloodlessly as we had this city. I could give Bilal his escape from death after all.

THIRTY

I hated the sea.

We set sail the next morning, Haytham supplying us with one of the ships from his reclaimed city and a crew to man it.

Last time I'd been on a ship, I'd been drugged and a prisoner on the way to the palace. It turned out that not being shackled wasn't much better. The deck of the ship was never steady, and after I lost sight of land, a strange panic set in. Ahmed found me the first night belowdecks with my head in a bucket. He sat patiently next to me, running a hand gently up and down my spine as I retched up the contents of my stomach.

I waited until I was sure I had nothing left before speaking to him. Even if I didn't quite dare lift my head from the safety of the bucket.

"How did you find me?" My mouth tasted like bile.

"Sam sold you out," he said as I slowly lifted my head. Ahmed handed me a skin of water. I took it with shaky hands and rinsed out my mouth, spitting into the bucket. "He said he hadn't seen you eat anything today."

"Should I be flattered he tore his eyes off Shazad long enough to notice anyone else?" I peeled a strand of my still-too-short hair away from my face.

"Here." He handed me a flat green leaf. "Chew on it. It'll settle your stomach. I got some from the Holy Father in Tiamat. I thought we might need it. It took me a while to find my sea legs, too, back when Jin and I first set off seafaring."

Tentatively, I put the thing in my mouth. It didn't taste bad—sweet and cool as it hit my tongue. I chewed slowly. Ahmed watched as I tried to get my feet under me.

"Amani, I need to ask you something." If Ahmed had more guile, I might've thought he'd deliberately come looking for me when I was shaky and vulnerable. But it was Ahmed. "After this is all over, I'm not going to take the throne."

That got my attention. "What?"

"At least not the way my father took it," Ahmed hurried on before I could start berating him. "Not by force, without giving the people a choice in who governs them. You were right about what you said in Sazi: I ought to listen to the people who know this desert. I'm going to hold a vote. Like they do in the Ionian republics, to let the people chose their ruler. Any man or woman who thinks they would make a better ruler than me can put their name forward, and if the people agree they would be better than me, they can choose that person instead."

I stared back at him, trying to take this all in. "Why are you telling me this?"

"Because"—Ahmed rubbed at the scar on his forehead thoughtfully; it was a habit of his when he was thinking—"I want to know what you think."

"Why?" I realized I was speaking mostly in single words. I didn't sound smart enough to lace up my own boots, let alone advise a ruler on this. But I had told him back in Sazi that he didn't know everything. That he ought to listen to me.

"Amani, you know this country better than anyone else in this rebellion. Do you think it will work?"

I thought about it. "What would you do about the Sultim trials? They've been used to determine the next ruler since the beginning. It's a hard tradition to break."

"I know that. But do you think I can?"

The Sultan had said something to me the night of Auranzeb, with his firstborn's blood still on his hands. He'd said that the world was changing. That the time of immortals and magic was ending. That they should not be allowed to rule our lives anymore—we should rule theirs. The Sultan was a cruel, self-serving man. But I didn't know that he was wrong when he said that. Maybe it was time to change. Maybe the desert was ready to choose its own ruler.

"Yes." I nodded slowly, my head still swimming a little. "I think it might work." Ahmed's shoulders sagged in relief, and I realized he'd been nervous about what I would say. He pressed his knuckle into the spot on his forehead.

I reached up to his hairline, moving one of the dark curls away from the spot he'd been worrying at. "Where did you get that?" I asked before I could stop myself. I knew most of the scars on Jin's body. Ahmed didn't have quite so many. But he had some.

"Oh." Ahmed laughed. "It was my fault. It was when Jin and I were very young, our first year on board the *Black Seagull.* I was learning to plot courses while Jin spent most of his time clambering up and down the rigging. I made a mistake one day. We sailed into a storm that we should have been able to avoid. I could've shipwrecked us. As it was, I was lucky—I just split my head open on the deck when we nearly capsized. I thought I was going to die that day."

"Are you afraid?" I asked, dropping my hand. "Of dying?" I felt the memory of Zaahir's kiss tingling on my lips.

"I don't know." He considered. If anyone had asked me the same question, my answer would have been quick and certain. *Yes, terrified.* Did that make me selfish and cowardly? "I've seen a lot of the world, a lot of what people believe about death, and I don't entirely know what I believe waits for us after. But I do fear things in this life. Not dying, but losing. That I'll have been the one to lead us into the monster's mouth, promising it was a cave of riches. That others will die, and that those who have already died for me will have done so for nothing. That everything that has happened and everything I have done will have become entirely insignificant and forgotten."

But then we were all more selfish than Ahmed. That was why he led us. And he was right. We weren't in this for ourselves. For this life. We were in it for what we could make for the future. The rest of us could die for this. But Ahmed needed to live.

If I used Zaahir's kiss for Bilal, Ahmed might still fall at the eleventh hour. He might die leading us to victory. But I was frightened that if I didn't use Zaahir's kiss for Bilal, I'd be far too tempted to give it to Jin instead.

Because I would always be more selfish than Ahmed.

• ● •

IT TOOK US three days of sailing to reach the northern edge of Miraji, and another two before we were close to port again. As we sailed toward Ghasab, we passed near enough to the coast that the shadow of the middle mountains fell over the ship. Everyone came on deck to watch as we sailed by, crossing the frontier from eastern Miraji to west, a long way from where we'd crossed over the other way.

We were close.

So close to getting Rahim to his army, to snatching them away from Bilal and marching them on Izman.

I'd only been to the port city of Ghasab once—twice

if you counted the time I was dragged through it unconscious by my aunt. But I hadn't exactly gotten to see much
of it then.

Ahmed sent the twins out ahead to report back the
day before we would dock. It might be a few days to Iliaz
on foot but it was only a few short hours as the shape-
shifting falcons flew. They were back before sundown.
Maz landed on the crow's nest and scrambled down the
mast in the shape of a monkey, while Izz misjudged his
landing and catapulted into a roll that only didn't break
his neck because he became a snake at the last second before turning into a very naked boy at our feet.

Izz reached us first. "There's an army," he said breath-
lessly, yet with a wide-eyed look that couldn't quite hide
his exhilaration at beating Maz to us.

"Were you two racing?" Shazad asked, tossing Izz a
shirt, which he tied around his middle, for our sake.

Izz beamed momentarily. "I won."

"I can see that," Shazad said, handing a pair of trousers
to a disgruntled-looking Maz, as he reached the bottom of
the mast and changed back to a boy. "What's this about
an army?"

"Iliaz," Maz said, fastening his trousers. "There's an
army camped at the western base of the mountains, by
the look of it."

"There are blue flags," Izz added.

"The Gallan," I said, feeling my blood go cold. "What
are they doing here?" I'd found my seasickness was better
if I stayed on deck, where the air was less stale. And the

plants Ahmed had given me had helped some. I'd taken to sleeping on the deck, falling asleep under the stars. Jin was usually there at night, too, manning this monstrous ship I didn't understand or like with the whole of his attention.

I'd been avoiding him ever since Zaahir had kissed me, since any temptation to kiss him would be a decision bigger than I was ready to make right now.

"Probably running a supply route to Izman through the mountains." Rahim crossed his arms over his chest, leaning back against one of the huge masts. "It's what I would do if I were laying siege to the city. You'd think they'd have the decency to stay out of our country while we fight this out among ourselves."

"How many?" Shazad asked, growing grave now. She checked around quickly, making sure no one else on board was close enough to hear.

Izz and Maz traded sheepish looks. Izz scratched his blue hair, making it stick up at the back as he faced us. "A lot?" he guessed.

"I'd say at least twice that many," Maz nodded along seriously.

"So too many to fight outright," Jin interpreted for the rest of us.

"Any way we can walk through under an illusion?" Shazad turned to our Demdji princess.

"I don't think I can hide this many people." Delila chewed her lip as she glanced around. "Six people is one thing, but we're close to three hundred now."

The wind off the water picked up, riffling its fingers through all of our hair, dashing a few stray strands over our general's face, deep in thought.

"We could fly over them." Ahmed was pressing that spot on his hairline again.

"Only in small numbers, though," Jin pointed out, leaning on the helm as we moved gently through the water. I stared out across the narrow band of sparkling blue ocean. We had finished passing the mountain now. The coast wasn't green fields and orchards of sweet fruits anymore. It was blistering golden sand. It was desert. My desert.

"It would take too long." Rahim agreed for once. "And it's a risk to split everyone up."

"Rahim, you know these mountains; is there a way around?" Shazad asked.

I found myself reaching for the sand almost without noticing it. The pain in my ribs answered, but so did the desert, shifting as I drummed my fingers against my side. I had the beginning of an idea. I just couldn't tell whether it was the kind that would get us all killed or not.

"The mountain is well defended," Rahim was saying. "No roads, only paths. There is one way we could try, but we'd lose at least a week and—"

"What if we go through?" I interrupted Rahim. "Not around, not over, but"—I made a small forward motion with my hand, like it was a knife cutting through silk, and even this far away, I felt the sand shift, like a current through water—"through." The wheels in my mind were still turning, wondering if we could really do this or if I was losing my mind.

"No." Ahmed was already shaking his head. "You heard Shazad: a fair fight would be suicide with our numbers, and I won't risk it."

But Shazad knew me well enough to know that even I wasn't reckless enough to suggest fighting our way through. She was watching me, mind turning quickly, trying to see what I was thinking. "You're not talking about a fight, are you?"

"Not a fair one, at least." I could feel the excitement bubbling up. "What if we sailed through?" There was a moment of complete silence as everyone stared at me like I was insane. Everyone except Shazad, who understood instantly. Jin caught up to her a moment later.

"So, just to be clear." Jin leaned forward so that I was pinned under his gaze. He was speaking slowly. If I knew him any less well, I might've thought he was chastising me. But I did know him. He had that smile on his face. Like we were about to get ourselves in real trouble and he wouldn't have it any other way. "You're suggesting sailing a ship through the sand with your Demdji gift?"

"You really think that will work?" Shazad asked.

"The sand runs deep enough," I said. I could feel the rush of being back in the desert. "I think I can try."

"You know a ship isn't flat, don't you?" Jin said, but that spark was still there. "You'll have to keep it balanced."

"Without the full force of your powers?' Ahmed asked. "Amani, it's a risk."

They didn't trust me. Not entirely. I could see the doubt hanging on every single one of their faces as they looked at me. That I wasn't strong enough. They thought I was too confident. But if my power was draining out of me and my days were numbered, then I might as well use the dregs of it to do something big. I might as well pour it all out of me before I died.

"Everything we do is a risk," I said. "And we've got a bigger fight than this one waiting for us in Izman. I don't want to lose any more time."

"You're sure you're up to this, Bandit?" Jin tightened his hands on the wheel.

I raised my shoulder. "What's the worst that could happen?"

"We could all die," Rahim answered.

"So, what else is new?" I asked.

I watched the circle of people around me as the idea that we might actually do this settled on us, one by one. What it might mean. That it might even be possible.

"It'd be one hell of a battering ram," Shazad admitted.

"If Amani can do this—" Rahim started.

"She can," Jin said, eyes on me. He was on my side, along with Shazad. We only needed one more person. Everyone looked at Ahmed. He was unreadable. A family trait he shared with his father. His head tilted forward in thought for a long moment.

I was about to say something else, to keep fighting

for it, keep making a case that I could do this, when he lifted his head. And the Rebel Prince had slipped away. He didn't look like his father, I realized, he finally looked like a Sultan.

And he nodded.

THIRTY-ONE

T he sun rose bright and brilliant to the east side of the ship, the wind coming from the north, tugging at the sails.

"It's good weather for sailing." Jin tied a rope around my waist. He was so close, the sun blazing behind him, making me squint when I looked up at him.

Everyone was tied to the ship, harnessed so that if I lost control of the sand and the ship toppled over, they wouldn't be thrown overboard. Jin fastened the rope tighter.

We waited until the first light crested over the edge of the water before Ahmed nodded to us from where he was harnessed to the mast.

Jin started calling orders, like we'd planned—

instructions I didn't understand about sails and jibs. We started to move, the sails swelling, waves lapping against the hull below us, as Jin maneuvered us straight toward the shore.

I took a deep breath and felt the sand on the floor of the sea swell lazily in response, trying to fight the heavy water clinging to it. I shut my eyes, pressing my palm downward, pouring my focus into it as we picked up speed on the water.

I felt the sand strain against me even as the pain in my side doubled, almost toppling me over the side as I fought to cling to my power.

"Now!" Jin called.

I pulled on my powers at the same moment that the sailors pulled on knots. Sails billowed to their full swell out into the wind, and the sand rose up to meet us, lashing into the bottom of the ship.

The whole thing rocked unsteadily under us, listing to the left. A few screams rang out across the deck, and I gripped the ship, fighting to regain my balance and balance the ship at the same time, letting the sand drop out from below us for a moment. Letting the water take back over even as the desert rose ahead to meet us.

We were running the ship aground. Except I was hoping I'd be able to keep it running.

"Amani, now." I heard Jin's voice again, and I knew we were out of time. I needed to get this right or we would hit a lot worse than a bad swell in the water. I whipped my hands up and forward, dragging every bit of sand I could find up around us like the swell of a storm just as we reached the shore.

We hit the sand with a force that sent every one of us jolting against the railings and the mast, everyone bracing for impact, worried that we'd topple over as we hit the sand of the desert and crash, our bodies shattering among the debris of the ship.

And then we kept going. The sand didn't stop us. It swelled around us, like waves, carrying the ship over the shore and into the desert.

We were sailing on a sea of sand.

The shock came over me so quickly that I almost lost control of the desert. I grabbed hold of it again as I stared at the sand banking the ship on either side, swelling up around us high enough to keep the ship steady. Driving us forward like the current with the power of the wind on our side. We were speeding ahead.

A bubble of frantic elation swelled in my chest through the pain. This was impossible. But I was doing it.

I shifted us, correcting the angle a little, as Jin called out instructions I only half heard. We were flying over the unforgiving desert. We were skimming across the Sand Sea.

And in a second, I understood what it was that Jin missed about this. The freedom of gliding through the world, forgetting for a moment where you had come from and not worrying about where you were going. Being, just for a moment, nowhere at all.

I couldn't help it. I let out a whoop. Shazad took it up

next. She was beaming into the wind with a smile like I hadn't seen on her since we'd rescued the prisoners from Eremot. The rest of the ship quickly took up the cry, cheering as they released their white-knuckled grips on the ship. As they realized we were really doing the impossible.

The Gallan camp came into view over the rise of sand, line after line of tents appearing in our path like islands in the sea of sand. But I didn't have any intention of stopping.

As we got closer, I could see men in foreign uniforms dashing out of their tents, running frantically out of the way at the sight of us. The sand swelled below us as we crested nearer and nearer.

"Everyone get ready!" Shazad called as I steered the ship toward the dead center of the tents. "And raise our colors!"

I saw something bunched in one of the young rebel's hands. It looked like a flag. She attached it to a rope on the mainsail and started pulling, raising it high above us as Shazad and Rahim both started shouting orders about drawing weapons and Jin started bellowing new orders at the ship.

But I didn't hear much of it. Because there, unfurling high above us at the top of the mast, was a dark blue flag stitched with a golden sun. Ahmed's symbol. A declaration of the Rebellion.

A signal to the Gallan of who was coming for them, a signal that this country wasn't theirs to take. It was ours.

All around us, rebels were pointing guns over the edge

of the ship, using the bannister as support, angling the firearms downward. I saw cannons appear through port-holes around the hull. The ship wobbled a little bit as I lost my focus. But I kept us going. Straight and steady toward the sudden chaos blooming from the Gallan camp.

"Everybody brace!" Jin shouted as the front of the ship hit the first of the tents.

I felt the tent splinter below the hull like firewood under my boot.

"Fire!" Shazad called the order as we plowed forward, shattering tents ahead of us. Suddenly the air was filled with gunfire and the boom of cannons. Shrapnel tore through the air, shredding everything in its path. The wind caught a tent, whipping it away from the ground and casting it high in the air. The sun struck it as it soared over us, piercing through a hundred tiny holes in the dark blue fabric, so that for a moment it looked like a hundred stars peering down on us. And then the canvas was dashed away.

To my left, a bullet struck a cache of gunpowder, sending up a blossom of flames to one side of the ship. It caught across the camp, looking like paper men going up in flames.

The sand picked up a soldier in its wake, reeling him toward us, making him disappear under the bow of the ship. And I thought of a soldier like him marching through Dustwalk when I was a little girl, boots kicking up dust as he dragged a man out of his house and shot him in the name of their occupation. And I didn't feel sorry.

I fought through the pain in my side. Even if I loosened my grip on the desert a little, the wind would carry us until I grabbed it back. But now I forced the sand around us to swell, overcoming the Gallan like a wave. And then I looked up. Straight ahead, the sand ended, giving way to stone as the ground sloped up, as desert turned to mountains. Panic set in.

"Jin!" I called.

"I see it," he shouted back, already motioning for the sailors to bring in the sails. Already trying to slow the ship.

"There's a mountain!' I shouted.

"I see it," he said again.

I had to do something. I watched everyone scramble. "Everyone hold on!" I shouted. But my voice was lost in the gunfire. I caught Shazad's eye, raising my hands just a little. She took up the cry. But she was muffled, too. I watched as she made the decision. Pulling out a knife, she sliced through the rope at her middle. I cursed her under my breath.

Untethered, Shazad made her way down the line of gunmen, repeating the order, telling people to hold tight. Forcing them to drop their guns to their sides as they laced their arms through the bannisters or around masts, anchoring themselves as she ran down the line toward us.

I waited. Shazad needed to get closer. She needed to get to safety. I waited. I waited. Until I couldn't wait any longer.

I twisted my power, yanking the sand around in one

violent twist, changing the course of the ship at a hard angle, wrenching up the desert on either side to buttress us. I reached for Shazad as the ship listed hard to the right.

She was too far away. I could already tell as the ship tipped, preparing to send anyone not firmly attached over the edge.

Jin got there first.

Letting go of the useless wheel, trusting his tether, he launched himself down the incline of the ship, running down the deck as it became a steep slope. As I fought to keep the ship propped up.

He reached Shazad a second before the ship tilted too hard, grabbing her to him as the ground beneath them gave out, pulling the rope around his waist taut.

I breathed in relief as he anchored her. The two of them swung like a pendulum while the chaos turned to stillness around us as the ship settled in the sand, flat on its side. Everyone was still on board by the grace of a good rope.

I could barely breathe though the agony, but I heard Rahim call out, "Is everyone still alive?"

"Yeah, call out if you're dead," Sam added. And Shazad laughed. Then I was laughing, too. And I couldn't stop.

Because it was ridiculous and impossible, what we had just done. But I had managed it. And we were all still alive.

And we were almost at the end.

THIRTY-TWO

We struck camp halfway up the mountain, at the last village before the fortress of Iliaz. Bilal had to know we were coming, but our path hadn't met with any resistance. The people of Iliaz knew Rahim from his days in service to Lord Bilal's father, and as we made our way up, they came out to stare. When we stopped for the night, the locals welcomed him like a long-lost son. The whole village came out, carrying platters of food and pitchers of the wine that had made Iliaz rich. There had been no news from the fortress in weeks, the people said. Some said Bilal was already dead.

"He's not dead," I said, glancing up at the fortress above us. I could see stone towers through the crags in the mountains, casting their shadows over the green vines that dominated the hillside. We would be there before midday tomorrow. Bilal was still alive. I had the choice to keep him that way. We wouldn't need to turn his army against him.

I hadn't told anyone about Zaahir's gift. Not even Shazad. I wasn't sure why. But I really ought to say something now, as Rahim set out the plan for tomorrow on how to approach the fortress. He was calculating how many of his soldiers he thought he could count on to lay down weapons right away when a young girl's voice came from outside. "No!" she was screaming. "I need to talk to him!"

We were all outside in the space of a few heartbeats. The little girl stood in the doorway of the house we'd taken rooms in. She was about eight years old, her dark hair in a tightly coiled braid around her head, and she was thrashing and screaming as our guards hung on to her. "I need to speak to the commander! Please!"

"Mara." Rahim pressed out into the small town square, where he could see the little girl properly. Her head twisted at the sound of her name.

"Commander Rahim!" She wrenched forward to meet him, though one of our rebels still held her. "Let me go!" She turned, and with all the force in her tiny body, she slammed her heel down on his instep, forcing him to let her go with a violent string of curses far from fit for a little girl's ears. Not that she was listening anyway. She was already bolting toward us.

"I like her," Shazad said. "Here's hoping she's on our side."

"I taught her that," Rahim said, with a hint of pride in his voice. I could imagine he had. Separated from his little sister, whom he would've given anything for, he'd found another young girl to replace Leyla. He dropped to his knees to meet Mara at eye level as she barreled straight for him.

"You have to help!" She was breathing hard, her tiny face flushed. "I ran all the way here. He's going to kill them! He's going to kill them all!"

Rahim looked at her, brow furrowed. "Who is?"

"Lord Bilal." She swallowed, trying desperately to spill out all the words fast enough. "He knows you're coming. He knows he doesn't stand a chance. And there's this girl, a princess, they say, who's been whispering terrible things into his ear for weeks." Leyla. Damn her. We'd taken her out of Izman to keep her from causing trouble, but somehow she'd managed anyway. "He's going to poison the whole garrison so you can't turn them against him."

We all stared at the little girl as the words sank in, the horror of what she was telling us. And then we started to move as one.

We pieced it together as we went.

Mara worked in Lord Bilal's kitchens. She was the little sister of a young soldier in the Iliaz command. Lord Bilal had seen us coming. Using a ship as a battering ram wasn't exactly inconspicuous. He'd announced to the garrison that there'd be a feast that evening in our honor.

Mara had been hard at work in the kitchens with another servant. The other girl was new. She didn't know she wasn't supposed to sample the wine. Or she didn't care. Mara had watched the girl drop dead right in front of her.

It seemed Bilal had decided that if we weren't about to give him a Demdji to save his life, he wasn't going to let us take his army. He was ready to kill hundreds out of spite.

We wouldn't be able to make it on foot. Jin, Sam, Shazad, and I scattered, looking for Izz and Maz, as Ahmed started to leave instructions for what to do while we were gone. Rahim stayed with Mara. We found the twins quickly enough, and it took a handful of words for them to burst out of their human shapes into those of giant Rocs. By the time we returned, Shazad had grabbed the weapons we needed. I caught the gun she tossed me almost without looking as Jin pulled me onto Maz's back.

Rahim also climbed up, settling Mara with us. The little girl let out a scream as we launched into the sky.

It was a matter of moments before we were soaring over the walls of the fortress, the last of the sun touching the horizon as we did.

The courtyard was eerily empty when we landed, and the walls we'd flown over were unmanned. But it wasn't deserted. Ahead of us, doors that led into the main hall were flung wide open. Light and noise and celebration spilled out invitingly into the gloom as we slid off the twins' backs.

"Is it me," Sam voiced what we were all thinking, "or does this seem like a trap?"

"It's not you," Shazad said.

"Well, waiting won't change anything," Ahmed said, making the decision. "We go in now."

We fell into a formation naturally: Rahim and Ahmed taking the lead, little Mara still clinging to Rahim's sleeve, Shazad and me flanking them on either side, Sam and Jin taking up the rear, with the twins slipping in and out between us, now in the shape of cats.

We passed below a huge arch made of the same red stone as the rest of the fortress. Two heavy wooden doors sat propped open, guiding us into an immense stone hall. Inside it stretched up two levels, painted wooden beams supporting the ceiling high above us. By the light of hanging oil lamps, I could see faces and animals carved into the beams, gazing down on the scene below. Two dozen tables set up in a great horseshoe curved around the hall. They were lined with soldiers and heavy with food and pitchers of wine. I hadn't seen this hall when we'd been here before, when I'd been invited to Bilal's private rooms. But now he'd emerged, it would seem, and he sat at the very end of the hall on a dais above the rest of his men, in a chair that was more like a throne, a huge, twisted seat made of wood painted to look like gold and stacked heavy with pillows.

It took a moment for the first of Rahim's men to see us.

"Commander Rahim, sir!" a young soldier at the far end of the table exclaimed, standing up and knocking over his chair. It crashed onto the tile floor loud enough that several other heads turned our way. Shazad's hand strayed to her side at the same time as I touched the trigger on my gun for comfort. But the soldier strode forward, embracing Rahim, as he let out a relieved laugh and then, seeming to remember himself, released him and offered a lopsided salute. "We thought you were dead, Commander." The hall was quieting now, and almost every pair of eyes in the place was turned toward us. Including Bilal's.

His eyes were sunk so deep that all I could see were shadowed pits there. His hollow-looking face made him look crueler than he ever had. Bilal was fading fast. He was so emaciated that he looked like a small boy sitting in a too-big seat his father had left him, trying to hold it against a prince, who held more power than he ever would.

For a moment I felt a stab of pity for him. But as I looked around, I could see that the men's wine cups were full but untouched. They had been well trained, most of them by Rahim. And Bilal was ready to kill them all.

"It's not that easy to get rid of me," Rahim said, clapping his soldier on the back. His words were jovial, but his eyes, fixed on Bilal, were anything but. "What's happening here?"

Looking at his crumbling body, I hadn't been entirely sure Bilal would be able to stand, but he rose to his feet gingerly. "A celebration," he declared, his voice still carrying across the halls in spite of his illness, "in anticipation of your arrival. And your annihilation of the foreign threat." He signaled one of the servants, who rushed forward with a tray of wineglasses for us.

"Funny, that." Rahim took a full wineglass without hesitation. "Here I'd heard rumors of you striking alliances with foreigners. I'm sure your father would have marveled at that."

Bilal's eyes danced to me and Jin and Sam. I felt the memory of the burn of Zaahir's kiss on my mouth. If I was going to say anything, do anything, now was the time. I could save Bilal; I could end this without bodies. I glanced down at the wineglass that was being offered to me and kept my lips sealed.

"Yes, well," Bilal said, after letting Rahim's accusation hang a long moment in the air, "I am in good company, making alliances our fathers would not be pleased at."

Rahim started to advance toward the dais, walking slowly, deliberately. "A toast, then," he said.

We all watched as hundreds of men raised their glasses obediently, Rahim's army falling in line. "A toast," Bilal agreed. "To our esteemed commander Rahim, on his victory and return."

"To the commander," the crowd echoed, bringing the glasses up. I was about to cry out, to stop them, to warn them. But Rahim got there first.

"Wait." He held up his hand. It was an order called out in a room full of soldiers, and it had been issued by their leader. Their true one. Every single one of them stopped in an instant.

And surrounding Lord Bilal stood an entire room of men silently reminding him where their true loyalty lay. That this was Rahim's army. He held out his cup to Lord Bilal. "You don't have a drink, my lord. You can't drink to my health without it. Besides, it would be rude of your men to drink before you."

Rahim stepped onto the dais, pulling himself up to his lord's level. Except Rahim stood a head taller than Bilal, at least. He didn't break his gaze as he held out his own glass for his one-time friend.

Finally Lord Bilal reached for the cup. As both their hands closed over it, Rahim leaned in close to Bilal. I saw his lips move, saying something to him in a low voice. A sad smile spread over Bilal's face, but he didn't say anything. He just pulled back, prying the glass from Rahim's fingers.

He raised the glass. "To your victory," he said again. "And long life."

And then he drank, deep and long. He hadn't finished draining it before his legs gave out. He was dead before he hit the ground.

THIRTY-THREE

I found Leyla in Bilal's rooms.

I hadn't expected to. I didn't need to be involved in the aftermath of Bilal's death. Rahim and Ahmed and Jin and Shazad could take care of that. So I'd gone to Bilal's rooms looking for his books. I was hoping that he had more on the man in the mountain. That I might find answers about the Sin Maker.

It had been an easy thing to think of giving away Zaahir's kiss to Bilal. But now . . . if I was going to give it to someone I really cared about, I needed to know if it was a trick. He'd promised they would live to an old age. But I knew Djinn's ways. It could mean that whomever I gave his gift to would age a hundred years when I kissed them. It could mean I would grant them a cripplingly ancient life so they were forced to watch everyone around them die. I couldn't do that to Ahmed. Or to Jin.

I came desperate for answers.

Instead, I found a princess curled up like a little girl on Bilal's bed, letting the smoke from his funeral pyre billow through the open window.

I paused in the doorway, looking at her tiny figure in the dark, knees tucked to her chest, bare feet burrowing into the stitching of the heavy blanket covered in hunting scenes that was sprawled over the bed. I knew she was aware of me, but she didn't turn around.

"It was you, wasn't it?" I asked Leyla's back. "You poisoned his mind into the idea of killing all those soldiers so that we couldn't have them. So that your brother couldn't go to war against your father. How did you do it?"

Leyla's shoulders shook silently, like in a laugh. It was the first sign of life I'd seen from her. "You have seen me fool and manipulate you and others dozens of times. You have seen where I grew up, within those walls, with women who used their bodies and their minds like weapons." Slowly she turned to face me. She looked different from the girl we'd left here. The burning, indignant anger in her had turned to a twisted, ugly kind of rage. "And yet, after all this, you still think I'm too innocent to play this game?"

Her eyes were rimmed with red. I didn't know whether it was from crying or from the smoke. I strode across the room, past the bed, to the other wall. From the window I could see down onto Bilal's pyre. It was surrounded by soldiers. Doing their duty to him even though he hadn't done right by them.

"I guess the Rebellion has made me more of an optimist about folks than I used to be," I offered. I closed the window and turned back to Leyla.

"Have you come to kill me?" she asked.

"No. Your brother will probably come looking for you soon. It would be too obvious who'd done it." It was a joke. Mostly.

I considered Leyla on the bed. I'd come here looking for information.

We'd had a plan back in Izman. Before Ahmed had been captured and Imin executed. Get an army, disable the Sultan's machine, take the city.

We had the army.

We had the words to free Fereshteh's captured soul from the machine and bring down the wall, and the Abdals with it.

Now we just needed the city. And for that, we needed to disable the machine.

I might as well ask. "If I free Fereshteh's energy, that machine's not just going to quietly turn itself off, is it?"

"Who knows?" Leyla slid back down onto the bed, like she was suddenly exhausted, propping her head on one arm. "It's never been tested before. It's all just a theory until you test it. That's what my mother taught me. Rahim thinks I don't remember her. But I think I've proved that I am more of both my mother and my father than he will ever be."

"And if you were theorizing?" I pressed, before she could stumble down some path I couldn't bring her back from.

"If I were theorizing"—she closed her eyes—"I would say no. I don't think it will."

Tamid and Leyla were both smart. And now that they'd told me the same thing, it was a safe bet they were probably right. It had seemed far away until now. But suddenly it seemed very near.

I felt myself reaching out for something to hang on to as everything seemed to spin around me. My hand closed around an earthenware pitcher next to the bed. It did nothing to keep me standing when it slid off the table and into my hands. Anger rushed in. Sudden, violent, irrational rage took over. Without thinking, I hurled the pitcher across the room, sending it splintering against the wall before I stormed out.

I wasn't sure whom I was looking for as I headed back into the courtyard, on the opposite side from the funeral pyre. Jin, maybe.

Instead, I ran straight into Sam. He caught me by the arms as I walked into his chest. "Well," he said, "isn't this very Leofric and Elfleda of us?" The love story he'd been babbling about back in Sazi. The one that ended with them both dying. "Meeting in secret in the dark . . ." And then he trailed off as he saw my face. That I was in no mood for jokes. "Are you all right?"

I glanced over his shoulder. The twins were standing there, looking at me anxiously. I must really not look all right. "What are you three doing out here?" I asked instead of answering.

"Oh, well." Sam stepped away from me, releasing my arms. "Rahim got the news from one of his soldiers. After we left here, my former queen, long may she reign, struck an alliance with the Gallan king, may he die a painful death and rot in a ditch." For once, Sam sounded serious.

So the alliance had gone through. Since we hadn't taken the captain's deal, they had gone and made another ally. Made Miraji their enemy. The Gallan hated our kind, hated anything that wasn't wholly human. Sam might've turned traitor on Her Highness, but his queen had betrayed a whole lot of her people by striking this alliance, too. "Captain Westcroft and the rest of all those nice fellows who want me dead marched down to join the siege three days ago."

"So we're going to scout things out," Izz interjected, chipper as ever. He was clearly glad to be moving; the twins hated being in one place too long.

"Shazad said we needed to use all our advantages now," Maz added.

"How come you both get to be the Blue-Eyed Bandit and we're known as *advantages*?" Izz asked.

"Yeah," Maz agreed. "We demand a better legendary nickname."

I forced a smile and got the satisfaction of the pair of them grinning back, pleased that they'd amused me.

I glanced at Sam, understanding. "You're going with

them?" The twins didn't need an escort to report to Shazad. Maybe Sam thought this would impress her, acting like a real soldier. But then I saw the troubled look on his face. He might be one of us now, but he was born in Albis. Those were his people laying siege to our city. He needed to see it.

"All right." I moved toward Izz. "Let's go."

They didn't need me with them any more than they did Sam. But they didn't question me coming with them, either. The twins burst into Rocs as Sam and I wrapped our sheemas around our faces against the wind. I had to see whatever was awaiting us down in the city.

· ● ·

NIGHT HAD FALLEN completely by the time we reached Izman, but we could still see everything from the air. The light from the dome of fire made it glow faintly in the dark. But more than that, the ground around the city burned like an ember.

The siege camp had been destroyed. The Gallan tents, which had stood in perfect military lines when we'd left just a few weeks back, were now smoldering ash. The bodies of the Albish who had joined forces with them would be among them, too. Thousands of men who'd lined up around the walls had been annihilated, the ground still burning from the force that had destroyed them: the Abdals turned against our enemies.

I couldn't see Sam's expression in the dark, but he would mourn his people, no doubt. In a way I couldn't. The Sultan might be our enemy, but he had dispelled Miraji's enemies.

Maybe it was right that it should end like this. This was a war between the people who belonged in this desert. Not the people who wanted to own it.

We would decide it for ourselves—no one else.

All I could hear were Izz's wingbeats as we soared over the city. It reminded me of the destruction Noorsham used to cause. Fire. Annihilation. A force that wasn't natural, that came from the Djinn, sweeping across armies and destroying everything in its path.

They'd dared to try to take power from the Sultan. So he'd shown them his true power.

This was what would happen to us if we tried to face the Sultan while he still controlled the Abdals. If we went to face armies of metal with an army of men.

We would burn, too. Everyone would: Jin, Ahmed, Shazad, Delila, Sam, Rahim, the refugees from Sazi, the soldiers from Iliaz, the hopeful men and women who had joined us in village after village.

Unless I dispelled Fereshteh's power. Unless I used the words Tamid had given me. The first language, in a voice that could tell no lies. The same tongue that had trapped the Djinn, used to free him.

Either I died or we all did.

• ● •

"ALL RIGHT, HERE'S what we do." A map of Izman was rolled out in front of Shazad. Rahim had taken over Bilal's rooms, but there was no time to clear them out. So for now, Shazad's room was our war room. "We can march from here to here in a day." She pointed to a spot on the map that she had marked, in the desert west of Izman. "That puts us out of sight and out of range of the city when night falls. We wait *here* for morning. At dawn, you two fly to the east." She pointed at me and Sam with the tip of her knife. "Get into the tunnels and to the machine. While you do that, our army marches under cover of one of Delila's illusions toward the city. When the fire drops, the Sultan will be unprepared for us to storm the walls. We want to break through Ikket's Gate first to get access to Wren Street before the army is fully mobilized." She pointed in turn at the streets of the city she had grown up in. "From there, we can take the western ramparts and have the upper ground. Trained soldiers should be on the front lines; the less trained should hang back in the artillery."

"No," Rahim disagreed. "We should mix as many of the untrained rabble among my soldiers as we can."

"That's too risky. It will be harder for untrained men to hold a line. The Sultan's soldiers will break through that much quicker."

"It's better than if they break through the first line to find no second line of defense," Rahim argued. "Our soldiers would be mowed down like wheat."

"So you want to throw untrained men and women in

the middle of soldiers so that they can draw fire away from trained soldiers." Shazad didn't raise her voice. It was a steady kind of anger.

"I didn't say that."

"But you know they're more likely to die."

"They're untrained—of course they're more likely to die," Rahim said, every inch the commanding officer.

"That's enough." Ahmed held up his hand, stopping both of them. He looked at me. He wanted to hear what I thought. I'd seen the city. The destruction. I knew what we were facing.

I still had Zaahir's gift. I could decide this battle here and now if I gave it to Ahmed. It wouldn't matter what we did, he would live. He would survive even if it was a massacre. But if I gave it to him, I couldn't give it to Jin.

"I reckon you should listen to Shazad," I said. "Don't throw bodies in your father's way to slow him down." They weren't just bodies. They were the too-eager farmer's sons and daughters who had laughed when Shazad tossed them in the dust like war was a game. The people of the desert who came to us because we were offering better than they had, and all we were asking in return was that they lay down their lives.

"We still need greater numbers." Rahim shook his head. "We might be able to win this fight if we're very smart and very lucky. But I don't like counting on luck."

"Well, lucky for us, I am very smart." It was Shazad's turn to interrupt him this time. A flicker of a smile flitted over Sam's face. He had been quiet since we'd seen the destruction outside the walls of Izman, but he was clearly enjoying Shazad and Rahim arguing.

"What about the people in the city?" I asked. I was thinking about the machine. About what disabling it would mean if it really did go up in flames. If a Djinni's dying energy really had razed cities and armies in the past.

"Amani's right," Shazad said. "There are still rebels in the city, and others who are loyal to us." That hadn't been what I'd meant, but the result was the same.

"We can't spread the word in Izman that we're coming," Rahim said. "If we lose the element of surprise, my father can annihilate us before we even reach the walls."

"But if we can get them out, then they can fight," Jin said, understanding what Shazad was saying where Rahim didn't.

"Fine." Ahmed nodded. "Sam and Delila"—he turned to the two of them—"take a small number down to the city with you and start evacuating." I knew why he'd picked them: Sam to get people through the tunnels and Delila to hide what they were doing. "Get as many people out as you can. Leave now."

I realized suddenly that this might be the last time we were all together like this. Some of us definitely weren't going to survive the battle that was coming. We'd already lost so many to the war.

But as I looked from them to Ahmed to Jin to everyone else around the table, I suddenly knew exactly who was most likely to die: the one of us who was least afraid. The one who needed to be saved the most.

When we were finished, everyone dispersed, leaving just me and Shazad behind.

"You should tell him, you know," she said when we were alone. I didn't need to ask what she meant. She wanted me to tell Jin what I was walking into under that city: possible death.

We'd made a habit of saving each other, Shazad and I, of having each other's back. Except I couldn't watch her back on the battlefield this time. And she couldn't save me from my fate.

"Yeah," I said, leaning toward her, looping my arm around her shoulders. I leaned my head against hers and dropped a quick kiss on her cheek. Like a gesture between sisters when one of them was headed away from home for a little while.

Except we weren't sisters. We'd chosen each other. And now that I'd given her that kiss from Zaahir, and the promise of a life longer than this battle, she wouldn't be coming anywhere with me. "I probably should."

THIRTY-FOUR

The Young Princes

Once, there were two princes who did not live like princes. Instead of a palace, they lived in three small rooms in a city far away from their father, the Sultan. Instead of fine clothes, they wore castoffs from other children that their mother sewed to fit them. Instead of fine spiced meats, they ate plain soups and bread.

And instead of food being plentiful, it was running out quickly. Their mother had no money, and soon she could no longer feed the children more than once a day.

One day, the two young princes were especially hungry. They had scarcely slept for their infant sister crying in the night. That evening they sat at the table. The first young prince watched his mother cook, and he saw her pull out only two bowls instead of three, since she knew there wasn't enough for two hungry children and a hungry mother.

Seeing this made the first young prince angry, because she was his mother—his true mother. His brother's mother was long dead in another country. And when the first prince looked across the table into his brother's bowl, he saw that his brother had gotten a spoonful more of rice.

The first prince saw this as a great injustice, and he said things that no brother ought to say to another. That it wasn't fair that one brother should get more food at the cost of another. That he wasn't even his mother's true son or his own true brother. That if anyone went hungry, it should be the other prince. That it was his fault that they were here and starving anyway. That they should send him away on one of the many boats in the harbor, back to the desert where they came from, and let someone else feed him.

The prince had never seen his mother grow so angry as she did at those words. She told her son that she was never to hear him talk like that again. That they were a family and that he should never be looking into his brother's bowl to see if he had more, but only ever to make sure he had enough. And in punishment, she sent her son to bed without food.

The young prince raged. He decided that he had had

enough. If his brother would not leave, he would. He was halfway through packing up his pitiful collection of belongings when his brother returned to the small room they shared. He turned out his pockets onto the bed, revealing that they were full of rice.

The second prince, feeling sorry that his brother had not eaten dinner, snuck every mouthful of his own into his pockets to bring to his brother later. The first prince was astonished to see that his brother was ready to go hungry himself and give everything he had to another—and to one who had wished him away only moments before.

It was in that moment that the first prince understood the goodness of his brother. That the second prince had a kinder, more selfless heart than he could ever hope for. And he vowed that though the first prince might never be as good as his brother, he would do all he could to protect him.

It was many years later that the girl known as the Blue-Eyed Bandit came to him, far from that table in the little home where they had grown up. And she asked him what he believed happened after death.

And he understood what it was that she meant to do.

He wanted to rage. To rage that his brother would get her life and that the Foreign Prince would be deprived of her in turn.

But he had made a vow on that day long ago.

And he would keep it.

THIRTY-FIVE

Jin did what he did best when I told him: he left me before I could leave him, joining Sam and Delila in the advance party headed toward Izman. He claimed to Ahmed that someone needed to take care of their little sister. I was grateful that he didn't tell our prince the truth. If Ahmed knew he was sending me to die by disabling that machine, he would try to save me. That's what he did, after all. He tried to save people.

That's what I was doing, too.

Jin had been gone three days when a lookout reported there was an army making its way up the western side of the mountain. Not from Izman. From our side of the desert.

Rahim moved into action immediately, preparing his

men to fight. They were used to this, to skirmishes in the mountains, though none of us had been expecting that we would need to defend ourselves before reaching Izman.

But as we stood watching from the walls in the early dawn air, over the crest of the hill below, a banner bobbed into view. Not one stitched with the Sultan's colors. Instead, we saw Ahmed's golden sun. A few moments later, the first figure came into view, and I realized that I knew her.

It was Samira, the daughter of the Emir of Saramotai. Or she had been until someone had overturned her father and killed him. We'd left her ruling her father's city. Clearly the role suited her.

"Hold your fire!" I ordered Rahim and his men, who were poised with their guns on the wall. "Don't shoot."

I rushed into the courtyard, and I was out the gates before anyone could stop me, Ahmed and Shazad close behind.

When she was near enough to be heard, Samira ducked her head in a quick nod to Ahmed as she reached the wall. "Your Exalted Highness, we heard you have need of men to fight. And women. I have a hundred with me who don't want to sit behind our walls and wait for our enemies."

"One hundred," Shazad said under her breath, standing next to me. "That's a good start." And then, speaking louder, she asked, "How did you know where we were?"

"General Hamad," Samira said simply. I felt Shazad tense beside me.

"My father?" she said, and for just a second she sounded like a little girl again.

Samira nodded. "News that the Rebel Prince can't be killed because he is protected by the Djinn reached even us in the west. And then the general rode through with news that if anyone truly wanted to defend their country, this was their last chance." She smiled at our startled faces. "Now, are you going to let us in, or do we have to storm your walls? I have to say, they don't look like much next to ours."

• ● •

SARAMOTAI WASN'T THE last city to join us. A bigger party arrived from Fahali two days later, sent into action by the general as well. The port city of Ghasab joined us a day after that. And more kept trickling in from small desert and mountain towns, where the news had spread. Ahmed was alive. The Rebel Prince had come back from the dead to free the country from foreign rule. Sometimes they came in large groups, sometimes one by one, to pledge themselves to his cause. Until we couldn't wait anymore. We were out of time to train new recruits. Out of time to get more weapons. We needed to march. Before the Sultan marched on Iliaz, and we lost the element of surprise.

"How many in all?" Ahmed asked that night, before we descended the mountain.

Shazad and Rahim traded a look. "Enough," Shazad said.

"Enough for what?" I asked.

"A fair fight," Rahim said.

"Our father isn't going to give us a fair fight, though, is he?" Ahmed said.

"No," Rahim replied. "I doubt he is."

• ● •

WE HAD MARCHED up the mountain with three hundred men and women. We marched with close to a thousand. We made our way down from Iliaz into the desert flats around the great city of Izman. We marched together to war.

The sun was just beginning to set when we reached the campsite where Sam, Jin, Delila, and the rabble they had managed to get out of the city waited for us, just out of sight of Izman, covered by Delila's illusion. There were a few hundred of them. I recognized our rebels and some other allies, but many more were strangers. I was all too conscious of how many people were left in the city if the whole thing went up in flames.

We pitched camp alongside them.

I didn't see Jin among the crowd. I desperately wanted to go looking for him, but that would be selfish when we were trying to let each other go. When only he really had to let me go. And I'd spent a lot of time learning not to be so damn selfish.

He didn't come looking for me either.

As night fell, I was summoned to see Ahmed and Shazad for a few last instructions before we went into battle.

This would all end tomorrow.

That thought hung over our army. By the next sunset, either we would all be dead or Ahmed would be sitting on the throne.

Before I could enter Ahmed's tent, the flap of his pavilion was flung open violently, blinding me for just a second as a blaze of light spilled into the darkness. I shielded my eyes instinctively, but I could still see through the gaps in my fingers.

I knew Jin from his outline alone. He was a dark silhouette against the light streaming from Ahmed's tent. Caught, frozen, holding the tent flap open. The glare hid his expression from me. What I did see was his free hand twitch out toward me. As if to grab me and stop me. To hold me back from what I had to do.

And then his fingers curled inward. Fighting the want. Fighting the need to stop me. The reaching turned into a fist that dropped to his side. He let the tent flap fall, plunging us both into darkness, as he walked past without touching me.

I didn't turn around as he went, as I listened to his footsteps fade in the sand. I waited until I couldn't feel him at my back before I pushed open the flap to Ahmed's tent.

• ● •

PREPARATIONS WERE RINGING around the sands when I stepped back outside. Rahim was running his soldiers and our rabble through drills. No one was going to get much sleep with a battle on the horizon, and Izman was an imposing inky-black silhouette against the stars in the distance. It loomed large next to our small tents that dotted the sands, a behemoth facing a scattering of scarabs. Like the Destroyer of Worlds' huge monster in the old stories, the great snake who had been slain by the First Hero. In the stories, it was always the monster who lost. But I knew better than anyone that stories and truth weren't the same thing. Shazad could talk numbers all she liked, but we were awfully bold to think we were going to win—a rabble of half-trained, barely armed rebels against the might of the Sultan and his unstoppable Abdal army.

The city had seemed to get bigger as the sky darkened, like it was growing into the night itself, shadowed edges blurring into the sky until it was blotting out even the stars, pulling me to it with its long shadow.

"There will be a great deal of death here tomorrow."

The voice slithered unexpectedly out of the darkness, making me turn around sharply. There was a man standing a few paces behind me. I could only see an outline of him against the light from the tents, but I could tell he was wearing one of the uniforms of Iliaz. One of ours, then. I relaxed.

I hadn't realized how far I'd strayed until I looked back. I was halfway between my people and my enemy's city, on the edge of straying outside the bounds of Delila's illusion. Now I saw it laid out below me, colorful tents dotted across the sands, lit up by the campfires and oil lamps. From here it looked like thousands of lanterns littering the desert, screaming defiance against the encroaching night.

"Did Rahim send you to fetch me back?" I asked the soldier. There was no other reason he'd be this far out from camp as well.

The silhouetted man seemed unnaturally still. "No, he didn't send me. No man commands me anymore."

It was a strange answer given in a strange accent. And it was strange that he had been able to sneak up on me, too. I drew back a cautious step, glancing behind him to see if I might be able to dodge around him, outrun him back to the tents. That was when I noticed he hadn't left any footprints in the sand. And I let out a breath. Not strange, then. Just not human.

"Zaahir," I greeted the Djinni.

"Daughter of Bahadur." I still couldn't see his face in the darkness. It was unsettling. "It seems you've discarded another gift I've given you."

"I didn't discard anything. I just gave it to someone else." If the Sin Maker's gift was real, Shazad was now untouchable in battle. "Someone who needs it."

He shook his head, like some mockery of a disappointed human expression he had seen and was doing a bad imitation of now. A sorrowful gesture without any real sorrow. "You wouldn't kill a prince. You wouldn't kiss a prince. What am I to do with you, daughter of Bahadur?"

"I think you've done enough."

He ignored me. "Luckily, I have one more gift for you."

"I don't want any more of your gifts, Zaahir." I was tired. Too tired to argue with him, to try to outsmart him in whatever game he was playing with me this time.

"Trust me, you want this one, daughter of Bahadur." He pulled a ring off his finger and offered it to me. I didn't reach out for it. This tasted of a trick. I just wasn't sure what the trick was yet. "Take it," Zaahir urged. "I made a promise that I am bound to keep: to give you what you want."

"And what is it that I want?" I asked.

"You want to live," Zaahir said simply. I felt the chasm of fear I'd been trying to look away from all these weeks open inside me anew. And even in the dark I could tell he was smirking. Because we both knew he was right. More than anything, that was what I wanted. He turned the ring so that it caught the light from the camp, drawing my eye. It was a bronze band with a single bauble mounted on it. But when I looked closer, I saw that it wasn't a gemstone or a pearl. It looked like glass, and inside there was a shifting, colorless light. "You want to release Fereshteh's soul and stay alive. Fereshteh's endless fire has to go somewhere. But you don't need to burn. It can be contained inside this ring. All you have to do, once you are near enough the machine, is smash the glass on this ring. And all that immortal energy, it will not lash out and annihilate you like an insect in the path of a fire. The ring will draw the fire instead. Absorb it like water dashed across the sand. Instead of swelling up to drown you. And you, little Demdji, you can live."

It still felt like a trick. I knew enough stories of the Djinn to know that if it seemed too good to be true, then it probably was. But it was too late to stop the jump of hope in my chest that came with his words. And as I stared at the ring, I could feel the hope seducing me.

I thought of being in Eremot with Zaahir. The way he had simply touched the Abdals and their light went out. It had been like watching their spark get sucked into a greater fire. I remembered how he had reached out a hand and Ashra's Wall had shattered harmlessly. He had some power over Djinni fire that I didn't understand.

And Zaahir was right. I didn't want to die. It didn't matter how far I'd come across the desert. A part of me would always be that selfish girl from Dustwalk bent on surviving.

My hand closed around the ring. And then suddenly, like a shadow disappearing into the night, Zaahir was gone.

And I was holding my salvation in my hand.

THIRTY-SIX

I t didn't take me long to find Jin. He was on the edge of camp, where he'd pitched his tent, as far as he could get from Ahmed without giving himself over to the desert completely.

His eyes were closed, and a bottle of something dangled loosely in his fingers. He didn't hear me, or if he did, he didn't care. He didn't even look up when I sank down next to him. His head tipped back against the side of his tent, eyes closed.

"So, are you planning on finishing the whole bottle, or are you going to share?"

His eyes snapped open. A long silence stretched between us as I turned my head so that our gazes met. Until finally he handed me the liquor. I took a swig and made a face. "You couldn't find something better?"

"Two weeks in Iliaz and you're suddenly an expert in fine wines?" His tone was light, but his eyes never left me, looking for answers to why I was here.

"I'm just saying"—I took another swig—"I know we've got something better than this around here."

"Yeah well, the good liquor is being saved to drink to victory tomorrow." Jin pried the bottle out of my hands, taking a swig. I read a whole lot in that silence. That there wasn't going to be a tomorrow for a whole lot of people. But we were all acting like this might not be our last night alive. And now that included me. "So, Blue-Eyed Bandit." He didn't look at me when he spoke again. "Did you just come to torture me, or is there another reason you're here?"

"Why?" I challenged, watching him carefully, my blood racing in my ears. I knew what I'd come for. I just didn't know if I was ready to say it yet. "You don't want me here?"

"You already know what I want, Amani." Jin's voice carving out my name was low and rough with feeling, and it shattered the last of my pretense, sinking a hook into my chest and pulling me toward him.

We'd kissed a hundred times before. But this felt different somehow. This felt like the first time all over again, when he'd pinned me up against the side of a train carriage that shook around us like it might fall apart at any second, as we clung to the only other thing in the world that seemed sturdy, both of us on that train rushing ahead into something we didn't wholly understand. When everything in me had seemed to come alive under his hands. When he turned me from a spark into a fire, and I didn't know how anyone could have enough power to do that to me.

My lips grazed his just slightly, like a match, seeing if it would strike. He tasted like cheap liquor and gunpowder and desert dust and, somehow, still of salt air. That first kiss and every kiss since hung between us. The desperate ones, the angry ones, the joyful ones. And now this one, a whisper of my mouth over his, a question. We might all be dead tomorrow. But we might not. And right now, we were alive.

"I've decided," I said, my mouth against his, "that I'm not going to die tomorrow. I reckoned you might be interested in knowing that."

It was a fragment of a story. Of what had passed between me and Zaahir in the desert. But it was enough. For now. And I felt him exhale, like some great weight had been lifted off him, a second before his arms went around me. They circled me completely, crushing me to him as his mouth claimed mine.

The match caught between us, and we turned from kindling into an inferno.

The bottle fell out of my hands, spilling the wine into the sand. I was lost in him. I didn't know how I could've made any other choice but him. It would have been impossible. I slid my hands under his shirt, across his back, up his spine. I anchored him to me, my fingers digging into his bare skin. I didn't just want him. I needed him.

He stood suddenly, barely breaking the kiss, our bodies clinging together, his grip tight enough that he lifted me up with him easily. Sometimes I forgot how strong Jin was. It was a few staggering steps, but my feet barely touched the ground as we moved. I was dimly aware we were at the entrance of his tent as canvas hit my back. My feet found the ground long enough to stumble inside.

My head bumped something—a hanging lamp. We broke apart as I cursed. Jin laughed, rubbing the spot at the back of my head. "Are you all right?"

"Fine." My breathing was shallow. I was very aware that we were alone together in such a small space.

"You're very graceful. It's one of the things I love about you, Bandit." He reached past me, steadying the lamp I'd struck, releasing me just for a second. Just long enough to set a match to the small amount of oil left in the light. The tent was filled with a warm glow. And I could see him now, more clearly than in the dark of the desert, the faint stubble on the planes of his cheeks, the way his dark hair fell into his dark eyes, the way his broad shoulders rose and fell in his white shirt when he breathed, revealing his tattoo. We'd known each other long enough that I was used to him now, but in this moment it was like I was seeing him for the first time again, fascinated by him without entirely knowing why. When his hands came back to me, they were gentler, pushing my hair away from my face so that he could look at me. "God above, you're beautiful," he breathed.

"You don't believe in God," I reminded him, my voice low.

"Right now, I think I just might."

I needed more of him. I slid my hands under the hem of his shirt, pushing it up. He shifted obligingly and tried to lift it over his head. But the tent's ceiling was too low. He dropped to his knees, pulling me down with him. His shirt came off in one smooth motion, and he discarded it to one side.

I had seen Jin half-undressed a hundred times. But everything felt different now. And for the first time since that day in the store in Dustwalk, I was keenly aware of how much of him there was. He was a whole kingdom of bare skin and ink under my hands. I leaned close to him, tracing the outline of the sun over his heart.

I felt the ragged exhale of breath into my hair as I did. He lifted my face up and kissed me again, curling his fingers into the fabric of my shirt. Neither of us spoke as his hands ran the length of my sides, pushing the cloth up. My stomach rose and fell under his callused thumbs; his fingers grazed my ribs one by one. My breathing came harder as his thumbs brushed higher, and then in one quick motion, a break in our kiss, my shirt was over my head, away from my skin, landing in a tangled pile with his. And there was nothing between my skin and his hands.

I suddenly felt shy, intimidated by the certainty of that movement. "You've done this before." I tried to keep my tone light, joking. But it was too late for that. The skin of his stomach was pressed to mine as we breathed. There was nothing left between us. No lies or pretense or secrets.

"Yes," he said seriously. He traced a scar on my shoulder with his thumb, one of the places my aunt had cut the iron out of me. He was being careful—careful not to cross any lines I didn't want crossed. He met my eyes steadily. Like he did when we stood in Ahmed's tent planning something, or in a fight, checking what the other one was doing as we moved together. His dark gaze was serious. "Does that bother you?"

I wasn't sure whether it did or not. That there had been other girls before me, girls who were better at this than I was. Jin had worn my sharper edges smooth in the year since we met. But now I felt them there, still under my skin, holding me back from him just a moment longer. "Does it bother you that I haven't?"

He let out a short huff of air, a relieved laugh that tangled into my hair. "No." His thumb had moved away from the scar on my shoulder now, and it ran the length of my jaw, mapping it out like I was uncertain territory. "But if you don't—" He cut himself off, like he was picking the right words. "I meant what I said about saving the good liquor. I'm planning on surviving tomorrow." He pressed his mouth to the dip in my throat. "And now I'm planning on you surviving, too. We don't have to do anything tonight. This isn't our last night. You and I, we're going to get tomorrow, and the next night, and a thousand nights after that. For now, it can be enough that I am yours." He kissed me gently. "All that I am I give to you, and all that I have is yours. Because the day that we die, it's not going to be tomorrow."

He said it with the certainty of a Demdji truth-telling even though he was entirely human. His calmness always tied me together—like he was holding me firm in a sandstorm. He was sure, I realized. He was sure that he wanted me. And I was sure that I wanted him. And it was more than a want.

I leaned in, struggling to hold myself together inside my own skin when I felt like I might shatter out of it if I touched him again. But I would break apart entirely if I didn't. I pressed a kiss against his mouth softly and felt him smile against me. "I'm yours," I offered back. I traced my mouth along the line of his jaw. "All that I am I give to you." I dipped my head, my mouth exploring his collarbone and the lean, muscled line of his shoulder. "All that I have is yours." I felt his hand curl into a fist against my bare back. Like he was grasping for something to hang on to, to anchor himself. But all he could find was skin. Finally I leaned my mouth against the tattoo over his heart. "Until the day we die."

Whatever thin barriers were left between us disappeared. I was keenly aware of everything as it happened, though later, it only came back in flashes. Like I was drunk on him. On us together. I remembered some advice I once heard a mother give her daughter on her wedding day back in Dustwalk: to lie back, close her eyes, bear it, and wait until it was over. But I didn't want to close my eyes. I wanted to see everything.

Together we shed pieces of clothing until we were nothing but skin. His hands questioned when they were not sure. As he shifted over me, I caught sight of the ink that went across his hipbone, the tattoo I had only seen an edge of before, above the line of his belt.

It was a star, I realized. A small circle bursting with light on all sides like it was breaking apart. I drew the line of it with my finger. I heard Jin make a sound like I'd never heard before as he pulled my attention back up with his mouth on mine. He kissed me deeply until I heard myself saying his name over and over in my shallow breaths, like a plea, or a prayer. He whispered my name back to me against my lips like a secret that belonged to him. My breath came in small, ragged gasps, and I sank my fingers into his back. We were burning together as one single flame, bright enough that we could defy the night.

Until finally the last of the space between our bodies vanished.

I came apart in his hands, and he in mine. Both of us shattering into sand and dust and sparks, until we were both just infinite stars tangled together in the night.

THIRTY-SEVEN

THE DEMDJI AND THE PRINCE

Once there was a boy from the sea who fell in love with a girl from the desert.

The boy knew she was dangerous when he met her, with a gun in her hand and no care for her own life in a dusty desert town at the end of the world. She was all fire and gunpowder, and her finger was always on a trigger.

He guessed he was in trouble when those same fingers danced across the stories inked into his skin without seeming to understand how much power she had in her. Or how much power she could have over him. He knew it for sure when he woke up with a headache, missing the girl, and found that he was glad she had given him an excuse to go after her.

He knew it when she drove him across the desert for fear that losing her would tear him in half. He knew it when he did lose her, and he would have torn the whole world apart looking for her.

But he wondered if a boy from the sea and a girl from the desert could ever survive together. He feared that she might burn him alive or that he might drown her. Until finally he stopped fighting it and set himself on fire for her.

THIRTY-EIGHT

Something was wrong.

I woke suddenly, completely certain of that.

Only my waking mind wasn't as sure as my sleeping mind had been. And for just a few seconds, it didn't seem like anything could be amiss. I was lying in the circle of Jin's arms, fitted against him like we were two pieces meant to fit together. There was a heavy blanket between me and the morning air that I remembered Jin pulling over us last night. My head rested on the tattoo over his heart, listening to its steady beat, as he drew lazy patterns with his fingers across the bare skin of my back underneath the blanket.

And then I remembered that today was the day we were all going into battle.

Jin felt me wake up. "What's wrong?" he mumbled tiredly into my hair. I lifted my head enough so I could see him. His lids were heavy with sleep, his hair disheveled, but his eyes were as sharp and ready as ever, watching me. I wondered how long he'd been awake.

"I'm not sure," I said. But even now I couldn't shake it. It was there, an unsettled feeling in the pit of my stomach. Like there was some danger coming that I couldn't see yet. I sat up abruptly and smacked my head against the lamp, the same one from last night.

I cursed, rubbing my head, as Jin laughed from where he was still sprawled lazily on the ground. "You've got a new enemy. The Sultan and his army will have to wait until you've defeated that lamp."

I stuck my tongue out as I pulled the blanket off him, wrapping it around myself like I'd just stepped out of the baths in Izman, before venturing outside the tent. Dawn was only just putting on its face, the faint pink of the sky igniting Izman to the east of us. But even in the half-light, I could see there was something else between us and the city.

I squinted, trying to get a better view of the shifting, blurred thing on the horizon. It almost looked like—

It hit me all at once. That feeling of wrongness wasn't just fear—it was coming from my Demdji side.

I pushed my way hurriedly back into Jin's tent. He looked up from where he was pulling clothes on. "It's a sandstorm," I said, suddenly breathless. I started searching for my own clothes. "The Sultan, he knows we're here."

I found my trousers, pulling them on quickly under the blanket. "He's using the Abdals to—he's doing this to keep me here." I grabbed my shirt out of the pile, hands shaking. I could already anticipate the pain of trying to hold back a sandstorm long enough to make it a fair fight. I knew I couldn't hold it back *and* get into the city. I yanked my shirt on.

Jin pulled me to him. "Calm down." His steadiness made me still. "We have armies and other Demdji. You're not alone in this fight. However"—he hooked his hands under the hem of the shirt I had just pulled on—"I am going to need my shirt back, because I don't think I'm going to fit in yours." I just had time to realize he was right—I'd pulled on his shirt without noticing, and I was drowning in it—before he stole a quick kiss from me and pulled the shirt back over my head, tossing me mine instead.

It was a lot harder to believe you might lose a war when you could still laugh on the morning of the last battle.

I stepped out of Jin's tent just as the storm reached us. I took in a breath as sand rushed closer, encircling the camp, pushing toward the tents. I raised my arms, hands steady as the storm got close enough that I could feel the sands lashing at my skin.

I pushed back with everything I had in me.

The storm stopped its invasion all at once. Sand strained against me at the edges of the camp. The desert that usually obeyed me was fighting back. I couldn't get it to disperse, couldn't wave a hand and scatter the storm back into the dunes where it had come from. Instead, the sandstorm whipped around the camp in a cyclone, like a wild animal prowling on the outskirts of a cage, nipping occasionally at the edges of tents, making them tremble in the air.

This was a standstill.

"God, there you are!" I opened my eyes at the sound of Shazad's voice to find her, Ahmed, Rahim, and Sam running toward me, all of them looking unsettled as the storm raged around us. "I tried to find you when I saw the sandstorm, but I couldn't track you down." Shazad's eyes slid to Jin, standing in the opening of his tent just behind me. We both still looked disheveled from more than just sleep. The sly look on my friend's face told me she understood now she'd been looking in the wrong tent. But her mind slid quickly back to the present. "Amani, how long can you hold this?"

"I don't know." Not as long as the Abdals could, that was for sure. I was already starting to feel the strain, the risk of the wild storm slipping its leash and tearing through the camp. And the power controlling it on the other side came from machines. I was only flesh and blood. "What do we do?" I asked, breathless. I needed to go to the palace; that was the plan. I had to deactivate the machine. If I didn't we would be helpless against the Sultan's metal soldiers. But if I left, the sand would rush in and drown us. And it would all be over.

"I'm not sure," Shazad said, watching the sand circling us. We all stared at her, even as I could feel my knees threatening to give out.

Sam spoke first. "Did she just say she's not sure, or am I hallucinating?"

"I'm thinking." Shazad's voice was still level. I could see it going through her mind, the cost-benefit analysis of what was likely to get the fewest people killed. It shouldn't be her decision to make. And it wasn't. It was Ahmed's.

"Amani needs to go to the palace," he said, taking the decision away from her. "My father is obviously doing this to keep her here, which means he's afraid of what will happen if Amani does get to the machine."

"People will die." One of my knees buckled, and suddenly Jin was behind me, steadying me. My arms were shaking. No matter what we decided, the reality of my failing power might decide for us. But I wasn't giving up that easy. "You can't fight in a sandstorm." I could feel the power of it pressing against me, threatening to swallow the camp whole.

"And we can't fight at all so long as the Sultan has this power to wield against us," Ahmed said. "The plan remains unchanged. Now, if everyone can—"

The sensation hit me so suddenly that I doubled over. It wasn't the pain I normally felt when using my powers; it was more like a sudden blow. Power suddenly slamming into mine, knocking the storm out of my hands.

I lost control. Whatever Ahmed was going to say was lost in the rush of the sandstorm.

I braced myself against Jin, my body radiating pain, as I waited for the sand to swarm in, to consume us.

But that didn't happen.

Instead, the sand rose, spiraling far up into the air, up toward the clouds. For a moment it hung over us like a huge, dark cloud, blotting out the sky, a swirling mass that could easily crash down and crush us all. I started to reach for it again, even though I knew it was hopeless.

And then, suddenly, the sand scattered through the air, falling harmlessly like rain around us.

"What's happening?" I gasped, pulling up my sheema to shield my eyes from the sand. The others were doing the same. All except Sam.

"I think . . ." His eyes were turned westward. The rest of us followed his gaze. There, on the horizon, stood row upon row of green uniforms. "It's the Albish army."

THIRTY-NINE

I t was far from the whole Albish army—a dozen men out of hundreds. But a dozen men wielding powers were better than nothing.

"Captain Westcroft." We met him at the edge of the camp as he marched, leading what remained of the men we'd seen in Iliaz. The young soldiers behind him looked battered. "We figured you'd been annihilated."

"Many of us were." The captain nodded gravely. "But I thought it prudent to keep some of our soldiers separate from the Gallan." Their Demdji. They might have forged an alliance with the Gallan, but hundreds of years of prejudice didn't disappear just because two regents had signed some paper far away. The Gallan thought all magic was the work of the Destroyer of Worlds. The Albish had a different kind of faith. "We were luckier than most of my men." The captain looked sad, tugging on the ends of his moustache. "And now it seems like you could use some cavalry, so to speak."

Ahmed considered the foreign man. I knew what he was thinking. Allying with foreigners had been the beginning of his father's rule as well. It had been the start of us handing the country over to the Gallan and their greater force. We could not make that mistake again.

"We will happily accept," Ahmed said finally, "provided you can follow orders from my general." He nodded to Shazad. He wouldn't make his father's mistakes. If he could make them pledge themselves to us not as allies but as those who would obey, then we could do this.

I could see her already tensing, ready for the raised eyebrows that came with her being a woman. But Captain Westcroft just nodded. "If we can take orders from our queen, then I'm sure we can manage that. After all, she does outrank me if she is indeed your general."

Shazad's brain worked fast, unsnarling everything into the smooth fabric of a plan. "Okay, here's what we're going to do."

• • •

SAM AND I were ready all too quickly. We didn't need much: A few weapons. Izz in the shape of a huge Roc. For the Albish to direct a little bit of cover my way. For me to stay alive to the end.

Suddenly we were standing in a circle, all of us keenly

aware that this might be the last time any of us saw one another alive.

"This is it." I checked my gun for the hundredth time.

"It seems like someone ought to make a speech or something," Izz said, wearing only a blanket, ready to shape-shift for us.

"Something suitably heroic," Maz agreed with his brother.

Around us, the noise of the camp getting ready for battle reigned, men and women arming themselves, rushing into position to face the Sultan's men and machines. Orders were shouted down the lines to the rhythm of guns snapping into place against uniforms. A few prayers were going up.

Our people would fight on the defensive until Sam and I could bring the wall down. And the Albish would provide a sandstorm. They might not be able to control our desert, but they could control the winds enough for it to look like I was still with Ahmed's army as it closed in on the city.

"Speeches are best saved for the dead," Shazad spoke up. She'd been unusually quiet. "That's what my father used to say, at least."

I embraced Ahmed, then Rahim, both of them whispering a prayer of good luck in my ear.

I turned to Jin. There was nothing either of us could say now that we hadn't said last night. He just ran a thumb along the line of my jaw. "I'll see you again, Bandit," he promised before kissing me.

Shazad embraced me last. "Bring each other home safe," she said finally, before letting me go and looking at Sam.

His mouth pulled up at the side, and I recognized the prelude to a joke—some gallows humor before we all headed off to try our hardest to stay alive to see another dawn like the one rising behind us now. But before he could say anything, Shazad grabbed the front of his shirt and yanked him toward her abruptly, kissing him squarely on the mouth.

And suddenly everyone else was looking at their feet. Or at the sky. Or just about anything that wasn't Sam and Shazad.

That was one way to shut him up.

Finally the two of them broke apart. "Well," Sam said, looking flushed and unbearably pleased with himself as he riffled his hands through his hair. "That's one hell of a motivation to come back alive."

We climbed on Izz's back, and in a few quick movements, we were catapulted above the approaching army, toward the city.

Izz flew over the dome of fire, spreading huge blue wings wide as he soared over the rooftops, leaving the battle behind.

We landed a little way from Oman's Gate, the easternmost entrance to the city. When we'd left through the tunnels, there had been a Gallan army in our way. Now there was nothing but blackened sand.

I stood in front of the gates, a little way back, carefully not to touch the fire. Did I have anything left in me? If I didn't, we'd have to dig our way in. I drew my power to me, pulling it together between my hands as I pressed them in front of me before splitting them open in one violent gesture that sent me to my knees in agony. The sand parted, scattering away from the huge gate. And sure enough, there, underneath, was one of the bricked-up tunnels.

Sam stepped onto it, and sand cascaded down as I released my power, breathing hard. Cautiously he pushed his foot through the hard stone before pulling it back. Like dipping a toe in the water to test it. He turned toward where I was standing, still on steady desert ground, extending one hand to me. "Shall we?" he asked, like we were headed into a party and not a death trap. I took his hand, stepping down onto the top of the tunnel with him.

He pulled me to him, like we were going to dance. Suddenly the solid stone below our feet started to give. I felt the soles of our boots slip through, slowly at first. Then we started to drop. Fast. I just had time to hold my breath and shut my eyes before we plunged through the roof of the tunnel, like a pair of stones sinking through the water.

We hit the ground hard, in a heap. Sam grunted loudly below me as my elbow caught him in the stomach. I untangled myself, rolling away from him. It was dark and cool down here. The only light was above us, a long narrow metal wire that was incandescent with Djinni fire, feeding the wall from the palace. But it wasn't much to see by.

I didn't know how long we walked for. We moved as quickly as we could through the tunnel, aware that every moment we wasted here was another moment our people were on the defensive on the battlefield.

Sam was faster than I was. He was running ahead, his blond hair glowing dimly in the light, when suddenly he stumbled, sprawling into the dark. I caught up with him in a few short steps as he picked himself back up. "Are you all right?"

"I tripped," Sam said. He groped around for a moment in the dark before his hand closed on something, and he held it up to the light. It was a gleaming bronze face. I drew back without meaning to. An Abdal. Or part of one. The eyes were blank and sightless. It was just a piece of a machine, I reminded myself. It was nothing without the spark of fire lighting it, without a word in the first language marked across it, giving it life.

"We're under the palace," I said out loud. "We're close." I stretched my hand out backward, searching for the stone wall. It met hard metal instead.

"The walls are lined with iron." When I said it out loud, my voice echoed against the metal unsettlingly. "Seems like the Sultan's been hard at work since we were last here."

In the faint light of the wire, I saw Sam reach up and lay a hand flat against the stone ceiling. He could reach it, but just. "So we're trapped," Sam said, too cheerily. "Excellent."

"Not trapped," I said. I nodded at the path marked out by the wire. "Just one way to go."

We moved more carefully after that, picking our way forward in the dim light. The farther we went, the more discarded pieces of Abdals there were. Bronze and clay hands and torsos. Early tests. Experiments that hadn't quite worked before Leyla got it right. There was an articulated leg that reminded me of the one she had made for Tamid. And then there were those that looked almost whole, metal men slumped on the floor like discarded dolls or tired soldiers. The light glanced eerily off one of them. "Sam." I grabbed his arm, making him jump. "I think that one just moved."

Sam looked where I was pointing. "A trick of the light," he said. But he took hold of my hand all the same, leading me forward a little bit more quickly. I heard a small whirring sound as we passed another.

"That wasn't a trick of the light," I said to Sam. And then the Abdal sat up.

We staggered back as the thing started to drag itself to its feet like a broken puppet being pulled up by its strings. We ran, bolting down the tunnel, following the wires. As we dashed past another metal body it moved, too, seeming to snap to attention. I stopped as we passed by another, pulling my knife out as I did. In one violent motion I pried the bronze cover off the back of its foot and drove the knife through the word that gave it life. I tried to wrench the knife back out, but it was caught in the mess of gears and wires that lived under the Abdal's skin.

"Amani." I heard Sam say my name, and even as I looked up I realized there was another Abdal coming toward us, blocking us off straight ahead. Sam had his gun out. Three quick shots, but the thing didn't even falter. Instead it raised its hands toward us in an inhuman imitation of Noorsham blessing his people back in Sazi. I could feel the heat swelling around it as it prepared to burn us.

We turned to run the other way. To retreat. The light from the wire dashed across the gleam of bronze behind us. Two more Abdals were closing in on us, slowly raising their hands. The heat around us was building. We were trapped.

For once, Sam didn't have anything smart to say. I just felt his hand, looking for some comfort, his fingers squeezing mine. Something hard pressed against my knuckle. The ring that Zaahir had given me.

The ring that was supposed to save me when I released Fereshteh and turned the machine off.

I thought of Zaahir back in Eremot and the way he'd simply extinguished the Abdals' flame with a touch. His last gift was not meant for this. But the Abdals were getting closer. Inching toward us, the heat building to an almost unbearable point.

I wrenched my hand out of Sam's death grip, flinging it toward the wall instead.

The glass smashed.

And I felt a shockwave, an emptiness, a void. Like a wind that swept up the fire of the Abdals and then snuffed them out, sucking all the air out of the space. Smothering them.

As one, they dropped like ragdolls, falling to the ground.

Sam stared at me. "What just happened?"

It doesn't matter, I tried to say. Except that wasn't true. It did matter. I glanced down at the shattered ring in my hand. Now whatever magic had been in that ring had fled, and I was left with nothing to face the sheer power of Fereshteh. I had no way of freeing him except the words I had used to free Zaahir.

But before I could answer Sam, I heard the sound of distant footsteps. Of metallic feet scraping along stone. There were more. And they were coming. We weren't there yet.

"We have to go," I said.

And then we were running again, bolting down the metal-and-stone corridor. We didn't make it far before we crashed into another wall. The end of the tunnel. The bright wire passed through a tiny gap, disappearing to the other side. To the machine. Our hands slammed into cold metal.

Now I was sure I could hear noise behind us. The whirring of gears, and something that sounded terribly like the slap of metal feet. I banged my fist angrily against the metal.

"What do we do?" I turned around, desperately looking at Sam. But he wasn't looking at me. His hand was flat against the ceiling. And then he was reaching through, the edge of his fingertips disappearing through the stone above us. "I can't reach that," he said, "but I think I can get you through."

I blinked at him for a moment, not understanding. He could lift me through the stone. But he wouldn't be able to follow.

"No—" I started to argue, but Sam was one step ahead of me.

"You have to go," Sam said urgently. He grabbed my arms in a gesture that seemed like something he'd read about in storybooks. "There's no time to argue. One of us has to make it out of this alive," he declared dramatically. He really did sound ridiculous, even when he was about to throw himself at death.

"Shazad—" I heard myself say. Shazad had told us to bring each other back. Not for him to save me. For us to save each other.

Sam's mouth pulled up a little on the side. "Didn't I tell you?" He forced a broad smile. "All the greatest love stories end like this."

I could feel the last moments slipping through my fingers before death came for us. I couldn't just leave him. But I couldn't find the words either.

"Sam." I flung my arms around him. Like we'd stood when he'd pulled me through the wall to the Sin Maker. Like we might be going through the wall together again. Even though this time he wasn't coming with me. "I'm sorry." It was the only thing I could find to say as I embraced him.

I'm sorry that I drew you into this. I'm sorry I led you here. I'm sorry you're here with me. I'm sorry that it ends here.

Sam tightened his arms around me, I felt the solidity of him that would be dust in a few moments. "I'm not," he said as he pulled away.

And then he was on his knees in front of me, hands locked together, his back to the wall for balance. I could hear the sound of the Abdals getting closer. If I left him . . .

But if I didn't, everyone died. Everyone out on that battlefield. Jin and Ahmed and Rahim and Delila. Sam was laying down his life for us.

I steadied myself on his shoulders, putting my boot in his linked hands, and Sam lifted me. I only just had time to hold my breath before my head met the stone. It gave way as Sam pushed me up, and suddenly I was halfway through, shoulders and arms above the stone ceiling. I braced my arms, pushing, yanking the rest of my body through the floor even as Sam kept hold of me. And then I was on the other side, my legs pulling out of the tiles of the palace floor. I just had time to see the tips of Sam's fingers disappear.

FORTY

THE ONCE NAMELESS BOY

O nce, in a kingdom far across the sea, there was a boy born with no name.

As a child at his mother's knee, he heard many stories of men from the great land where he was born who made names for themselves, through prodigious acts of valor and heroism. And so, as he became a man, he began to search for a name of his own. Eventually his quest took him far from the shores where he was born, to a desert where others like him had come from nothing and found names.

It was there that he began to fight in the name

of another man. A man who had many names. The Prodigal Prince. The Rebel Prince. The Resurrected Prince.

It was in the name of this man that the nameless boy fell.

Some might say that the boy's quest had failed. For he would forever be nameless in his own land. A pale girl he had once loved would think of him sometimes, on a bright spring day in her cold stone castle. But she would never speak his name. A family in a small, dark cottage would mourn their lost son when the war ended and he did not come home. But none of them would ever know how his end came, and as years passed they would wonder out loud about his fate less and less until they stopped altogether.

And when they were gone, too, his name would never be spoken again in the land of his birth. No mothers would tell their sons and daughters his story as they held their children on their knees in front of the fireplace. No singers would compose odes to his deeds. And the queen of the kingdom across the sea would never know that a boy from her island met his end alone in the dark, fighting another ruler's war.

But not so in the desert.

In the land where he fell, they would speak his name around campfires, along with the other heroes of their country. Children would be told tales of his feats of heroism and clap their hands when they heard of his many tricks to fool the Rebellion's enemies. And they would go quiet when the story came to how he died. Some would even shed tears.

He would be remembered long after those who had known him joined him in death.

In the desert, the boy would never be nameless again.

FORTY-ONE

I was alone.

Sprawled across the fine marble floor of the palace, I pressed down on the tiles, like I might be able to tear them up and reach down for Sam. To drag him to safety with me. But it was too late. It was just me now, and the mosaic of Princess Hawa staring down at me from the wall.

The first daughter of my father. The first girl to fall in love. The first girl to die for it.

Sam's words from below the mountain in Sazi crept back to me, when he first told me that all great love stories ended in death, and I felt a sob inch its way up my throat. I fought it down. There was no going back now. He had made his choice in those tunnels. I had, too. I'd see him in death soon.

My side ached with the strain of using my power as I dragged myself to my feet. I pressed my hand against Hawa's, silently calling on my sister through a thousand generations to help me. The door yielded below my hand, admitting me to the vaults.

The first time I had come down here, it was too dark to see. Now the vaults blazed with light from the machine, so bright that I could barely see anything else.

I shielded my eyes as I felt my way down the stairs. I thought I could hear voices calling out to me—the other Djinn I had imprisoned here. But I couldn't make them out from one another over the whirring of the machine. I had to get close enough to it. As I reached the bottom of the stairs, I could scarcely see any more—the light was too bright. Even when I closed my eyes it seemed to burn.

I scrambled for my sheema, loose around my neck. It came free easily in my hands. I wrapped it around my head, covering my eyes twice, until the light didn't burn against my eyelids, knotting it at the back of my head. I extended one hand in front of me. Moving forward slowly, carefully. Trying to find my way blind.

The whirring grew louder as I got closer, until I was close enough that I heard the swish of one of the blades of the great machine next to my skin. I drew back, dropping to my knees, feeling my way along the ground until I found the metal of the circle below my fingertips.

I pressed my fingertips to the ground.

I felt the jagged glass of the ring, still on my hand, scrape against the stone floor. Useless now. I remembered the rush of relief and hope and joy that had flooded me last night, when I thought that I would get to live. I'd been so certain that I'd get to see more than one last dawn when I'd gone to Jin. Would he ever forgive me for going and dying on him after I'd told him that I wouldn't do that to him?

I should have known better. We both should have. This was a war. If you didn't die in one fight, there was always another one that might get you. Zaahir's gift had saved my life and Sam's long enough for us to get to the next fight. For Sam to die in that one, to save me. So that I could die in the one after that.

That was what we did. Survive one fight to get to the next. Over and over again until you didn't survive. And all that you could hope for when dying was that some people wouldn't have to see another fight. That eventually, somewhere, this country would find peace.

I couldn't wait. Every second I waited, others were out there losing this fight against the Abdals. I had to do it now. I said the words in a rush, before I could lose my nerve. The same ones I had used to free Zaahir. I shouted them over the drone of the machine, my voice rising in angry defiance until I reached the last word, until I reached Fereshteh's name.

And then the whole world turned to light.

Even through my blindfold I could see the blazing white of immortal fire, and I could feel pressure all around my body. Heat on my skin. A scream in my ears.

Then, the light vanished in a blink.

The heat went with it.

Left behind was a kaleidoscope of colors that I could see even behind my blindfold. I scrambled to untie it. To see whatever it was that had stopped Fereshteh's freed soul from incinerating me.

As I pulled it away, I started to make out colors in the glare. Like pillars of blue, red, gold, and a dozen other hues around the too-violent fire that had once been Fereshteh. I saw shapeless figures of flame encircling the machine. Standing around it. Caging it. Shielding me from it. Shielding the whole city from it.

● ● ●

I REALIZED SUDDENLY that I was lying on my back and opening my eyes. The rushing sound in my ears was gone. Above me, dust was dancing in the air through the sunlight. I could taste metal.

I pushed myself, shaking, onto my elbows. The light in the vaults was different now—not blinding white anymore. It was the familiar buttery color of early morning sun.

The motes floating through the morning light—they were what was left of the machine. It hadn't just shattered. It was like the metal had turned back into dust of the mountain it was mined from.

There was nothing left of Fereshteh, either. His soul had fled the prison Leyla made for it. And maybe tonight it would inhabit the sky, along with every other dead Djinn from the First War.

The pillars of colored fire that had encircled the machine were gone, too. Where they had been stood a circle of Djinn in the shape of men instead.

They had saved me.

They stood in somber silence with bowed heads, my father, Bahadur, among them. The ground beneath their feet was scorched black. I expected them to vanish, the way Zaahir had at Sazi. Instead, one of them turned his head toward me, blazing gold eyes catching me in his sights.

"So," he said in an ancient voice, "Zaahir has sent an assassin after us."

As one, they turned toward me, and suddenly I was caught under a dozen immortal gazes.

"I'm not—" Speaking was a struggle; I'd hit the ground hard, and my lungs felt raw. "I'm not an assassin."

"And yet you bring weapons here," one of them said. He didn't move, but I felt the air stir under my hand, lifting it as if some invisible grip were guiding it. And I realized they were all staring at the now useless ring that Zaahir had given me.

"We made that weapon for Zaahir"—it was my father who spoke now—"when we imprisoned him below the mountain. We gave him a promise of freedom if he would repent for what he did."

"But we gave him a second path to freedom, too, should he want it." Another one of the Djinn stepped in. "We gave him that ring so that he could chose his own death if he wished to. If, in a moment of desperation, he should wish to escape, all he needed to do was break the ring and he would be released from life."

I understood in one perfectly clear moment. This had been what Zaahir had intended all along. To use me to exact revenge over those who had imprisoned him. To kill them in the same way they had given him to kill himself. He had given me a weapon that could end an immortal and then sent me into their midst.

He hadn't lied to me. It would've saved me. It would've taken Fereshteh's energy away safely—as well as snuffed out the fire of every other Djinni here. As it had the Abdals. As it would have him, if he'd chosen to end his own immortal life.

This had been his intention from the beginning.

He had played a long game with me. He had given me a way to save Ahmed, but he knew I would never kill a prince with the knife. He had given me a way to save Bilal, but he knew I would be too late to use the kiss. And only then did he give me the ring to save myself. He had made me desperate enough, with one promised salvation after another, so that I would to accept this last gift without question. Too close to the battle to wonder for very long about his generosity. To realize that he was sending me in against his old enemies, the Djinn who had imprisoned him.

"She will need to be punished," the one with molten-gold eyes said.

"I didn't know." I was breathing hard, and everything hurt. Slowly I tried to drag myself to my feet.

"But you knew that you should not release the one your kind call the Sin Maker," another one said, turning violent blue eyes on me, ones that reminded me of the color of Izz's wings in the sun. "And so you allowed him to trick you."

"We should punish Zaahir," another one disagreed. This one had dark purple hair that looked almost black. "Bahadur's daughter does not need to die."

My father stayed silent, neither agreeing nor disagreeing.

I had managed to get myself to standing now, as they all looked on, sizing me up with their unnatural gazes. "A balance, then," a red-eyed one said. "She should not die for Zaahir's crimes. But someone should."

There was a nod from around the assembled Djinn. And when the red-eyed Djinni looked at Bahadur, he, too, inclined his head just ever so slightly.

"We are nothing if not just," another Djinni with eyes as unnaturally white as a flame spoke. "You chose to release Zaahir from his prison. You can make this choice, too."

"A choice?" I wasn't sure if it was a question or if I was just repeating the word. But it came out a low, angry, breathless hiss. He might burn with an infinite number of the small sparks that burned in me, but just then I'd swear there was enough fire in me to set the both of us alight.

The red-eyed Djinni didn't wave a hand or say words like the market performers did before revealing the grand ending to their great trick. But I felt it all the same, the shift in the air the moment before they appeared across from me.

Side by side, staggering, fresh from the battlefield. Two brothers. Two princes.

Ahmed and Jin.

"A choice of which one will die."

FORTY-TWO

*T*his would be a whole lot easier if I were still the same selfish girl you met in Dustwalk.

I'd said that to Jin about another choice, on another day. Or maybe it was really about the same choice. Because I'd made this choice so many times before without knowing it. A hundred small choices on the road that had led me to this one, this final choice. Between what I wanted and what I ought to do. Between myself and my country.

When I'd chosen not to flee Fahali, to save my own skin. When I'd chosen not to let Jin die in the desert after the Nightmare bite. When I'd chosen to face down Noorsham. When I'd chosen to let Shira die. And to let Hala die. And let Sam die. And when I'd chosen to free Zaahir.

It was a choice between what I wanted to do and what I needed to do.

"Amani," Ahmed spoke, glancing around the vaults, confused. "What's happening?" But Jin never took his eyes off me.

"It is your choice, daughter of Bahadur," one of the Djinn said, "which one dies today. Or don't choose and they both die."

A faraway part of me knew I ought to beg and plead, to rail against fate and the whole world for bringing me here. Against the Djinn, who made humanity and then played with us like this, with their deals and their tricks that they called justice. Who were taking more from me than I ever had from them.

But I didn't. I didn't rage or cry as I watched Ahmed's mouth forming words I couldn't hear. As I saw Jin standing perfectly, impossibly still, eyes closed as the understanding of what was happening, and the pain of it, struck him. I was standing in the same stone vaults, but I was far away.

Suddenly I was standing in a crowded barn on the other side of the desert all over again. One bullet left. Two bottles. Both—I needed both of them alive. But I couldn't cheat my way out of this one.

It was an easy choice, really. Even if it was the hardest choice I'd ever have to make. Because I wasn't that selfish girl anymore.

Ahmed was shouting something, I realized. I forced myself to focus on him, to hear him from somewhere far beyond the roaring in my mind. He was telling me to take Jin and get out.

To let him die.

Jin wasn't saying anything. He knew me. I didn't take my eyes off Jin as I spoke. And though my voice was barely more than a whisper, I heard it echo around the vaults. "Let Ahmed go," I said.

Jin let out the breath he'd been holding. Like it was a relief.

"No!" Ahmed's voice ripped from his throat. "Amani." He was on me, his hands tight around my arms. "Don't do this. It's not worth it, there are other ways—"

"Ahmed." His name came out more prayer than plea. "It's done." The tears were coming hard and fast now, streaking down my face.

Ahmed looked shocked, his hands digging into my arms. "But you love him," he said softly. "You love him, and you should save him. That's what people do with those they love, Amani—they save them."

No, it wasn't. Sam had taught me that. Great love stories ended in death. *All* stories ended in death sooner or later. Ours was ending sooner.

I could feel grief hammering at me now, like waves against a ship. Like the sandstorm tearing at the walls of the camp. "I'm making the choice he would have made." The words wouldn't come anymore. "The choice we all made. That we would die for you."

"Ahmed." Jin still couldn't move, but he found his voice. "I would always have died protecting you. You must know that."

Ahmed's chest rose and fell like he was trying to catch

his breath. He moved over to Jin shakily. He placed a hand on Jin's shoulder. "I would've died for you, brother. In a heartbeat."

"I know," Jin said. "But you're not going to." And then he embraced him. They gripped each other like they were still young boys, like they could pour every bit of strength and life they had into each other. "Go do something worth dying for," Jin said, releasing him.

The red-eyed Djinni raised his arms.

I saw the rising panic in Ahmed as he scrambled for everything he wanted to say to his brother. "Jin—" He stepped forward urgently just as the Djinni brought his arms down. And just like that, Ahmed was gone, air rushing in to fill the space where he'd been. Jin's shoulders sagged, the strength leaving him, everything he'd been holding on to for Ahmed's sake fleeing him.

His eyes landed on me.

I closed the distance between us, Jin pulling me close to him as soon as I was within reach, until every single part of us was pressed together and I felt whatever strength I had left leave me, too.

"I'm sorry." The words came out a sob into his shirt as he tightened his arms around me. "I'm so sorry."

"I'm sorry, too." He spoke into my hair, pressing his mouth close to my ear. "I promised to teach you how to swim. I don't like breaking my promises."

The laugh that came out of me was short and ugly through the sobs. But I saw Jin smile as he tilted my head back up toward him, his thumbs wiping away the tears.

He smiled faintly. I knew what he was thinking. I had some salt water in my soul after all. "You should go," he said. *You shouldn't have to watch this.*

"No." *I'm not going to let you die alone.*

He pulled me suddenly, violently forward. There was no gentleness in that kiss. Nothing but desperation and anger and fear. Knowing it was our last.

"I love you. I love you. I love you." I wasn't sure which one of us was saying which words. Pressing them hard against each other's mouths, in the last moment we had left. I could feel tears streaming down my face. I could taste blood.

We were ripped apart. Not by hands, but by air. By a power greater than us. And I was staring at him, suddenly dragged far away from me. I watched him through tears. A blade appeared out of nowhere. It wasn't made of iron, I realized. It was made of sand—a sharpened blade made from the desert itself. The Djinni holding it was Bahadur.

My father gazed at me with ancient, pitiless eyes. "You don't have to watch this, daughter. We can send you far away."

"I'm staying," I said, never taking my eyes off Jin, trying to drink him in until the very last second. "Until the end."

And then my father plunged the knife through Jin's stomach, driving it in to the hilt. And I felt my own insides rip open.

FORTY-THREE

I was bleeding.

It was soaking through my shirt and onto my hands. My fingers were stained bright red. And somehow I'd fallen to my knees.

I realized it all distantly, as if I was in a dream where everything was a little bit less clear.

I wasn't just imagining the pain. My hands were wet with blood as I pulled them away from my stomach.

I pushed my shirt up hurriedly. There was a slice in my side exactly where the knife had gone into Jin. Exactly where my scar from the bullet in Iliaz was. Like an old wound torn open. Except this one was brand-new.

The Djinn were looking down at us curiously. Even after all this time, they seemed unable to tear their eyes away from us. From our pain. Our anguish. All the experiences they hadn't known before we brought them into the world.

"You married him," one of the Djinn said matter-of-factly.

No.

Except the denial wouldn't come.

All that I am I give to you, and all that I have is yours.

We had never knelt side by side in front of fires with my face covered, but we had said the words. Not in front of a Holy Father, but last night, tangled up in Jin's tent.

Until the day we die.

It was the words that mattered. I had tied our lives together when I said those words. When I made them truth. And I'd knotted our deaths, too.

"Your daughters tend to lose their hearts very easily, Bahadur." One of the Djinn spoke to my father, a hint of mockery in his voice. "And their lives with them."

With those words, he was gone. Blinking out of existence. Already forgetting us as he vanished back to the desert. Another Djinni blinked out after him. And then my father after him, without so much as casting a glance back our way. And then another. One by one, they vanished from the vaults that had held them for so long against us.

Until we were alone.

Blood was pooling around me, warm on my fingers. My hands crawled away from it across the stone floor, feeling blindly. Something solid wrapped itself around my fingers.

Jin had caught my hand. I clung to his.

I lifted my body from the ground, screaming in pain, dragging myself the last few feet between us. I pressed my hand against my wound as I moved, until the side of my body was against his, our knotted hands trapped between us.

I shifted so I could see his face.

So this was how this story would end. The resurrected Prince Ahmed would win the war. When he took the palace, he would descend into the vaults again. And there he would find us twined together in blood on the stone floor.

They would burn us. And maybe they'd even remember us. But it would be some distant, false, nameless version of us. The Blue-Eyed Bandit and the Foreign Prince. Not Amani and Jin.

The stories might tell that we loved each other. But the stories would never remember what that felt like. They would never know that when we lay together in his tent the night before we died, he traced the small scar along my collarbone. That when he kissed me, he smiled against my mouth. Or what it sounded like when he said my name. We contained our own stories. A thousand tiny parts of the story would die with us.

The world was starting to fade away into unconsciousness. No—into death. I wanted to tell him I was sorry. But I was and I wasn't. I wanted to tell him I didn't want him to die, that I loved him. But he knew that.

"What do you think happens?" I said instead. "When we die?" Jin didn't believe in gods. He didn't believe in heavens or hells or worlds after. Just in this world. Just in now.

Jin traced my face, like he was trying to remember it. "I think they burn us and we become dust and ash." He ran a finger across the edge of my lips. "And I think that the dust that was me will spend until the end of time trying to get as close as possible to the dust that was you out in that vast desert."

Something that was neither a sob nor a laugh came out of me, and Jin's fingers clamped around mine.

I only had time to press back before the darkness came.

FORTY-FOUR

THE YOUNG DEMDJI

Once, at the dawn of a long-ago war, the First War, the immortal Djinn created life. And alongside it there was death. They gave their creations bodies that could be hurt and destroyed and scattered like sand and then lit them with a single spark of Djinni fire that would one day extinguish.

But among them, there were those who had a greater spark of fire than had been granted to most mortals. They were called Demdji. Many said it was because they had more fire that they burned so much brighter and quicker than most.

That they all died so young.

Princess Hawa took her last breath on a wall overlooking a battlefield.

Ashra the Blessed took her last breath facing the Destroyer of Worlds when no one else would.

Imin of a Thousand Faces's last breath came wearing the one face that death was truly seeking.

Hala the Golden breathed in freedom one last time so that she would not have to take a thousand more breaths as a prisoner.

And the Blue-Eyed Bandit took her dying breath in the vaults below a city at war, clutching hands with the man she loved as the world faded away around them.

And then, after her last breath, she took another one.

FORTY-FIVE

The dark cleared like a sudden burst of fire, and for a moment all I could see was light.

I was dead. Death wasn't darkness and dust and nothingness, like Jin thought. It was blinding light.

Then I realized I could see the outline of a shape through the light, and it was making my eyes water. My lungs were burning for air, and I could feel blood and hard stone under my hand. I sucked in a panicked breath. A breath that felt like the first one in a long time. I bolted upright, rasping, coughing, sputtering.

The light wasn't death, I realized. It was the sun, shining through the well into the palace vaults. And I wasn't dust in the desert. I was exactly where I had died. My hands were still sticky with my own blood, my face stained with tears. This was a whole lot more ordinary than death. I was alive.

And then my eyes focused on the single thing that had changed. The room wasn't empty anymore. My father was there.

Bahadur was crouched across from me, watching me with those unreadable blue eyes that matched mine perfectly. Like we were one person. Like I really belonged to him. He waited patiently as I found my footing back in the world of the living. Like I'd seen other parents watch their children take their first steps.

"I'm not dead," I said, and I felt the words slip out like only the truth could.

"No," Bahadur agreed. "Not anymore."

There was a sort of quiet then, as he let me settle into that notion. As he let me take another breath, realizing that for a few moments, at least, my lungs had stayed still. That my frantic heartbeat had slowed to a stop. And for a moment I'd been gone.

We'd both been gone.

"Jin." My eyes slid sideways frantically, looking for him. His figure was still slumped in a puddle of blood. Not moving. Not sitting up. I scrambled over to him, fumbling to push up his shirt, sticky with blood.

But as I ran my hand across his skin, I could tell already that it was unbroken under the swath of blood. It was only then that I noticed my side didn't hurt anymore. I touched it, looking for the wound, but it wasn't there. More than that, the skin felt smooth. The scar.

The one from when Rahim had shot me in Iliaz, where the last piece of metal had been pulled from, where the pain radiated from every time I used my power—it was gone, too.

I rested one hand on Jin's chest. It rose and fell under my palm. Just slightly, but enough. Enough for me to know that he was not dead.

"He'll wake shortly," my father said from behind me. I twisted around so I could see him over my shoulder. He was still crouched. If I hadn't known better, he'd have looked like any desert man by a fire. Except he was too still. Like his muscles didn't feel any strain from sitting like that. He was not flesh and blood. Not human. "He needs a little longer than you. He's not made quite the same as you are." I wasn't entirely human either.

I turned so that I was facing him fully, one leg sprawled in front of me, the other tucked under. One hand still on Jin's heart, like I had to hold on to him so he didn't disappear. "You saved us," I said. *How?* Only that was a stupid question. My father was among those who had made us. Created humanity out of desert dust and fire. I had watched Zaahir lift Noorsham's soul from his very body. It wouldn't take a whole lot to pull some torn pieces of humanity together—like stitching a tear in a ragdoll. "Why?" I asked instead.

He rubbed his hands together. It was the closest thing to a human gesture I'd ever seen from a Djinni. A small tic, a moment to buy time to think. "You asked me once if I remembered your mother. You seemed to believe I wouldn't.

That I wouldn't care enough to. But you were wrong. I remember everything. I remember the day I tasted fear as I saw hundreds of Djinn fall to the Destroyer of Worlds. And I remember the first woman I loved, who gave me my first child. And I remember watching that child die on the walls of Saramotai. And I remember that your mother had a small scar just above her lip that pulled when she smiled." He touched his mouth, the exact place where it had been. I remembered that scar. Even though I didn't remember her smiling much. "I remember everything, daughter of mine. Sometimes I think we feel things more deeply than mortals ever do."

I felt Jin's chest rise and fall below my hand. "You don't know what I feel," I said.

He smiled. "No," he granted, bowing his head gently. "I don't. But I do feel as well." We were silent for a moment, as he let that hang there. I had only lived seventeen years, and sometimes I didn't believe that I could contain everything I'd seen and lived and thought. No one ought to be made to contain an eternity. "I also remember the wish your mother made for you. What she asked for when I told her that she could have one thing she wanted for you."

"What was it?" I couldn't help it. I had been wondering what my mother had asked for since that day in the prisons with Shira. I had feared knowing since Hala had told me of her own mother's selfish wish, and since Noorsham had left his body.

"I had hundreds of children before you, Amani. Their

mothers wished for many things for them. For glory and wealth and joy. But your mother wished for none of that. Though she was desperate to get out of a town that would kill her one day, she never thought to ask for an escape, or for great riches to pave her way out with gold. Her wish was simple: that you should live." He smiled then, sadly. "That you should live like she hadn't."

That I should live. It seemed such a small wish. When she could have asked for riches or power or a great destiny for me. But with my heart still beating when it had no right to, I understood it wasn't small at all.

"It was a wish I hadn't heard for centuries. Not since my first daughter."

He meant Princess Hawa. My sister. We were separated by centuries, but she was my sister all the same. Daughter of another mother who wished for nothing but life for her daughter in the middle of a difficult war. "But Hawa died."

"Yes." He dropped his head. "She did the same thing you did. Fell in love with someone who stood too close to death." Bahadur's eyes flicked to Jin, and for a second I felt like an ordinary daughter whose father didn't approve of the boy she'd chosen to marry. "She tied her life to his, because she knew I would have to protect him. That if he died, she would die. And I did. I protected him in battle a hundred times over. In the end, it was her I wasn't watching. My eyes were on him instead of her, when an arrow strayed from the battlefield. It was through her heart before I could do anything." He paused. "I saved her a hundred times, but I couldn't save her the last one."

"But you saved me." I suddenly understood why he'd been the one to wield the knife. An arrow through the heart had killed Hawa on the spot. A wound to the stomach, though—that was slower. Slow enough for him to save me without anyone noticing. "You didn't have to." It came out more ungrateful than I meant it to. "I mean"—I stumbled to catch up to my words—"my mother asked for me to live . . ." Djinn thrived on technicalities. On gaps in wishes that they could wriggle through, obeying to the letter but no more. "That promise was kept when I drew my first breath. You could've let me die any time after that if you'd wanted to."

"If I'd wanted to," Bahadur repeated knowingly. "Fathers will always do what they can to protect their children. I can do a great deal when I need to."

"Well." I cleared my throat. I had no business crying when I was alive. "I suppose bringing me back from the dead goes some of the way toward making up for seventeen years of not doing a whole lot."

Bahadur surprised me with a laugh. It was a deep and honest sound, and I liked it. And suddenly, stupidly, I wished I had more time to hear it. That I could have a father who would sit across from me and talk to me like this whenever I needed one. And for just a second, I felt that bone-deep wanting I hadn't felt in a long time. Since leaving Dustwalk. The one that came with longing for something you feared you might never have. The price

I paid for being alive now was that after today, I might never be called *daughter* again. Djinn couldn't be regular fathers, after all.

"And the rest of them?" I looked away quickly, worried he might read what I was thinking in my traitor eyes, like Jin had an uncanny ability to do. "When they find out we're not dead . . ." Will *they punish you?*

Bahadur brushed my words aside. "My kind do what they can to keep from crossing paths with yours. We hope the day that we all must will never come again. I hope that even more since your brother's death." His eyes had a faraway look. He knew, I realized, what Noorsham had done. "We fight separate wars. And now it is almost time for you to return to yours." I could feel that he was right. The strange sense of suspended time that had hovered around us was fading. The world was leaking in around the edges.

Under my hand, I felt Jin take a shuddering breath. His eyes snapped open, and he stared at me, blinded by the light pouring down the well of the vaults now. "We're not dead," I blurted out as he focused on me. "We're still alive. Both of us."

Jin searched my face, eyes wild, hand reaching up to me. "Now would be a terrible time to start lying to me, Bandit."

And then suddenly I was laughing and crying and kissing him as I helped him sit up. I turned around, looking for my father. Wanting to say something else—I wasn't sure what. But he was gone. There were only dust motes dancing in the light where he'd been crouched a moment earlier.

I felt something like invisible hands tugging at my clothes. And I remembered what he'd said. It was time to go back to the fight.

FORTY-SIX

We were the enemy at the gates of the city.

Jin and I emerged onto the palace walls to find a real battle below us. Our people weren't on the defensive anymore. They were attacking.

The Sultan's unnatural wall was gone, and the city ramparts were scattered with bronze bodies—fallen Abdals, their spark vanished with Fereshteh's release. The Sultan's soldiers made of flesh and blood were scrambling to get into position, reaching for their weapons. More rushed through empty streets toward the palace. We matched them in numbers, but they still had the higher ground.

A scream from above drew both of our heads up. Izz flew overhead, releasing something from his claws, a bomb that struck the wall, exploding as it landed, taking stone and soldiers with it but still not shaking the gates open. The Rebellion needed a way in.

I reached for the desert.

And there was no pain. No struggle. My power flowed easily, like it was breathing a sigh of relief as it invaded my whole body.

Involuntarily, I touched the smooth skin of my stomach. My father had healed that old wound, too, along with the new one.

But it was more than the absence of the ache. For the first time ever, I felt my power like it was part of me. Truly in my soul. Not a weapon at my fingertips but like another heartbeat.

I didn't so much as twitch my fingers as I grabbed full hold of the desert. Of *my* desert. I *was* the desert. And it would answer to me.

I pulled with everything I had, raising the sand like the surge of the sea. It crashed into the Eastern Gate, splintering the stones, scattering soldiers, and opening the gates.

I flooded the city with the Rebellion.

The streets turned into a battlefield as we raced down from the palace walls. We were unarmed except for my gift, and Jin hung behind me as we entered the fight.

A soldier turned as we rounded a narrow corner, his gun rising to meet us. I moved faster than he did, the sand at his feet surging up around him, blinding him, choking him.

Jin shifted past me. In one swift motion, he knocked

the soldier in the face, grabbing the rifle out of his hands.

Suddenly there came a gunshot behind us. Jin and I turned as one. But the bullet hadn't been aimed at us. Sprawled on the street was a man in a soldier's uniform. Above him in a window was a girl in a gold khalat, her hair tied back off her face, a gun in her hands. She was shaking, and her eyes looked wide with the shock of what she'd just done. She'd just saved us.

Her gaze met mine, and she gave me a small nod. I felt a surge of hope. The Rebellion hadn't been extinguished inside the city while we were gone.

We had to get back to the rest of the battle.

Shazad's plan had been to split the Sultan's soldiers up, divide them among the streets and alleyways, where numbers wouldn't matter and we could push them back until the palace was in reach.

We started to see the first signs of fighting on Red Reed Way, the thoroughfare that led through the city from west to east.

Jin braced the rifle against his arm, taking aim even as I gathered the sand to me, guiding it together until it would arc like a blade against them.

Together we fought through the fray like a knife through water.

A dozen times a blade skimmed by my neck, close but not close enough. I saw a gun raised toward me even as I brought the force of the desert down on the head of the solider who wielded it. I should have been dead a hundred times over. I wasn't. I felt like I was untouchable. Like no bullets could hit me. No swords could strike me as we cut through the fight, back to our own side.

Then I saw her in the middle of the fight, dark braid swinging as her sword caught a man in the throat before she dropped to her knees, slicing her blade along the back of another man's leg, downing him before she executed the killing blow, a knife to his neck.

Shazad had always been a force to be reckoned with, but watching her now it was like she was barely human. She was a firestorm, and she would burn the Sultan's armies to the ground before she fell to them.

When she spotted us in a lull in the fray, her face shifted. She grabbed me, pulling us toward her as we rounded a corner into a small impasse, temporary shelter. "You're alive," she said, embracing me even as Jin took up a position watching the streets around us, rifle at the ready.

"I'm alive," I agreed. "Shazad"—I drew away from her— "Sam didn't—"

Jin's rifle went off suddenly, cutting me off with a bang. A cry came from the street near us as the threat fell.

"We can grieve the dead later." Shazad shook her head quickly, guessing what I couldn't say. But her voice still sounded tight. "For now, I need a barricade across the palace road and Golder's Way to stop the soldiers retreating any farther than the river. The streets start to climb up there; we're lost if they gain higher ground. Can you get me that?"

"Yeah." I nodded, glancing quickly up above us. "I think I can. But listen, Shazad, I think you might be able to get reinforcements out on the streets. The people of Izman—we got them to riot once. If you can get them out in the street in Ahmed's name, then we outnumber the soldiers. I think we can end this."

"We don't exactly have time to go door to door," Shazad said as something exploded nearby. None of us flinched.

"The Zungvox," I said. "I reckon it's still in the great prayer house." I remembered seeing it, the wiring of Leyla's invention curled around the inside of the dome like a snake, designed to allow one man to speak to the whole city. For the Sultan to threaten and control us. But we could use it another way. We could get the fallen Abdals to speak for us.

Shazad's eyes darted quickly in that way they did when she was working out a plan faster than any of us could. "All right, here's what we're going to do: Amani, you get me some barricades so we can keep fighting. And flag down the twins, get them to move as many of the Abdals away from the walls and into the city as we can."

"Yes, General." I saluted her. And for the first time, Shazad didn't correct me on her title.

"Jin," she called on him, "how about we get your brother to the great prayer house. It's about time the city knew he was alive."

"We can manage that between the two of us." He drew back into the shelter of the alley, reloading his gun. "Any sign of the Sultan?"

"He's on the battlements." She squinted up at the walls. "But I haven't been able to pin him down. The orders are that if anyone gets the shot with the Sultan in their crosshairs . . . take it."

Jin and Shazad darted out of the shelter of the small street, back toward the fray, even as I turned to the nearest door. It took one burst of sand to shatter the locks, and then I pushed through. The ground floor of the house was empty, but as I pounded up the stairs I could hear voices and small whimpers and cries from behind doors. But I wasn't here to hurt anyone; I just needed higher ground.

I burst onto their roof. From up here, I could see the end of Golder's Way. Shazad had made us all memorize the map of Izman. I could already feel the desert rising below my hands. The sand roared to life, answering my call as it surged in a storm up from the ground and slithered over Izman like some great swarm.

I brought it crashing down at the place where Golder's Way met the river, building an immense blockade that no soldier would get past, stopping their escape short.

I glanced eastward. I couldn't make out the palace road from here, the other point of retreat. I needed to move. I would lose precious time running back into the streets and fighting my way through. But it was too far to jump to the next roof.

A thought struck me, and quickly I gathered a handful of sand toward me. I tightened the grains into a bridge that I arched to the next building. I ran across it without hesitation or fear that it might give out below me. And sure enough, not a grain of sand faltered as I dashed to the next building and then the next after that.

Finally I could see my target, the end of the road where the ground sloped up. And sure enough, men in gold uniforms were moving toward it in something that looked like retreat. I cut them off, a wall of sand halting their escape.

A little way off, Izz soared above the city. My heart leapt as I grabbed at the sand, sending it up in a burst in his path, trying to get his attention. Izz veered violently to avoid it, but he saw me standing on the roof, waving my arms at him.

He soared down toward me, turning into a boy and landing in front of me. "You're alive." He grinned gleefully.

"For now," I said. I didn't have time to celebrate. I told him quickly what we needed, and in another moment he was gone again, launching himself from the roof, a boy plunging down into the streets.

A moment later a huge blue Roc rose back up, talons around one of the dead Abdals, their spark of Djinni fire gone with the release of Fereshteh. But the Zungvox was Gamanix technology, not Mirajin magic. I had to pray it still worked.

I caught sight of one of the Abdals lying on the street below me. I picked it up in a surge of sand, carrying it as far as I could, like a leaf on the wind, before I lost sight of it.

Izz returned, plucking another Adbal off the wall, narrowly avoiding a bullet as he did. We worked as quickly as we could, Maz joining us after he noticed what we were doing, dispersing the Abdals as far and wide as we were able. Scattering the Sultan's mouthpieces across the city.

All the while, every passing moment that we didn't hear Ahmed speak, I repeated the same thing under my breath over and over again.

"Jin is alive. Shazad is alive. Ahmed is alive. Jin is alive." So long as I could say it out loud, it was true. So long as I could say it out loud, it meant they were still fighting their way through the crowd to the great prayer house.

And then I heard it on the air. Ahmed's voice.

"People of Izman!"

I glanced west toward the prayer house, relief crushing my chest. He had made it to Leyla's invention,

"People of Miraji." Ahmed's voice carried through the thousands of fallen Abdals. "There is fighting on your streets. But we do not come as invaders. Instead we come as saviors. My father has ruled you with fear and with foreign steel. He has turned you over to enemies and hung your daughters and your sisters from his walls. He has killed his enemies in cold blood. He has killed his own family, his father and his sons alike. He has taken this country from you and enslaved you. We are here to return it to you. And if you would fight with us, for your freedom and for your country, we would welcome you."

It was as if the city shifted below me. Not in some cataclysmic moving of the earth, as Zaahir had done in the mountains, but in some way that was purely human. The

First Beings might be all-powerful, but they had made us for the one thing that they could not do: to lay down our lives for what we believed in.

It was the shift of an entire city remembering what we were made for and standing up at once.

And we stood up and fought.

I wasn't conscious of time as the battle of Izman raged on. Once I rejoined the fray, I stopped being one girl and melded with the Rebellion, like they were part of me. Moving obstacles out of the way, cutting a path to our enemy. From time to time I heard Shazad's voice taking over the Zungvox, giving orders and guidance to a city that would fall to chaos without them.

The fighting carried on for hours.

Soldiers belonging to the Sultan clashed with our people.

Then there came a scream from the sky.

It was a hideous noise. And when I looked up, I saw a horrifying sight.

Izz was writhing in the air, high above us, thrashing amid flames. A lit arrow had caught his left wing. It was burning a violent mix of blue and red flames as his feathers ignited.

He screamed and plummeted his way toward the water to extinguish himself, trailing smoke behind him in a black train.

Cries went up around me. From somewhere a few streets away, Maz shot into the air after his twin, shifting shapes frantically, from kestrel to Roc to sparrow, looking for the place where Izz had landed. For a way to help his brother.

Suddenly it was as if I were watching it all from far away. As if only half of me was standing on the battlefield and another half of me was standing in a green palace garden on a warm day, a lake full of birds in front of me, pulling back an arrow to strike one down.

Except that I wasn't the one holding the bow now.

I tracked the arc that the arrow must have come from. I was a good shot. I would find it. And sure enough, there he was.

I saw the Sultan before he saw me. He was standing atop the wall, armored and dressed in uniform. I drew my gun and took aim. I knew it was impossible that he heard the click of my pistol, but his head turned my way. His gaze was hot, his stance cool. His head tilted ever so slightly as he drew his bow back, aiming for me now. His throat was just a little exposed.

I could make that shot. I dropped my pistol, gathering the sand to me instead.

I pulled my power backward, like a bullet in a gun. Like I had just one bullet left and everything riding on it back in the pistol pit in Dustwalk.

I saw his hand tense to release the arrow even as the sand flew from my hand, heading for exposed skin, tearing toward my target with all the force of the desert behind it.

I was a good shot.

I didn't tend to miss.

FORTY-SEVEN

THE RULE OF THE GOOD PRINCE AHMED

O nce, in the desert country of Miraji, there was a
prince who took his father's throne.

Many people told many stories of that day.

They said that the Rebel Prince Ahmed fought a glorious battle against a cowardly opponent, his father, who
hid behind his walls and let his soldiers fall in waves.
They said that such was the Sultan's cruelty the people
turned on him as well. And that when the Sultan fell, his
armies laid down their weapons at the prince's feet and
surrendered to their new ruler's mercy gratefully.

They said that when the Rebel Prince Ahmed entered

Izman, flowers rained from the windows, thrown by jubilant people grateful to be freed. His Demdji sister, Delila, who had begun this fight with her birth, blew kisses to the men as they passed, happy to at last be returning home to the palace she had been forced to flee. And the Blue-Eyed Bandit caught the flowers, weaving them into a crown for her prince as they advanced toward the palace.

But those were stories. They would never tell the truth of what I remembered of that day.

I remembered carnage on the streets, not carnations. The confusion after the Sultan fell, as men continued to fight. Good men, not wicked. Men who were just following orders given to them by a dead ruler. Men whose families would pour from their houses later to weep over their bodies. I knew how the Sultan fell, because I killed him, and I would have nightmares about that for months afterward. And sometimes his face would change to Hala's. Sometimes to Shira's. Or Sam's.

But the storytellers would never know that. No one would know that except for Jin, who would wake in the night when I did, ready to fight until he realized that the threat was in my mind and he couldn't defend me from it.

Even if people had known the truth, they wouldn't have been interested in telling it. Flowers pouring from windows like falling stars made a better tale.

The stories would never tell that after the Sultan fell, as we crossed the city, we were reminded of the cost of war with every single body. That as I pushed my way through the streets, I found Samir, a bullet through his chest. A kid from Dustwalk, like me, who'd joined us in Sazi. It didn't matter how well we had trained him. War took lives and changed the ones that were left behind.

The stories would remember that Izz survived his fall at the Sultan's hands but not that his mangled, burned wing would turn to a mangled arm that would never fully heal, no matter what shape he took. He had a limp when he was on all fours, and his wing flapped hopelessly when he tried the shape of a bird. Maz stopped shifting into creatures that could fly altogether, because he didn't want to go somewhere his brother couldn't follow.

I remembered how thick the air was with the smoke from funeral pyres that night. We burned as many bodies as we could. And we burned four empty pyres, too.

The first one was for Sam. There was nothing left of him to burn, though we tore up the tiles of the palace looking all the same. But it was only ashes and collapsed Abdal bodies down there. If I hadn't known better I might've thought he'd just slipped away through a wall after all, run off to some other adventure. Captain Westcroft told me that in Albis they believed that when you died and were buried, your body blossomed into a tree or a field of flowers. A new life. So we covered Sam's funeral pyre in flowers, cut from the vines in the harem. The same kind Sam had plucked the first night I met him.

We set a ring on Hala's empty pyre, gold for our lost golden girl.

For our Demdji of a thousand faces, we used one of Shazad's khalats that Imin had liked to borrow.

A crown for Shira, our dead Sultima.

Bodies long lost because they died in the war, not this battle. Other ones. But we finally had the time to mourn them now that it was over.

We burned the Sultan, too, and his sons stood next to the pyre as they ought to do. Even if they were the reason he was dead. But that was the way. We were mortal. Sons were always meant to replace their fathers.

The pyres burned until the moon wasn't visible through the smoke.

I remembered finally collapsing into a bed that was familiar because I had slept in it when I was a prisoner of the harem. I didn't know where else to go in the huge empty palace we had conquered. I woke to the noise of the pillow moving under a new weight as Jin came and lay down. I shifted just enough to let his arms curl around me and pull me to him.

"No men allowed in the harem," I remembered mumbling half-asleep into his shoulder as he tried to get comfortable. When he laughed, I felt it through my whole body, and the joy at still being alive swelled so quickly through me all at once that I thought I might shatter.

"I think they make an exception for princes," he said into my ear before kissing me.

I remembered noticing that we were both still wearing our weapons and wondering how long it would take for the fight to really leave us, even now that we had won.

But the stories were not made from our memories; those were of interest only to us. The stories were made to tell a tale people wanted to hear. And people wanted to know that we had won and that all was well.

Ahmed became a legend across the desert within days: the Resurrected Prince, come back from the dead to save the city. The whole country. The stories said that he had burned the foreign invaders in his path before taking on his father.

But it was the Sultan who had done that. Who had dispelled our would-be occupiers. He had helped us and made Miraji safe from foreign rule. The massacre of the Gallan was the only reason we were able to seize the city at sunset without risk of losing it at dawn.

But stories liked things to be simple. The Sultan was the villain. We were the heroes. And we had given the people of Miraji a new prince, kinder than his father. A new desert, free of occupation. A new dawn.

* ● ●

I STRUGGLED TO clasp the sun-shaped medallion around my neck as I walked, fumbling awkwardly with the chain for a few moments before I finally had to stop moving.

I was late.

I leaned against a mosaic of some swans that stretched the length of this hallway through the palace, facing a line of arches that opened onto a placid-looking pond as I fumbled with the tiny hook at the back.

I'd never owned a piece of jewelry before, and I would've happily carried on that way if Ahmed hadn't given me this medallion. It marked me as one of the new Sultan's advisors on the temporary council he had formed to untangle the business of making a new country. It was symbolic, which was exactly why I was supposed to wear it.

I tilted my head forward, making the hair Shazad had so artfully arranged fall over my face. It had grown out since it had been shorn in the palace all those months back. It was long enough now to snag in the clasp of the necklace if I didn't take care. Long enough that I could've put it up, but Shazad hadn't allowed that. Instead she'd run her hands through my dark locks a few times with that knack she had, and a hint of oil on her fingers, until they looked artfully disheveled to her satisfaction. She'd done my makeup, too, smudging dark kohl hastily around the eyes and red across my mouth so that it matched the khalat I was wearing, which was the color of a sunrise. Red like the dawn, but edged in gold braiding twisted into the shape of the skyline of Izman along the hem. I looked like I'd come fresh from battle. Which I realized, as she left, was the whole idea. Shazad looked slicked and sleek—a leader, a general. I was playing the part of the Blue-Eyed Bandit, roguish and not entirely fit for polite company. We were all half character now, for the rest of our lives, anytime we appeared in public. It was a fair price to pay for victory.

Finally the clasp closed with a satisfying snick. I tossed my hair back over my shoulders and ran as fast as I could without losing my shoes, heading to the gardens.

The Shihabian celebrations had begun at dusk. Here and throughout the city, the night was made bright by lanterns. Lit with oil this time, not stolen Djinni fire. There had been talk, though, of replicating what Leyla did without needing to murder First Beings. Of having light without fire. Of making some more Abdals who could defend us if we needed. We were still at war with Gallandie, after all. Though I guessed it would be a long time before they rallied together and came for our country again. There was talk that their empire in the north was crumbling. The marriage alliance and peace with Albis had failed. They were a falling empire surrounded by enemies. Including us. And Albis. Ahmed had forged a tentative peace with the Queen of Albis. Fighting for a different peace than his father had forged with the Gallan. One where we still ruled ourselves. We had allies now. Not occupiers.

Meanwhile the Gallan Empire's easternmost regions were rebelling for independence. For freedom and the right to a country where the Gallan religion, and the hatred of First Beings that came with it, wasn't imposed on them.

But if the Gallan did come again, we would need to be ready. Leyla's creations had changed the world, and there was no going back.

Even Ahmed, who fiercely resisted doing anything that might remind his people of his father, had used Leyla's Zungvox once more. To announce the election to the city of Izman.

His father, and his father before him, all the way back

442

to the first Sultan, had ruled without the people's voice. He wanted to change that. He would let them decide if they wanted to allow him to stay as Sultan. He did not want to be a conqueror of his own country. He asked them to chose.

And so an election was held.

Nobody was surprised when Ahmed won. We had declared that anyone could put themselves forward as a contender for the throne. Several of the Sultan's other sons had stepped up against Ahmed, along with one or two of the emirs. A dozen men against Ahmed in all. We spread the word around the whole country, sending out the men and women we trusted most to collect votes from every city, town, and tiny village. In some places where they couldn't read or write, they had to vote with objects instead of names. It was a strange collection that was brought back to Izman to be counted: names scrawled on paper by the hundreds next to bags of colored stones and pieces of painted wood. But in the end it was easy to know the outcome. We were Demdji—after we counted, when we said that the most votes had been cast for Ahmed, it was true. We didn't make mistakes.

Ahmed was elected the leader of Miraji for the next decade. Long enough to build the country he had promised, but not so long that power might corrupt him.

In the garden, men and women milled around in spectacularly colored clothes. They were people whom Ahmed needed to support his rule now. Emirs and their wives and children, Rahim of Iliaz and Haytham of Tiamat among them, setting a good example for others to follow. Though we knew there were already mutters of dissent behind Ahmed's back. Captains who were now serving under a general both younger and more female than any among them, who needed to be wooed into obedience. General Hamad had stepped down in favor of his daughter. He was growing older and had fought two great wars. Seen two Sultans die. One of whom he had betrayed. Ahmed was arranging for him to be paid a handsome retirement. He said that it was a rare privilege to retire instead of die on the battlefield. And it was time for a new generation to rule.

Shazad had started to change things already. One of the garrisons had been set aside for women, and it was filling up slowly. Many of the new female soldiers were rebels who had fought with us in the battle of Izman and decided not to go home. But a few were new recruits, trickling in from the city, a few even from Sara's Hidden House. The captains would not accept their new general or their new recruits overnight. But they weren't exactly being given a choice. The world was changing; they would have to change with it.

We had won the war, but we all knew there were still a thousand little fights like this waiting for us. But tonight, there were laughing voices drifting through the garden on the cooling night air, and there was good wine. And for a few hours, there was rest.

I lingered at the edge of the celebration, unnoticed in

the shadows as I scanned the crowd, looking for Jin. But another brother found me first.

"A different celebration than we had last year," Ahmed said, appearing at my elbow from inside the palace. At least I wasn't the only one running late.

"You could say that." Last Shihabian we had been in the Dev's Valley. In hiding. Without a kingdom. Without a single real victory. Without so many deaths. Last Shihabian we had been surrounded by a whole lot of people who were now just dust in the desert.

Ahmed was wearing a black kurta with gold braiding. His hair was carefully combed back, making him seem older than his nineteen years. He looked every inch a ruler.

Since the election last month, he'd spent all day of every day locked in some meeting or other, untangling the country he'd won. I was in some of the meetings, but not all. Today Rahim and Ahmed had conferred to decide what to do with our traitor princess, who was still imprisoned in Iliaz. The rest of us had made ourselves scarce. No one wanted to be called on to take sides over whether to treat her like a sister or an enemy.

"Any decision?" I asked, even though I wasn't sure I entirely wanted to know.

But Ahmed just shook his head gravely. "We're still at odds. Executing Leyla is what my father would have done. Shazad says we should make an example of her. Rahim wants me to spare her any grave punishment, of course. Though she hasn't so much as spoken to him since . . ." He trailed off and ran his thumb along the rim of the glass. "He brought more news of her from Iliaz. She's carrying a child."

Bilal's, I realized. I wouldn't put it past Leyla to have planned this, too. As a way to keep herself alive. She had to guess that Ahmed would struggle to deprive a child of its mother, no matter what her crimes. Not after the Sultan had taken Ahmed and Delila's mother from them.

"I don't know." Ahmed sighed, casting his gaze over the party as we lingered on the outskirts for a few moments longer. The light and noise lapped out of the party, just barely brushing at us, inviting us in. "I don't think there's any possible victory against her. I'm beginning to understand my father better after his death. Making choices that he would be hated for because the alternative was worse."

"You're not like your father," I replied, leaning against the cool stone palace wall. But he wasn't wrong. If he killed Leyla, some would call him cruel and some would call him just. If he imprisoned her, some would call him weak and some would call him kind.

"What would you do?" Ahmed asked, catching me off guard.

"To Leyla?" I asked. "There's a whole lot of things I can think of, but I hear you're supposed to be nice to pregnant girls."

Ahmed smiled, but he didn't give way either. "You know that's not what I meant." He tapped the golden medallion around my neck. "I gave you the post of advisor for a reason. I want you to advise me."

"I'd exile her." It slipped out before I could think. But as soon as I'd said it I knew I meant it. Enough people had died in this war. Too many. And all to build this: A better place. A new dawn. A new desert. "Send her to Albis," I said, the idea getting clearer in my mind. "Or back to her mother's homeland in Gamanix, just make it clear that she can't ever set foot back in the desert again. Send the message to everyone that the worst punishment for treason isn't death, it's living somewhere other than the great country that you will build. It's what I'd be most afraid of, having to leave my home." Ahmed regarded me, a faint smile playing over his mouth. "What?" I asked defensively.

"Nothing. Just . . . it would have been an unbelievable waste to us all if you had spent your life stuck in that town at the end of the desert." He offered me his arm. It was time for us to wade into Shihabian.

"Don't worry." I looped my arm through his, as I'd seen Shazad do at polite occasions. "Even if I was still stuck there, I would've voted for you."

We walked into the celebration together.

• ● •

FULL DARK CAME at midnight, as it always did. Snuffing out the fire. The moon. The stars. For just that moment, it was like being dead all over again in those vaults.

Total darkness. And then Jin's hand found mine. Reminding me that we were alive. That we were just a flicker of flame in a very long night. But we were here now.

Maybe Jin was right, down in the vaults on the day of the battle for Izman. Maybe there was nothing after this life. Maybe he and I would just be dust, forever searching for each other in the wind. But that wouldn't be all we were. We would be stories long after we were gone. Imperfect, inaccurate stories. Stories that could never even come close to reality.

I had already started to hear the tale of how Jin and I were saved from death by the grace of the Djinn, who were so moved by our great love that they fed us flames until our bodies reignited.

Later, the stories would say that the Blue-Eyed Bandit and the Foreign Prince would fight many more battles for their country. And their adventures would be recounted to children around campfires at night. And the stories would say that when death finally came for them again, at the end of very long lives, it would claim them together, side by side, in a desert they had fought for.

But they would never tell that the Foreign Prince kept his promise to the Blue-Eyed Bandit and taught her how to swim. The stories would forget the small moments that she would remember: the way his fingers felt on her spine when he lifted her against him in the water of the baths in what used to be the harem. That it always made him smile when he kissed her and she tasted of salt. That she fought to learn for his sake, even though she felt like a flame being doused in water. The stories would only tell of the day the Blue-Eyed Bandit was on a ship in a storm and how she leapt from the deck as it sank and swam her way to the shore. And that from there she sent a wave of sand to save the sinking ship. But no storyteller would ever think to wonder how a girl from the desert learned to swim.

Every story of the rule of Prince Ahmed would speak of his goodness and the prosperity he brought to his country. They wouldn't ever know of the long nights burning oil making difficult decisions, the days that the Blue-Eyed Bandit would storm out of his chambers because she thought he was making a mistake. Or the nights he would spend sleepless, worrying the same thing.

Everyone would know that when he stepped down from the throne after ten years, the country elected another prince, one of his half brothers who had grown up in the harem. Then, the storytellers would drop their voice as they recounted what came next: though this man shared blood with the Rebel Prince, he could not have been more different from his brother. And it was not long before he tried to seize power for himself and began taking the lives of those who disagreed with him. And soon he declared that he would rule not just for a decade but for his whole life, just as his father had.

But, the storyteller's voice would rise now, one night as the usurper prince sat gloating at his victory in his palace, a knock came at his chamber door. When he opened it, he found the Beautiful General standing there. He was shocked for he had had sent an assassin for her and believed her to be dead. But the assassin had failed; the general had killed him instead. And when she discovered what was happening, she marched her army through the night and took the city back as he slept. And she had done it without firing a single shot or even drawing her blade. But she drew it now, as she stepped into his chambers and ended his tyranny.

That was a story that every girl who signed her conscription papers to the join the Mirajin army certainly heard as a child.

But no one would know that on the eve of that bloodless battle for Izman, eight people would gather together for the first time in many years. And they would remember every time they had done this before, when they were younger. The Foreign Prince would ask, *Didn't we already win this war?* And his brother would wonder out loud if they might always be fighting for freedom against men who desired power. And then the Beautiful General would clap her hands together and say, *Okay, here's the plan.* And the Blue-Eyed Bandit would laugh because she hadn't heard that in a long time.

The stories would only tell that a new election followed the dethroning of the usurper. And it was the Beautiful General who was chosen to rule the desert next. She became the first Sultana elected in Miraji, and she would defend her country for another ten glorious years.

And when she stepped down, the boy known as the Demdji Prince would be chosen by the people to rule. He was the adopted son of the Rebel Prince, though by blood he belonged to the blessed Sultima. Some stories even said that he shared blood with the Blue-Eyed Bandit, too. Though most said that was an absurd fabricaton. But they all agreed that his rule had been prophesied even before he was born, and that his great lineage meant he was destined to be a great ruler.

But the Blue-Eyed Bandit, who remembered where he and the Blessed Sultima had both come from, knew that the Demdji Prince had not been made great by his bloodline. He was kind because the Rebel Prince would pick up his son and soothe him when he fell and scraped his knees instead of chastising him for weakness. And the Foreign Prince taught his young Demdji nephew that he didn't need to share blood with anyone to call them family. The Blue-Eyed Bandit herself would teach him how to shoot and when to think instead of pull a trigger. And the legendary commander of Iliaz would show him how to sit a horse and remind the young prince that soldiers were owed respect, not just orders. The Demdji princess and the legendary Demdji twins would be the first to help him understand, when he was very young, the powers his father had left him. The Beautiful General would teach him to strategize instead of fight his way through a problem. And those near him would know the truth that the stories didn't tell, that he was a great ruler because he was the best parts of all the men and women who raised him.

And no stories would ever tell how one day, when the Demdji Prince was still a child, the Blue-Eyed Bandit would find herself far in the south, sitting on a stone warmed by the sun, next to a Holy Man who had only one leg. Both of them watching the young prince play in the same dust they had grown up in, with cousins who shared his blood but who would never really understand what his life was like in a palace far away. When the boy's grandmother picked him up, the Holy Man said that he reckoned this would have made the Blessed Sultima happy if she could have seen it.

The tales would be imperfect; the legends would be incomplete. And each and every one of us standing in the garden that night would take an entire universe of stories with us when we died, the accounts of every small moment that did not seem grand enough to storytellers, which would disappear in smoke when our bodies were burned.

But even if the desert forgot a thousand and one of our stories, it was enough that they would tell of us at all. That long after our deaths, men and women sitting around a fire would hear that once, long ago, before we were all just stories, we lived.

Ahead of us, in the garden, a fire flickered to life.

And the storyteller began.

ACKNOWLEDGMENTS

First, to my parents. I could write a million books and thank them at the back of every one and it still wouldn't come close to being enough thanks for the last three decades. You're still the best parents any girl could ask for.

I will always be grateful to Molly Ker Hawn, who goes above and beyond what it means to be an agent. I am beyond lucky to benefit from her passion for books every day. Amani wouldn't be where she is without her.

To my editors Kendra Levin and Alice Swan. I would have given up, lain down on the floor and stayed there a dozen times over if it wasn't for them. I am completely indebted to them for their patience, their energy, and their belief, especially when I had run out of all three. Thank you for helping me get to the finish line.

My thanks to Ken Wright, Leah Thaxton, and Stephen Page for being so supportive of me and this trilogy over the past three years. It means the world.

Thank you a thousand times to my publicists extraordinaire, Elyse Marshall and Hannah Love, who are both filled with boundless energy and optimism and enthusiasm and make everything look effortless even though I know how hard they work.

I am grateful to the whole of the teams across both sides of the pond who helped root the devil out of the details: Maggie Rosenthal, Krista Ahlberg, Natasha Brown, and Susila Baybars. And for taking a sloppy-looking Word document and making it into a real and very good-looking book, my thanks go to Theresa Evangelista, Emma Eldridge, and Kate Renner.

For getting the book out there, I owe thanks to the whole of the marketing, social media, and publicity teams across both countries. Bri Lockhart, Leah Schiano, Kaitlin Kneafsey, Emily Romero, Rachel Cone-Gorham, Anna Jarzab, Madison Killen, Erin Berger, Lisa Kelly, Mia Garcia, Christina Colangelo, Kara Brammer, Erin Toller, Briana Woods-Conklin, Lily Arango, Megan Stitt, Carmela Iaria, Venessa Carson, Kathryn Bhirud, Alexis Watts, Rachel Wease, Rachel Lodi, Sarah Lough, and Niriksha Bharadia.

And for getting the book to shelves, my thanks go to the whole of the sales teams, including, but certainly not limited to, Biff Donovan, Sheila Hennessy, Colleen Conway, Doni Kay, David Woodhouse, Clare Stern, Kim Lund, Miles Poynton, and Sam Brown and the Faber reps.

I am so very grateful to the whole of the Bent Agency and all of their co-agents for putting the story of Amani and the rebellion on shelves across the globe. And to all my foreign publishers for bringing these books into your respective countries.

I live in terror while doing acknowledgments that I will forget people in my life who have helped. So, friends, colleagues, countrymen, please be assured, I still think you're awesome.

But in particular, I want to thank Amelia Hodgson. She has read more than one draft of this book when she didn't have to and given up entire days of her weekend to help me troubleshoot it in great detail. If you liked the scene with ships sailing across the sand, that was her suggestion.

Michella Domenici, who is the best book-cheerleader anyone could want.

Anne Murphy, who is the sort of person who knows exactly how to head off a stressful time at the pass with a small gesture that always makes a big difference.

Sophie Cass, who has the misfortune of working around the corner from my publisher, and will drop everything and buy a girl hot chocolate in a time of publishing need.

Meredith Sykes, who finished this book and immediately sent me a tear-stained selfie, which arrived just in time to pull me out of a particularly bad dark night of the soul.

Justine Caillaud, who has been my creative partner in mischief since we were six months old and is the best at reminding me not to feel bad about how much creativity takes from us.

And of course Rachel Smith, naturally, who's still got my back.

Thank you to all my Penguin Teen on Tour companions for making being on the road a good time. And especially to Renée Ahdieh, who is 50 percent responsible for coming up with the title for this book (specifically "The Fall" part).

Over the pond, my thanks go to Roshani Chokshi, Jessica Cluess, and Stephanie Garber, the best people to have at the other end of a text/email/DM in times of authorial trouble when you just need to talk it out.

And on my side of the pond, my thanks to my Author Partners in Writing/Crime/W(h)ine Samantha Shannon, Laure Eve, Cecilia Vinesse, Katherine Webber, Melinda Salisbury, Katy Birchall, Lisa Williamson, Non Pratt, and many more I'm sure I'm forgetting. I'm sorry, I'll buy you a drink.

And last but certainly not least, to all the booksellers who have put this series into a readers' hands, the bloggers who have encouraged others to pick it up, and all the readers who have embraced Amani and the rebellion. I can write all I like, but a story really needs to be read to become more than just my words, and so thank you all for bringing this one to life by cracking its spine.